BUGS

Other books by Theodore Roszak

Person/Planet: The Creative Disintegration of Industrial Society

The Making of a Counter Culture: Reflections on the Technocratic Society and Its Youthful Opposition

Where the Wasteland Ends: Politics and Transcendence in Postindustrial Society

Pontifex: A Revolutionary Entertainment for the Mind's Eye Theatre

Unfinished Animal: The Aquarian Frontier and the Evolution of Consciousness

Editor and contributor

The Dissenting Academy

Masculine/Feminine: Readings in Sexual Mythology and the Liberation of Women

Sources

BUGS

Theodore Roszak

DOUBLEDAY & COMPANY, INC.
GARDEN CITY, NEW YORK
1981

ISBN: 0-385-17410-1
Library of Congress Catalog Card Number 80–2625

BUGS

THE BEGINNING

It began as a bubble of steel swelling higher and higher beside
the Potomac until it was one of the world's largest geodesic
domes. Distantly across the Washington Channel, it mirrored
—some said eclipsed—the stately contour of the nation's capi-
tol. Later, when its naked framework was clothed in a rich
tracery of textured marble, there was no mistaking the intended image. The National Center for Data Control brooded
over the city like a vast, disembodied cerebrum. At night,
bathed in the rippling luster of a programmed lightshow, it became a small mountain of gray matter pulsing with thought.

Inevitably, it was called the Brain.

Its planners, having carefully designed the visual metaphor,
welcomed the name. So much more colorful than the bland in-
itials "En-See-Dee-See." And so much more to the point. The
Center was meant to be nothing less than the brain of the nation.

Its critics (there were many both aesthetic and political)
called it garish. It *was* garish, a shameless eye-catcher. But perceptive observers conceded that the Brain had every right to
stake its claim boldly on the Washington skyline. From the
outset, it was more than another government office building. It
was the symbol of an era. Like the Eiffel Tower before it, or
the Palace at Versailles, or the Parthenon in ancient Athens, it
was a monument built to an ideal.

At the ceremonies that marked its formal opening, the President described the Brain as "our national cathedral of information, a milestone in man's age-old quest for good government
and civilized order."

And he threw a switch. Infinitesimal rivers of electricity
coursed silently through billions of microprocessors. The Brain

was officially alive and thinking. History turned a corner. "We are entering a new Age of Reason," the President announced. "Science has finally endowed our technological sinews with the controlling intelligence they require."

In its brawling youth, the industrial world toiled for its bread with the muscle power of strong machines. In its comfortable maturity, it retired into the care of smart machines. Just as men once invented mills and dynamos to do the work they could not do with their own frail hands, so they invented computers to think the thoughts they could not think with their own fallible minds. And, at last, the Brain was invented, a massed and disciplined phalanx of electronic intellect that brought the computer to perfection as thinker, planner, problem-solver.

To the casual visitor walking its corridors, the National Center for Data Control might have looked much the same as any other busy government agency: a little, neon-bleached and air-conditioned universe of esoteric offices and specialized departments. But the Brain concealed hidden depths, an inner sanctum where extraordinary powers were gathered. There, in a glass-walled chamber where the noise and the heat and the grime of the outside world never intruded, twelve Sygnos 7000 computers stood in a tightly linked ring, solemn guardians of the public good, as lordly as the monoliths of ancient Stonehenge.

Within that charmed circle, enough fact and logic had been concentrated to serve all the cabinet level departments in Washington, the needs of the Congress, the federal courts, the regulatory agencies, the FBI. Two hundred years of Supreme Court history had been reduced to several magnetic memory bubbles. All the records of the Internal Revenue Service had been etched into a handful of silicon wafers. In the Brain, Big Government had become a few neat stacks of microchips.

But the Sygnos ring was only the vibrant core of the Brain. From there, its power radiated across the continent. A subtle telecommunications web fanned out in all directions from Washington to connect the Brain with nearly five thousand key computer terminals in military bases, universities, banks, corporate boardrooms, police headquarters, government offices. This was MASTERNET, the Brain's data transmission network. In turn, MASTERNET reached skyward to the boundaries of outer space, where three CONCERT satellites bridged the seas to Western Europe, Japan, Latin America. The Brain was the citadel of an invisible electronic empire grounded in its society's insatiable appetite for hard data and swift decision.

And it was something more. It was a vision of the world to come. Its lobbies had been cleverly designed to serve as a showcase for the most advanced hardware and programming techniques computer science had to offer.

Inside the Brain were computers that drew pictures, composed music, sang songs, wrote stories. Computers that played games and solved puzzles. Computers that invited the public to simulate space missions and to test strategies of war, to improvise impossible geometries and experiment with fantastic architectures.

A program named SPORT permitted people to match all-star teams of their own selection in imaginary contests, to pit famous fighters, golfers, tennis champions, race horses of the past and present against one another.

A program named DOCTOR offered its users the consolations of cybernated psychotherapy.

A program named SHERLOCK re-enacted routine police work, allowing the public to collect clues, trace criminals, enforce laws.

A program named UTOPIA gave visitors the chance to design social policies and conjure up ideal worlds.

Still other programs demonstrated the possibilities of computerized law, medicine, counseling.

At one level, the Brain was a futuristic penny arcade filled with the world's most expensive pinball machines. But behind even its most whimsical amusements, there stood one central purpose: to present the computer as a real intelligence. The machine that most people still knew as little more than a high-speed number cruncher or a glorified filing cabinet was displayed at the Brain as a *mind* capable of learning and teaching, innovating and predicting, planning and creating.

Offered the opportunity to attend and admire, the public flocked to the Brain and dutifully learned what it was expected to learn. Within six months of its opening, it was outdrawing the Smithsonian Institution. Within a year, visitors to the capital ranked it as a greater attraction than the Congress. Schools were especially welcome at the Brain and accounted for most of its traffic. Field trips came from as far away as Philadelphia, Richmond, Baltimore.

Three times each day, Monday through Saturday, tours roamed through the Brain, absorbing its wonders and amazements. Their guides had been carefully trained; everything they did—the pet names they used for computers, the anecdotes and jokes they threw off—was aimed at the one goal of making the machinery of artificial intelligence familiar, benign, inviting. A number of the guides had once worked in zoos and animal shows. They were found to have a peculiar gift for humanizing the non-human. Snakes, tigers, crocodiles—they knew how to make dangerous beasts seem as harmlessly charming as Walt Disney creations. But in this case, in their work at the Brain, they were expected to carry the experience one step further—from friendly trust to willing deference. People came to the Brain to be entertained; they went away converted.

Sometimes—most times—in the little games they played with visitors, the Brain's computers would outwit their human partners, but always in ways that were kindly, unthreatening, even comic. They were programmed to correct people politely for their mistakes, to apologize for their own superiority. The visitors liked that. They liked these ingenious machines that blinked and winked and talked, that took push-button orders and said "please" and "thank you." It brought them a certain aristocratic satisfaction to be treated so courteously by servants that were obviously more clever than they. People welcomed having the inevitable presented to them as if it were a matter of their own choosing.

As each tour ended, visitors were left in the care of an IBM 370/188 computer nicknamed Rembrandt. Rembrandt was equipped with an optical-graphics component that allowed him to make a lightning-fast, chiaroscuro portrait of anybody who stood in front of his goggling purple eye. For a small fee, visitors could punch their names and addresses into Rembrandt's transistorized innards and, while he made his sketch, he would speak to them by name.

"I hope you enjoyed your tour of our facility, Phyllis," he would say. "Please give my regards to everybody back in St. Louis. It's chilly and raining today in St. Louis but you'll be pleased to know that the Cardinals' beat the Pirates last night."

If the visitor had tried any computer games on the tour, Rembrandt already knew the results. He complimented those who did exceptionally well; he might even have run a quick search of the Brain's social data that allowed him to add, "The University of Missouri class of '65 would be proud of you." Then out would slide a plastic card bearing Rembrandt's artistic handiwork, together with the visitor's name and vital statistics coded upon a microchip. "Here's a little souvenir for you to take home, Phyllis," Rembrandt would say.

Invariably, people thanked Rembrandt for their souvenir. And Rembrandt would say, "You're very welcome. Do visit us again."

As for those who had done poorly at the games—which was usually the case—Rembrandt had a consoling word to offer. "Please don't let it worry you," he would say. "After all you're only human."

One had to listen closely to hear which of the last two words in his message Rembrandt had emphasized.

1

Timmy the Electronic Turtle circled swiftly to the left, leaving a loop of black ink on the carpet-sized sheet of paper. With painstaking care, the tiny robot artist neatly closed the curve it was drawing, forming an egg-shaped oval. For a moment it paused, alertly awaiting instructions from its computerized brain. Then, with a busy hum, it wheeled around and, along one ingeniously selected trajectory, quickly inked in a grinning mouth, a pair of lopsided ears, and—with a final, confident plop! plop!—two jelly-bean eyes.

"Snoopy!" the small crowd of astonished children cheered, immediately recognizing the familiar cartoon. "Snoopy! Snoopy! Snoopy!"

The woman from "Wonder/Wander" leaned forward, instructing the videotape editor to cut to a close-up of the children's faces on his monitor. "There, that's it," she said. "Oh, that's lovely. Look at the amazement in those eyes. It's exactly what we want."

Her name was Kayla Breen, a taut, hard-edged woman in her early forties. The producer of a major network success, she carried off the part with aggressive self-assurance. "Don't you agree, Tom?" she asked the man beside her in the editing room, a question that was clearly a decision. "*That's* our opening. The little turtley thingamabob doodling around; then Snoopy; then those marvelous faces."

The man offered no objection. "Whatever you say, Kayla," he replied indulgently. "You're the expert here."

She registered his answer with a quick smile as she rushed along, skillfully stitching the sequence of her show together. "And then we can mix in Jenny Penny's voice-over intro. 'Good afternoon, children, blah-blah-blah. Here we are at the National Center for blah-blah-blah.' All right, Jerry, let's try that."

The editor threw an audio switch. A woman's voice, light and frothy, floated in above the children's laughter.

"Good afternoon, children, and welcome again to 'Wonder/Wander.' Today, we're visiting the National Center for Data Control in Washington, D.C., our nation's capital."

The woman's face emerged on the monitor, young, pert, smiling. Miss Jenny Penny, America's favorite television school teacher. She reached forward with a grease pencil and wrote four large letters on the plastic see-through screen between herself and the camera. "D-A-T-A. Data. That's a funny little word, isn't it? But it has a *big*, important meaning. And today we're going to learn what that word means from 'Wonder/Wander's' very special guest, Dr. Thomas Heller. Dr. Heller is going to tell us all about this *great*, *big*, marvelous building we're in. And he's going to tell us all about little Timmy the Turtle, who just drew that supernice picture of Snoopy for us. Welcome to our show, Dr. Heller."

"Did she say 'supernice'?" Kayla asked her editor.

"She said 'supernice,'" the editor answered.

Kayla groaned. "Lord, that girl! I told her no more 'supers' for the rest of the month. She's way over her quota." She sighed with resignation. "Okay, now let's have Tom up close on her introduction. Oh, that's good. That's a good, strong smile to start with. Tom, you were born for the medium."

Before him on the small screen atop the editor's videotape recorder, the man saw his own face being drawn up closer and closer by the camera until his hairline and shirt collar were cut away at top and bottom. It was by now a familiar public image of himself: Thomas Heller, well-known television talking head. An impressively good-looking head it was for television—as he had been told many times. The high forehead and heavy-rimmed glasses lent an air of cool professorial authority, but the eyes were intense and penetrating, the features shrewd, well-chiseled, memorable. The face was a curious mixture of diffidence and cunning, the voice that went with it was measured, commanding, smoothly articulate. Together, they made him one of official Washington's most sought-after media personalities, a man many times interviewed, often tapped for major documentaries.

Heller had long since perfected the role he was about to perform for Kayla Breen. He was going to expound the virtues and powers of the new National Center for Data Control—*his* Center, the all-knowing, all-powerful Brain. But this time, there was a difference. The authoritative head, while no less self-possessed, was confining itself to words of one syllable. Because "Wonder/Wander" was the great American children's hour, the guaranteed largest audience of under-eights (and their mothers) in the Western world. While he was before its camera eye, Heller was expected to make everything about the science of information sound primer simple. It was a new assignment for him, one for which he had let himself be carefully coached by Kayla Breen and her production staff through several weeks of preparation.

> "Dr. Heller," Miss Jenny Penny was explaining to her audience, "is the director of the National Center. That makes him a *very* important man here in Washington. And we're going to be talking about a lot of exciting things with him. But first of all, Dr. Heller, I'd like to ask you about little Timmy here. He

doesn't actually look much like a turtle to me. He looks more like a vacuum cleaner that lost its bag. I wonder how you decided he was a turtle."

"Well, when Timmy here was first invented four years ago," Heller answered, deftly moving into the prearranged repartee, "he wasn't very fast at all. It took him half an hour just to draw one Charlie Brown. So we called him a turtle. But then he got better and better, and faster and faster. I guess he moves way too fast for a turtle now. Maybe we should change his name." He kneeled down beside one of the children, a shy black girl with two front teeth missing. "If I had a chance to name him, I'd call him Billy the Beaver."

Miss Jenny Penny knelt on the girl's other side. "Or maybe Ronny the Rabbit. What would you name him, Loretta?"

After some coaxing, little Loretta timidly suggested Jacky the Cow.

"We'll drop that," Kayla remarked sourly. "The kids don't always score for us," she apologized to Heller. "Cut to take 137 where Tom brings in the robots."

The editor punched a number into the VTR Computer. The tape flashed forward to pick up Heller saying,

"Actually, Timmy is a robot. That's a clever machine that takes orders and does what it's told."

"You mean like R2D2 in *Star Wars*?" Miss Jenny Penny asked.

"That'll grab them," Kayla commented.

"Exactly," Heller replied. "Except that the only thing Timmy can do is draw pictures. But he's very good at that. He can draw nearly one hundred cartoons and comic strip characters." While Heller spoke, Timmy was busily tossing off sketches of Mickey Mouse, Bugs Bunny, Darth Vader . . .

"One hundred cartoon characters!" Miss Jenny

Penny chirped. "That makes him just supersmart, doesn't it?"

"Superscrew that girl," Kayla muttered.

"It's not really Timmy that's so smart," the Heller on the television monitor was explaining as he moved across to the far end of the exhibit. "It's his brain. Now, Timmy doesn't carry his brain around inside him the way we do. His brain is all the way over here in this metal box. This is called a computer. This is where Timmy gets his orders. The computer thinks for him, it tells him what to draw, and where he is on the paper, and how to get from one place to another so he makes all his markings in just the right way."

"Is that what you call 'data'?" Miss Jenny Penny asked. She and Heller were standing alongside the CYBER 600 computer that held Timmy's memory.

"Yes, that's right," Heller said. "Data is information, facts, orders. All the information Timmy needs to make his drawings is in this computer. Or rather, it's in the program that's inside the computer. That program is called MICKEY. It's named after Mickey Mouse. I guess that sounds sort of comical, but Timmy's program is really very clever. It's called a bubble memory, and it contains over ten million bytes of information on three silicon wafers no bigger than your fingernail. Timmy gets enough data out of those microchips to solve tens of thousands of free-contour, non-co-ordinate plotting problems . . ."

Kayla reached out to push a button. The videotape stopped dead with Heller's face frozen in mid-sentence. She pursed her lips and shook her head. "No, no. Sorry. That's getting too thick. Let's lose everything after 'Mickey Mouse' and then cut to where Tom explains what a program is. That's 219." Turning to Heller she said, "The bytes and the wafers—we have to get into that slowly. It's too much at once. Also 'non-co-ordinate'—that's a no-no for sure." Cutely, she wagged an admonishing finger at him. "Remember, Tom. Nothing over three syllables unless it's a proper noun."

Heller looked suitably contrite. She reached over to pat his hand. "Don't worry, you're doing just grand. We've got tons of material from you we can use. Jerry, run that nice section where Tom does his Brain talk." Her hand was still on his; it stayed there, holding firmly while the editor cued his tape. Her grip reminded him they had a dinner date after the editing session. It would be their third evening together in a week, all on Kayla's expense account. She was a more than slightly predatory woman; over the past several days, while she and Heller worked on the show, she had been moving in close and fast.

Now on the television monitor, Heller, Miss Jenny Penny, and the children were grouped around a computer in another part of the Center. Heller was making a joke about this department being called GOD, the Government Operations Division. "Drop that," Kayla instructed the editor. "Bound to be offensive to Moral Majority families. The Lord's name in vain, you know—23.8 per cent of our audience. Pick up just after that— on 'why is this building nicknamed the Brain . . .'"

With surgical precision, the editor cut a few seconds further into Heller's remarks, picking up on the line,

> "Do you know why this place is called 'the Brain'?" There was an eager flurry of response from the kids. "That's right. Because we *think* with our brain— that's *our* computer up here, in our heads. That's where we learn things, and remember things, and do arithmetic and geography and spelling. That's where we keep all the important facts we know—like people's names and their addresses and their birthdays. Well, that's what the United States government does here in this building—it thinks. About everything. About people and jobs and money and schools and freeways and airports and space satellites . . . about all the biggest problems in the world. This building, with all the computers you've seen here today, is the

biggest brain in the world. And it's getting bigger every day.

"Do you know how many important computers all over the world are connected with our big Brain here? See all those little red lights on the map up there?" The camera swung to a map of the world above Heller's head. "Every one of those lights is a computer place like this one, only smaller. Now we call that— all that put together—a 'network.' That's a good word for you to learn: network."

Miss Jenny Penny broke in to give the sequence more visual variety. "Let's all say that new word together. Net—work." The camera panned the children's faces as they responded. "Net—work. Net—work." Then it returned to Heller.

"Network. That means a whole family of computers all in touch with each other, all thinking together. We call that network on the map MASTERNET. It's the biggest computer family in the world. Someday, this Brain and all the little helper brains from MASTERNET will know just about everything there is to know about everybody and everything in America. And why is that important? Because it will help the government help people. The Brain will know where people work, and how many times they've been sick, and what kind of car they drive, and what kind of blood they have. It will remember if they paid their bills, or if they ever did anything dishonest and got arrested."

Heller paused, remembering that he had been instructed to interact with the children as often as possible. Leaning forward, hands on his knees, he put a teacherly question to them.

"Now, do you remember what we call facts like that when we put them all together, all in one big bundle?"

Several voices chirped back, "Data!"

"That's right, data. That's what the government,

and the police, and school teachers, and doctors and hospitals need to do a good job and make people happy. Lots of good, dependable data."

While Heller studied his performance on the monitor, Kayla bent over her clipboard, making fast notes on all that went by, keeping up a steady stream of complimentary comments. "Yes, very good . . . we'll keep that. Just right . . . wonderful."

Heller agreed with her enthusiasm. He also liked what he was seeing. He was carrying the job off nicely for someone who rarely dealt with children. Normally, his work restricted him to the bracing company of top decision-makers and academic specialists. The last twenty years of his life had been spent in high administrative circles, negotiating the powers and privileges of the Brain with congressional leaders, fighting off the attacks of political opponents and hostile civil libertarians who insisted upon seeing the NCDC as the beginning of an American police state. Now, for Kayla's young audience, he was stepping down several levels of discourse. More demanding than that, he was projecting a new Thomas Heller—good-natured, fun-loving, avuncular, a man he had never shown the world before.

He knew there were those who refused to believe there could be a humane side to his character, people who distrusted the Brain, and Heller, who was its builder and boss. That was exactly why he had initiated the visitors tours to the Center and the special schools program; it was why he had invited Kayla to bring "Wonder/Wander" to the Center. No sooner had the NCDC been authorized by Congress, than public relations became one of Heller's commanding priorities. He prided himself for being so alert to "the human factor" in the Brain's future.

"We've got to put a human face on the Center," he argued in policy sessions with his staff. "We've got to open ourselves up to public experience and curiosity. It's extremely important to establish an outgoing, hospitable atmosphere. We'll let the public get close to the beast, learn the Brain is their friend. We can't afford to look too 1984-ish, especially not now at the outset. There's too much co-operation we need in assembling our data bases."

His staff had been reluctant about the proposal. Kids were bound to get underfoot, and rubbernecking tours would burn up valuable time on the equipment. In some areas, where the Brain housed classified information, there would be tricky security problems.

Still, nobody resisted too strenuously. The staff understood Heller's concern. They knew as well as he how seriously the future of the Center could be threatened by the pressure of a determined opposition in the press and the Congress that continued to denounce the Brain as a dangerous concentration of power, the threshold to the Brave New World. In political cartoons accompanying severely critical editorials, newspapers as influential as the New York *Times* and the Washington *Post* frequently portrayed Heller as a glowering "Big Brother Watching You." The American Civil Liberties Union had borrowed that menacing image and was using it as part of a nationwide "Campaign Against the Brain," which cast Heller in the role of a psychotic snoop. *Time* magazine had run a major feature on the Center; it had been favorable enough, but its cover illustration caricatured Heller as a bug-eyed, elephant-eared robot named "Peeping Tom." The name had stuck; Heller knew it was what the Washington bureaucracy and press corps called him in private. It wasn't only the Center that needed a human face.

But fighting free of the Peeping Tom image posed some tough problems for Heller. This was because the characterization, while it usually came at him as a crude accusation, was largely true. He *was* bent on creating a national data network of unprecedented size and power; he *was* fanatical about his commitment to the role of the Brain as a central organ of government. What his critics missed was the idealism and intellectual exhilaration that underlay Heller's project. Above all, they failed to see the computer as a quantum leap forward in rational decision-making that offered the modern world its one best chance of security and salvation.

Heller knew he could not be entirely candid about that conviction. It was a truth and a faith that few people were ready to hear. Phrased with all the passion Heller might wish to lend it, his private vision of the future was bound to be distrusted, even feared. How else could people react to an ideal that broke so radically with the past? Heller belonged to a small, brave band of daring minds—computer scientists and cyberneticians, psychologists working on the frontiers of artificial intelligence, logicians experimenting with advanced programming theories —who were the secret apostles of a new gospel of progress. Until the world at large was prepared to accept the full import of their message, they had to serve their cause with the utmost tact, settling for marginal gains, unobtrusive victories.

Heller knew that strategy was bound to prevail. Day by day, in every walk of life, ingenious new data techniques were making their way forward, permeating the society with the power of a superior mentality. Once, less than a generation ago, the computer had been an exotic and mysterious machine that few people might expect to see or touch. Now, shrunk down to the size of microprocessors no bigger than a fingernail, computers were suddenly everywhere. They were commonplace, homely. They had become toys, gadgets, amusements. There was hardly an appliance on the market that did not contain its own tiny chip or shred of man-made intelligence. Already, in America, Europe, Japan, computer technology had reached such density that its critics had no choice but to yield ground; they were at a loss to imagine any other way to package and process the data on which the modern world depended. They grumbled, but they gave way. It would not be long before their surrender was total, and they acknowledged in the Brain, not an adjunct to government, but government itself, at last free of bias, misjudgment, and corruption.

That was the hidden agenda behind Heller's public relations campaign. It was not simply a matter of winning friendly opinions for the Brain, but of teaching a new conception of life and mind to a species that was the old, failing order of life and mind.

For the first several weeks after the Brain opened its doors to the world, Heller's personal involvement with the public was intense. At least once each week, he shepherded visitors through the Brain, explaining, demonstrating, entertaining. He even took charge of school tours. The task cut severely into his busy schedule, but he enjoyed the role of welcoming host, relished seeing the Brain become a popular and accessible feature of the city. By the time "Wonder/Wander" came to film, Heller had hired a small corps of professional tour guides and was giving the public little more of himself than an occasional wave if he was on hand when visitors trooped by his office or passed him in the halls. But he had saved "Wonder/Wander" for himself, a platform for his new public image. And, of course, it was Heller, the Brain's top man, whom Kayla Breen wanted at the center of her show.

2

"MIPS and BIPS? Oh, Tom, you're putting me on. What are MIPS and BIPS?"

Kayla Breen was working on her third martini while she and Heller waited for a table in the Four Georges. It was not the first time that Heller had seen her tight; at day's end, Kayla rushed to ensconce herself in an alcoholic haze, growing more flirtatious with each drink. She confirmed his impression that television people got drunker faster than anybody else, including politicians.

"MIPS means *millions of instructions per second*," Heller explained. "BIPS means *billions of instructions per second*. It's a measure of how fast a computer computes. The current generation of computers is into BIPS. We're way beyond MIPS. That's what the microchips are accomplishing for us: a revolutionary improvement in speed and precision every eight years. Soon it will be every five years. You see, the computers are moving too fast for their critics."

"MIPS. BIPS. Sounds like baby talk. But no," Kayla objected, her words already slurring at the edges. "That's too sophisticated for our kids; we'll have to leave it out. Most of my audience can't even count past ten."

She was wedged up against him at a corner table, much closer than she had to be even in the thronging bar. Kayla did not become troublesome when she was drunk. On the contrary, Heller found her cute and playful, an easy person to unbend with. She made no secret about coming on to him, and he appreciated her frankness. Since his divorce eight years ago, Washington society generally ranked him among its more eligible bachelors, a man of good looks and great influence. It was a status that frequently forced him into some artful maneuvers to preserve his freedom. With Kayla, there was no need for maneuvers; she let it be known she had no permanent arrangements in mind. She was only passing through town.

"Well, the way I try to teach the kids about MIPS and BIPS," Heller continued, only half-seriously trying to make the conversation sound businesslike, "is to give them some simple instruction—like to add two and seven . . ."

"Eight!" Kayla answered with a sloppy snap of her fingers. "Don't tell me that's wrong. It's close enough for all normal human purposes."

"Or I ask them to untie and tie their shoelaces."

Kayla lifted one shoe, brushing her leg against Heller's and displaying a slender ankle. "Sorry, no laces, just buckles. How about getting out of one's pantyhose? Will that do instead?"

"Carrying out that one instruction," Heller continued, "usually takes the kids several seconds. Then I tell them that our very slowest computer at the Brain can carry out one billion instructions every second."

"Amazing!" Kayla exclaimed. "I didn't even know computers wore shoes." Leaning forward on his shoulder and batting her eyes, she fell into a comic imitation of Miss Jenny Penny. "And now tell me, Dr. Heller, are BIPS just the most superfast things there are?"

"No," Heller answered. "After BIPS comes TIPS."

Kayla burst out laughing. "TITS?" she squeaked loud enough to draw attention. The game she and Heller had come to play when they were together after hours was for him to talk shop with mock persistence while she tried to distract him with sheer irrelevance and sexual innuendo.

"TIPS," Heller corrected. "*Trillions of instructions per second*. That's the new generation of computers. But they're .

tricky. They use Josephson circuits. Very costly. A whole new technology."

"You're not going to tell me what Josephson circuits are, are you?" she asked with exaggerated distress.

"Why not? I thought you said this was supposed to be a working dinner?"

"It is. It is. Can't you see how hard I'm working?" She rested her chin on his shoulder and drew his arm tight against her chest. "You're just not co-operating."

Playing his part, Heller continued, "We do have a new Josephson computer on display at the Brain. You might want to include something on that. You see, the core has to be kept in liquid helium, more than 250 degrees below freezing centigrade. That usually impresses the kids. We tell them that it's colder inside that computer than . . ."

". . . than inside Dr. Heller's heart." Kayla finished his sentence. "You know, there are rumors around this town that Thomas Heller is as frigid as they come. Just all brains and numbers. Is that true, Tom? Are you a Josephson circuit?"

"What do you think, Kayla?" he asked, reaching up to stroke her chin with his knuckle.

"I'm beginning to wonder."

"You've only been in town for a week."

"Such a long time to spend in lonely hotel rooms. Haven't you heard, Dr. Heller? Things move fast these days. Faster than a speeding BIP."

The rumor she mentioned was all too familiar to Heller—part of the negative public image his opponents used against him. It was no secret how his unsparing ambition in creating the Brain had destroyed his marriage; but broken marriages were par for the course in Washington. There were other, more irksome stories that portrayed him as unfeeling, ascetic, a disembodied calculating machine. Those stories hurt. They wounded his pride. Worse, they made him an easy target for critics who rushed to defend "human values" against the computer.

Accordingly, with cool deliberation, Heller had set about outflanking his critics. He budgeted time for the effort. He joined a few athletic clubs, took up tennis and cycling, maintained a regular social schedule, showed up at well-publicized cultural events. He also made it his business to be seen in public with handsome women once or twice a month. Kayla was part of that strategy. Her flirtatious attentions at carefully selected restaurants and night clubs around Washington were meant to enhance his virility in the public eye. She might not have guessed she was being used that way; Heller suspected she wouldn't care if she did. It was likely she had little more in mind than Heller did: a transient few nights with no risks and the benefit of some prestigious companionship in prominent places. She was safe for Heller, a woman too deeply caught up in her own soaring career to be looking for more than he cared to offer.

After they had taken a table and ordered, Heller said, "I know there are people around town who think I'm a pretty cold fish." He allowed a carefully calibrated amount of wounded feelings to show behind the remark.

"But you're not," Kayla hastened to console him. "Tell me you're not."

"Well, it's the stereotype every mathematician has to struggle against. The irony is: computer science is really based on a very different idea about life than the public thinks."

"Screw the public!" Kayla said. She was now mixing the cocktails she had drunk with a prodigious amount of wine. "That's all just envy. Envy and resentment. Listen, you should hear what they say about women who make it in television. You know what they say? Dykes, that's what they think we are. Outrageous! What's your idea aboout life, Tom? Tell me your idea."

"The whole reason we need the computer," Heller explained with more enthusiasm now than their little game required of him, "is exactly because people—including you and me—*aren't* machines. We *aren't* computers. We weren't meant to be. We can't be that rational, that logical. It's biologically impossible for us."

"Right," Kayla agreed, fixing him with a glassy stare. "I'll drink to that." She did. "What *are* people like, tell me, Tom."

Amused by her increasingly soggy attention, Heller pursued his now slightly intoxicated end of the conversation. "People are fuzzy-minded, sloppy, imprecise."

"You can say that again," Kayla commented.

"People are slack. Their will and their concentration fatigues. That's why we need another intelligence in the world to carry on for us, to take over from us. We've created an economic system that's gotten beyond us. It needs an intelligence that never forgets, never weakens, never gets confused. Brains that never get tired of thinking. That's what computers are for."

"And us, we're for fun and games, right?" Kayla added. "I like that, Tom. Here's to fun and games." She drained her glass, cradled her chin in her hand and gazed seriously at him across the table. "But listen—can we trust these machines? That's what I want to know. Tell me the truth, just between us experts. Do we really *want* them to take over?"

Heller answered flippantly, but the words sprang from a profound conviction. "Do we have any choice? They *are* taking over. They're already in charge of everything important."

"You mean the bombs. They're in charge of the bombs."

"Yes, the bombs. And the banks, and the factories, and all the records and all the numbers. They've been sneaking in steadily for twenty years. Government, military, business, schools, medicine. But nobody noticed it happening until it *had* happened, because the microprocessors are so small, and so very seductive. They make everything so easy for us. And we *like* giving up responsibility." He winked knowingly at her. "Our weak spot."

"But will they be kind to us, when they take over? Will they . . . respect us?" She was making a face that mimicked deep philosophical concern.

He could no longer tell how seriously to take her questions. Everything that passed between them had taken on a tone of semi-inebriated frivolity. Moreover, under the table, her shoeless foot had been probing his calves through most of dinner.

"We'll program them to respect us," Heller answered.

"That's our only hope really. After all, we want to be fondly remembered."

"Remembered?" she asked with an inquisitive squint.

"Evolution is on the side of brains," he said, not expecting her to catch the point. "And the best brains around aren't ours any more."

She pondered the remark. He thought he saw a flicker of disapproval move across her face. Or maybe it was only an uncomfortable shiver. Quickly, he covered up his grim forecast with a laugh—as if he were only joking. In fact, he wasn't. He had just told her one of his deepest beliefs, his vision of the coming human obsolescence. Perhaps something of the Arctic landscape that often filled his thoughts of the future had touched her, chilled her. He reached across to fill her glass. Obligingly, she raised a toast. "Here's to brains, Tom. Which aren't always everything."

Even as she drank, her eyes were on him with a searching, remotely curious gaze. She might not have been as drunk as he thought. Tactfully, he steered the conversation toward less sensitive subjects. But there was really only one other direction to go. It was Kayla's last weekend in Washington, and there were expectations waiting to be honored like outstanding debts. Having come this far with her, he could not send her back to New York suspecting the rumors she had heard about him were true. He caught her foot between his ankles and the subject of computers slipped away for the evening.

3

Their dinner had hardly been a working dinner, but their breakfast the next morning in Kayla's suite was all business. From the moment she woke him with a dry kiss and an approving smile, she was a different woman. She shook off her liquor and her affection with an efficiency Heller could only admire.

At breakfast, she passed him a résumé of the videotaped sequences still available for inclusion in the show. "We'll be choosing from among these, I think," she said, checking off a half-dozen possibilities with a red marking pencil. "The Star Wars computer game is a must. I also like the video gizmo that lets the kids drive through the towns. What's that called?"

"Oh yes," Heller said. "That's TOURIST." She was referring to a multimedia exhibit that allowed visitors to simulate a drive through any one of forty American and European cities. On a projected visual display, they could call up information, view historical monuments, even check the menus of restaurants. "I thought that came off very well," he said.

"Yes," Kayla agreed, "but then there's that House of the Future sequence—with all the computerized gadgets. Actually, I think that's pretty silly. I mean who has that much trouble turning on their own lights or adjusting the thermostat? But that's where you explain so well about microcodes. We really ought to include that."

There was an item on the list she had left unmarked. "What about this sequence here where I talk about the UIM?" he asked.

"The UIM?"

"The Ultra-intelligent Machine."

"Oh that." Kayla paused and thought, then shook her head firmly. "I don't think that quite worked. You actually made it sound a bit too menacing—all that about computers becoming smarter than people. If you want my opinion, Tom, it's not good public relations to push a point like that too hard—even with children."

"I agree," Heller said. "I wasn't aware I had."

She smiled wryly. "You tend to get carried away sometimes. Not many people want to think of the human race being replaced by metal boxes, no matter how smart they are."

Nervously, Heller backed off, returning to the résumé. "All right, what about SHERLOCK?" he asked.

"Ah, SHERLOCK is definitely in. In fact, I want to close with that. Place of honor."

Heller was puzzled by the decision. "Really? Why?"

"You don't remember? Well, wait and see."

Later that day in the editing room, Kayla ran the sequence for Heller. Heller remembered he had used it in the show to explain what a program was, drawing out the difference between hardware and software. Programs like SHERLOCK were software, the instructions and the logic that told a computer what to think and how to think about it. In this case, the program was a game that allowed the kids to simulate some basic detective work. The game finished with the children watching their own personal statistics being entered into the Brain's criminal justice memory bank. As Heller explained,

"When you leave here today, the Brain is going to know all kinds of things about you. We'll put everything right there in the computer. It will know your name, and where you live, and what school you go to, and even what grades you got on your last report card. We'll give it a picture of you to keep and your fingerprints. And it will know what your voice sounds like. It will put all that data right beside what it knows about your mother and your father and your whole family—all on a little chip, just this big, see? Made out of, guess what? Sand. That's right, sand. Or silicon, as we call it. And the Brain will give you your very own Social Security number, which you can keep for the rest of your life. And if you ever get lost or sick, it will help the police or the doctor find out what they need to know."

One of the boys asked, "If a little kid gets losted, could it find him, the Brain?"

"It can help find him, oh yes," Heller answered. "The Brain has helped find lots of lost children."

"If a little kid gets kidnapped, could it find him too?" the boy asked again.

"The Brain can help," Heller repeated. "For instance, it might be able to tell the police who the kidnapper is. It might recognize his fingerprints or his voice on the telephone. The Brain keeps track of lots and lots of bad guys. You see, this is where the police from all over America keep all their data about criminals."

Another kid piped up, "Does the Brain know who robbed our television?"

"Well, it might. The robber's name could be in there somewhere, if he ever stole anything before and got caught."

"Then why don't it catch him and make him give it back?" the kid wanted to know.

"The Brain can't catch people," Heller explained. "The police have to do that. What the Brain does is to *think* for the police, you see? It's like a detective. Someday it will be the world's smartest detective, once we get all the data in and all the bugs out. Which will take a while yet. Because even the smartest computers always have lots of nasty bugs in them."

Suddenly, from off-screen there came a sharp little "Oh!" of distress. Heller's television face stopped talking, a frown of surprise traveling rapidly across its brow. As he watched his reaction on the screen, Heller recalled the incident, but he did not know how much of it had been filmed. He saw himself register puzzlement, then ask, "What?" as he looked out before him at the two dozen children who were sprawling on the floor. The camera, responding, was pulling unsteadily back and to the right.

"Okay, go with this," Kayla instructed her editor. "I'm so glad we caught this. Follow back and then in. We'll lose all this and cut to . . . there."

The camera picked out a little girl, a pale and fragile six-year-old wearing thick, goggling eyeglasses. "Do they bite?" she was asking, her hands drawn up to her mouth, her slightly crossed eyes opened wide with worried concern behind her blurry lenses.

"Bite?" the television Heller asked, now off-camera.

"The bugs that's in the machines . . . do they bite?"

The camera swung back and was once again tightly focused on Heller's face as he grinned broadly and fell into the condescending tone adults assume when they are amused by the misapprehensions of children.

"Oh yes," he answered. "They certainly *can* bite. They can be lots of nasty trouble. Oh, they can eat you up . . . cost you days of work. And then we have to stop and take everything apart and chase those bitey bugs away."

"And then where do they go, when you made them all run away?" the little girl asked.

On the screen, Heller walked over and bent down to rest his finger on the tip of the girl's nose. "Well, I'll tell you a secret, sweetheart. They run away and hide in all the other computers all over the world. And zip! there they are again, jumping out just like that when you least expect it. Pinch, pinch, pinch!" And he tweaked her cheek between two fingers.

"But," the little girl insisted, her voice tense and quavering, "you should . . . you should . . . the 'puter peoples should stamp down on them, and squish them, and kill them, and make them all dead."

Around her, other children began to act out her advice, gyrating about, stamping and squishing in all directions, while some pincered with clawlike fingers at legs and shoes, yipping, "Pinch, pinch, pinch!" The little girl went on, "You should spriss them all over with poison, like behind the sink when they come. Because they could bite you and eat you. They could bite little children up."

Heller's television face chuckled. He took hold of kids on both sides and drew them to him, reaching out to stroke the little girl's hair. "Well, no, that wouldn't work with these bugs. Because they're ever so tiny, you can hardly see them at all. And you never know where they might be, so you can't kill them. But I'll tell you what we can do. We can have lots of good computer people on guard all the time. And when they catch any bugs, they'll right away shoo them off and make sure they don't do too much harm."

Kayla rocked back in her chair laughing, clapping her hands together. "Lovely," she said, "just lovely. Oh, that's priceless. Look at those eyes, those expressions. Our grownups will get such a kick out of this. That's 17.3 per cent of our audience. We can spare them that much."

The camera was panning the faces of the children. Wide worried eyes, open mouths, one kid here and another there holding up fingers and thumbs, going pinch, pinch, pinch.

"You want to leave that part in?" Heller asked.

"I wouldn't cut it out for the world," Kayla answered. "It's perfect, very televisual. It moves, it's spontaneous, and so *human*."

Yes, Heller thought so too. It *was* human. Dr. Thomas Heller caught off-guard, responding with just the right mix of wit and fatherly affection, honestly confessing to the limitations of his science, but in a way that was sure to show confidence, invite trust. He liked that picture of himself, the real man relating to real kids with genuine, unscripted humor, his arms about them, tousling their hair.

That, Kayla and her production crew agreed, was how the show must finish, with the odd-looking little girl asking her question, and Heller making his little joke, telling her oh yes, the bugs could bite, they certainly could.

And two weeks later, just after "Wonder/Wander's" visit to the Brain had been broadcast, the first one did.

2

1

It didn't look like a bite—not at first. It looked like a light rash. A programmer from the Law Enforcement Division checked into the Center's infirmary complaining of a prickly skin irritation over her hands and forearms. The rash was hot and pesky and she could not keep from scratching at it. The medic on duty gave her a salve and sent her home early. The next day she was back on the job, but over the following week, four more people appeared with the same complaint. Then the programmer from Law Enforcement returned with a more severe outbreak. After that, there was never less than one case a day and sometimes as many as three.

Heller did not learn about the rash until it had been around the Brain for nearly a month; he may have been among the last to hear of it. It was not unusual for him to drift out of touch with minor details of that kind for several days at a time when more urgent matters claimed his attention. The early spring was one of those periods. A European junket, a conference in Tokyo and, most pressing of all, a congressional hearing that promised to become a highly publicized confrontation between him and the civil libertarians.

Through most of May, the hearings kept him away from the Brain for all but a day or two of each week. Then, toward the end of the month, he had occasion to call in his head of Credit References. The division owed him a report detailing the safeguards surrounding the Center's use of sensitive financial data.

Heller needed the information for the hearings, and it was two days late. Why? "Sorry," he was told, "it's this damned rash. It's got me way off schedule."

"What rash?" Heller asked.

Lee Miller, head of the Law Enforcement Division, was in Heller's office at the time. "The stuff is all over the place," he volunteered. "I'm a couple days behind in my section too. Picked up a little of it myself last week, see?" He showed the backs of his hands to Heller. They were red and marked with several small welts. "Sometimes it itches like crazy. Surprised you haven't heard about it."

"These hearings have had me tied up round the clock," Heller explained. "How long has this been going around?"

"I'm not sure. It started maybe a month ago . . . a little less. I think our division got hit with it first."

That morning Heller phoned the infirmary. After searching his records, the physician in charge reported ". . . some twenty-five cases, including maybe a dozen repeats. Of course, some people may not have checked in here; they may have gone to their own doctors. I sent a memo about this to Berny last week. I thought we should have a specialist come in for consultation."

Berny was Bernard Levinson, Heller's general factotum at the Center. A sharp, meticulous administrator, he shouldered most of the day-to-day responsibilities of the Brain. Levinson was ten years—or roughly one computer generation—younger than Heller. Otherwise, their careers ran a close parallel. Both had graduated at the top of their class from MIT's Laboratory for Computer Science. Both had rapidly piled up formidable research records and had been brought to Washington as whiz kid consultants to the military. Their paths had crossed in that capacity some fifteen years ago when Heller first became thickly involved in the fight to gain congressional authorization for the Brain. They recognized one another at once as natural allies aggressively committed to advancing the political role of the information sciences. When Heller took over as head of the Center, there was no question who his second in command would be.

"I thought I should keep this odd little matter out of your way while you were busy with the hearings," Levinson explained when Heller contacted him about the rash. He had already acted on the infirmary's recommendation and sent the latest batch of cases, four people in all, to a dermatologist. "I should have a report tomorrow. I also checked with the personnel offices of a few other big installations in the city to see if anything similar has turned up. Right now, it looks as if we're the only victim." As usual, Levinson had been thorough.

"Well, let's get on this fast," Heller instructed him. "It's beginning to cost us."

Automatically, he sought to clear his mind of the problem, consigning it to the status of a minor housekeeping detail, nothing he need give a second thought. But the matter would not be dismissed; it nagged him that day and the next while his thoughts should have been concentrated on the hearings, which were emerging in the media as major news. The sight of Lee Miller's inflamed hands kept breaking in upon him, demanding a label, an explanation. But Heller could not find a neat, logical slot where the problem might be filed and forgotten.

More annoying still, the morning after the rash had been brought to his attention, he waked out of a restless sleep with a prickly sensation over his arms and chest. Rubbing at himself, he hurried to the nearest mirror. There was no sign of a rash on him, the itchiness was gone. He had had a dream . . . something unpleasant associated with the discomfort that woke him. What was it? A crime . . . an escape . . . an ambush. Children chasing him or being chased, playing cops and robbers. He went through breakfast trying—unsuccessfully—to piece the taunting fragments of the fading dream together. Then, catching himself at the task, he snapped his mind to attention. Irked to the point of anger, he sharply reminded himself that brooding over dreams was not the sort of thing Thomas Heller wasted his time doing.

A day later when Levinson brought in the dermatologist's report, he was more eager to hear the results than he cared to admit.

"It's some kind of allergic reaction," Levinson explained, "but the doctor can't say to what. Something people are handling around here. Everybody's got it on exposed surfaces. The hands and arms. Some of the women who wear skirts have it around the ankles and calves."

"No idea at all what it might be?"

"None. As far as I know, everything people handle around here is the usual run of office materials. Metal, glass, plastic, vinyl. Pens, pencils, paper. Nothing exotic."

"What about the ink on our print-outs?"

"I thought of that. But the people who work most with our inks haven't been especially affected. It's the standard product —magnetized printer's ink. I rubbed some on my hand last week. I asked a couple others who've had the rash to do the same. Nothing. We can check that anyway. I'm asking the dermatologist to spend a day over here next week. Maybe he can spot something we're missing. There were four cases of the rash yesterday, three the day before that. That's a two-day high. The latest cases seem to be worse. Larger welts, more irritation, lots more complaining. Also a few people this week claim to have the rash under their clothes."

"Are people worrying about it?"

"Sure. Everybody knows about it by now. There's lots of bitching. It's even picked up a name. 'Data pox.' Cute. Several people have been hit twice. There's a secretary in Credit References who's come down with it three times. She's making a lot of noise. Says she's ready to quit."

To himself Heller thought, Stupid business! I have no time to waste on this. But he gave instructions to Levinson coolly, without the least sign of peevishness. "I suggest we make a serious show of urgency and concern. Let it be known that I'm on top of this, giving it my full personal attention, and so on. Let's get a couple allergists in here to work with the skin doctors. Make it a complete survey—out in the open. Let everybody see it happening."

"One more thing you may want to know," Levinson added.

"What's that?"

"The dermatologist says he checked with a couple of his colleagues in the city to see if they were turning up anything similar. Guess what? One of them had—two kids from Lafayette High, about ten days ago. Brother and sister. That was just after they came through the Center with their class on a field trip. Of course, there might not be any connection."

Heller thought a long moment. "I hate to consider closing the Brain. That's drastic. It could attract too much attention. We don't want to exaggerate this. To begin with, unless we have good reason to do otherwise, we should keep this strictly in-house. Look, let's reschedule all visiting to twice a week until we clear up the mystery. Let the schools in on Tuesday and the general public on Friday. And instruct the guides to steer their tours around any sections where there's been lots of rash."

The dermatologist and the allergists spent two days examining the Brain and then reported to Levinson. He summarized the results for Heller. "They were absolutely thorough, but not very illuminating. They all agree it's an allergy, but they weren't able to find anything particularly suspicious on the premises. They agreed we should have our inks analyzed. But I've had a dozen more people rub the stuff on with no sign of irritation."

"I've tried it myself," Heller said, holding out his hands. "Same result. I doubt there's anything there."

"Also nothing unusual about the soaps or paper towels we use," Levinson went on. "No strange plant life around the offices, nothing in the air conditioning, nothing unusual about the fluorescent lighting. There are a couple dozen buildings in Washington constructed out of much the same run of materials we've got around here. I've checked with our architects, especially about insulation, paints, carpeting. They've had no complaints of this kind with other projects. Nor have their suppliers and subcontractors. The doctors talked to everybody who's had the rash. The only thing they have in common is that they all work here. They haven't been going to orgies together or anything like that."

"So the bottom line is zero."

"Except for maybe one new thing. When we were talking to the rashees, several of the recent cases—I counted nine—said they were sure they'd been stung."

"Stung?"

"Stung . . . bitten. Those are the words they used. They said the day they got the rash, they kept feeling little stinging sensations on their arms and ankles or under their clothes, like something biting. They'd slap at it, you know, the way you would at a mosquito. Fact is, I've seen people doing that around the place over the last week or so."

"Did anybody manage to swat anything?"

"No, nothing. But it's curious: none of the earlier cases could remember anything like that. The rash just suddenly appeared with them."

"What'd the doctors make of that?"

"Well, they certainly didn't see any insect life around the place, so they thought it must be an illusion. They said inflamed nerve ends can produce that feeling—as if things were crawling over the skin surface. It's just funny that we're getting that report now, not earlier."

Heller allowed a long pause to settle in. He wondered if he and Levinson had the same thought in mind. Both men were intimately familiar with the data processing and electronics industry. They knew its science, they also knew its folklore.

"You're thinking what?" Heller asked.

"You know the old rumor about the telephone company."

"Cable lice?"

"Yeah."

Heller knew the story. It had been circulating for more than two generations through the journalistic twilight zone. Every few years a lurid exposé would appear in a weekly scandal sheet like the *National Enquirer* about the lice or mites that supposedly infested the telephone company's switchboards. Usually, there were photos of girls identified as telephone operators showing arms and legs covered with nasty lesions. Legal action was reported to be in progress by the former employees; they were suing for damages, but the phone company was hushing up the case. There were unpleasant descriptions of the phone lice, sometimes magnified photographs. People Heller knew in the telephone industry dismissed the rumors as totally absurd, an attempt to extort money from the company. They referred to the problem as "delusionary parasitosis."

"That's only gossip," Heller replied.

"Ma Bell *says* it's only gossip."

"And you say . . . ?"

"I say maybe this is how gossip begins. First you get a real rash with no explanation why. Then you get imaginary lice to account for the rash."

Heller saw the point. People try to make sense of things. The more mysterious the situation, the more cockeyed the conjectures. And data pox was becoming very mysterious.

"All right," he decided. "Get another team of allergists in here to go over the ground again. And this time get someone up here from the Atlanta Center for Disease Control to lend some authority to the investigation. Put out the word that the rash has been diagnosed by a team of medical consultants as an allergic reaction of as yet unknown origin, that we're continuing a top priority survey of the Center to find the source, that we invite full participation by the staff. Anybody having information or leads about possible causes is to report to you. If anyone starts talking lice, or gremlins, or rays from outer space, come down on it fast. Find out who said what to whom, and have them all in for questioning. Make them say where and when, and find witnesses. Show concern, but be firm about evidence. If there's none, then make them agree they were seeing things. Until somebody catches a computer louse, they don't exist."

2

Later that day, on his way to the hearings, Heller pondered what Levinson had said about the mythical phone lice. There were executives he knew at AT&T who believed the rumor was part of a left-wing conspiratorial effort to discredit the company. Could the same be true of data pox? Could someone be spreading the stuff around the building, perhaps rubbing poison oak on people's clothes and equipment, trying to sabotage operations and break morale? That might be worth checking into. He made a note to increase security and surveillance at the Center, possibly to run an informal personnel survey to scout out malcontents or subversive types. The idea sounded more than a little paranoid, but the elusive nature of the problem invited such speculation, especially now, when Heller and the Brain were under renewed critical pressure. The hearings before the Senate Committee on Judicial Affairs, now in their second week, were proving to be a rough exercise for him. They were generating more alarmist reports in the media than he found comfortable. This was no time for the Center to be experiencing mysterious new troubles.

Senator Merrill Cory of California, chairman of the investigating subcommittee, was an old enemy of the Brain. Heller regarded him as the sort of doctrinaire opponent he stood no chance of winning over or discouraging. People like Cory would fight on the same line until they either got their way or had to retire from the scene. There would always be some grievance or rumor that gave them an excuse for public recrimination. Heller had learned that he simply had to work around such opposition, angling to outflank and outlast it. Ideological harassment came with his job; each year he budgeted a generous amount of time and energy to cope with it. A sad waste of his talent, but he charged it up to public relations. His strategy was to stay cool under attack, hasten to offer reasonable co-operation, keep the matter low key, play for time and wait for the crisis to subside. Eventually, barring a first class scandal or persistent public outcry, he knew the Congress would wrap the problem in red tape and pass on to more urgent business.

Heller was wisely reconciled to the fact that an operation as novel as the Brain had to expect a certain rhythm of controversy. Each time its appetite for data grew, each time it reached out to take on a new responsibility, there was bound to be resistance. Especially so since it was widely known in Washington that Heller was maneuvering to make the Brain an independent executive bureau, with full powers to deal in classified information and to exempt part of its personnel from standard civil service procedure. Only the military intelligence agencies held a comparable status. Whenever Heller inched toward that goal, enemies like Cory opened fire.

It was Heller's continuing push for maximum independence that had touched off the current hearings. Friends in the executive branch and the military had proposed legislation to remove the Brain from the Department of Commerce, where it functioned as part of the Social and Economic Statistics Administration. That was far too humble and exposed a position to suit Heller's tastes. His immediate objective was to rehouse the Brain within the National Security Council, where it could operate under a military cover and avoid constant scrutiny. Cory, always quick to decry Heller's intentions, responded by dramatically proclaiming a Citizen's Charter of Privacy that would impose strict legal limits on the Center's access to data and the use that could be made of it. It was the sort of liberal grandstanding the senator specialized in. Predictably, the civil libertarians, led by the ACLU and Common Cause, rushed to support the idea, comparing it to the charter that governed the FBI. They argued: if the FBI can be restricted in its vital activities, why not the Brain?

The answer was clear in Heller's mind, but it was not a line of defense he could press too openly. The Brain was not primarily a law enforcement agency like the FBI. The police work it did was actually one of its low grade functions, totally pedestrian and far below the state of the art. The Brain's true purpose went far beyond mere record keeping and data retrieval; its mission was nothing less than to provide a worldwide industrial economy with an unprecedented higher order of governing intelligence. Data was the fuel and lubricant which that new intelligence required. It had to have the fullest possible access to information of every kind.

Precisely because it so awesomely surpassed human intellect, the Brain had to know more, far more than any government had ever known before. But exactly what and how much it might have to know at any given time, no one could say in advance. Could a person of average intelligence predict what a genius might need to know to carry through a great intellectual project? By the same token, the Brain functioned at levels of complexity that even human genius could not imagine. Only if its operations were left wholly unrestricted, could it demonstrate its superiority and deliver its full benefits.

And that was the rub. Heller had no doubt that, once the public grasped the limitless potentiality of computer intelligence, it would endorse—more than that, it would *clamor* for its maximum application. No society would willingly sacrifice so immense a promise of security and abundance. But in order to reach that point of public acceptance, the Brain had first to prove itself; it had to establish a record of accomplishment. That meant it had to expand its control and influence without hindrance. It must not be hobbled in its forward thrust by timid minds having no conception of its brilliant and beneficent future.

That was why the charter which Cory and his supporters were championing would be a disaster. It would slow the development of the Center down to what a few mediocre recalcitrants saw fit to allow. And who were these opponents but little, bitter, envious men who knew they were being left behind in the dust of a great historical advance? Though he had never committed the idea to print, Heller saw the new information technology as no less than an evolutionary transition that was bringing a higher species to supremacy. Just as the kingdom of the vegetables had once given way to the animal, and the animal to man, so now man was yielding his dominion over nature to forms of machine intelligence that were his own finest creation. That was why Heller viewed the carping criticism of his enemies with such secret contempt. It was worse than ignorant and insulting; it was a biological throwback. The unreasoning fixation of his opponents on trivial issues of personal privacy was the pathetic resentment of sea creatures as they witnessed the first amphibians leaving the ancient habitat, daring to breathe the air and walk the earth.

But this was clearly not the way Heller could argue the matter in public debate. He had to deal tactfully with the cultural lag that confronted him. He could not openly contend that

Cory and the civil libertarians had no legitimate issue. Where they demagogically invoked the right to privacy, their appeal struck deep emotional chords. The society was still largely swayed by the irrational rhetoric of backward-looking humanists like Cory. Heller had to allow for that.

So he turned to a line of argument he had worked out over many years, reaching back to his early career in computer science at MIT and the RAND Corporation. With painstaking logic, he argued that, in a complex modern society, the traditional conception of "privacy" as an absolute property right in personal information was simply untenable. For the sake of the national defense, internal security, effective law enforcement and competent social planning, data of every kind had to be freely assimilated into the public domain. He pointed out that, as a matter of plain fact, this was already happening in a multitude of covert, often illegal ways. Data banks, both public and private, were steadily eating into the private lives of people. There was no longer any reliable way for ordinary citizens to keep secrets. Nor would they want to—not if they knew what that might cost in the way of sound policy-making and efficient management.

Late one night, while he lingered with Heller over perhaps one drink too many, Levinson had asked only half facetiously, "Listen, Tom, just between you and me and Johnny Walker, what exactly *is* the difference between us and Big Brother?"

Heller had answered, "Big Brother was fiction. We're not."

The reply did not mean Heller failed to respect the dangers that came with the Brain's position in society. Rather, he was confident that there was a more responsible way to address the challenge of the computer than Senator Cory's stance of fanatical rejection. In the future, the only rational safeguard of information, public or private, would be the professional ethics of data technicians working under a binding oath like that sworn by physicians and lawyers. In Heller's view, that was a dependable, yet flexible guarantee which would allow the Brain to move rapidly forward in its mission without endangering constitutional rights. People were willing to trust their doctors, psychiatrists, priests with intimate details of their lives; they must simply learn to see data technicians in the same way—as duty-bound professionals.

But none of this would come to pass if the Brain once seriously failed to discharge its responsibilities with the utmost reliability. Heller's enemies would use any failure against him mercilessly, with every intention of crippling the progress of the Center. This was why data pox nagged at his mind so stubbornly. It could provide his opposition with a second line of criticism. Besides the issue of privacy, there was the question of simple efficiency. Anything that slowed the Brain down, anything that interfered with its accuracy even in the slightest had to be treated with maximum urgency. The Brain and MASTERNET were rapidly becoming the single channel carrying the entire national information flow. Heller had always known there was a risk in centralizing the nation's computer power so tightly; he also knew there was no other way to create the governing superintelligence he wanted. But if MASTERNET crashed, the most vital data services of the society crashed with it.

Heller had colleagues in computer science who had been dubious about the Brain from the beginning. They had warned him that he was flirting with disaster; the system was too vulnerable. If it pricked its finger, it might bleed to death. But he had taken the risk, and had persuaded the government to follow where he led. In the face of such fears, he insisted on the possibility of designing a national information center that could withstand any imaginable emergency. The system itself was its own most powerful defense. It contained programs meant to cope with every possible contingency from blown fuses to thermonuclear war. There were crisis scenarios in the Brain that had been traced out in detail by the finest minds in the profession using the most advanced computers in the world. The Brain was designed to be self-correcting in depth, one step ahead of every problem that might arise.

But Heller knew there was nothing in any of its contingency programs that dealt with a mysterious little rash that would not go away and could not be cured. What if the rash got out of control, began to spread in epidemic proportions, grinding down morale, upsetting the Center's schedules? Of course, he was exaggerating. Still, the bizarre, wholly unforeseen character of the problem troubled him.

Data pox. Such an absurdity! Who could have predicted it? But at once Heller reminded himself that he had no defense along that line. It was his official responsibility to predict it. And he hadn't. Just as it was the Brain's official responsibility to be omniscient. And it wasn't.

3

The second group of allergists came to the Center and left, producing no better results than the first. Yes, the rash looked like an allergic reaction. No, they could not identify a likely cause. After another two weeks and no let up in cases, Heller ordered a third medical team to investigate. But now he knew he was spinning his wheels—looking busy, getting nowhere. All the while, data pox continued to spread through the Brain. A month after the first doctor had been consulted, more than two hundred people—over a third of Heller's staff—had come down with the rash, many for a second or third time. Three resignations had already been traced to the complaint; absenteeism was on the rise. Around the offices, people could be seen regularly now swatting at their ankles or arms, as if chasing off pests. Everybody who had picked up the rash over the past month described its onset as a sting or bite, but Levinson had picked up no mention of insects as a cause. Not until the end of the third month. Then somebody finally saw one.

3

1

It was a black cleaning woman named Polly Johnson who saw the first bug. Toward five o'clock one afternoon in mid-June, she had begun polishing the glass doors of the Internal Revenue Division. Suddenly she let out a hoot that could be heard across the building.

"Get offa me, bug," she screamed, batting at her arm with a wet sponge. She leaped back, upsetting her cleaning cart, spilling powders and pungent fluids across the floor. At once, a small group of people rushed out of the IRD to offer help.

"Get offa me, you hear!" Polly cried again. Then she gave a harsh, gargling screech. "It went *in* me! Ooh, that insec' bitin' his way *in* me!" And she began to rub and slap furiously at her left forearm. "He bitin' right into me. Git him out! Git him out!"

In a moment, the foyer of the Center was a chaos of excitement. People on their way home, streaming toward the exits, were brought to a halt. The large black woman, keeping up a steady yammer of pain, crumpled against the wall and slid to the floor. Two programmers from IRD, slipping precariously in spilled detergent, pulled her back to her feet and steered her down the stairs toward the infirmary. Within minutes, Berny Levinson was there.

"Can you see anything?" he asked.

The doctor who was studying Polly's arm shook his head. He sprayed the skin with Novocain and fed Polly some pain-killers. She sat on the edge of the examination table, rocking back and forth, moaning, her free hand mopping her brow and cheeks. She was clearly in great pain.

"Nothing," the doctor said. "She's got a bite all right. Big as a bumble-bee sting. But I don't see any stinger in the wound, just a good-sized welt." He applied cold compresses to the swelling, then scrutinized it through a magnifying lens.

"He went right *in* me," Polly insisted. "I seen him."

"Exactly what did you see?" Levinson asked.

"I see him go in me." She shivered each time she repeated the report.

"What kind of insect was it? What did it look like?"

"Jus' a tiny, little white old bug, no bigger'n an ant. But soon's he bit me, it hurt like fire. Like a bee sting."

"Where did you first see the insect?"

"He on the door I was cleanin'. On the inside there of the IRD, you know. I seen him runnin' along the glass, sort of jitterin' aroun' like, you know. I never seen no bugs roun' here before, so I jus' watchin' him go. An' then he come over to where the crack is in the door, you know, an' he slip right through like that where there hardly any space at all. But then he on the outside, an' he come right on me. I feel him hit right there on my cheek, an' then on my arm, an' he start bitin' right at me."

The doctor inspected the place on her cheek where she said the insect had first landed. "Yes," he said, "there's a mark there, just a small nick. And then you saw it go *into* your arm? It didn't jump off maybe?"

"No, sir," Polly answered emphatically. "He go into me. I swat at him, an' he start drillin' his way right in. An' then he *gone*, an' I can feel him goin' right on bitin' his way in."

"Do you feel anything now?" the doctor asked.

"Jus' a big hurt," she said.

"Any more biting or stinging?"

"No, jus' like a kinda burnin' an' an itchiness all over. Like when I had the rash. That's what it feel like now, like I got the rash again."

She had made the connection Levinson was both eager and fearful to hear. "When did you have the rash, Polly," he asked.

"Las' month, I had the rash twice, Mr. Levinson. An' now I'm gonna have it again." Her answer was an angry and sullen accusation.

Levinson asked the doctor, "Do you know of any insects that behave like this?"

The doctor shook his head. "When her arm stops hurting, I'll probe the wound a little, see what I can find." He acted as if he were dubious of Polly's report.

"You git that thing outa me, is all," Polly ordered. "You jus' git him out."

But the doctor found no bug in the wound. The next day, Polly stayed home, phoning in to say she had "that rash" again all along her arm, insisting that the insect had given it to her. As with most other cases, the worst of it was over in forty-eight hours. When she reported back to work, Levinson checked with her to offer a friendly word. His solicitude did nothing to brighten her mood.

"If I get that rash one more time," she warned, "I'm quittin' this place, Mr. Levinson." And then, as he was leaving, she muttered after him, "That bug still inside me somewheres, that's what I think. I seen him go in, all right. I been *infested*."

Levinson had reported the incident to Heller, but several days passed and no more bugs were seen in the Brain. They decided to write off Polly's bite as an oddity unconnected with the data pox. Perhaps, Heller conjectured, she had been drinking on the job, seeing things. "Maybe," Levinson agreed, "but we all saw the bite." Meanwhile, the school term had ended, and, without calling attention to the decision, Heller was able to suspend the children's tours scheduled for the summer. He cut back to one visiting day each week, hoping to diminish the risk of the rash spreading to outsiders. The last thing he wanted was to order the Brain quarantined.

In mid-July, for the first time since the spring, there was a marked falling off of cases. Eight one week, five the next, two the next. Cautiously, Heller allowed himself to hope the worst might be over. Perhaps the rash would leave as mysteriously as it had come.

He hoped, but he more than half feared it was too much to expect. Before the month was over, Heller's crisis had ceased to be an in-house problem.

2

It was the third day of a near-record heat wave. The air over Washington had congealed into a warm jelly; even the best air-conditioners in town were balancing on the edge of overload. At a few minutes after four o'clock, the last public tour of the Brain was coming to an end. The guide had finished her remarks about the Public Opinion Polling Division and was leading her group toward Rembrandt in the muggy entrance lobby. She had just halted to make her final remarks when there was a brief scream from the rear of the line, then a man's voice calling for help. A man and a woman rushed from the polling division, struggling to get through the heavy glass door into the lobby. The man was brushing frantically at the woman's blouse and skirt. Several staff members and a few visitors came running behind them. The woman was flailing her arms, whining and yipping with panic.

"Insects . . ." the man shouted. "All over the machine in there . . . the computer. Please . . . they bit her. They're on her. Call a doctor!"

In the infirmary several minutes later, Levinson and Heller talked with the couple as the wife's bites were treated. Their name was Frankyl, tourists from Pittsburgh spending a few days in Washington. The woman had several ugly welts on each arm, on her shoulders, back and chest. "I can feel them in there," she repeated over and over. "They're crawling around way inside." She was trembling and white with shock.

"What did you see?" Heller asked urgently. "What did they look like? Where did they come from?"

The husband answered for her. "They were little white things, fleas I guess. We saw them crawling over the front of that last computer the lady showed us. The one that answers questions about public opinion, you know. We were finished with that exhibition and everyone was leaving. Jackie and I were at the end of the line. We saw these fleas—just a couple of them at first. And then we saw more, coming up out of . . . I don't know where. Wherever there was a crack or a seam in the metal, and from around the switches, or whatever you call them. It looked funny to see insects on a machine like that, so we watched them awhile after the tour moved off. Then one of them sort of jumped or flew off the computer onto my wife's arm. And it started biting her right away. And then another one jumped on her . . . and then they all started jumping, at her, and at me, and everywhere. So we ran. See, I got a couple bites, there and there. God, they burn like fire. They got all over Jackie."

"They bit right into me," Mrs. Frankyl said again from behind the screen where the doctor was examining her. "Right under the skin. I could see them getting under there, squirming around and digging in. I can feel them in there." She was repeating Polly Johnson's description, and in her voice too there was the tension of hysteria barely under control.

"I think we better get her to a hospital," the husband insisted. "I think we should get those things out of her quick."

"I can't see anything under the skin," the doctor said.

"I don't care what the hell you can't see," Mr. Frankyl retorted sharply. "It's what she feels that counts. She could be infected. Those things could be poisonous."

Levinson was already at the telephone. "I'm calling an ambulance now, Mr. Frankyl. We'll have both of you taken to Southwest Community Hospital for treatment. The Center will be fully responsible."

"I should hope so," the husband replied petulantly. "Christ! We only came in here to get out of the heat. What luck!"

Karen Short, a programmer in the Public Opinion Polling Division, had come with the couple. Heller asked her, "Did you see these things . . . these insects?"

"Yeah," she said. "It's just the way he told it. There were little white things running all over the front of the Cyber 2300. Maybe about the size of ants . . ."

"Smaller," Mr. Frankyl corrected. "Not that big. They were definitely fleas. You couldn't make out any features on them they were so small. But, God, could they bite!"

"Yeah, well maybe smaller than ants," Karen continued. "And they made this sort of clicking sound."

"Clicking?" Heller asked.

"That's right," Mr. Frankyl agreed. "Clicking. They clicked."

"Sort of click, click, click," Karen tried to imitate the sound. "Reminded me of a computer printer. Very metallic, mechanical. You couldn't hear that until there were lots of them together. Click, click, click."

"How many of the insects were there?" Heller asked. "Many?"

"Thousands," Karen estimated. Mr. Frankyl nodded agreement. "A couple thousand easy."

"Did anybody catch one?"

"Hell no. They bite."

"Or step on one?"

"People were trying to. I saw Chuck Peters trampling all over the place. Somebody must have gotten one."

"My wife seems to have caught several of them—in her body," Mr. Frankyl reminded Heller.

Levinson hung up the phone. "There'll be an ambulance here in minutes. They'll take Mrs. Frankyl to emergency, and then find her a private room if necessary. One of our people will go with you to arrange about the billing and other expenses. Also to find you hotel accommodations, Mr. Frankyl, if you need them."

"We're extremely sorry about this," Heller added feebly. "Please assume that your expenses for this visit to Washington will be handled by the Center. It's the least we can do."

Mr. Frankyl looked up from his wife's injuries. His expression showed no willingness to be bought off by Heller's favors. "What the hell kind of machines do you have around here?

We've got computers in my office . . . I never saw any insects coming out of them. This place could be a menace." Heller could see "lawsuit" written all over the man's angry face. Lawsuit . . . publicity . . . scandal.

That night, knowing the newspapers routinely covered admissions to the emergency ward, Heller and Levinson worked late preparing a press release. They had rapidly rounded up and questioned everybody on the staff who saw the insects, but without finding out more than the Frankyls had told them. Most bewilderingly, nobody had caught or killed a single insect; they had all disappeared back into the Cyber 2300. Chuck Peters among others claimed he had stomped on several of the insects. But when he lifted his foot, they scurried away unharmed or leaped at his legs. He had suffered a few nasty bites around the ankle.

When they were finished drafting their statement, Levinson remarked, "What we've got here is four windy paragraphs adding up to zero information. Not a single answer to any obvious question."

"We can't tell them what we don't know," Heller said wearily. "All we can do is display concern—vigorous concern."

"We could take the computer out and shoot it."

"They'll have to accept our word for it. It's a freak accident."

"Yeah, until it happens again. Freak rash, freak attack of freak bugs. Only one thing is solid. The pattern still holds."

"What pattern?"

"Escalation," Levinson said. "Step by step, it gets worse."

3

The next day, the Public Opinion Polling Division was closed and the Cyber 2300 disassembled. An entomologist from Georgetown University was asked to be on hand in case any insects showed up. He was a lanky young man, bearded and slightly long-haired. He wore bright, modish clothes: flared slacks and high-heeled boots. His name was Schifman, and he watched the proceedings with a wry skepticism. Neither Heller nor Levinson much liked his looks, but he came highly recommended. He had worked on classified projects for the military; he could be expected to be discreet.

"People saw these things come directly out of the computer?" Schifman asked Levinson as the computer was torn down piece by piece by a contingent of slightly nervous technicians.

"That's right," Levinson answered. "Karen here and some other employees observed the attack, as well as the Frankyls."

Schifman turned to Karen. She was standing by with a canister of insect spray. "And then, after the attack, they all scooted back into the computer?"

"Uh-huh," Karen answered. "They were gone in a flash. I couldn't even tell where they were going in. They were just vanishing like that, around the edges of the VDT screen and around the keyboard and printer."

Schifman had been studying parts of the computer as the technicians handed them over. "I don't know . . . looks like pretty tight metal seams. You say these things were how big? About the size of fleas?"

"Yeah," Karen answered. "And they clicked."

"Clicked?"

"Everybody who was here agrees they clicked," Levinson explained.

"Clicked . . . like crickets, maybe?" Schifman asked.

"No," Karen said, "It was very mechanical sounding. Sort of clickety-clickety-click . . ."

"Hey, do that again," Schifman requested, amused by her attempt to reproduce the sound. She tried again, finishing in embarrassed laughter. "That's real cute, the way you do that," Schifman remarked. There was an undercurrent of flirtatious banter passing between them. Levinson delivered a heavy, censorious sigh, loud enough to be heard across the room.

"Okay, and then what, after the clicking started?" Schifman asked, obediently returning to business. "How did they get on the people?"

"They jumped," Karen answered.

"How far?"

From the front of the Cyber 2300, Karen paced off a distance. "Well, with the display equipment, we only let one or two people get close at a time. The rest stay behind the barrier and watch. That's where the Frankyls were—maybe even a little farther back. About here."

Schifman estimated the distance. "Four feet . . . maybe more. This little flea jumped over four feet?"

"Yeah. Some of them jumped farther than that."

Schifman wagged his head and grinned at her sardonically. "Whatever kind of grass it is you folks have been blowing around here, I'd change my brand."

"We didn't ask you here to make wisecracks," Levinson snapped impatiently. "We've got a lady in the hospital since yesterday covered with bites—severe bites. Maybe we've got a bad lawsuit on our hands. This is no hallucination, Professor."

"Okay, okay," Schifman said placatingly. "Just catch me one. Insects that live in computers . . . that's worth a Nobel prize."

But they found no insects. Inside, the computer was a microscopic jungle of silicon wafers and dense electrical circuitry. When the inspection was completed, Levinson escorted Schifman into Heller's office.

"To the best of your knowledge, Professor," Heller asked, "is there any form of insect life that could survive inside that computer? Is there any literature, any research that would lead you to believe that's possible?"

There was a sober, crisply professional side to Schifman's personality; in Heller's presence, he decided to display it. His answers were succinct and precise. "Insects are living organisms, just like human beings. They have all the same basic biological needs and functions. They eat, breathe, metabolize, eliminate wastes. What I see inside this computer comes close to being a completely sterile environment." He was turning over a few fragments of the Cyber 2300, some memory planes, some pieces of a printing chain. "This stuff is what? Quartz, silicon . . . lots of metal, plastic, electronic wiring. There's nothing any organism could eat or drink. I wouldn't expect to find a bacterium holding out in there. Besides, I gather it gets pretty warm inside these machines, and there's electrical current flowing through, right? That's just not a viable habitat—shall I say, for life as we know it?"

"Can you imagine any kind of mutation that could adapt to that habitat?" Heller asked.

"Imagine? Of course I can. But that's science fiction. That's not what you're paying me to provide. The fact is we didn't find any sign of life inside there. No hives or nests, no eggs, no waste materials—nothing."

Levinson had a question. "What about the pattern of attack—drilling into the body? What insects do that?"

Schifman wagged his head. "I talked with the lady in the hospital—Mrs. Frankyl. Checked her wounds over. Superficially, they look like large sting marks—from a good-sized wasp or hornet. Which doesn't check out with the size people say these things were. If you look more closely, magnify the wound, it looks all torn up, not like a sting, but as if something chewed into her, the way, say, a chigger might. A chigger makes a pretty vicious little attack, but never this big. I've asked the lab at the hospital to send me a tissue sample from the inflamed areas. I might be able to identify some toxin. There are tropical fleas that burrow under the skin to lay eggs, but that's just subcutaneous. And, if you look, you discover eggs, which we don't find here. Drilling or eating straight down into the body, through muscle tissue, and so fast . . . in a couple of seconds, I don't know of any insects that behave like that. I'll ask around, but right now, I can't even make a wild guess."

Heller stared out his window for several seconds. "This is serious, Professor. Very serious. I'd appreciate your discretion—especially with the media."

Cutely, Schifman turned an imaginary key locking his lips. "The fact is, Dr. Heller, with the exception of the bites Mrs. Frankyl is carrying around, I'd say I haven't come across anything here that isn't more likely to be a hoax or an illusion."

"You're sure you can't offer us any help at all at this point?"

"Catch one," Schifman said. "Then I can help."

4

Over the preceding weeks, the troubles at the Brain had not gone unnoticed by the media. Levinson, an experienced hand at dealing with the press, had done a deft job of fending off the occasional curious inquiry about "some kind of infectious rash you've got over there." He had mastered just the right blend of friendly interest and expert obfuscation. "Rash, you say? Well, a few of our people came down with some poison oak after a picnic last week. Is that what you mean? Oh, I see —something contagious. We've had some summer flu going around the Center, the usual office epidemic, you know. Maybe that's what you've heard about. It has slowed us down in a few departments. Do you think that's worth reporting? I'd be glad to dig up some figures for you, if you care to call back."

Now, after the attack on the Frankyls, there was no way to keep the story buried any longer. There was bound to be legal action. Even before the Frankyls began talking to lawyers, the Brain was hit with a barrage of phone calls from local reporters who had picked up word of the incident through Southwest Community Hospital Emergency.

Unable to side-step, Levinson admitted to a "minor infestation of insects" in one of the Center's divisions and read his prepared press release, which was intended to make the event sound like an inexplicable curiosity. No, the insects hadn't been identified as yet, but they seemed to be some kind of migrating tick or flea, probably brought in from the outdoors and temporarily nesting in some part of the Center. There were specialists on the job, and the problem was sure to be cleared up by next week. Meanwhile, the Center would be closed to the public. No, there would be no interruption in its data processing responsibilities. The Cyber 2300 involved in the incident was part of a public exhibit, not an on-line computer. The NCDC was more than sufficiently prepared to carry on through a minor inconvenience like this.

That evening, the CBS evening news gave the story a brief,

semi-humorous report. "The National Center for Data Control in Washington seems to have found some real bugs in its computers . . ." Heller played along with the joke, granting a short interview, looking quizzical and concerned before the television cameras, but always keeping a smile on the story. Luckily, the Frankyls turned out to be a timid couple who preferred to stay out of the public eye. They gave no interviews to the press and returned to Pittsburgh two days after the attack. They were accompanied to the airport by the same senior staff member who had taken them to the hospital; he returned to the Center with the Frankyls' assurance that Mr. Heller would hear from their lawyer about any further medical expenses.

For the time being, the attack looked too outlandish to be of any use to Heller's critics: nobody wanted to invest too much energy in what looked like a single, offbeat incident. A few of the Brain's enemies even helped out—inadvertently. In an interview, Senator Cory insisted that "we should not let one bizarre accident like this distract us from the *real* issues surrounding the NCDC and MASTERNET," and then quickly turned to his familiar list of grievances.

Heller knew this was not a line of defense that could hold for long, and it did nothing to restore morale at the Center. His employees were justifiably anxious, afraid of the machines they worked with, angry about the rash that would not stop happening, and which they were now convinced must be caused by the insects. Within a few days of the Frankyl attack, the Office Workers Union, which represented about half of Heller's employees, presented a demand for an immediate shutdown and inspection of all computers.

In Heller's eyes, it was the union's usual self-righteous overreaction, demanding more than he could possibly agree to. Under pressure, he grudgingly agreed to have all the Cyber computers in the 2300 series taken off-line and inspected, once again with Professor Schifman standing by. That action alone would cause more than enough disruption, crippling the work of three major divisions. Data traffic was beginning to back up at the Brain for the first time in its brief history.

Once again, the technicians went to work, dissecting the

computers. Over a two-day period, the result was the same: no sign of insect life, nothing out of the ordinary. For another day and night, the Cyber 2300s stood gutted and idle while their frames and panels were treated with insecticide. Heller wondered: should he feel relieved or worried at the negative reports coming in from his technicians? At one level of his mind, he realized he needed a positive finding, something new and solid that could lead to decisions. Yet, irrationally, he welcomed drawing blanks—as if that might prove the insects were unreal. He resisted the idea of finding them, suspecting intuitively that when he did, nothing about them would make sense.

4

1

At the Brain, data pox had a name and a history. Heller might not know what the disease was or where it came from, but he could pinpoint its beginning, trace its progress. So many cases in so many months, all grouped together as "a problem." As baffling as his crisis was, it had an identity.

In the world beyond the Brain, data pox did not exist even as a mystery. It was there, unknown to Heller or Levinson. But nobody had a label for the queer and bothersome rash that began to interrupt the work of offices, banks and schools that summer. It was a complaint that went by no name or by too many different names. Or it simply went unreported and unremembered. Nobody thought of the occasional mild itch on their hands or ankles as the first symptom of a national emergency.

In Minneapolis, just before the close of the school term, the rash broke out among three classes of students working with a new, statewide computerized instruction network. A few kids were taken to doctors; the doctors diagnosed their problem as hives, poison oak, sunburn. It was gone in a few days and forgotten.

In Dallas, the rash struck checkout clerks in a highly automated supermarket chain. The clerks, talking it over among themselves, concluded that they were picking up burns from the new laser scanners the stores had installed. Their union demanded an investigation.

In Boston, the rash appeared episodically among patients passing through General Hospital's MUMPS System—the Mass Utility Multi-Program System used for preliminary diagnosis. When they mentioned the rash to their doctors, the doctors told the MUMPS computer, which entered the complaint into the patients' medical records as an allergy and promptly scheduled them for skin tests.

In Seattle, Phoenix, Atlanta, the rash hit mechanics adjusting automobile microprocessors. At newspapers in St. Louis and Miami, it flared up among reporters as they worked at word processing consoles. In New York, Kansas City, Denver, it broke out among travel agents using computerized ticketing systems.

In cities everywhere, it struck bank tellers, insurance adjusters, air traffic controllers. And in private homes, where computer games and data terminals were now familiar household gadgets, the rash came and went and came again. The cases were light and brief, momentary discomforts identified as a dozen different skin irritations.

All this was invisible to Heller, just as his troubles at the Brain were largely invisible to the rest of the country. Nobody was keeping track, nobody was adding it all up. With one exception. Here and there, among the growing number of computer hobbyists in their local clubs, there were a few people who began to wonder about scattered outbreaks of the rash among club members or among people using computers in the schools and offices where they worked. Some created new files in their data terminals—records of exact numbers, times, places. A few, picking up reports or rumors of data pox at the NCDC, began—just dimly—to see the big picture.

Outside of the Brain, inquisitive computer jocks were among the first to ask, "Could it have something to do with the computers?"

2

Ziggy Champolsky worked at the Brain, but he had not heard of the data pox. He had not even heard of the attack on the Frankyls. There was no time in Ziggy's life for the mere news of the day. He inhabited an elevated realm of the mind where the pure, crystalline logic of microcircuits was more real than flesh and blood.

Every major computer center had one or two Ziggies connected with it. They were called "computer junkies," strange, scruffy, sometimes wild-eyed young men who haunted the premises as dolefully, as insistently as compulsive gamblers are drawn to casinos. Dropped-out types who had no professional standing, the best they could do to gratify their addiction was to beg, wheedle, connive to use the equipment.

Junkies like Ziggy were either the madmen or the visionaries of computer science; it was not always possible to say which camp they belonged in. In their heads, they carried dreams of impossible programs, vast logical structures of infinite complexity designed to force the computer to new heights of achievement. Usually, the ultimate program they pursued was of such astronomical intricacy, there was no sane hope that they would ever complete it. It was a mathematical Shangri-la, a logical El Dorado. Computer junkies were modern alchemists, looking for the Philosopher's Stone in an electronic jungle.

There was only one reason why computer centers tolerated their presence: Junkies could be used. For such minds, the most challenging projects were child's play. They took on any assignment hungrily. Promise them the occasional late night shot at a first class machine, and they were your slaves. Like all addicts, computer junkies would sacrifice anything— their jobs, health, families—for one more fix.

As would only be appropriate for the NCDC, Zbigniew Tadeusz Champolsky, its resident junky, was very likely the most brilliant of his kind. That was why Heller had given him special privileges at the Brain; he was one of the gems of the staff. A Polish logician and chess champion, Ziggy had fled to the West just a few years before the Center was opened. Heller first met him at MIT holding down a low level coding job at the Computer Science Laboratory. He was a small, disheveled, more than slightly uncouth young man, who may not have come near a comb or a bar of soap in years. At the time, he had no reputation, except as an unpleasant eccentric—snappish, ill-tempered, his face perpetually screwed up in an expression of pain or distaste. Everybody could spot him as a junky, but Heller was the first to recognize his genius and to gamble on giving him the free play he needed.

In Ziggy's case, his great fantasy was to develop a program for Go, the Japanese board game which vastly surpassed chess in its complexity. From there, he intended to generalize his work to include all games of strategy. For such a purpose, no one program could ever suffice. Ziggy would have to develop whole systems of programs, a grand, kabbalistic scheme that was bound to be the work of years.

Heller could not say how successfully this project was coming; he did not really care. Every computer scientist he had mentioned it to regarded the task as impossible. For all he knew, the nights Ziggy spent hacking away at the Center were a hopeless waste. Still, he treated Ziggy generously and paid him well—because his services as a programmer and analyst were invaluable. In two years at the Center, he had helped redesign major sectors of the country's air defense and had revolutionized the strategies of submarine warfare. Currently, he was at work on the programming for a new, mobile missile force that was being deployed throughout the western United States. He could write subsystem assignments like this almost offhandedly, unscrambling the toughest problems with astonishing ease. The Pentagon had more than once tried to lure him away to one of its facilities, but the Brain had the hardware Ziggy claimed he needed. That was an exaggeration; Heller knew it, so did the military. The Government Operations Division where Ziggy worked offered vastly more computing power than he could use. But for a junky like Ziggy, privileged access to the Brain was a matter of high prestige. It was for him what it would be for a Catholic priest to serve mass at the altar of St. Peter's.

There was no telling when Ziggy might show up at the Center. Sometimes he was away for weeks; at other times, he would put in a solid forty to sixty hours at a computer console, catching an occasional daytime nap on a cot in the supply room. It was always touchy having Ziggy around during normal working hours; he was surly and obtuse with people who crossed his path, a shambling wreck of a man who might appear barefoot and in pajamas at any hour of the day. Regularly, Heller had to take him aside and scold him tactfully, reminding him of the basic social courtesies. Ziggy respected Heller; he would promise to behave, knowing that Heller had the power to take from him the one thing he most craved. But his promises never held for more than a few weeks at a time. Inside Ziggy Champolsky, the brain of a genius floated uneasily atop the personality of a spoiled six-year-old.

The night guards at the Brain had special orders for dealing with Ziggy. They were to admit him at all hours, escort him to his workplace, take his cigarettes away and then more or less baby-sit him while he was there. Unanimously, the guards loathed Ziggy, and, one and all, Ziggy loathed the guards. He resented their supervision, mocking and needling them at every opportunity. When he entered the building, it might be with a shout as he reached for the sky western-style. "Okay, sheriff," he would yip in a thick Polish accent, "you frisk me up, bang-bang. No cigarettes, no six-guns, yes?" Later, the guards might find him immersed in his work, a Coke bottle and a mustard-dripping sandwich balancing precariously atop a piece of million-dollar equipment. When they took his snacks away, he would hurl nasty Polish curses after them.

Finally, the guards decided among themselves the only way they could control Ziggy's movements was to lock him in at his console and let him ring Central Security when he wished to leave the room. Ziggy did not like that. "What I am in here? Computer Gulag?" he shouted. "You lock me up, I piss on the floor. I shit on the keyboard."

At first, his response to the arrangement was to ring for every little thing on the telephone intercom—and for nothing at all, just to make himself annoying. The guards were not above threatening physical force, which finally reconciled Ziggy to his semi-confinement. He grudgingly accepted the fact that he could not gain the guards' attention more than once an hour.

On the night Ziggy made his last visit to the Brain, it was Jimmy Willis who heard his final, urgent signal in Central Security. It was a little after 4 A.M. and Willis had just returned from escorting Ziggy to the men's room ten minutes before. "Fuck you, Ziggy," Willis grumbled, turning up his transistor to drown the persistent buzzing of the intercom. He was determined not to answer. The signal was coming from the Government Operations Division where Ziggy was working that night on his targeting project; it continued, frantic bursts of sound one right after another, then a long unbroken buzz. Overlapping it came a second signal from the front desk of the building. Willis answered that. It was another guard asking, "Hey, you gonna take care of that mother or not? He's buzzin' the whole damn place."

"Okay, okay," Willis agreed. He pushed the GOD button. "What you want, Ziggy?" he barked.

The only response was a torrent of Polish that sounded like an angry tirade. Willis switched off in disgust; but then the buzzing started again. Angrily, he hauled himself to his feet and trudged off toward the stairs. "Ziggy," he muttered, "tonight I swear you gonna get your ass waxed."

3

The bodies were found shortly after 7 A.M. A security guard, making his final round before the workday began, checked the Government Operations Division. The scene he discovered there suggested a fight: chairs overturned, desk tops in disarray, books and files scattered. The IBM 370/158 computer at the center of the room was on, the video display still flickering with an exchange that finished "SYNTAX ERROR—REPEAT INQUIRY." Ziggy's notes and papers were all over the room.

Across the middle of the floor, leading away from the intercom phone was a trail of blood. It ran to the opposite side of the room and through the fire exit, a heavy door opening on to a narrow metal staircase. Behind it lay the bodies of Ziggy and

Willis. Ziggy was crumpled at the foot of the stairs against the outside door; Willis was sprawled face down, halfway to the bottom. His gun lay on the stairs below him, two cartridges fired.

Security called for an ambulance and contacted Levinson at once.

The police doctor, who was on the scene within the hour, fixed the time of death toward 4:30 A.M. Ziggy's head had been severely fractured at the right temple. That in itself, the doctor decided, might have been enough to kill him. He was speculating about the possibility of a fight, with Ziggy being hurled downstairs by Willis. But he was puzzled. "These wounds—on both men. And their eyes. What in God's name happened here? How could two men do that kind of damage to one another?"

Both bodies were covered with deep lacerations; their faces were a horror, traces of white bone showing through at the jaws and brow. Where their eyes should have been were raw sockets clotted with blood. The doctor was baffled, but Levinson had already reconstructed the incident in his mind. The bugs had attacked Ziggy massively. That accounted for the wild appeal the guards had heard on the intercom. Finally, already severely injured and bleeding, he had bolted for the fire exit. But the bugs had blinded him; he stumbled and fell the full length of the staircase, crushing his skull. When Willis arrived—no doubt taking his time—he may have heard Ziggy calling from the fire stairs or seen the trail of blood and followed it toward the door. By then the bugs must have been out of the room, pursuing Ziggy. When Willis appeared, they went for him—again, first of all for the eyes. Blinded, he panicked and pulled his gun, perhaps trying to attract help by firing off two rounds. Then he collapsed.

Levinson kept the scenario to himself. He was playing for time, trying anything that might delay painful explanations. He kept siding with the idea of a fight, even though there was no way to make the picture consistent. "Possibly Champolsky got hold of Willis' gun," he suggested.

"You think they had some kind of showdown?" the police inspector asked. "There were hard feelings between these two?"

"Ziggy didn't get on well with any of the guards," Levinson said. He realized it was a dirty trick, trying to implicate Willis in Ziggy's death. He had no right to do it—except that the story had no chance of holding up, not once the bodies were examined in the hospital or morgue. But perhaps for a few days, a few hours . . . until he and Heller had a chance to talk.

"I don't know." The inspector shook his head dubiously. "This doesn't look like a fight. Neither man was shot. Anyway, no two people could maul each other like that." Then he asked, "Haven't you been having some problems around here with insects? I thought I heard a story on the news the other week . . ."

As soon as the condition of the bodies became known to the press, the story of the Brain's infestation began to leak out and then flood from countless sources in and around the Center. Fact, rumor, speculation reaching back four months to the first harmless rash mingled freely in the reports. The Brain was besieged with inquiries. Heller and Levinson had nothing to defend with except the freakishness of the matter. An unprecedented problem . . . what could anyone expect of the Center's leadership except concern? But in official Washington, concern was cheap, and it purchased no mercy.

There was no question but that the work of the Center would have to be suspended, the computers shut down. Heller now accepted that and moved swiftly. Within a day, the Brain lurched to a dead halt; at once, entire sectors of the Washington bureaucracy and public services across the country registered tremors as the MASTERNET system began to reroute and adjust. Heller and Levinson had to assist in carrying out the lock-down; the morning following the two deaths, the Office Workers Union called a strike. The Center was left with only its senior administrators on duty, and they were rapidly sucked into a maelstrom of activity, issuing instructions, assurances, press releases in all directions. Yes, Heller agreed, there must be a complete investigation. He welcomed it, initiated it, offered full co-operation. Of course, something must be done.

Plans were being drawn up, emergency procedures implemented. Meetings were scheduled at the highest level. Heller expected to see the President within twenty-four hours. Perhaps the Brain should be fumigated . . . yes, that was a serious possibility under discussion.

But all this was only temporizing, trying to put a good face on a disaster. With the deaths of Champolsky and Willis, Heller's awkward public relations problem had become a media sensation. He found himself chained to the telephone, struggling to clarify a nightmare.

In the midst of the chaos, a single word of good news broke through. A bug had been caught. Just one.

4

It was found in Ziggy Champolsky's clothing following the autopsy. Levinson had warned the hospital to watch for insects on the bodies—or in them.

The bug dropped out of a heavy metal truss; Ziggy wore the device to control a severe rupture which may have accounted for his chronic bad temper. A medic sorting out the clothes dislodged the insect; it leaped onto his arm and nipped him. It was quickly brushed off, falling on one of the steel examination tables. Before it could right itself and leap away, the medic slapped a specimen jar over it.

As soon as Levinson got word of the capture, he contacted Schifman, who agreed eagerly to clear his schedule and give the bug top priority. It reached him at Georgetown by the late afternoon. There was no quick response. Toward eleven that evening, Schifman phoned to say he was transferring the examination to his lab facilities at Walter Reed Research. "I need more equipment," he explained; he would say no more. Heller pressed for information, but Schifman became a stone wall of irritation. "Sorry, Doctor, no journalistic tidbits. We do the whole scientific trip, no shortcuts." His voice was crisp with impatience. The phone clicked dead.

The next morning he was back in touch, sounding no more

encouraging. He was ready to make a report, but not on the telephone. "You've got to see this to believe it," he said. "Even so, I'm seeing it, and I don't believe it."

The Schifman that Heller and Levinson had first met at the Brain had been relaxed, wry, slightly flippant—too much so for Heller's taste. The man they met that morning was alert and tightly concentrated, the total professional hard at work. He was also edgy and impatient after a full night in the laboratory. When he spoke, there was a mean crackle in his voice; it was not due to lack of sleep, but to painful frustration. His first words were, "Do you know what this fucking bug is made of?" He tapped a microscope on the lab table beside him. "Guess what it's made of. *White stuff.* Solid white stuff. That's all I can tell you after eleven hours in two laboratories. Take a look for yourself."

Heller and Levinson took turns staring down the microscope. Under the lens, they saw nothing but a blank white expanse filling the iris aperture below. Automatically, each sought to adjust the focus, searching for a recognizable image.

"Don't fool with the focus," Schifman snapped. "It's focused, take my word. What you see is what there is. That's 1200 magnification on the best phase-contrast microscope you're gonna find in town. You're looking at a section of the insect taken from the torso. I've got others—from the legs, the head, the interior of the body. All the same. White stuff. If you stain it, it becomes the color of the stain. Undifferentiated red stuff, undifferentiated blue stuff."

He gestured toward a second microscope on another table. "Under the ultramicroscope, you get the same picture—a solid blank nothing." Heller and Levinson checked the slide beneath the microscope. It was as Schifman said: the same white surface, unmarked, featureless. When they were finished, he led them across the lab to a small television monitor which seemed to be a flickering blank screen. "Okay, where do we go from there? The scanning electron microscope—that's 100,000 magnification. What you should be seeing on that screen is structure—molecular structure. There's nothing wrong with the equipment. This is the same result I got at Georgetown.

Solid stuff. Absolute density. At maximum magnification, the thing has no cellular structure, no biochemical structure. Nothing penetrates it—ultraviolet light, electrons, nothing."

Heller made the lame, obvious comment. "That's not possible. It's a living thing."

"Oh, it's a living thing all right," Schifman said. "After I sectioned it into eight pieces, it was still alive. Head off, legs off—still alive. Ten legs, incidentally. What the hell kind of insect is that? You take it apart, all the parts keep moving. It can be immobilized by removing the legs, but not killed. The head is still alive, alive enough to bite. That I can show you. Look."

Through another, smaller microscope, Heller peered down at a pinpoint specimen on a slide. At once, he pulled back from the eyepiece to reprove Schifman for the adolescent prank he was playing. But Schifman was not laughing. His face was grim and stiff. Heller returned to the microscope. What he saw in the lens was a smooth, cone-shaped head with two black dots for eyes and a slit-like mouth filled with dagger-sharp teeth. The object might have been modeled out of soap or clay. It might have been a toy. But then the mouth opened and snapped shut several times. The thing moved; it was alive. Its grotesque simplicity was comic, but at the same time hideous, like a bad caricature that had been brought to life.

Levinson, waiting to get a look at the head, asked with marked concern, "You cut the thing up?"

"Sure I did," Schifman answered. "How the hell else are you gonna analyze it? But don't worry, I've got all the pieces. And I've got photographs at every stage of dissection—the whole bug and all its parts. With this thing you don't have to worry about decay. It doesn't decay. For all I know, you could stick all the pieces together, and it would be back in business. You know what the standard definition of an organism is? Something you can *not* take apart and put back together again. In between, it's supposed to die."

Heller, passing the microscope to Levinson, asked, "What in God's name is that? It doesn't look real."

Schifman shuffled through the photos he had taken. "I have no name for it—except 'bug' . . . 'data bug.' There's no insect species of this description, not remotely. There's no living thing of this description."

Schifman's words were careening through Heller's mind like beads from a broken string. They did not cohere or connect; they made no pattern. "Please," he said, "can we run this through from the beginning—slowly?"

Schifman blew out a spastic sigh and poured a cup of coffee. "Okay, from the top. When the specimen arrived at Georgetown, I assumed my first order of business was to identify it. Simple. For that, I shouldn't need anything more than my Sherlock Holmes magnifying glass. But here's what I saw, and right away I knew I was in trouble."

From his stack of photographs, he drew out a picture of the whole insect, a flat, white oval with its cone-shaped head and ten wiry legs. The photograph looked like the rough outline of an insect waiting to have all its physical details filled in.

"I wasn't sure the thing was an insect at all. Certainly, I never saw anything like it. But I assumed you wanted me to tell you more than that. So I'd have to cut. But before I did, I ran an ultrasound probe to get some idea of its insides. That was the first real shocker. The scan showed a solid, homogeneous medium—like a piece of marble. I had to stop to test my equipment. It was functioning all right. The bug simply has no internal structure. Nothing. That's what I confirmed by cutting. Which, incidentally, turned out to be no easy job. So far I've worn out three ultramicrotomes dissecting this thing. It's like slicing rock. I finally had to make the major separations with a laser scalpel."

"I don't understand," Heller said. "What do you mean there's nothing inside?"

"The body is solid all the way through. The mouth just ends at the throat. No esophagus, no stomach, no gut. No circulatory system, no sex organs, no nerves. The thing has no musculature, no bones, no metabolism. It can bite, but it doesn't digest. It'll bite anything you give it. I fed it other insects—ants, termites, aphids. I fed it worms, caterpillars. It doesn't eat them, doesn't digest them. It couldn't. It just chops them up into pieces, like a buzz saw cutting through wood. Likewise, the thing's eye. It has no structure. It's just made of black stuff, absolutely solid, same as the white stuff. I tell you, the thing is a fucking cartoon."

"Have you run any other tests on it?" Heller asked.

"Of course. Everything I could think of. I ran it through a protein analyzer—both at Georgetown and here. There's no DNA in the thing, no amino acids." Schifman spread out a section of graph paper; all the lines upon it were straight and undisturbed. "There's no organic chemistry to the thing. Strictly speaking, it's made of nothing, nothing that registers on any instrument."

Heller could see that Schifman was hotly agitated, a man driven beyond the limits of his professional skill. Anger and frustration were mixed in his voice.

"That's when I decided to come to Walter Reed and recheck my results. Also to run an x-ray diffraction analysis. Same result. Blank. Zero. This thing doesn't just violate the laws of organic chemistry, it violates the laws of physics. It has no atomic structure. No cells, no molecules, no atoms. A blob, that's all it is. If you try to burn a piece of it, you get no chemical spectrum. In fact, it doesn't burn. I've held the head in a Bunsen burner, and there it still is. You can't dissolve it in carbolic acid; it doesn't react with any standard solution. As far as I can see, there's no way this thing can reproduce and there's no way it can be killed."

There was a long silence. Finally, Heller said, "We need other people to run tests on this." It was all he could think of saying. His characteristic response: call in more experts. But the idea sounded hollow and dispirited. "May we ask you to bring in some colleagues to consult?"

"If you say so, sure," Schifman answered with a sullen shrug. "With help, there are some more exotic tests I can try, though I wouldn't be hopeful. Nuclear magnetic resonance, maybe. But if it's got no atomic structure . . . Anyway, I just didn't know how far you wanted this to go."

"What do you mean?"

"I know you've been sitting on this matter hard. Okay, that's your decision. But what I'm finding out here isn't going to be reassuring to anybody. This is a new life form. It lives in computers on nothing at all. It bites, kills, but can't be killed. We don't know what it is, where it comes from, what it's made of. Once that gets around . . . well, I'd rather have you decide who says what to whom, and where it goes from here. It's a neat bit of pure research. But the Brain is politics, right?"

Schifman was right; Heller appreciated his concern for discretion. But there were not many choices available now.

"Yes, that's so," he agreed. "But we have to find out all we can, fast. I'd like to keep this low profile. No press releases, no shoptalk, you understand. Try to deal with people we can trust in that respect. Berny will make any necessary arrangements—travel, fees, any facilities you need. Whoever you call in, the main question is how do we stop it?"

"You mean kill it?" Schifman asked.

"Kill it, get rid of it . . ." Then, almost pleadingly, he added, "Make it go away . . . make *them* go away." That was weak, defeated. It was the sick and sinking sensation inside him speaking. Ahead of him as far as he could see into the future, Heller saw meetings, conferences, urgent committee work, heated argument. Very well. He was used to that kind of pressure. After twenty years in Washington, he knew how to address crisis. One defined the problem, analyzed its parameters, took soundings, rallied support, drew a line and fought on it. All this he knew. But what was his line to be now? What could he recommend, even provisionally? For the first time in his career, he felt more than threatened. He felt caught in a vacuum, a man in free fall through empty space. No sense of direction, nothing to cling to. And meanwhile, the Brain, MASTERNET, the electronic infrastructure of the government and economy was crippled and limping. The vulnerability of centralized data processing had been indisputably established. He could not come out of this without irreparable damage to his prestige and influence.

In his distraction, Heller only heard part of what Schifman was saying. The words brushed against the edge of his attention. ". . . might have been designed by some amateur god who didn't even know his high school chemistry. As if he just said, 'Let there be' . . . with no idea *how* such a thing could be. You know what this is like? It's like you asked a kid to invent an insect, and he came up with a crawling thing that bites. A bunch of legs and a mouth. Period. That's all."

The words clicked in Heller's brain. Something remembered, suddenly sliding into sharp focus. Eagerly, he spread Schifman's photographs across the lab table, picked out one of the whole insect. Of course. He had seen this bug before. He had a picture of it in his office.

1

Back at the Brain, Heller ransacked his office: desk, closets, filing cabinets. He would not tell Levinson what he was searching for until he found it—at the back of one of his secretary's files. A rubber-banded wad of crumpled papers streaked with color. He spread the bundle across his desk for Levinson to see. They were children's drawings in pastels, crayon, runny watercolors. Most of the pictures were stick-figure people surrounded by various boxy objects meant to be computers.

"The kids drew these," Heller explained. "Reports on their visit to the Center. The teachers sometimes send them in. I asked Della to keep some of them for a lobby display."

Among the drawings, Heller found what he was looking for: a large page, folded over, filled with oval shapes standing on stick legs. At one end, each had the head he and Levinson had seen under Schifman's microscope: sharp-nosed, shark-like, with two spots for eyes and a row of bayonet teeth. He placed Schifman's photograph beside the drawing; the match was perfect. At the bottom of the drawing there were the awkwardly formed letters "BUSG." At the top were more letters bunched together, possibly a name in random order: "DPNHAE."

After a moment, Heller said, "I remember now. It's a little girl . . . thick glasses, slightly crossed eyes. She asked about bugs in the computer. I made a sort of joke about it. Kayla used the incident on the 'Wonder/Wander' show last March. She—this kid—was the first to see them."

"See them?" Levinson asked. "You think she *saw* them?"

"Of course. How else could she draw them?"

Levinson looked dubious. "But how . . . ?"

"Well, look, damn it!" Heller snapped impatiently. "There it is, exactly what we saw in the lab this morning. That's it. That's the bug. That's why the kid was so scared. She'd actually *seen* the insects. And then when I mentioned them . . ."

Levinson was shuffling through the other drawings. "Interesting," he mused. "Look here . . . on these pictures." He had spread out four or five other drawings and was pointing out patches of little dots and dashes—on the computers, the floor, the stick-figures. "Think those could be bugs too? Maybe they all saw them. Look at this one—could be people chased by a troop of bugs coming out of a computer."

Heller studied the pictures. "Hard to tell on these. But this one is definitely what we saw this morning. We've got to find out where this kid saw the insects."

Levinson, looking at the BUSG drawing, was doing a quick count. "Ten legs. Ten legs on every one of them."

Heller was already on the phone putting through a call to Kayla Breen in New York. When he reached her, he asked for a lead on the children who had been on the show with him.

"Oh, that'll be easy to find," Kayla assured him. "Why don't you come up to town this weekend, and we'll go through the files together?"

Heller thanked her for the invitation, perhaps too curtly. "You may have heard we're having some trouble here at the Brain."

She had. She offered condolences. "I thought I might be able to take your mind off all that for a few friendly hours."

Heller thanked her again, less curtly this time. "Sorry, Kayla. I've got to stay on top of things here."

She breathed a resigned sigh along the phone line. "I was hoping to get an encouraging firsthand report from you. After all, I have a vested interest in the Brain. I've got your show scheduled for an off-season rerun in September—first week of school. Should I suspend it until I know you're in business again?"

"I'm sure we'll be back on line by then," Heller said. To himself he thought, And if not, a gap in "Wonder/Wander's" schedule will be the least of our worries.

Before the morning was out, Kayla called back to tell him that the children she had used for her program at the Brain were a special group. "It's a mix of kids we've featured before in things we shot in Washington. Bright, responsive . . . they show up well in front of the camera. Lots of personality and back-talk. Some came from advanced classes in the city schools, others from private schools in the area." She remembered the incident with the little girl and the bugs. "Don't tell me there's a connection between that and this trouble you're having."

Heller explained about the drawing. "We think the girl may have seen the bugs somewhere around the Center before the first outbreak."

"I see. Oh, good idea." After checking her records, she was able to find the child's name on a list of the participants. "That scrambled name on the picture you have must be 'Daphne.' There's a Daphne Saxton listed—from the Hartmann School. Oh yes. That's a rather unusual private school on Cathedral Heights. Highly experimental, specializes in the arts. We've filmed a few sequences there for other shows—art classes mainly. Also, I remember about a year ago, we did a midsummer program there. The kids performed a sort of seasonal celebration with dances and chanting. Very colorful, very imaginative. The head of the school is a remarkable woman— Leah Hagar. German, Hungarian background. She's put together a strange mix of educational ideas. Do you know anything about the Hartmann system? Mostly that, plus some Montessori, some Rudolf Steiner, some Wilhelm Reich. I've used her as a consultant on 'Wonder/Wander' a few times. Very charismatic type."

Heller asked another favor of Kayla. Would she contact the school, ask for the child's address, find out whatever she could about her? Kayla agreed and phoned back promptly with an address in the Adams-Morgan district of the city.

"The little girl is six years old, going into the first grade this fall. She lives with her mother, who uses two names. The married name is Saxton, but I gather there's been a divorce or separation. The new name—or maybe it's her maiden name—is Hecate, like the goddess. Hecate is a goddess, isn't she? Or a banshee or something? Anyway, at the school, she's Miss Hecate . . . or *Ms.* Hecate. She teaches there. I think I've met her—as part of the midsummer program we did. Very striking woman, I recall. A little fey, but very good with children."

At once, when Kayla had said good-by, Heller phoned the Saxton-Hecate home. There was no answer. There was no answer when his secretary phoned several times through the rest of the day. Heller could feel his anxiety rising with each failed call. Had the woman and her daughter gone off for the summer? He had his secretary check with the Hartmann school. No, they did not believe Miss Hecate had left town, but they could not say when she might be home.

Heller, careening through a hectic schedule of emergency meetings and telephone conferences, struggling to reassure worried public officials and government agencies across the country, began to grow exasperated with this faceless woman and her child. There was vital information he needed from them. Irrationally, the more times he failed to reach Jane Hecate through the day, the more convinced he became that she was the one person who could help him most. Conceivably, she— or her daughter—held the key to his problem; they might know the source and nature of the insects. Perhaps he was that close to solving the mystery. If so, he must hold off on other commitments, weigh his statements carefully, delay and evade. And that was becoming more difficult by the hour.

Already, pressure from the media was mounting steadily. How long would the Brain and MASTERNET remain locked down? What happened to the nation's data processing in the meantime? Was there any further information about the insects? Had any of them been caught and identified? On this last point, there were conflicting reports. Sources at the hospital said that some of the insects had been recovered from the bodies; Heller was flatly denying that this was so. It was an unfounded rumor, he insisted, not wanting to reveal the baffling nature of the bug until he could give a more encouraging report.

The press, drawing nothing but blanks, sensing evasiveness, was beginning to sound aggressively suspicious. Since the Watergate period, "cover-up" was the standard interpretation of all ignorance and delay in high places. Heller, maneuvering to pacify the media, countered with vague talk of having the Center fumigated, a possibility that sounded positive, hopeful. He had instructed Levinson to place inquiries with a number of exterminators in the city. A few were already scheduled to visit and offer bids, but their reservations were unanimous. It would be a colossal job, and, without knowing what the pest was, nobody would guarantee the results.

That put Heller in a bind. Having denied that a bug had been captured, he could not pass Schifman's specimen along to the exterminators. In any case, there was no point in doing that. If Schifman had not found a way to destroy the bug, there was no chance a commercial exterminator would.

2

In the late afternoon, Heller reported for his scheduled meeting with the President. He had requested the visit; it had been announced to the press. But he went with little enthusiasm, knowing the meeting was only the standard Washington charade of concern and prompt action. He would get no real help from the White House; it was unlikely he would even see the President. He would be meeting with Walter Turnbull, the White House chief of staff, the man who screened—and buried—most of what was intended to reach the President.

Turnbull was not a man Heller respected, nor for that matter was the President. They were part of a slack, complacent administration that had shown little leadership. In the normal course of events, Heller had as little to do with the White House as possible. He preferred to keep his dealings at the second and third level of the various Washington hierarchies, working through specialists and technocrats who knew how to shape policy in subtle, non-official ways, and who, like himself, were outside the province of political campaigns and elections. These, he had learned many years ago, were the people who lasted and mattered; they could often do more with an interoffice memo than the entire Congress could do with legislation.

In their first meeting three years ago, Heller had needed only sixty seconds to size up wheelin'-dealin' Wally Turnbull for what he was: A windy bore whose intelligence was wholly invested in low, opportunistic cunning. He had been the President's campaign manager, and that was the level at which his talents were pegged. No matter what issue came his way, he could be relied upon to place public imagery and political logrolling ahead of sound policy. Installed in a key administrative post at the President's right hand, he handled the job in a sloppy and devious way, trying always to shield an incompetent President from hard decisions and bad news.

It was typical of the Administration that nobody, least of all the President, wanted to register the full gravity of what was happening at the Brain. As far as Heller could tell, the two deaths and the shutdown were being treated as a temporary inconvenience that could be left to the technicians to clear up. Heller seriously doubted that anybody at the White House grasped how critically dependent the government was on computerized data processing. Several times over the past few years, when important decisions had to be made in support of the Brain and MASTERNET, Heller had been forced to work through his connections in the Defense Department and the military in order to gain the leverage he needed.

In Heller's eyes, figures like Turnbull and the President were sad, classic examples of a defunct politics, remnants of the precomputer era. But just now, their dereliction was welcome to him; he could use it. He needed time, a few days at least to follow up his lead about the Saxton child, to find out what he needed to know, possibly to rescue the situation without spreading further alarm. If there was one thing he could always get from the White House, it was procrastination; all he had to do was throw Turnbull a few hopeful sops.

"Now this problem you're having over there at the Brain," Turnbull asked when they met, "it isn't gonna cause us any real trouble, is it?" The question indicated the answer he wanted.

"We have more than enough redundant computer capacity within the MASTERNET system to absorb the Brain's responsibilities—temporarily."

"Good, good. The President will be glad to hear that."

"Of course, I'll need the President's approval to activate the REDIRECT program. You'll receive a formal request to that effect by tomorrow morning. I'd appreciate a prompt response."

"REDIRECT. Now let's see . . ." Turnbull was squinting strenuously at Heller, wondering if he should recognize the term. He should have, but of course he didn't. Briefly, Heller explained.

REDIRECT was the Brain's major contingency plan for reassigning its workload to other computer facilities under disaster-mode operations. The program was essentially a vastly expanded version of the Brain's day-to-day use of multiprocessor systems for distributed data handling. Under normal circumstances, even the largest computer facility might find itself periodically overloaded, and even the best hardware could experience occasional breakdowns. Whenever that happened, a prodigious array of stand-by processors throughout MASTERNET was programmed to take over instantaneously and to reroute data services to other computer centers. The transfer might only last for mere seconds at a time, or for as long as several hours. Backup processing of this kind ordinarily cut in and out automatically several times each day at any of the Brain's divisions, swiftly and unobtrusively reallocating its responsibilities to several alternative computer facilities around the country. In cases of extreme data congestion or equipment failure, there were arrangements that allowed the Brain to draw upon CONCERT, its high-speed satellite link. CONCERT extended the Brain's emergency backup capacities as far as West Germany and Japan.

REDIRECT, an essential part of the Brain's initial design,

would phase in all of these stand-by capacities as part of an intricately co-ordinated plan; but that plan had been predicated upon disasters that attained the magnitude of social revolution or thermonuclear war. REDIRECT had always been envisaged as part of a total reorganization of government. At that point, a serious breakdown of data technology would be swallowed up in a widespread national convulsion. Short of an emergency on that scale, the massive transfer of responsibilities which REDIRECT called for was bound to be embarrassingly visible to critical eyes. Heller had never expected that to happen. From the outset, he had regarded REDIRECT as part of the Brain's public relations—a theoretical guarantee to the nation that its most crucial information services would not be interrupted even in an extreme crisis.

But now REDIRECT had to be activated; it was the only alternative to a complete stoppage of data transmission. No doubt it delighted Turnbull to be reminded that the program existed; no doubt the President would be eager to order it into operation. But for Heller, resorting to REDIRECT amounted to a surrender of the Brain's near monopoly of information processing. It was an open confession of failure.

"That's excellent!" Turnbull exclaimed when Heller had finished his quick sketch of REDIRECT. "I've got to hand it to you technical boys. You don't miss a trick. But listen—this REDIRECT thing, won't we need a copy of that? Something to wave at the next press conference if questions come up?"

"I have that right here," Heller said. He pushed a small mountain of papers across the desk, a full description of the Brain's contingency plans. He enjoyed watching Turnbull frown uncomfortably at the weight and technical density of the material. The man would not be able to cut his way through the first three pages of what Heller had given him.

"Yes, that's excellent," Turnbull said. "But haven't you got something a little less . . ."

Heller had come prepared. He sailed a two-page résumé of REDIRECT into Turnbull's lap. It was the words-of-one-syllable version with key technical phrases underlined and defined in footnotes. "You can probably reduce this to a short para-graph for the President," he said with thinly disguised disdain. By now he knew exactly how far he could go with Turnbull in the direction of veiled insult.

"Very good," Turnbull said, his face brightening. "The President will surely appreciate that. You know, he's got this damned Algerian thing hanging over him, keeping him up day and night. Now, you aren't gonna be down for very much longer at the Brain, are you?" Again, the question asked for an upbeat reply.

"We're running a check on all our equipment," Heller explained. "That'll take a week or so. Meanwhile, we did catch one of the insects. It's being studied now."

"Hadn't heard about that," Turnbull said. "Well, that's good news, isn't it?"

"Not exactly," Heller answered. "It's proving difficult to identify. Something rather exotic. A sort of flea, it seems—but we can't tell what kind as yet. My advice is to keep this under wraps until we can say what the insect is and how to get rid of it."

Turnbull was uncertain. "Can we keep this insect secret for that long?"

Heller knew what Turnbull was concerned about. He did not want to involve the White House in suppressing information that might leak out at any moment. "If you wish, Wally," Heller proposed, "you can forget I told you about this for the next few days. The man who's examining the bug is reliable. He only knows he's researching for me, and he's perfectly secure. I'll assume full responsibility."

Turnbull deliberated. "All right, Tom. Let's postdate this information by forty-eight hours. I can't see any harm in that. If the thing's still under study by competent authorities, I'd say we had the right to complete our investigation. No need to bring this up with the President until he can make a full, positive statement. You know, that's what the public likes. Nice, neat solutions. They want the solution even before they know there's a problem." Turnbull laughed. Heller gave a small, bitter grin. "Now in the meantime, you wouldn't say there was any danger of more people getting killed at the Brain, would you? We wouldn't want that. That was very bad news about this black man getting killed, you know. The President sent off a personal letter of sympathy to the man's family."

"What about Champolsky?" Heller interjected.

"Who?"

"The other man who was killed."

"Oh yeah, the Polish fella. Did he have a family?"

"Probably, somewhere in Poland." Heller was not making the point seriously. He was teasing Turnbull, who, he could see, was adding up votes in his head.

"Well," Turnbull decided, "maybe, if you could find us an address, we could send off a letter. . . . Wouldn't want the Polish-Americans to feel left out."

Almost flippantly Heller said, "If I can find an address, I'll send it over."

"Good, good! But the important thing is—no more people getting killed over at your place. Now that's got absolutely to be avoided."

Heller bridled at letting Turnbull lead him along the course of least political resistance. He wanted to stand up and shout in the man's face, "Don't you recognize a state of national emergency when you see one? Are you going to sit there counting the Polish-American vote when the central, decision-making technology of the government may be collapsing?" Instead, picking up the easy lead Turnbull offered him, he answered, "The Center is operating with a skeleton crew: senior staff and a few secretaries. The computers are locked down and under guard. There's no danger of another attack." Fighting back a faint blush, he added, "We're looking into the possibility of fumigating the entire building."

Turnbull liked that; Heller knew he would. It was simple and obvious. "Of course! Fumigate the place. That ought to do the trick. Well, I'd say we've got this problem well in hand, wouldn't you, Tom?"

Before Heller left, Turnbull offered him a few words with the President. It was his reward for presenting no rough edges. Listlessly, Heller agreed. It would help with the press to say he had talked to the President personally. Not that the Washington press corps had any higher opinion of the President's competence than Heller did, but a White House audience was the going standard of decisive action. It would be reported as such.

Several minutes later, the President bustled into Turnbull's office; he was a man who specialized in bustling—and in beaming radiant confidence. Everybody agreed: as a presidential type, he might have been ordered from central casting. At once, he clasped Heller's hand in both of his. It was the usual excessive greeting he had years ago perfected for canvassing votes in Texas shopping centers. "Tom, a rare privilege to see you! Wally tells me we have this problem at the Center well under control. I'm truly glad to hear it. The Center is, of course, vital to all of us—a major priority. You'll keep us posted."

"Yes, sir," Heller answered sullenly.

"Of course," the President continued, "us country lawyer politicians'd like to think there are still some good old-fashioned ways to keep our fingers on the public pulse beat that are just as good as any computer." With one hand now thrown across Heller's shoulders, he used his free hand to thump his chest above the heart. The President repeated this remark every time he met Heller. Heller waited for it and flinched; then he retaliated by repeating, to himself, the thought that invariably came to him whenever he was smothering under the President's theatrical exuberance: *Every nasty thing they say about this man is true. It wouldn't take even a minicomputer to replace political leadership of this caliber; a cut-rate pocket calculator would do.*

"Now, Wally tells me," the President continued with a thoughtful frown, as if he were taking up a deep line of policy, "that you'll be fumigating the Center. Good move."

"We're considering that," Heller said. "We may . . ."

"Good move. I'm glad to hear we have a positive alternative. And keep us posted." Turnbull reminded him of the paper he was holding in his hand: the résumé of Heller's contingency plans. "Oh yes, and thanks for this." He clearly had no idea what the paper was.

"For the press," Turnbull reminded him.

"Right. Very good. We'll have this on hand for the next press conference. Excellent—uh—formulation. I wish we could talk longer, Tom, about more long range plans. But I'll have to get back now." He dropped his voice to a confidential whisper. "This problem with the Nigerians, you know."

"The Algerians," Turnbull corrected.

"Exactly," the President said, never breaking stride. "The Algerians." And he was gone.

3

Heller drove away from his presidential audience depressed, yet boiling with anger. The meeting had been a shabby exchange of pretense and deception—exactly the sort of politically convenient obfuscation he deplored. All he had really done of any value was to enlist the Presidency in a stopgap public relations ploy to calm fears and avoid obvious questions. It had been contemptibly easy to do; but it contributed nothing to solving his problem, except to give him a few more days to locate the Saxton girl and find out what she might know. It troubled him to realize how heavily he was leaning on that frail hope. Was he deceiving himself, snatching at straws?

From the White House, he was scheduled to return to the Brain, meet Levinson for a fast dinner, and then put in an evening with his senior staff, reviewing and tightening contingency plans. To his own surprise, he turned his car away from the Brain, north toward the Adams-Morgan district. He was heading for Jane Hecate's house, where nobody had answered the phone all day. It was a decision dictated by sheer nervous anxiety, and by his need to escape, if only for a few hours, from the relentless pressure at the Center.

The address he was looking for turned out to be a modest, clapboard bungalow with a large wooden porch; it stood at the end of a run-down, narrow street that echoed with the noise of children playing. The sidewalk in front was badly buckled and the yard was dirt and weeds. He rang at the door; nobody answered. He moved his car to the shaded side of the street and waited, suffering the damp heat of the waning day. Trying not to meet the eyes of residents on nearby porches, he ran through the reports and position papers he had with him; the material slipped from his mind as soon as he read it. He was killing time, drifting. The supper hour came and passed. He walked to a nearby diner for coffee and from there phoned Levinson, instructing him to take over the staff meeting. Vaguely, he said he would be tied up for the evening. He was being evasive. It wasn't like him.

Toward eight o'clock, a battered Volkswagen van pulled up outside the house. Two women and four children got out. The oldest kid might have been twelve; Heller recognized the youngest as Daphne. The women, he estimated, were in their mid-thirties, dressed for the out-of-doors in tee shirts and jeans. The one was stout and dark, the other small, fragile and fair, glowing with sunburn. They began to unload packs and baskets, some playthings from the back of the van. Heller left his car and crossed to them before they unlocked the front door. He started to call a name and stumbled on the first word. Miss? Mrs.? What did he call her? He started again, avoiding the title. "Jane Hecate?"

The small, fair woman turned. Her eyes struck him at once; they were deep and hazy, a calm, slightly hypnotic gaze.

"My name is Thomas Heller," he explained as he approached the porch. "I'm from the Center for Data Control. I'm sorry to bother you. I called earlier. No one was home. It's rather important."

The two women passed puzzled glances between them. Jane Hecate answered, "Is this a survey? At this hour? We're really very tired. We've been out all day with the children."

Heller went on, "It's a problem we're having. It's hard to explain. If I might have just a few minutes . . ." He was fumbling to give her his card.

"Can't this wait?" she asked, pleading. "Really, we've got to clean the kids up and get them to bed."

"I could come back later—in an hour. Or just wait out here. Please, it's extremely urgent."

She took the card he was holding out to her and read it. When she looked up at him again, her eyes had changed, had deepened and cooled with recognition. "Oh yes," she said, slowly with a dark weight. "Mr. Heller. Of course." She passed the card to her friend, and they again exchanged glances, this time more solemnly. The two youngest kids, Daphne and a little boy, were romping on the porch, jumping on and off a creaky swing. After a long moment, Jane Hecate said, "I'm sorry, I'm not interested in talking with you, Mr. Heller." Cold, direct, firm. Heller was startled and hurt. How long had it been since anyone said that to him—or even implied it? Three hours ago, he had been with the President at the White House; now he was being refused an audience on Belmont Street in the Adams-Morgan.

"Please . . ." he begged, groping to find a persuasive phrase, something to drive home the gravity of the situation. He drew himself together, paused, then went on, trying to mirror her strong calm. "Lives are at stake."

She had not expected that. Her brows arched, and her eyes brightened with concern. "Lives . . . ?"

"It's that serious," he went on. "If it weren't, I wouldn't be here, waiting for you this long." He tried to angle the remark just right, to give it more humility than arrogance. An important man, coming to a place like this, in person, sacrificing his valuable time . . . can't you see how urgent this must be?

It worked. She relented. "Can it wait until we put the children down?" He agreed. She unlocked the door and invited him into a small, stuffy living room. There was no air conditioning in the house; the heat was as oppressive indoors as out. She opened some windows, turned on a dim lamp and asked him to be seated. Then she and the others disappeared into the back of the house down a long hallway.

The room he was in was minimally furnished: a bare floor, two dilapidating chairs, some cushions against the wall. Was it squalid or merely simple? He could not decide. What took his eye at once was a table against one wall—a heavy, raw wooden plank balanced on three large stones. On it stood a small, ceramic figurine about a foot high. It might have been very old or a modern abstraction; it possessed that sort of ambiguity. The features had been worn down or modeled away, leaving the bare outline of a woman's form wearing a dramatically horned headdress. At its feet were two crossed knives, the handle of one pearl, the handle of the other ebony. Behind the figure there was an oil painting that echoed its shape: a shadowy female form with a crescent moon rising behind its head.

There were several other paintings in the room, mainly small, unframed canvases done in the same style, evocative combinations of curves and angles in muted, earthy colors. Hidden skillfully in the complexity of the works, there were several dreamlike motifs: the horned woman, an exploding star, an ascending bird, the crossed knives. The paintings were well executed, but it was not a style Heller liked; it was too murky and undefined for his rigorous, mathematical tastes. Yet there was a strength to the work and a haunting vibrancy. In the lower right hand corner, each painting was signed "J. Hecate."

For the next half hour, he was alone, listening to the sound of children at the rear of the house, laughing, whining, splashing about in a tub. He examined the one bookcase in the room. It was made of several fruit crates, stacked and painted bright colors. In it were books dealing with art, psychology, dreams, occult lore. Books he had never read, subjects he did not know. Uneasily, he began to realize he had strayed a long way from familiar ground.

He turned to discover the little girl Daphne peeking at him from the doorway. Shyly, slowly, she crept into the room, naked and dripping. She stared at him as she came forward, as if trying to recall his face. She was the same pale, intense child he remembered, with great hollow eyes behind thick lenses. He smiled at her, a stiff, false smile.

"Hello, Daphne," he said, trying to sound casual. "Remember me?" Cautiously, the girl walked over to him, her fingers curled at her mouth. When she was before him, she reached up with one hand as far as she could. He bent down to her gesture. As he did so, she caught the skin of his cheek tightly between her thumb and finger, pinching hard, until it hurt. Heller tried to brush her hand away; she pinched harder, digging her nails in. A hard, fearful panting came into her throat; her face became agitated, almost savage. He pulled back, taking a mean scratch across his cheek. The girl's mother called from the back of the house and Daphne, still making the little gasping sound, turned and ran across the room. At the door, she turned and looked back, her gaze worried, as if she thought he might be coming after her. Reaching out, she made awkward, tight little pincers of her fingers. "Pinch, pinch," she said, then turned and ran.

Heller discovered his heart racing with agitation, his breath locked in his throat. That kid . . . that little girl . . . how much of all this, the worst crisis of his career, traced back to her, to what those wide, goggling eyes had seen that nobody else had seen? He wanted to grab her, shake her, make her talk. Instead, he stood rubbing his sore cheek, holding his temper.

Within a few minutes, the mother returned to the living room. She was barefoot now, wearing a long, blue gown loosely tied at the waist. Her hair was free; it fell about her shoulders and well down her back. She wore no makeup; her face was gifted with smooth, mask-like good looks, a sharp nose and strong cheekbones. But the skin was drawn back too tightly at the mouth, making her teeth prominent—the one flaw in a beautiful face. She drew herself up gracefully on a large cushion against the wall and said nothing. Her quiet eyes probed his face. She was leaving it all up to him. He would have to calibrate his words precisely.

"I don't know how much you know about the Center," he began unsteadily. "We process data for the government and for various agencies around the country. A lot of things are tied into our computers. We're a pretty big sort of operation."

There was a warning at the back of his mind—not to overdo his importance. She won't be impressed or intimidated. Be careful. Keep it modest, low key.

"Everybody in Washington knows about the Brain, Mr. Heller," she replied in a cool, ungiving tone. It was a gesture of recognition, a connection. It helped. He went on.

"Well, we've been having an odd problem at the Center over the past several weeks. Perhaps you've heard about it on the news. An infestation . . . insects of some kind. They've gotten into some of our computers."

He noticed it at once: the flash of surprise that lit her face, the sudden intensification of her eyes. He had touched a nerve. What did she know? "That's what I came to see you about." He left a pause, waiting to see how she might fill it. After a moment, she asked, "You said somebody's life was at stake. Whose life?"

"It's rather unpleasant," he continued. "I don't want to upset you. These insects I mentioned—as it turns out, they're pretty vicious. They've attacked people. Two nights ago, they attacked a couple of our employees—a programmer and a security guard—and killed them. You haven't heard about it . . . ?"

Her distress was now undisguised. He could see her throat working, trying to swallow down her anxiety. "Your machines killed somebody . . . ?"

"No," he corrected, "the bugs, the insects, they attacked the two men. They went for their faces and eyes, blinded them. One man fell down a flight of stairs and struck his head. The other man . . . well, he was badly mauled. About a week before that, the insects attacked some visitors, bit them up severely."

She turned her head toward the wall, hiding her face, running one nervous hand over her hair and down her neck. "Terrible . . . terrible machines. Deadly things."

"No," he insisted, "it wasn't the computers. It was the insects—they came out of the computers, you see."

She looked up to search his eyes, suspicion and concern mixed in her expression. "Death in your machines. Now you see that. You can't blame it on . . . on anyone else."

He struggled to be patient with her. He could see that, behind the calm eyes, she was shaken. He decided to shift his ground. He reached into his briefcase and fished out Daphne's drawing.

"Your daughter visited our Center last March—with several children from your school. It was filmed for television."

Quietly, darkly, she murmured "Yes."

"Afterward she drew this—part of a report on her visit. See? It has her name on it. This is what the insects look like."

Jane took the drawing and studied it with a troubled frown. "This is what they look like? This is a child's drawing." She stared at him incredulously, as if she thought he might be playing a bad, tasteless joke.

"Yes, I know, it's strange. I can't explain it. We caught one of the insects just yesterday. It's the only one we've seen. I know it sounds a little crazy, but it *does* look like that . . . only in three dimensions. Actually, as if it got up and walked off that page."

She continued to gaze at him uncertainly. "You have an insect that looks like this—like a stick drawing? You've actually seen something that looks like this?"

"Yes, I have," he said as earnestly as he could. "I really have. Just yesterday morning. You have to see it under a microscope. It shows up like that. We don't know what kind of insect it is as yet."

She was more puzzled. "You think Daphne saw this under a microscope?"

The thought had never occurred to him. How would the girl be able to draw the insect if she hadn't seen it magnified? "Well . . . no. I don't know . . . possibly . . ."

"My daughter has never been near a microscope."

He swallowed hard, feeling foolish and off balance.

"Mr. Heller, what exactly are you trying to tell me?" Her eyes were challenging.

"I can't explain all this," he went on. "I can't make sense of it yet. What I know for certain is that your daughter drew that picture. And that there *are* insects that look like that. I've seen them—or *one* of them at least. They're in our computers. What I'm wondering is—where did your daughter see these insects? At the Center? Or before? That's really all I'm here to find out."

Jane rose and walked to a dingy brick fireplace at the far end of the room. She pressed the palms of her hands across the mantel, gathering her thoughts. With her head tilted forward, her long, sandy hair fell about her face like a hood. Heller could tell she was thinking with great urgency, choosing a course of action. She turned and studied him, then said, "You frightened Daphne at the Center. Do you know that? You told her there were 'bugs' in the machines. She's always been afraid of insects—unfortunately. I've tried to dispel that fear, make her at home with all living things. But insects have always distressed her. It was the wrong thing for you to say."

"I'm very sorry," Heller apologized. "She misunderstood what I meant. It was only a little joke . . ."

"I suppose I'm not entirely free of blame," she went on, as if she had not heard what he said. "I didn't want her to go on this field trip." She threw Heller a distinctly defiant look. "I don't approve of your Center, of your machines. I don't think you have any right . . . I suppose I may have made Daphne apprehensive. Perhaps I said something about the machines being dangerous, something like that. Then you teased her about the bugs. I saw it on television. You made her afraid, you made all the children afraid. You sent her home like that. She had bad dreams . . . nightmares. That's where she saw the insects—in her dreams."

Heller's heart sank with remorse. "Oh, I am sorry. I didn't realize. But she was dreaming of something she saw. The bugs are real, you see. They exist. What I said to the children about bugs—you realize those weren't real bugs. It's a metaphor."

She stared across the room at him with rising anger. "You don't think the fears of children are real?"

What did she mean? Heller struggled to grasp what she was saying.

"The fears of children," she went on, "the bad dreams of children—if we listened to what they have to teach us, if we built our world to heal those fears, to eliminate them, we'd be much better off. Those fears never leave us. They're in all of us. They have *meaning*, but we forget that. Your machines wouldn't understand that. Machines can't make a world for children. They're at the farthest extreme from childhood. They're dead things. Children are the beginning of life; machines are the end."

Heller could not take this in. It sounded murky and emotional, the sort of talk he found intolerably irritating. But he must remain patient, keep things friendly. He made a show of trying to understand. "No doubt you're right. Did you ever talk to Daphne about her dreams? Where she might have seen the insects she dreamed about?"

"You don't understand," she said, wagging her head with exasperation. "*You* put the bugs into her head and into her dreams. She saw them because you mentioned them. You told her they were in the machines. She dreamed about what you told her."

"Yes, but you see, the bugs *exist*," Heller repeated. "It's not just that I mentioned them. They're not simply subjective. They exist."

"And Daphne's dreams exist," Jane insisted heatedly. "Her fears exist, the human imagination exists, moral intelligence exists, the visions of saints exist . . ." She stopped herself short, realizing that she was rambling. Sullenly, she added, "The world isn't just what you can touch and measure."

"Well, yes," Heller agreed, fighting down his impatience. He knew he was close to something important, something she knew; but she was clouding things, leading him astray. "All I mean is that the insects *really* exist. I mean . . ." What did he mean? How should he put it? This was no time for a lecture in basic epistemology. Besides, he suspected that, in her present state, demanding too much clarity would only antagonize her. The woman was confusing things in ways he despised, but he must control himself, stay in touch.

"All these things 'exist,' Mr. Heller," she continued more calmly. "Daphne's dreams were real to her—real enough to frighten her. We did what we had to. One can't stand by and watch a child suffer."

Heller groped his way through her words searching for meaning. Who was the "we" she spoke of? "I don't follow you, I'm sorry. Please, may I talk to Daphne?" Her eyes turned defiant. He hastened to explain. "It doesn't have to be now. Tomorrow maybe. I'd like to have a few people talk to her with me.

There's an entomologist who's helping us at Georgetown University . . ." He could feel her withdrawing.

"No, Mr. Heller," she said with a slow, determined shake of the head. "My daughter won't be put through that again. It's bad enough you're here, reminding her. We've healed her fears. I won't have her frightened again."

This was tricky. She was defending the child. He recognized he must respect her concern. He had to navigate carefully. "You see," he explained again gently, "it may be that Daphne knows where the insects come from. She may be able to lead us to a nest, a source . . ."

She gave a contemptuous half chuckle. "You really don't understand. I've tried to tell you."

Deliberately letting some irritation show, he replied, "Perhaps *you* don't understand—how vital this is, what's at stake. The Center is a major facility of the government. If it stays closed down . . ."

Her face brightened with amazement. "You've closed the Center? You've actually closed it?"

"Yes. Because of the deaths. We can't risk another tragedy. That's why we have to get rid of the insects, find them and destroy them. Miss Hecate, I didn't come here to ask a minor personal favor. This is an authentic public emergency. I was at the White House this afternoon discussing the situation at the Center with the President. He agrees we must do everything in our power to prevent more deaths." He could see her mind working rapidly, adding up and retotaling all he was saying. He played the one card that seemed to matter most to her. "More people could be hurt. I'm sure you want to prevent that."

Almost to herself, she said, "It's not Daphne's fault. She can't be blamed for this. She's a child, a frightened child."

"Nobody's to be blamed," he assured her. "That's not what I mean."

"Nobody's to blame?" Her voice took on an offended edge. "'Bugs' in the machine. Such an odd phrase—'bugs.' Who makes up an odd phrase like that? Not Daphne. Not you either. Nobody. It simply appears, doesn't it? Spontaneously.

Just a metaphor, you say. But you know, Mr. Heller, meta-phors, poetry—they don't occur by accident. They have their own reality. The way, long ago, people—women—thought of the earth as a mother that bore fruit. Was that *just* a meta-phor? It had meaning and power within it. It taught women how to cultivate the earth, because they could hear the power in the word. Sometimes that power is a gift, sometimes it's a warning. All the symbols we speak with and think with, all metaphors, all poetry are filled with secret meanings. Even your own thinking, Mr. Heller. So mechanical, so mathe-matical. But there's poetry there, down underneath. Most of us lose touch with poetry. But children are still very close to it. They hear what words really mean."

Again, Heller could not follow what she said. Was she really saying anything sensible? All this could be garbled nonsense. He didn't know enough about Jane Hecate to judge what lay behind her words. Perhaps only a kind of nuttiness which could put on a sincere and impressive surface. She seemed to be trying earnestly to tell him something, but it melted away when he reached to take hold. Her language was not his. He had to cling to what he knew. The bugs really existed; the lit-tle girl had seen them. He must talk to the girl. He labored to stay patient and polite, knowing that the way to the child was through the mother.

"Yes, I see . . ." he said soberly. "Well, of course, no one would think of blaming your daughter. If anyone is at fault here, it's obviously me. To tell the truth, I've never reflected on the phrase . . . 'bugs.' Maybe I'm only at home with num-bers and FORTRAN—computer language. I'd appreciate your help so greatly. Perhaps you could talk to Daphne for me. There are only a few things I want to pin down."

A reflective shadow passed across her face. For a moment, she stared blankly out the window. Then, "Tomorrow. Come back tomorrow. I'll try to help. But not tonight. I want to prepare Daphne for your questions."

"When tomorrow?" he asked. "In the morning?"

"No. Daphne has a class in the morning. I don't want to interrupt her routine—especially for something as unsettling as this. She's . . . delicate, very sensitive. Please remember that. I'm not boasting, but she is very special, very unusual."

"I'm sure she is." His hand went to his cheek. The scratch the girl had given him still burned there.

"Come in the evening," she said. "After seven."

"There's no chance of seeing her earlier? I hope I've made the urgency of the matter . . ."

"Please," she cut him off, politely but firmly.

He worked mightily to control his impatience. The child was only a few rooms away; he was desperate to talk to her, if only for a few minutes. It wrenched to be leaving without finding out what he had come for. But what if the child was, as she said, sensitive, perhaps unbalanced? The wrong approach might ruin everything, make it impossible to gain the information he needed. He had no choice but to do as the mother required. He waited through a thoughtful pause, then, reluctantly, agreed to return tomorrow. She moved to escort him across the room.

"Interesting paintings," he remarked as he crossed to the door. "Your work?"

"Yes," she answered.

"Interesting," he said again, then winced to himself, realizing how feeble the phrase sounded. He was out of his depth talking about art. The subject was a foreign language to him. Usually, when conversations turned in that direction, he would offer some flippant, defensive remark about the progress that was being made with computerized drawing and painting— achievements like Timmy the Turtle. He would have been embarrassed to mention that to her; and there was not much about computers that embarrassed him. Still, he wanted badly to connect on some level with her before he left. "That image —the horned figure—it's in several of the pictures. What is it?"

"A fertility symbol," she answered. There was a mildly teasing tone to her words, as if she wondered what he would make of that. "It's a traditional form."

"I see. A goddess?"

"Yes. The goddess."

Blindly, he hazarded a guess. "Hecate?"

She showed surprise. She had not expected him to make the identification. "Yes. She has many names. That's one."

"One of your names too. After the goddess?"

She did not answer at once. Studying him, she pulled thoughtfully at a strand of hair. He could see she was gauging how much friendly small talk she cared to make with him. "It's a professional name. I began using it for my painting a few years ago, after I . . ." She did not complete the explanation. "I've been using it for about four years now, since I started exhibiting."

She had brought him out on the porch, closing the screen door behind her. He might simply say good night and leave now, but he found himself searching for ways to prolong the moment. Why? Perhaps it was only to find out something more about how her mind worked, the mysterious logic by which she traced the insects to her daughter's dreams.

But no, that was not the real reason he lingered on the porch. She was leaning against the wall beside the door, her hands behind her, her hair draped softly at her shoulders. And he realized he had not yet fully taken in the delicacy and strangeness of her features. It was her beauty that held him, and her deep calm. Now that he was on the point of leaving, her eyes had become less guarded. She was not, after all, a severe or hostile woman. Under her softening glance, he found himself unaccountably relaxing, loosening. She could not know she was offering him this moment of transient ease; still, it made her company precious to him. He rapidly tunneled back into his undergraduate English. "Hecate . . . Let's see. Am I right? It's from Shakespeare, isn't it? *Macbeth?*"

"Yes," she said. "There's a Hecate in *Macbeth.*"

"One of the witches."

She sighed wearily. "That's a distortion. Long before that in ancient times, Hecate was the goddess of magic."

"Witches are magic, aren't they?"

"In a shabby, sort of hand-me-down way. At least as most people think of them. 'Eye of newt and toe of frog.' Not the real thing."

"The real thing . . ." There was no way he could connect the phrase with the concept of magic. "So Shakespeare got it wrong?"

"Like most Christians. Like most men."

He smiled. But no, she was not offering the remark facetiously. When she smiled back, he knew it was at his own bewilderment. She had turned and entered the house before he realized he had forgotten to say good night.

1

He had to know more about Jane Hecate. The Brain gave him that much of an advantage. With Levinson's help the next morning, he rebooted enough of the system to program through a general inventory that compiled material stored in a dozen different data bases: census, internal revenue, health and welfare, driver's license, credit references. Bit by bit, in a matter of minutes, the Brain deftly pieced together the life history of Jane Saxton/Hecate.

As he ran the search, Heller reflected uneasily on the testimony he had given only two months ago before the Cory committee. He had explained how, in order to protect the privacy of citizens, the information collected for the Brain was aggregated and quantified to strip it of individual associations. Routinely, it was milled into faceless and nameless numbers. For, after all, the National Center for Data Control was not interested in petty, personal details. It dealt in vast, anonymous statistics that were viewed from the Olympian heights of public policy.

What he was careful to leave unsaid was that the Brain, if so commanded by authorized parties, could just as easily individualize anything it had ever aggregated. That was what Heller was doing now, as he reclaimed the buried image of Jane Hecate from a slag-heap of social data. The Brain could be the consummate snoop.

Nothing extraordinary came back from the search. He learned that she was thirty-seven years old—older than he would have guessed. Upper middle-class background. Father— Dr. Anthony Collins, a Baltimore physician. College—Bryn Mawr. Postgraduate work with teaching credential—Columbia. While at Columbia, married to Paul Saxton, social scientist and systems analyst now at Princeton. One child from the marriage, a daughter now eleven. Divorced—seven years ago. (The divorce came eleven months before Daphne's birth. Who was the girl's father?) Employment—several years of off-and-on teaching in New York, California, Princeton, mainly paralleling her husband's academic appointments. Received small amounts of Aid for Dependent Children for a year or so after the divorce. For the past four years, teaching at the Hartmann School in Washington. Three parking tickets and a minor traffic citation. Some IRS delinquencies. A few scraps of medical data: psychiatric care in California and Princeton; one federally funded abortion three years ago.

There was a second search Heller made—a Class One security check. This involved the use of highly sensitive data the Brain stored for the FBI, CIA and military intelligence as part of a classified program. Here he discovered that her name as Saxton and then Hecate appeared on the mailing lists and membership rolls of several organizations. Heller could recognize most of these as environmental, feminist and anti-nuclear groups. There was one local organization he could not place. "Earthrite." Possibly another ecology group, but it published a quarterly journal bearing an unlikely title: *Crystal Egg*. Before he left for his evening meeting with Jane, he was able to find Earthrite listed as a tax-exempt, "traditionalist" church with branches in California, Canada, England and Switzerland. That more than anything else confirmed what he suspected. In dealing with Jane Hecate, he was treading a narrow bridge across a yawning chasm. What he could see on the far side was both alien and distasteful. If only the bridge held firm long enough for him to get to the daughter . . .

2

When Heller returned that evening to the small house on Belmont Street, he found it dark and deserted. The windows were locked shut, the Volkswagen van was gone. He waited on the porch swing until nearly eight-thirty and then inquired at the neighbors. A woman across the street told him she had seen the van being packed that morning. The two ladies who shared the house had driven off with their children about noon. No, she had no idea where they had gone; sometimes they went off for days at a time.

Driving home angry and insulted, Heller began to shape plans for locating the mother and daughter. In the morning, he would inquire after them at the Hartmann School and at Earthrite. It was unlikely he would gain much help in those quarters. Where did he go then? The former husband perhaps —at Princeton. Or he might try tracing the other woman in the house. He could run a check on the Volkswagen van . . . on Jane's welfare payments and bank account to see if she ever used other addresses. He would use everything he had—police, FBI, private investigators if necessary.

Along the way, he stopped at the address he had for Earthrite. It was an area of small shops and boutiques along the C&O canal below M Street, less than a mile from his own townhouse in Georgetown. The church was a modest two-story building; Heller must have passed it countless times on his way to the Brain and back each day.

The ground floor was a tiny bookstore, now closed for the day. From the outside, he could not tell much about it. By the glow of a dim night light, he made out a few bookcases, a desk, some chairs. The shop looked as prim and austere as a Christian Science reading room. The front door bore the name "Earthrite" in small, discreet black letters burned into a wooden panel. Below that was a sign giving the hours of weekly lectures and services in the church upstairs. The display in the front window was unprepossessing, but now immediately familiar to Heller: the small, horned figurine cut from white stone, standing on a black cloth at the juncture of two crossed knives.

"Hecate the Witch, Hecate the Bitch," he mused to himself. And where was she now?

When he arrived home, he found three consecutive calls from Levinson on his phone recorder, each more urgent than the last. The final message, an outburst of impatience, simply said, "Come on, Boss Man, get on the stick!" Heller phoned back at once. Levinson's voice was unusually brittle. He had received a call from Lyman Touhy, the Secretary of Defense.

"He knows about the bug. He found out from Wally Turnbull. How did that happen?"

"I mentioned it to Wally yesterday," Heller answered. "Supposedly it was postdated information. Not that I'd be surprised to learn that Lyman picked it up out of the woodwork as soon as I opened my mouth. The eyes and ears of Washington."

"Well, he's mad as hell we let Schifman examine the thing. He wants access to it right away."

That took Heller off-guard. Where did Lyman enter the picture? "Yes? Why?"

"Exactly what I asked. It wasn't easy to get an answer. I told Lyman it was our problem and our bug. Why shouldn't we handle it our way? All right, here's the big news. Don't drop your teeth. DoD has been experiencing data pox for nearly a month in a couple of its major data processing operations. Specifically, Lyman mentioned PAVE PAWS, NORAD and B-MEWS. They've been keeping it under wraps, treating it as possible espionage. Suspicious sons of bitches! I put out a call on this last April. They never breathed a word, just sat back and watched us sweat it out at the Brain. I don't think Lyman is telling us everything he knows yet—just feeling us out."

"Are you sure it's the same problem?" Heller asked.

"No question. In fact, I was more sure than Lyman was; we have more details about the symptoms than DoD has put together. Lyman's data pox is apparently still at an early stage—the point where people start talking about creepy-crawly feelings. That's where we were in May. Nobody at Defense has seen any bugs yet, if we can believe what Lyman's telling us, which we very likely can't. The rash seems to be working through the same sequence of phases. I'm inclined to take soundings again among major computer installations around the country."

"DoD hasn't done that?"

"If they have, Lyman's not saying. My impression is he's only gotten urgent about this in the last few days—maybe since the two deaths at the Brain."

Heller agreed to Levinson's proposal. "All right, take the soundings. And try some installations abroad as well. This time, be persistent. Make sure you turn up everything you can about rashes, pox, bugs. Also see if there are any direct personal vectors involved: people carrying the pox from one place to another. Maybe it's contagious. We've also got to pin down some dates. Has anybody experienced the rash before we did? If not, then Daphne Saxton was the first person to see the insects. We need to know where and how."

As for the bug, Levinson reported that Schifman had shown it to two other specialists, one entomologist, one biophysicist. All the tests had been repeated; in addition, the bug had been examined with a field ion microscope. The findings—or nonfindings—were the same. "This is going to be damned difficult to keep quiet," Levinson warned. "The insect is a real freak of nature. I can tell the scientists are aching to break into print. I've asked them to be discreet, even hinted that this is classified. But that's not official. I can't bind them with an oath. I think we should make a firm decision about the bug— how secret it is, or how public it is."

Heller pondered the matter. He still clung to the hope— though less securely now—that, with a few days' time to locate Jane Hecate and her daughter, he might solve all his riddles and get the Brain back in operation before anyone was the wiser. "All right, Berny," he said, "start making arrangements with Lyman to place the bug under a Department of Defense cover. DoD already suspects possible espionage; that should be enough to make them play along. But make sure Schifman stays close to the specimen and keeps in touch with us. I don't want this slipping away from us into Lyman's control. If anybody finds a way to kill this thing, we should be the first to know."

3

As Heller expected, neither Earthrite nor the Hartmann School would give out any information about Jane Hecate. But he had little trouble finding her. With the help of her former husband, it took less than two days.

Paul Saxton was a social scientist with a modest reputation in government circles. Levinson, digging to remember the name, finally placed him as part of a committee he had worked with some years back on a classified, counter-insurgency project for the Army. Saxton was not a heavyweight in his field, but he managed to punctuate his teaching career with prestigious stints at RAND, MITRE and other military think-tanks. On a few occasions, he had testified for the Defense Department at congressional hearings. He was an ambitious academic, still eagerly prowling the fringes of official power, looking for a way in. In his eyes, so Heller suspected, a call from the Brain was bound to look like an inviting opportunity to be of service. He could be counted on to provide information. Heller was right. All it took was a friendly phone call from Levinson asking for confidential advice.

"This is a bit delicate, Paul," Levinson explained, improvising rapidly. "It's part of a security check on someone who seems to be connected with an odd religious group your ex-wife belongs to. We'd like to know about the group, maybe get in touch with her . . ."

Saxton, overdoing it, offered to drive into Washington if necessary. But Heller, taking over the line from Levinson, assured him that a few minutes on the phone would serve. From there, the conversation wandered freely; Saxton was more than willing to talk about his ex-wife's bizarre interests—perhaps to clear himself of any compromising associations. With exaggerated distaste, he rehearsed all he knew about her feminist and religious involvements. As he saw it, "the rot" set into their marriage about eight years ago. He was in California then, at RAND for the second time and getting well mixed into policy-making circles. Saxton began to dilate upon his success; Heller had to move him along with his wife's story.

"Jane couldn't take the pressure," Saxton explained. "She didn't like *this*, she didn't like *that*, she didn't like any of the people I worked with. Finally, she just stopped being part of my world, began painting, picking up her own friends, joining offbeat political groups—which created some pretty serious problems for me." It was clear that Saxton saw all this as vindictive, spiteful. "The climax was she drifted into this weird church—first in California, then, after we broke up, back in Washington. Jane always had a weakness for things like that—mystic stuff, clouds of unknowing. We never really related on that plane."

Saxton knew little about Earthrite. Jane had kept it to herself. He saw it as "one of these trendy, intellectualoid, occult operations. Typical religion of the oppressed. I have this image of middle-class lady pagans, sitting around sticking pins in pictures of their husbands and boyfriends. Well, that isn't exactly fair. Jane's a bright girl, very well read. Eccentric maybe, but no bubble-head. Fact is: I really don't know that much about what goes on in the church. The few pieces of writing I've seen from the group are reasonably scholarly. Incidentally, the church isn't all women. There are a few men in it. God knows what kind of specimens they must be. I don't want to be a rumor-monger, but I gather the men are there for certain sexual rites. Jane got involved in that at some point . . . part of the reason for our divorce." Daphne, he hastened to add, was not his daughter. She had come along since Jane joined the church "as part of the sexual mumbo-jumbo." He considered Daphne a "strange child, obviously in need of competent psychiatric care—which she isn't likely to get." The girl was being raised in the religion, according to "some pretty bizarre educational ideas." He clearly disapproved.

Saxton knew the church owned some property in the Dolly

Sodds area, well into the West Virginia mountain country. If Jane had left town for an extended stay, it was likely she had gone there; she used it as a second home for weekends and vacations. He didn't know the exact location.

"When you're in town next time, look me up for lunch," Heller said, trying to bring the call to a quick conclusion. Saxton was unabashedly eager. He proceeded to bore Heller with several minutes of talk about some second-rate research he was doing. "Listen," he finished, "let me send you a few papers I've done on psephological programming. You do expect to be back in operation before the elections . . ."

The rest of what Heller needed to know about Jane Hecate came from Earthrite itself. He had his secretary put in a call for him. She posed as an old friend of Jane's passing through town, desperately wanting to get in touch. Earthrite, clearly not very expert at keeping secrets, told her Jane was staying at Gaia Lodge, its mountain retreat. Might she have directions for getting there? Yes, of course.

It was clear in Heller's mind that he would have to handle Jane and Earthrite on his own. He knew, in some way he could not bring into focus, that she and her daughter were at the center of his crisis. But that conviction was based upon a phrase or two Jane had dropped, on a few subtle gestures of recognition and fear. It had nothing to do with the clear logic he might have embedded in a policy memo. For years now, even in his most personal affairs, that had been his touchstone: could he phrase his choices and decisions in the dispassionate administrative prose that passed between him and his colleagues in their official communications? Could he make a tight argument that ran from fact and number toward a persuasive QED? That was hardly the case now. He was working from intuition, and that was unfamiliar to him. He had no idea how he would explain to anyone what he was seeking through Jane Hecate and her church. He would be embarrassed to try.

He made rapid and not very graceful arrangements to be away for at least a day, leaving Levinson to improvise excuses for his absence in the midst of a burgeoning emergency. So far, he had not told Levinson anything more about his visit to Jane Hecate than that it was a "promising lead" . . . if only he could get to the child. But, of course, Levinson was to keep even that little to himself.

Before he left Washington, Heller made one stop. He visited the Earthrite bookshop to round up some reading material. It was a tidy, ordinary store; its small collection of literature was mainly scholarly and neatly organized. The few pictures and decorations around the walls—ceramic pottery, macramé hangings, wood carvings—were modest and well done. Toward the rear of the shop there was one small painting he could identify as Jane Hecate's work. The title on a small card alongside was "White Goddess."

As he moved about the shop, flipping through books and periodicals, Heller tried to look academically curious. He had no idea what questions he might ask without arousing suspicion. The woman in charge of the store seemed puzzled by him, but she remained forthcoming and pleasant. When she asked for the second time if he wanted help, he could only think of asking if she had any books dealing with psychic phenomena. Frowning uncertainly, she asked what he meant. He rummaged through his limited vocabulary on the subject. "Oh, mind reading . . . things like that." It was all he could think of; it didn't sound too bright.

She smiled a little nervously. "I'm afraid we don't carry anything like that. We're not very psychic."

"I thought that would be important to your church," he said.

The woman looked faintly irritated. "No, not really. Why did you think so?"

"Uh . . . I had the impression . . . from some things I'd read."

"Well, that's not very accurate. Are you familiar with Dr. Hartmann's writings?"

"Dr. Hartmann . . . no."

She sighed, still smiling politely. "You don't seem to know

much about us." She took a periodical from the rack behind her. "This issue of our journal gives some background material on Earthrite."

It was a copy of *Crystal Egg*. Under the title, it said "A Journal of Traditional Studies." The cover picture was a severe face, gaunt, hollow-eyed, framed by a bushy, unkempt head of hair. Underneath was the name "Dr. Immanuel Hartmann" and the dates "1868–1937."

"Thank you," Heller said. "It's a form of witchcraft, isn't it?"

"What is?"

"Earthrite . . . the church." Again, she frowned disapprovingly. Awkwardly he added, "That is, witchcraft in the best sense, the true sense." He wondered what he meant by that.

The woman gave him a dubious stare. "You're not from the newspapers, are you?"

Heller was jarred. "Oh no. I'm from Georgetown University. Doing some research on . . ." On what, he wondered. "On traditional religions."

The woman was looking more uneasy, but she remained courteous. She went around the room collecting pamphlets and periodicals. "I don't know what you understand by 'traditional.' However, these may help you learn something about Earthrite. I think you'll see we're not any sort of witchcraft, or spiritualism, or voodoo. Dr. Hartmann was quite a distinguished philosopher. We've tried to preserve that character in our studies." She stacked the publications on her desk. "If you'd like to look through these . . . You may find we use the word 'wiccan' occasionally for some of our seasonal rites. It's an Old English term which is sometimes translated as 'witchcraft,' but we prefer not to use the word. We feel there is an important distinction between a modern philosophical system like Dr. Hartmann's and the sort of folk customs and popular superstitions people have in mind when they speak of witchcraft. It's rather like the difference between, say, the vulgar practice of alchemy and C. G. Jung's study of hermeticism, if you see what I mean."

"Oh yes," Heller agreed, having no idea what he was agreeing to. She had taken the discussion into an area where the discriminations she made were meaningless to him. He bought all the literature she had assembled for him and left rapidly.

4

Along the four-hour drive into the West Virginia mountains, Heller stopped three times for coffee, each time loitering over the publications he had bought at the Earthrite bookshop. *Crystal Egg* was well produced and attractively illustrated. In its back issues, he found articles on ancient folk rituals, the cosmology of European stone circles, women's mysteries, fertility rites, the use of occult symbols in modern psychiatry. There was one brief essay signed by Jane Hecate dealing with native American childbirth chants, also a notice of her paintings on exhibition at a small Washington gallery. The subject matter of the magazine and of other Earthrite publications was wholly alien to him, but it was all of a restrained, markedly academic tone. It gave him no common ground with Jane Hecate, but it did not lead him to write her and her church off as hopelessly eccentric.

In several of the issues of the magazine he came upon articles by Leah Hagar, head of both the Hartmann School and the church. They dealt with education, children's art and games. One continuing series by her reviewed the work of Immanuel Hartmann, about whom Heller knew nothing. From the series, he learned that Hartmann was a German philosopher who had moved through a number of occult societies, groups whose names Heller could not identify. The man had finished his life in Leipzig in the late thirties, the founder of a small, quasi-religious sect called *"Erdrecht"*—in English "Earthrite." He was a prolific writer and lecturer; Leah Hagar's articles carried long bibliographies of his work, all of it published by the Earthrite Press. The movement he headed was generally referred to as "traditionalist"; occasionally the phrase

"Old Religion" was used. The German for that was *Urglaube*, which Heller recognized as a stronger, less precise term: the ancient or primordial faith.

Skimming the series and other writings, he concluded that Earthrite was a sort of eclectic, pagan revival. There were references to pagan deities, especially to mother gods of many names; there were exercises for the contemplation of nature; there were numerous rituals, chants, spells. Heller might have dismissed what he read as nonsense, but there was a marked intellectual sophistication to the writing and a good deal of respectable scholarship. Some articles were signed by university professors, others by psychiatrists. It almost annoyed him that what he found in the literature he bought was not outright cranky. He wanted a convenient slot to put Earthrite in. He hadn't found it.

As he covered the last few miles to Gaia Lodge, Heller still assumed Jane Hecate had gone into hiding and would be difficult to find. He was mistaken. He had no trouble locating the lodge or getting onto the grounds. The entrance, at the end of a short cinder road, was clearly marked, the gate open. What had he expected—a walled sanctuary guarded at every point? He parked his car among several others, one of them the old Volkswagen van.

The retreat seemed to be a collection of simple log and clapboard cabins surrounded by several acres of pine forest. It reminded Heller of a boys' summer camp, perhaps its former use before Earthrite took it over. On the porch of the largest cabin, he saw a group of three people. To his relief, two were men. The people on the porch watched as he approached: neutral faces, neither inquisitive nor hostile. He felt expected. One of the men called into the cabin; before Heller could speak, the screen door opened and Jane came out. She was dressed as he had first seen her, in tee shirt and jeans, her hair drawn back in a tight bun. She offered him a faint, nervous smile and led him off into a nearby wooded area without making any introductions.

"This is a little sooner than I expected," she said as they walked. "I would have liked a few more days."

"You didn't do much to cover your tracks," he explained, almost apologetically. "I only had to ask a few questions . . ."

"I didn't come here to hide. I don't suppose I could hide from someone in your position. I just wanted time to think. And I needed some advice."

"Have you worked it out?" he asked.

They had reached a small clearing shaped into a pentagon by fallen logs at the edges. In the center, on a large tree stump, there stood an earthenware version of the horned goddess, the two crossed knives at her feet. Off to the left, Heller could see a group of children at play, running among the trees. He spotted Daphne among them.

Jane sat down on one of the logs, her back against a tree. For the first time she looked directly into his eyes: a firm, decisive gaze. "We think you should talk to Leah." She made it sound like a major concession, but she did not even bother to give Leah's full name or explain who she was. Why did she presume he would know? He feigned a mildly arrogant ignorance. "Leah?" he asked.

"She's the head of our church here in the United States."

To himself, Heller commented wryly, With, no doubt, a congregation of sixteen and a half members.

"But first," Jane continued, "I'll tell you what I can. That's what we've decided—to tell you all we know."

"I appreciate that," he said.

"It's no special favor really," she explained. "We're not any sort of secret group. The only secrets we care about look after themselves. Open secrets. Some people have the eyes to see, and some don't. If I was reluctant to tell you very much the other evening, that was because of Daphne. I was worried that you might demand to question her, that you had the power to force that. That's the one condition I insist upon. You must leave her out of this. I don't want her troubled. I can tell you all there is to tell."

Heller nodded. "I agree, certainly."

She drew her knees up and paused for a long moment. In the late afternoon, the woods were hypnotically tranquil—warm, fragrant, filled with the high, bright cackling of birds.

At once, as he settled into Jane's company, Heller found himself touched by her calm. A stubborn tension deep inside him surrendered, and his breath flowed easily. He wondered if he might not have trouble staying awake in the deep, narcotic comfort of the moment. He had not experienced serenity like this . . . he could not say in how long. Years. He would almost have been willing to believe he had wandered into a sacred grove.

"All this that's happened," Jane began, "the problem you're having with your machines—you must understand that nobody at Earthrite intended that. Until you told me about the insects, I would never have conceived of such a thing. This much I can tell you for certain: Daphne never saw those insects anywhere before you mentioned them to her. I've questioned her carefully about that. She saw them in her dreams, in her fears —no place before that. That's what she drew in her picture— things she'd seen in her nightmares, things you told her were in your machines."

Heller tried to form a question, but let it pass. He must be careful not to sound challenging or skeptical until he heard her out.

She went on. "I know you find that hard to understand. Frankly, so do we. I should tell you that none of us here in the church—certainly not me—have any extraordinary powers, psychic talents, anything like that. We make no such claims. We call ourselves a 'traditionalist' church. That means we try to re-create some of the old rites and ways of nature worship. For some of us—like me—it's largely an aesthetic outlet. That's how I was drawn into Earthrite—through my painting. The church brought me something moving and beautiful, a new way of seeing the world. It's one of our fundamental teachings that natural things are 'supernatural' enough, without any extra added attractions.

"At the same time, it has always been Leah's conviction— part of the Hartmann philosophy—that all people are born with many so-called 'extraordinary' abilities, powers that we may later speak of as 'psychic.' Leah believes that children get educated away from those abilities by standard schooling; they get intimidated out of them as they grow up. Powers of imagination and insight, abilities of the mind that rise above ordinary reality—they lose them all. That's what the Hartmann system is all about—protecting those talents in children and letting them grow. I decided to bring Daphne up in the church because I wanted her to keep as many of those abilities as possible, right from the beginning. In fact, from even *before* the beginning. You see, she was conceived as part of our rituals. Her prenatal development was completely under Leah's supervision, as well as her birthing. I raised her to be free, creative, open. And she *has* become a remarkable child. But I didn't know how remarkable until you visited the other day. Now, frankly, I'm frightened at how different she is, at how different I've made her."

He saw a slight shiver run over her. Her eyes darkened and her tone became heavier. "After Daphne visited your Center, she came home filled with anxiety. She remembered only that one thing you had said—about the bugs. Such a stupid needless remark! She understood your machines were like great hives filled with dangerous insects. I remember telling her she must forget it, that it wasn't so. Perhaps I didn't do enough right there and then to calm her fears. And then the dreams began. She had these terrible dreams—for several nights. At first, she couldn't remember what she had dreamed—or, at least, she wouldn't tell me. Finally, I discovered she was dreaming about these . . . these things, these insects. I decided to ask Leah for help. We organized a healing exercise . . . a sort of exorcism, you might say. We told Daphne to send the bugs back where they came from, back into the machines. It worked. The nightmares stopped. We thought that would be the end of it."

After a moment, he realized that she was finished; this was what she had to tell him. She sat, staring grimly at the ground, waiting for his response.

"That's where you think the bugs come from?" Heller asked. "From Daphne's dreams, from her mind?" He tried to put the question gently, but a thrusting, dubious note entered his voice nonetheless.

She looked across at him shrewdly. "You say you've seen the insects. Have you been able to identify them?"

"No, not yet. But I'm not ready to believe they're figments of the imagination, some sort of ectoplasmic projection."

She seemed hurt and embarrassed by his refusal. "Then believe what you wish," she sighed wearily. "You came all this way to ask for our help. Why do that if you know better? That's what I have to tell you. Perhaps there's no point in talking to Leah."

Heller yielded. "I don't have any better explanations; I don't have any explanations at all. The bugs aren't any known life form. Forgive me—I'm out of my depth."

"And we're out of ours," she confessed. "What I'm telling you—it's the only way any of us can make sense of things. None of us has any experience with spells, hexes, things like that—except for aesthetic or psychological purposes. There are old rituals, seasonal rites and such that I find extremely beautiful. I enjoy them the way I do poetry and painting. I'm sure they have a healthy, balancing effect upon the mind. I've never assumed they had any power beyond that, never thought they could be used the way people use machines—to force the world to be different, to hurt people. Something's gone wrong, something's gotten out of hand."

For several moments, they allowed the silence of the woods to settle around them, broken only by the songs of birds and the distant voices of children. Looking across at her under the shadow-lace of the leaves, he was struck more than ever by her quiet beauty. And now, for the first time, there was a soft vulnerability in her eyes, as if she were asking him to understand and help.

Finally, when he realized she had told him all she had to say, he asked to meet Leah Hagar. He asked reluctantly; he would have preferred to stay with Jane in the quiet grove for the rest of the day—for a week, a month, a year. It was a physical strain for him to turn his mind back to the task that had brought him to this mountain retreat. Somewhere beyond the woods, in the frenetic city where his computers were, where the engines of progress never slept, the world he belonged to was threatening to disintegrate. And he had come here, not for solace, but to find out why.

1

If he had passed her in the street, Heller would not have given Leah Hagar a second look. A fragile, soft-spoken woman in her early seventies, dressed in severely dark and dowdy clothes, she hardly cut an imposing figure. Yet, he was no sooner ushered into the mountain cabin where she waited for him surrounded by a small corps of deferential followers, than he was struck by her formidable presence. Approaching her, he felt like a traveler from distant parts who had been granted a special audience with a tribal matriarch. Try as he would to assert his status, Heller could not gain a secure footing with her. The woman was all unnerving angles; her appearance, her manner worked subtly to keep him off-balance. Some stiffness or injury about the hips forced her to perch tensely on the edge of her chair, her weight propped on a cane that thrust her neck and shoulders aggressively forward. Her face, too, was oddly skewed, perhaps by a touch of paralysis at the cheek which sharply tilted her brow and jaw line. Her habit was to hold her mouth in a stiff, off-center smile that must have been meant to be ingratiating; it came across as a mocking grin. All the while, behind her heavy glasses, one eye, grotesquely magnified, goggled unblinkingly at him as if he were a specimen beneath a microscope.

Jane made introductions around the room; these too were oddly unbalanced to Leah Hagar's advantage. Heller was, very formally, "Dr. Thomas Heller of the Center for Data Control." The two men present were a "Professor Samples from George Washington University" and a "Dr. Fritsch." The women in the group were Samples' wife Alison and a Carol Aronson, both introduced as teachers at the Hartmann School. But Leah was simply "Leah." No title, no further identification—as if none were required. The casual touch lent her special status. That was awkward for Heller; it left him groping for a name to use, something that would preserve a protective distance between them.

"Dr. Heller," she greeted him, reaching with difficulty over her cane to take his hand. "So honored to meet you, though I wish it were under happier circumstances." Her accent hinted of Middle Europe—strongly German, slightly Hungarian. She gestured for him to take the chair beside her. It was a wobbly folding seat lower than her own, placing him uncomfortably under her penetrating, one-eyed stare. "I do hope Jane has told you—we are as surprised and distressed by this misfortune as you. You see, we only wanted to help the child. None of us expected our exercise to have more than a psychological effect. How difficult it is for us to learn that, indeed, nature is a seamless garment, all of a piece, mind and matter interwoven. Little Daphne's fears have entered the world—invaded it, perhaps I should say. Only a child's dream. But now, you see, it has become our nightmare as well."

Heller said nothing, but she read his skeptical silence perceptively.

"Of course, our conclusion is difficult for you to accept. I quite understand." The stiff smile widened to reveal several long, uneven teeth. "Well, perhaps we are wrong in our reasoning, perhaps too hasty. We only proceed from what you have told Jane. Have we misunderstood? Maybe before we go further, we should review our facts. Exactly how strange, how 'unearthly' would you say this phenomenon is? Does it qualify for a suitably strange explanation? Is it worth discussing with people like us—such a spooky bunch?" She chuckled and the others around the room smiled. Heller did not smile. "After all," she went on, "it may not be necessary to reach so far out of intellectual bounds. You must tell us. These insects—can you say what they are, where else they might be found?"

"No," Heller answered. "The insects are unique. We have no classification for them; we know of no other species that looks or behaves as they do." He held back what Schifman had discovered about the anatomy of the bugs, but even admitting no more than he did, he suffered a sense of defeat for the world he represented in this gathering. He was bringing them a phenomenon science could not explain. It seemed almost an act of treason.

"So," Leah continued with more relish than Heller would have liked, "we are dealing with a scientific impossibility. That is a definite fact, is it not?"

Heller agreed and went on to mention Schifman's characterization of the bug as a child's invention.

"Ah," Leah exclaimed, "more evidence, wouldn't you say? Even the biologist falls into line with our hypothesis."

"Possibly," Heller admitted, though he had no clear idea what "evidence" meant in this company.

"And we are right in believing that nothing like this rash or these attacks has ever occurred before among your machines until after Daphne's dreams?"

"Yes, that's correct. But what you're proposing is absurd. How could such a thing happen?"

" 'How' may be more than we can say," Leah answered. "First, we need simply to know *what* we are dealing with."

"I think we should let you know something about Earthrite, Dr. Heller." It was Professor Samples who spoke. He was about Heller's age, an alert, wide-eyed man, distinctly academic in manner. "A psychic projection like this—or whatever we might want to call it—is not part of our lore or belief in the church. We have as little experience with this as you. Please don't feel we have any interest in 'selling' you on the idea. The church has never been concerned with psychism. In fact, I dare say all of us here share your fear that we're up against something inexplicable and highly dangerous. The only difference may be that we're prepared to take the possibility of a mental or emotional projection seriously, and you're not. Your position is entirely understandable. In fact, I think you should stick to your skeptical guns simply to balance any excessive credulousness on our part."

"You have no knowledge of such a phenomenon in your work, Raymond?" Leah asked Samples.

"No, I haven't." To Heller he explained, "I'm a psychologist at GWU. I've done research in extrasensory perception and paranormal states of consciousness. All very modest things compared to this. There are many reports of various materializations—but nothing well documented by my standards. And surely nothing on this scale. The Tibetans, for example, claim that their adepts can project *tulpas*—creatures shaped from pure mental force. Not illusions, but flesh and blood entities having all the empirical qualities of living things. The legends say that *tulpas* are usually of a nasty, unpleasant nature, very difficult to control and to eliminate. These insects are rather in that category, but I'm afraid such reports go well beyond my research. My own inclination is to leave them in the realm of legend or traveler's tales."

Samples was being commendably cautious. Even so, listening to speculation of this order, Heller felt vaguely defiled, like someone who must stand by politely while his religion is obliquely insulted. Uneasy and defensive, he was finding it difficult to make eye contact with anybody in the room, except for Jane. He glanced across at her, trying to draw her into the conversation. She responded to the cue.

"We think we may have miscalculated about the healing exercise we used with Daphne. It may have been far more powerful than we realized."

Leah nodded solemnly. "I have used this exercise many times before," she explained. "It works well to calm the mind, to soothe fears. A traditional healing spell in Middle English. But who can say how old it is, or what its depth may be? Even our church is so cut off from the Old Religion that we must work from scholarly reconstructions. Imagine—a thousand years, ten thousand years from now, people of another age, another culture picking their way through the debris of our civilization. They find antique tools and machines, perhaps some remnants of your very clever machines, Dr. Heller. They push buttons here, there. One of these ancient implements is what . . . ? An atom bomb. They know nothing of its full power. They set it off, and boom! Possibly it is like this with us. I have never taken into account that where the spell speaks of 'casting out,' this could become a physical projection. Yet, under certain circumstances, with the right subject . . ."

"This is an important point," Dr. Fritsch broke in. He was a large man in his late fifties, bald, thickly bearded and imposing. "Daphne *is* a rather special subject. Perhaps Jane told you about her upbringing. She has been raised wholly within Hartmann theories of child development. Her creative and imaginary powers are extraordinary, though still quite erratic."

"You see," Leah interjected, "she could be *our* atom bomb." The remark brought an expression of undisguised distaste to Jane's face. Leah reached out to her at once apologetically. "Sorry, sorry, my dear. Only to say—such gifts must be handled with care. You understand, Dr. Heller, we do not suggest the power of this exercise lies in the mere words. That would be quite vulgar magic. *Ex opere operato*, yes? Rather, we say there is a subtle interaction between the exercise and the mind of the subject. In this case, a mind that was a specially prepared medium, far more receptive to the spiritual resonance of the ancient ritual than we could realize. Here, I believe, is where we made our miscalculation."

Fritsch continued, "I've been Daphne's counselor and therapist for the past few years. I'm a psychiatrist, incidentally, with my own practice in Arlington—child psychiatry mainly. I can safely say that, in my experience, Daphne is unique—in her sensitivity, in her powers of fantasy. But, as far as I'm aware, up until this point, there has been no indication of the paranormal. Of course, we may not have found it because we weren't looking for it. As Raymond mentioned, that isn't our orientation. My hunch would be that we inadvertently liberated resources within the child we never realized were there. I'm speculating, of course, but I gather that even you feel she plays some special part in the matter. Everything does seem to date from our healing exercise with her. There must be a connection."

Step by step, Heller could feel the discussion drawing him off in a direction he instinctively despised and dreaded—away from the clear, logical landscape that was his natural habitat toward the subjective, the psychological, the uncanny. Yet, within their own terms, the people from Earthrite were building a persuasive case. He must, for the moment, follow where they led. Fighting down his reservations, he asked, "Well, suppose there is a connection. What might we do about that? Have you something to suggest?"

"This, of course, is what we all wish to know," Leah answered. "But you will excuse me if I ask to examine the problem more deeply. Because I wonder if there may not be something more at work here than one little girl's fear of insects. We are, after all, discussing a rather critical state of affairs, so I gather. You must correct me if I exaggerate the crisis, Dr. Heller, but it is my understanding that these computing machines are now to be found everywhere. The government, the military, the business people—they all use the machines. Also, the schools, the hospitals, the police. To my way of thinking, we are dealing here with something more than a mathematical device. It is like a brain, a mind. Yes, a mechanical mind. And the entire body politic has come to rely on this mind. So that now, if this mysterious contagion, this infestation should spread beyond your Center . . ."

She let the phrase dangle, fishing for information he was not prepared to give. "Do you have any reason to believe it will?" he asked.

"None. But you will not say we can rule out this possibility, as fearful as it is to contemplate. I say, then, if the contagion should spread, it would be, for the body politic, like a disease of the central nervous system."

"Yes, you might put it that way." Heller's voice was hardly audible as he made the admission. He shuddered—he thought only to himself. But Leah picked up the response.

"So, I gather I am not being extravagant. Now, I ask—could so dramatic a result come from such a small cause—one child's peculiar phobia? You see, in the church, we have a strong sense of adequacy, of balance. To produce a great effect, there must be a great cause, a powerful cause. This leads me to believe we must look further than just to little Daphne."

"What do you mean?" Heller asked.

"You recall the 'Wonder/Wander' show from your Center? The moment you mentioned these 'bugs,' as you call them, Daphne cried out—yes. But you remember the other children?"

"They all reacted," Alison Samples observed. "You could see it in their faces."

"Yes," Leah went on, "those faces, big frightened eyes, so worried about the bugs. And the way you teased them, Dr. Heller."

"I'm very sorry about that," Heller apologized.

"Yes, but you see—what you said, it made them all afraid. This was again a matter of dealing with powers you did not understand—the psyche, the dream-life of children. Now imagine, Dr. Heller, this program, it is broadcast across the country. Millions of children are watching, many of just this age when the imagination is so quick, so alive, so different from the adult mind. And all the children hear this same frightening thing, you understand? All at the same time. And, as with Daphne, there is fear. Here is this important man, and he is saying that these machines are filled with dangerous bugs that jump out and pinch and bite."

"That's exactly how Daphne took it," Jane added. "Absolutely literally. Even I didn't realize how simple and literal she was being. I just tried to shrug it off, downplay it, distract her."

Dr. Fritsch picked up eagerly on Jane's remark. "There's such a complex interplay here between the literal and the figurative, it's almost impossible to say which realm we're in. I mean, in psychiatry—say, especially in dream analysis—we know that sometimes a stubbornly literal interpretation of a metaphor or an image is the most effective way of contacting the underlying symbolic significance. In this instance, Daphne and the other children—conceivably millions of them in the audience—came away with this idea that your machines were like great nests or ant heaps filled with angry insects. You see the imagery, don't you? The machines . . . inhuman things. And the way people get filed away inside them: they *are* a kind of ant heap. The bugs inside could be *us*—people who don't want to be treated like insects, who want to escape. The child takes the image literally, grows frightened, and just because she does so, grasps the essential truth of the matter."

Heller broke in with some heat. "And you want me to believe this could produce a tangible effect?"

"Somehow we must account for these insects, Dr. Heller," Leah insisted, resuming her line of argument. "These curious insects that are like no other living thing, and which the scientist tells you might be invented by a child. So, let us have a hypothesis. Here we have a remarkable little girl who has been educated to heighten all her imaginative and spiritual gifts. Suppose the mind of this child should now act like a lens. It focuses the fears of millions of children, all watching on the television this same program at the same time. Yes, perhaps we must take into account another remarkable machine, besides your mechanical brain, Dr. Heller. This television, which is like a single eye shared by millions, gathering all their attention to a point, magnifying what they see. Curious, is it not, how, at a certain pregnant moment, the machinery of modern life might come to work against itself. . . ."

Her voice trailed off and her face darkened as she seemed to wander after some unspoken line of thought. For a long moment, the room fell silent; Heller and the others waited until she returned to herself. At last, she picked up as if there had been no pause at all. "It is my thought that many times in history such a thing happens—one mind acting like a lens, gathering the energy of millions into a single event, a single powerful constellation. Perhaps that is what an avatar is, or a messiah, or a great saint. A gifted personality that magnifies what lies hidden in the hearts of many. And then we have a moment that is not like other moments, an intersection of forces never again repeated. Your science, Dr. Heller, wants always things that repeat, is that not so? Predictable patterns. But there is an older science that is more concerned with these special moments which it is not possible to make happen again. What is called 'revelation'—you follow me?

Of course, these moments—when one mind thinks with the power of many—this is not always a good and positive thing. In my lifetime, in the country I once lived in, we have seen one man, a man of extraordinary personal force, serve as such a lens. But for what? The hatred, the fear, the violence of a whole nation—for all that was demonic. In this case, we deal with children, millions of worried, troubled young minds all projecting the same image, the same simple picture: bugs in the machines. And suddenly through the imagination of one child this extraordinary thing happens, these fears are born into reality—*your* reality."

Heller blew out an exasperated breath. "But these kids . . . they watch television all the time. If what you say is so, we'd be living in a world of monsters by now."

"Maybe we do," Jane murmured solemnly.

"Very well, then," Heller said, impatiently resigning the point, "May I ask again—what conclusion do you draw?"

A sharp, inquisitive look passed over Leah's face. "This might yet depend, Dr. Heller, on how much we believe the fears of children have to teach us. What would you say? Is the innocence of children a form of ignorance—or a kind of uncorrupted wisdom?" He stared back blankly, refusing to be drawn by the question. "Well, to begin with, let us assume that we—in the church—have simply blundered, very badly. As badly as anyone who takes up power without sufficient knowledge. I assure you, we are deeply concerned for our responsibility in this tragic matter. It is not our place to throw the world into such disorder. We have no choice but to do what we can to repair the damage."

"By which you mean . . . ?" Heller asked.

"Undo the spell, if we are able, if it still lies within our power."

Heller fixed her with a look that was at once pained and perplexed. He had no idea what else she could have proposed; but now that she had made the only offer he might have expected, he was reluctant to dignify it with a word of thanks.

"Oh, never fear, Dr. Heller," she continued, once again reading his silence shrewdly. "We do not expect you to approve or endorse what we do. All this—such mumb-jumbo—is outside your world. We realize that. No, we will undertake this on our own, in no way implicating you. But you are also free, if you wish, to observe or participate, perhaps only out of curiosity. We are not a secret group. Our doors are open. We would take no advantage of your presence. In any case, whether you choose to join us or not, we will go ahead with our plans."

"What will you do?" Heller asked, more curious than he cared to reveal.

She sighed pensively. "This will take some research. Ours is a complex science. And, as Professor Samples has said, we have no experience with such a materialization, let alone with reversing it. There are others I must consult, and there is much study for us to do. We must proceed with the greatest care. We do not wish to blunder again. As soon as we are sure of our course, we will let you know, and then we will act—I hope soon."

One question troubled Heller. "How many people in your church know about what we've discussed here today?"

Leah gestured to left and right. "Only those of us here."

"And Anne," Jane added. "The woman who lives with me. She's looking after the children outside."

Heller ran his eyes around the room, trying to stamp some measure of authority on each member of the group. "You'll appreciate, I hope, that I must insist on the utmost confidentiality about our relationship—if there is to be one. The possible connection between the insects and the little girl—that's not for public consumption. It is, after all, highly speculative. It could give rise to some unfortunate rumors."

Leah grinned knowingly. "The data center and the mystic cult. No, they do not make a likely match, do they? I quite understand your concern, Dr. Heller. In this respect, we share common ground. I am also not eager to have Earthrite connected publicly with so serious a crisis. What good could come of that? Within our own small circle, we also have a reputation to consider. However, there are at least a few others I must contact. I assure you, people of the highest discretion."

"Christopher may have to know," Jane suggested.

"Yes, Christopher," Leah agreed, not explaining who Christopher was. "But, again, we can surely trust him to be discreet. So we finish, Dr. Heller, with that much in common."

Heller realized he had brought his conference with Earthrite to a conclusion, or perhaps to an impasse. What more could he ask of these people? There seemed nothing more to do than thank them and leave, but his intention was intercepted by Jane, who invited him to stay for supper and spend the night. There was a cabin he could have to himself. "Very basic accommodations," she said, "but clean and private."

Eager as he was to break off and get back among his own kind of people, it was an attractive offer. He was tired and hungry; the long drive back to Washington through a hot and sticky evening was hardly inviting. There was also the quiet charm of the mountain retreat, perhaps the last shelter he could expect for weeks from the crisis that tore at his life. But there was something more at the back of his mind—the prospect of sharing a few more hours of Jane Hecate's company. She had asked him to stay; he did not want to say no to her.

2

Twelve people gathered that evening in the main dining hall of the lodge. Heller and the six members of the church he had talked with that afternoon were joined by Jane's housemate and the four children she had been minding in the woods for the day. Later, Carol Aronson brought in an infant to be nursed at the table. Heller learned that she was trying the same child-rearing experiment Jane had undertaken with Daphne; that was why she had been included in the conference. Heller asked politely about the project; there was a certain irritating note of conceit to the woman's answer and to what Leah added. Glibly, they spoke of "woman-defined mothering," with the clear implication that the ills of the world were all to be blamed on the male domination of family and society. Heller was tempted to ask if unloading Daphne's lethal nightmares upon the human race was their idea of a "woman-defined" improvement. But, noticing Jane's obvious uneasiness, he backed off the conversation, and it was quickly dropped.

The group was as willing as he to avoid touchy subjects. He asked them a little about the church and about Immanuel Hartmann's philosophy; they asked him a little about computer science and the Brain. Heller recalled Paul Saxton's remark about Earthrite: "a trendy, intellectualoid, occult operation." But the people he shared the table with that evening were clearly well read and unpretentiously intelligent. If anything, they were overly respectful of him. At times, that made it difficult for him to maintain the distance he wished to keep. *Boundaries* he had to remind himself—he must make sure the boundaries between himself and them were well marked and closely patrolled.

To his surprise, he discovered that Leah Hagar had an impressive background in science. An advanced degree in biology from the University of Berlin, several years of research at the Charlottenburg Institute. "Of course, for such a career," she explained, "one does what is expected—the standard thing. In my case, enzymes. Or rather, one enzyme—pepsin. More and more minute analysis, until the vital form has become a mere collage of dead chemicals. But always for me there was another interest—very different, very risky. You see, I am not a completely loyal citizen of the twentieth century." And she described how, under the influence of Immanuel Hartmann and his movement, her research was diverted toward something she called "Goethean morphology." Was Heller familiar with the field? When he said no, she proceeded to explain. She spoke of "studies of biological form using projective geometry."

Heller could connect with nothing she told him. He knew a few computer programs that used projective geometry, but not in any way that related to biology. For all he knew, what she was saying might be totally inane. But it was both tactful and relaxing to let her continue, to listen uncritically, nod and smile. He wondered: would that make him seem more open-minded and tolerant in Jane's eyes. All the while Leah spoke, Jane's presence was never out of his mind. Frequently during the meal, he glanced across at her, offering her an open look, a smile. Each time, he noticed that Daphne's eyes were on him, a hollow, fixed stare through her heavy eyeglasses. Once he nodded pleasantly at her, but it did not soften her solemn expression. And once, uneasily, he saw her hand at her side, her fingers making the little, nervous pinching movement.

"Alas, for such unconventional research, one pays a dear price," Leah was saying, recounting the declining course of her scientific career. "In German, we call such studies *Naturphilosophie*. Natural philosophy. Very quaint. Very old-fashioned. It is a science for the sensuous eye, a science for artists. It builds no machines, no weapons. So what is its use? The further I went in this direction, the less time there was for the enzymes, yes? And so my career becomes less promising, less brilliant. And then, to be sure, there comes Herr Hitler, and I realize that the world does not need more science, more numbers. There were suddenly too many numbers."

She rolled back one sleeve to reveal a faded blue number tattooed on the inner forearm, the indelible emblem of the death camps. "So, after the war, I went in another direction. Inward and earthward." As she spoke the phrase, she pointed to her breast, then down toward the ground; it seemed a practiced, ritualistic movement, like the sign of the cross. Before the meal had started, Heller had noticed members of the group performing the gesture. "Oh, I had been, for many years, a student of Dr. Hartmann's. But it was only when the war ended that I became a disciple—when the true need became clear to me."

She paused. Heller found himself both moved and irked by her brief autobiography. Again, he had the sense that he was being unfairly, but skillfully disoriented. He could not help but feel for her plight during the war; but she had recounted the misfortune with a subtle tone of reproach. "The world did not need more numbers . . ." and Heller was, in her eyes, a man of numbers. Somehow he was meant to be implicated in the great evil of the age. Yet the point was not so overtly made that he could find reason to protest without seeming to admit a sense of guilt. He didn't protest; instead, he delivered a tactful yawn and glanced at his watch. Might he retire to his cabin, he asked. He would like to turn in early and be on his way before sunrise. Jane excused herself and rose to lead him from the table. Preparing his exit, Heller offered his perfunctory thanks to Leah. "I'm grateful to know you're willing to help."

"As you might suspect, this was not an easy decision for us," Leah explained as she accompanied him onto the porch, laboring awkwardly with her cane. "Obviously, your world and ours are very far apart. We belong to something quite old, something, by your standards, antiquated, defunct, superstitious, yes? But, you see, we regard your work as perhaps also a kind of superstition: a superstition of numbers. I hope that is not too harsh to say."

The stiff grin widened, becoming almost predatory. Heller stared back stony-faced. But he could not blame her for the jibe. He had wanted the boundaries between them clearly defined; she was defining them.

"We must be frank to say" she continued, we feel no obligation to rescue your machines. For my own part, I wonder if it might not be for the best if they should perish. But it is not our right to make such a decision. It would be too much power for us to wield. What concerns us is the danger to innocent people—like these poor men who have lost their lives at your Center. We had no wish for that. We do not wish harm to any living thing. That is our religion, you see. We have learned a great lesson from this tragedy. We have unleashed forces we did not understand. Maybe that is the way it is with your machines as well. You are also toying with powers beyond your control. So, we are all very human, very capable of the same arrogance and miscalculation. It teaches us humility, I think."

Heller nodded tersely—not in agreement, but to punctuate her remarks before they moved further into disputed ground.

It was not until he moved away from the porch that he realized how strained his temper had been by the presumption of Leah Hagar's parting comments. "Humility!" he said to himself. "There's not a humble bone in the woman's body."

3

"You must forgive Leah," Jane said as she led him toward his cabin at the far end of the clearing. "She's as uneasy dealing with you as I guess you are with her."

"Oh? Does it show?"

"A little. Actually, you were very considerate. I was hoping you and the others—especially Leah—wouldn't clash too much."

"We clash. But we also needed to talk. I suppose I didn't seem too grateful for the help I was offered. I hope you understand why. I don't want to believe I need that kind of help. I'm still not certain I do. I keep hoping this bug will turn out to be some ordinary kind of pest that can be caught and named and eliminated. I'd prefer to have DDT solve the problem."

"Yes, I feel the same. It's strange—you can spend years longing for something extraordinary to enter your life. A touch of magic, a small miracle. Then, when it does, it isn't what you bargained for. It's frightening."

They had reached his cabin, a small, clapboard building at the edge of the pines. Pausing on the steps, Heller retrieved a question that had been hovering at the back of his mind throughout the meal. "Odd, how all of you here always refer to them as 'machines.'" She frowned, not understanding. "Computers—you always call them 'machines.' Is that Leah's influence? A sort of catechism for the church?"

She remained puzzled. "Aren't they machines?"

"Well, yes of course. But it's so undiscriminating to refer to them that way—as if there were no difference between them and . . . well, steam engines or bulldozers or drill presses. You don't call all the trees and flowers and bushes you see around here 'vegetables,' just lumping them all together as if they didn't deserve names of their own or any special regard."

"And you think there is a difference, an important difference between computers and other machines?"

"Certainly there is. A vast difference. All the difference there is between mind and muscle. Computers are smart machines, not big steel brutes. They're delicate and subtle, even responsive. That's certainly what drew me to them. It had nothing to do with the machinery. The fact is, when I was a kid, I had no mechanical aptitude at all. Hated automobiles, model planes, rocket ships, all that. That made me something of an outsider among the boys. I suppose I was your typical mathematical prodigy—bright, arrogant, absolutely obnoxious. I wound up being pretty lonely, always the youngest in my class, the kid nobody . . ."

He brought himself to a sharp halt. He was wandering, free-associating back to his childhood—something he had not allowed himself to do in years. He glanced apologetically toward Jane. She showed no sign of minding the digression. She was listening sympathetically, waiting for more. But he felt too embarrassed to continue. "Anyway, what I'm getting at is: there's quite a distance in computer science between the theorists and the engineers. For me, the attraction of computers has always been their braininess. It's the challenge of seeing how clever we can make them. I like to think they were created in the image of our highest faculty."

"You mean logic, mathematics," she commented dryly.

Yes, that was what he meant. *Our* highest faculty meaning *his* highest faculty. He could see there was no hope of drawing her off in that direction. "Let's just say *thinking*—in general. Which some people believe implies some degree of sentience."

Her expression shifted to one of concerned curiosity. "Is that what you believe—that computers are sentient?"

"Well, I guess that's a matter of definition."

"A matter of definition—whether something is alive or dead?"

He had written volumes on the subject, but again he felt compelled to let the question pass. Odd, how she could intimidate him into silence by a glance, a word. A bit petulantly he remarked, "Well, I suppose your church prefers a strict and simple contrast in these matters. Natural versus mechanical. Good versus evil."

Her look softened, relented. "No, not evil. I don't want to say that about your work."

"It was one of the first things you said to me the other evening," he reminded her. "You called computers 'terrible, deadly'—as if they were weapons of war."

"But they are, aren't they? Isn't that the way they're used, mostly?"

"No, not at all. They're mostly used in business, hospitals, education, public administration. Oh, they can be used for war. But that's a political and ethical decision we're all responsible for making. We have to make choices like that about everything: atomic energy, aircraft, microbiology. . . . Anything can be a weapon."

She was pondering what he said. He realized he didn't really care whether she finally agreed with him or not, as long as he could prolong their time together. "I don't just mean military violence, I guess," she said. "There's also violence against people's privacy, against their freedom. Aren't computers mostly used that way—as Bob Fritsch said, to file us away like insects in a hive?"

"All right," he agreed, "I'll grant that they can be used in objectionable ways. But look—I notice you use two knives in your church. They symbolize something for you—good and evil, I suppose . . ."

"No. They represent darkness and light, life and death, masculine and feminine—polarities that have to be kept in balance. They're meant as an image of natural harmony. Each day we change the crossing: light over dark, dark over light."

Instinctively, Heller detoured away from the metaphysical obscurity he sensed in her answer. "Well, all I meant was—those knives could be used to do harm. They could be used as weapons. But you choose not to use them that way. You've given them a benign use. It's the same with computers. They could be a great blessing. They already are to many people.

There's a lot of idealism invested in them, a lot of brave hopes. In medicine, for example . . ."

She knew he was trying to close the distance between them, to make his work seem more humane and beneficent. She did not want to rebuff his gesture at friendship, but she was cold to his words. Looking away distractedly, she said, "I think there are enough machines—of all kinds. We don't need more, not until we've learned how to use them more wisely. They wound the earth and ourselves. You see, that's because machines come out of only one small part of our nature. There's more to us that needs to be understood, especially now. Even computers can't help with that." She looked back at him, her expression gentle and conciliatory. "I don't mean to say your computers are evil. They're just too much of one thing." Then, backing off, she said, "You must be tired. We'll try not to disturb you." And she was on her way back across the clearing.

He was tired, but he would have stayed on talking with her indefinitely if he could have found the words to hold her. Of course, there were answers he could give to her objections, logical inconsistencies he could point out, facts he could offer. He had argued these matters many times with weighty opponents. But he knew it would do no good to continue with her; she was divided from him by tastes and convictions he could not vanquish with his powers of reason. Nor did he want to. He had no wish to change her, argue her down, win her over. He only wanted to be accepted by her as she was. It was, at last, her strangeness that fascinated him, drew him. In every intellectual respect, she stood half a world away from him, and yet he wanted her to remain just what she was, impervious to his logic, unmoved by his authority. For the first time in his life, he realized how much one might lose by winning.

4

He drifted into sleep almost as soon as he stretched out on the narrow bunk in his cabin, even before he had taken off his shirt and pants. As his mind went dim, he noticed there was still light in the sky, a distant halo in the west. When his eyes opened again, the cabin was totally dark. What had awakened him? A dull, droning sound . . . he woke thinking it was a mosquito in his ear. No, it was a low hum of voices, talking or rather chanting. And there was a deep throb, a slow drumbeat. He recalled that Jane had said something about trying not to disturb him. But the unfamiliar sound had reached him, low and distant as it was.

He rose and went to the screen door, his clothes damp and sticking to his body. There was only the fragile remnant of a moon in the sky. Faintly, he could make out an unsteady yellow light between the trees. It came from the direction of the little grove where he and Jane had talked when he arrived. The thought struck him at once: the group was holding a ceremony, one of its rites. His curiosity was aroused immediately. Leaving off his shoes, taking care not to let the screen door creak, he made his way as quietly as possible toward the light. Nobody had forbidden him to watch anything the group might do, though it was the fact that he might observe something forbidden that drew him so powerfully. That thought made him feel sheepish; he tried to make his way with as little appearance of stealth as he could manage, still treading softly.

When he was several yards off, he could see the light came from a number of kerosene lamps placed on the pentagon of logs. Within the pool of yellow flame, he made out the shapes of people standing, holding hands, moving slowly in a circle as they chanted. He stopped short when he realized they were naked. His first reaction was to turn back, but he lingered for a while longer, fascinated by the unusual sight. He could not make out the words of the chant; it might not be English. Up close now, he could discern the pattern of the sound: a short phrase intoned by one voice—he could tell it was Leah Hagar—then a long choral response from the others. Leah was in the center of the circle, her small, bent figure swaying before the tree stump altar. The murmur of the chant was hypnotically soothing in the still night. He let it wash over him, reflecting that perhaps he was observing something very old—in spirit, if not in detail. Was it for such rites that, in ages past, people had been persecuted and butchered? He listened for several minutes, then turned to go. But as he turned, he discovered there was someone just behind him at his elbow. His heart surged and he gasped with surprise.

"Sorry . . . I didn't mean to startle you," Jane whispered. "I was on my way to join the circle."

Heller was grateful the night concealed his painful blushing. Had she ever heard him called "Peeping Tom"?

"Well . . . I hope I'm not doing anything I shouldn't," he apologized awkwardly. "I was awakened by the sound of the drum . . ."

Now he could see she was wearing the blue gown she had worn on the first night they talked, and her feet were bare. "And, frankly, I was curious," he admitted. "I've never seen a . . . ritual, is it? Nobody told me not to . . ."

"It's all right," she assured him. "We often have guests up here to stay the night. As I said: all our secrets are open secrets. This is a ceremony for the feast of Selene—under the sign of Leo and the waxing moon. You're free to join in."

Heller blushed more deeply. "Well, no . . . I don't think so . . ." Was she serious? Her tone sounded faintly taunting.

"Would it be whoring after false gods?" she asked.

"No, that's not it. I'm just not familiar with the ritual."

"It's really very simple. There's not much more to it than this. Nothing . . . extreme."

"The language . . . it isn't English."

"This chant is Celtic. Leah says it's very old. We use several languages, even some native American. It's a harvest song, thanks for fertility."

For several moments they stood watching. He became intensely aware of her beside him—a warm, sensuous presence in the damp heat of the night. She was murmuring the chant softly as she untied her hair and let it fall over her shoulders. He was moved to say something friendly and confiding, something about his perplexity, his need for help. But why should he think she would be sympathetic? Of course there could be nothing between them. But tonight, for these few moments, he was sharing some small part of her world—and she was permitting it. The moment drew him toward her, more poignantly than he could remember being drawn toward anyone in many years. At the same time, the warmth that flowed from her made him vividly aware of the knotted cold within him, the frozen core of his personality that anchored him to a way of life, an ambition that could be no part of this haunting rite.

Could that cold be thawed, he wondered for the first time in his life. Was this spell that reached out toward him strong enough for that? If so, he would yield. He felt his reluctance melting away; the sensation was dizzy and sweet. Then she reached out and pressed his arm softly as she moved away. Her departure jarred him painfully; he almost reached out to draw her back.

He watched after her as she moved into the circle of light. At the edge of the dance, she let her gown fall away and he saw the glow of the lamps take her body, edging it with gold. One part of him, struggling with immense embarrassment, wanted to turn his eyes from her nakedness; but he waited until she had gone once around the circle. Then, swiftly, he made his way back to his cabin, a strong heat descending upon him, covering his eyes.

He did not sleep until the sound of the chanting and the drum were gone, and then his rest was shallow, troubled. Her body, laced with firelight, moved sinuously through his sluggish mind, an image of mystery and desire. Had he been invited or tempted that night? The tension he felt within him, holding him back, binding him to his duty—was it a sign of courage or fear?

1

"You may find the hash brown patty a trifle greasy," Levinson observed, playing the mock gourmet. "But the Egg McMuffin is a masterpiece. Lukewarm, you can't distinguish it from USDA prime Styrofoam."

Fast food, takeout breakfasts lay before them in little white trays of solidified froth. Driving steadily from before daybreak, Heller had arrived back in Washington from Gaia Lodge just after 8 A.M.; he had phoned ahead to arrange the briefing with Levinson. Both men were haggard from the strain of sleepless nights. Levinson had been on the telephone almost continuously for thirty hours. Along with the plastic trays and cups of tepid coffee, he had deposited a stack of notes on Heller's desk, describing them as "the fruits of 156 phone calls." He was obviously curious about Heller's movements of the day before, but Heller side-stepped, promising to bring up what he had learned for discussion later.

"Okay then," Levinson began, "what have I got to brighten your day? To start with, the people's tribune, Merrill Cory, is once again gunning for your ass. Surprise, surprise! I don't suppose you caught the news last night?"

"No."

"Well, the senator has decided that mysterious insects that kill poor black security guards are a whole 'nother matter demanding a whole 'nother investigation. So we will be back up on the Hill very soon now to explain our inexplicable troubles.

Get this—Cory is now identifying the Brain as an environmental hazard. He wants the Environmental Protection Agency in on the hearings. In a way, that's lucky for us. It may take him a few weeks to get this new show on the road; so we get a little breathing space. That son of a bitch got top billing on two networks last night, 'I told you so, I told you so, I told you so.' And so on long into the night. He seems to feel he has scored a few points regarding the reliability of large scale data centralization. For once, I'm afraid I'd have to agree."

Impatiently, Heller brushed Senator Cory from the morning's agenda. He fully recognized the deadly accuracy of Cory's critical shot; but how effective this latest attack upon the Brain would be depended upon the skill with which he and his staff could now regroup their forces along a new line of defense. He moved quickly to that front. "How are we doing with RE-DIRECT?"

Levinson's answer started out encouragingly. "Extremely well. Surprisingly well. I wouldn't have thought we could gain so much co-operation and co-ordination short of a thermonuclear disaster. In fact, REDIRECT is working so smoothly, I'd almost be willing to bet we could come out of this smelling of roses . . ."

"Except . . . ?" Heller could hear the ominously pending qualification behind Levinson's answer.

"Except . . . are you ready for this? The rash is getting everywhere ahead of us."

Heller turned liquid inside. It was what he feared most. Levinson pulled a file out of his pile of notes. "I've had a telephone crew working on this full time since Saturday. Here's what I've been able to piece together. It's still sketchy, but there's a clear pattern. Within the last month to five weeks, there have been outbreaks of data pox at all these sites."

Heller ran his eye rapidly down the list. MIT, Case Western, Stanford Research, Bell Labs, Argon National Laboratory . . . a dozen more major computer installations. He recognized the pattern at once. "It's spreading through MASTERNET—as far west as Hawaii."

Levinson shuffled through his papers and fished out another list. "Also, as of the crack of dawn today, I was able to get some scattered returns from abroad. There are at least three installations in our European extension where the rash has occurred, along with two in the EURONET: Brussels and NORSAR."

Heller drew the somber conclusion. "So we can't rely on MASTERNET or CONCERT to pull us through." He collapsed wearily in his chair. "How the hell is it migrating? What vectors is it using?"

Levinson tossed off the only conclusion he could think of. "How else? It propagates along electrical waves—through thin air."

"But only between computers?" Heller shook his head despairingly. "What sense does that make? We use the same electricity as radios, television, toasters, hair dryers . . ."

Levinson had no answer. Instead he produced another document. "You recall I told you that a couble of DoD facilities had been hit? A couple—ha! It's a lot worse than Lyman was willing to let on the other day."

Heller glanced at the page Levinson handed him. Again he recognized the pattern at once. "The ARPANET too," he murmured. ARPANET—the Advanced Research Projects Agency—was one of the few computer networks in the United States still functioning semi-independently of the Brain. This was because it carried a great deal of classified information and was linked into military communications. A DoD operation, ARPANET had funded the most important computer science research of the past two decades and included many of the country's key computer centers. It was the network Heller had hoped would take over many of the Brain's lapsed responsibilities.

Levinson slumped back from the desk with a resigned sigh. "The rash is spreading through all the systems. At this point, we have no reason to believe anything or anyplace is immune. DoD is playing this close to the vest, but it's clear we're going to have to start comparing notes soon. We have a conference with Lyman and some brass at ten-thirty. Super urgent. So please don't disappear on me today. I think DoD may know more than they've told us."

Heller noticed that Levinson had placed little bracketed numbers and letters next to several of the computer centers on his lists. He asked what they meant.

"A small effort on my part to systematize the chaos," Levinson explained. "Those are levels of escalation. Stage 1 is a simple outbreak of the rash. That's where most of these installations are now. Stage 2 is the rash with reports of creepy-crawly feelings. Stage 3 would mean that bugs had been sighted. So far, there are no Stage 3s—except for us. The letters are rough approximations of magnitude. 'A' means light —a few cases. 'B' means medium—several cases over a few weeks. 'C' means very heavy. Of course, I could only get impressionistic ideas from the calls we made. Nobody has been keeping close track—just as we didn't at the outset. Nobody has begun to think of this as having an over-all pattern, except Lyman's people at DoD. They're beginning to piece together their own rather paranoid scenario, and getting pretty uptight about possible espionage. As far as I can tell, nobody besides us has more than a month to five weeks' experience with the rash. We're way out ahead—pioneering the apocalypse, you might say. We'd be at Stage 3C. Lots of cases, plus the only deaths."

Levinson shuffled through his papers and drew out one final item. "And finally . . . I can't say if this is good news or bad. I was on the phone with Alan Stern at IIASA early this morning. He recalls one of his Soviet conferees mentioning a strange rash that has been plaguing a computer facility in Leningrad."

IIASA was the International Institute for Applied Systems Analysis, a major international data bank in Vienna. It was funded jointly by the Americans and Russians for advanced research in the social sciences. "That's unconfirmed hearsay," Levinson added, "but it may mean data pox has transcended the ideological frontiers. Which frankly, I'd be relieved to hear. If true, it should make Lyman and the military less jumpy."

Heller realized he had a tough decision facing him before the morning was out. Lyman Touhy, the Secretary of Defense, was one of his strongest allies in Washington, a man who shared his own values and political style. Like Heller, he recognized information technology as the secret of modern industrial power; more than anyone else in the current Administration, he had fought to establish the Brain's data processing monopoly, especially its control of military systems. It was inevitable that, at some point, he would be drawn into the crisis. Heller welcomed that. He would need Touhy's clout and counsel to get anything significant done.

But how much was he to tell Touhy about Earthrite? If he held out now, he ran the serious risk of jeopardizing his relations with the man whose support he most needed. And there was no question in his mind that Touhy would expect to be told about Earthrite. He was a thorough man; in reaching decisions, he left nothing out of account. He would want Earthrite included in his deliberations; in his eyes, even the most tenuous connection with the church might be a compromising factor in future policy.

But that was the problem. Heller knew that Touhy could only see Earthrite as a bizarre and embarrassing complication. He could not bring himself to mention how far he had already gone with the church—all the more so since he could not dismiss the people he had met as cranks. Yet the one solid reason he had for taking Leah Hagar and her circle seriously was Daphne's picture, a child's drawing that traced back to a dream and then dissolved into wild parapsychological speculation. How could he talk to the Secretary of Defense and the Joint Chiefs of Staff about psychic projections and pagan healing rituals? They might think he was cracking under the strain.

No, it was impossible to introduce Earthrite into any official deliberations. Not at this point, not until he had at least consulted with Levinson, the one person he could imagine taking into his trust. He instructed Levinson accordingly, and they coordinated their stories to work around the drawing.

On their way to the ten-thirty conference in Touhy's office

at the Pentagon, Levinson delivered his last piece of news. "One more personal item," he said, drawing back his jacket and shirt sleeves. His arms were covered with a bright red rash. "It's cooling off a bit now. Came down with it the other morning—probably goosing up the computers for that search you ran on the woman. You know, it does feel like something crawling and stinging."

2

Lyman Touhy belonged to that special breed of all-purpose administrative mandarin who managed to transcend political parties and outlast presidents. He never lost a job; he simply shuttled between high-level assignments, a permanent feature of the Washington political landscape. It didn't matter what his title or office might be; he was simply a man of power, a maker of policy. His connection with Heller went back a long way. When Heller first began to make his mark in Washington, it was Touhy who took him into David Rockefeller's Trilateral Commission as a major consultant, and then allowed him to use the commission as a platform for his vision of centralized data processing. At the time, Touhy was still on the board at Exxon, but his career was blending gracefully and inevitably into official power. Two administrations ago, he had served on the National Security Council, and then as Secretary of Energy. In the previous administration, he had been Secretary of State. Now as Secretary of Defense during a lax and characterless presidency, he was indisputably the second most powerful man in government. Some close observers placed his influence slightly higher than that.

For Touhy as for Heller, efficient government was a science of exact numbers. Money, manpower, missiles, kilowatts, thermonuclear megatons—these were the realities of power, things that could be measured, counted and computed. The only quantitative experience of politics he lacked was that of winning votes. Running for office seemed distinctly beneath his dignity. He left courting the electorate to presidents; his interest was in governing the nation.

When Heller and Levinson arrived, they found three military officers waiting with Touhy in his Pentagon office. They knew two of them: General Haseltine, head of DIA, the Defense Intelligence Agency, and Major Kilraddin, an adjutant to the Joint Chiefs of Staff. They had never met the third. He was introduced as Captain Harlan Schaeffer of Naval Intelligence. Oddly, he wore large dark glasses all the while they talked.

Touhy wasted little time on preliminaries. By now, Heller knew his style to the letter. He spent no longer on small talk than it took him to light a cigar. When he had gotten a free draw and blew out his first cloud of smoke, it was the signal to begin. Everyone fell silent waiting for his cue. Touhy's looks suited his pre-emptory manner: blunt, tough, sober. His face had a prize-fighter's coarseness about it, the neck thrust pugnaciously forward, the shoulders hunched. He might have been one of the most cunning political operators in Washington; Heller had learned he was also a slugger.

The conference came down immediately to the rapid exchange of facts and figures, a hard-driving effort to define the problem with maximum precision. Heller quickly outlined the deteriorating status of backup processing in MASTERNET. He reported that REDIRECT was in full operation, but its capacity to absorb and reroute the data flow of the country was strictly provisional. Most of this Touhy already knew through his own sources.

On the DoD side, the situation was worse than Heller and Levinson had been told. Touhy now revealed that the first trace of data pox in his accounts reached back over two months: an outbreak at the Pentagon's National Military Command Center. Since then, computer personnel at CIA Headquarters, the Logistics Command Headquarters and LANTCOM, the Atlantic Command Headquarters, had been heavily afflicted with the rash. "Everybody working with computers at those locations has been hit by it," Touhy reported.

"Many severe cases and lots of repeats." He passed Heller a list of other military computer centers that were now seriously threatened by the pox. They included installations as important as Brookhaven National Laboratory, the Jet Propulsion Laboratory, and TOS, the Tactical Operations, the country's most advanced experiment in automated battlefield technology. The list also mentioned several computer centers in the DIANE network, the European counterpart of the AR-PANET.

"These outbreaks, plus what we knew was happening at the Brain," Touhy went on, "led us to believe we might be dealing with espionage aimed at incapacitating our data processing infrastructure. A week ago, when the first cases appeared at TOS, I was on the point of bringing our strike forces to full alert, assuming our equipment might be in danger of a wholesale flake-out." With characteristic understatement, he added, "We were concerned."

Heller made a guess. "Then you heard the Russians had it too."

Touhy displayed as much surprise as he ever permitted himself to show: a slight lift of the left eyebrow. "How'd you guess?"

"We got a hint of it via IIASA this morning."

"From Alan?"

"Right. Rumors of an outbreak in Leningrad—but nothing confirmed."

"Our information is confirmed," General Haseltine said. "We've received hard data through DIA and from West German sources. At least three Russian computer centers have been affected. One of them is their Western air defense headquarters in Leningrad."

"How can you be sure it isn't a fake," Heller asked, "to create the impression they also have the problem?"

"We of course considered that possibility carefully," the general explained. "We've checked and double checked. We're satisfied with our data. We don't know if the Soviets are hurting as badly as we are, but they are hurting."

"For which, much thanks," Levinson commented. "The bugs aren't Bolsheviks."

"Some consolation in that, I agree," Touhy went on. "But brace yourselves for the latest. We've suffered our first casualties . . . at Ames Research two nights ago. Captain Schaeffer can give you a report. He was there."

The captain explained he had flown in from Ames Research Center in California the preceding day. "Ames has been having data pox problems with its ILLIAC IV computer off and on for almost two months. That's a major terminal for the Seaguard project, anti-submarine warfare. Five days ago, an information officer working on the computer was attacked by the bugs and seriously injured."

"He *saw* the insects?" Heller asked, eagerly.

"Yes," the captain answered. "He was on his own at night. Something like a few thousand insects emerged from the computer and went after him. He was able to beat them off and escape, but his arms and face were badly bitten."

"Was he able to kill any of them?" Heller asked.

"No. Which was strange. But the ILLIAC was closed down and the Navy gave orders to disassemble and investigate. I was called in, also an entomologist from Stanford. We watched the dismantling. The investigation was not negative—as I gather yours have been here." He removed the sunglasses. His eyes and upper cheeks were rimmed with nasty lacerations. One eye was swollen almost closed. Heller noticed for the first time the bandaging under his collar and across one hand.

The captain continued with his account. "The technicians began at the front of the computer, removing a few small plates. They found nothing. Then they took off a metal panel that covered a good part of one side. At first, even with good lighting, nobody was sure what they were looking at. I certainly had no idea what the inside of a computer looks like. But the technicians showed surprise right away. Under the panel, there was a solid surface with a knobby white or gray texture. I thought it was a second, inner panel—some sort of insulation. One of the technicians reached out and gave it a push with his finger and it rippled . . . swayed like a curtain. You could see this undulation run back and forth through it. And then there was a clicking sound, like lots of clocks ticking all at once. I heard one of the technicians say, 'What the hell is this . . .' and just then the panel started to move and come apart. The thing was alive. It was all insects hanging there together . . . like the inside of a hive. Solid sheets of insects covering the whole computer. They started to scramble around and over each other, and slide down onto the floor. Waves of them, just tumbling out of the machine, living waves. It took us all by surprise. They blanketed one of the technicians immediately. Before we could do a thing, they started leaping toward everybody else in the room. They could jump a long way, six or eight feet. I was a few yards back, but they got to me in a second, went straight for the face, the eyes and ears. Everybody scattered in all directions. Some of us were able to beat the things off. There were four security guards close up to the computer who were overwhelmed and went down right away. They were bitten to the bone all over—as if by an attack of tropical army ants. An officer from Ames, Commander Keeley, was blinded. The Stanford entomologist was also killed. The rest of us suffered less damage, but there are three men still in the hospital. Under these clothes I'm pretty badly bitten up. They got through to the bone here at the clavical. I'm not sure they retrieved all the insects from me."

There was a long silence. Heller's throat was dry and working hard. After a moment, Touhy resumed, as cool as ever. "Three insects were recovered from the bodies of the casualties. Interestingly, they were all found in various prosthetic devices, which parallels your experience with Champolsky's corpse. One was found in an artificial hip joint, two in some bridgework. We're having the bugs studied on the West Coast—at the University of California Medical Center. So far, our results look as if they'll be the same as your man Schifman has come up with. No known life form. No chemical structure, no molecular structure, no atomic structure.

"What happened to the rest of the insects?" Heller asked.

"We can't be sure," Captain Schaeffer answered. "Everybody ran, most of us trying to protect our eyes. The bugs just seemed to scatter and vanish in all directions. Personnel in other parts of the center say they saw groups of the things heading into other computers, including small desk models. There were millions of them, but except for the three we caught later, they all disappeared."

"What's the status of Ames now?" Levinson asked.

"Semi-quarantine," Touhy answered. "The ILLIAC IV is down indefinitely. Its functions have been transferred to Stanford Research, and some of its non-classified work will be assigned to the IBM center in San Jose. We're limping along as best we can. It's a crippled facility." He turned to Heller. "In response to Berny's request, we've classified the bug. Professor Schifman and his colleagues have been so informed. Of course, we don't know whom they may have talked to already or how reliable they are."

"Schifman can be trusted," Heller said. "We had no idea when we caught our bug what this would turn out to be. We were just madly curious to identify the thing, so we did what seemed obvious: turned it over to a specialist."

"From here forward," Touhy instructed him, "all information about the rash and the bug will be routed through DoD. We're giving out nothing about what happened at Ames—though we're under pressure from the entomologist's family to explain his death. Our story will be that there was a fire and his body—along with the other victims—was badly burned."

"*Have* you burned the bodies?" Heller asked.

"Yes."

"That option wasn't available to us after our deaths here."

"I realize that," Touhy agreed. "We clearly can't control your personnel at the Brain very effectively. Most of the story here is already running wild through the media. It's likely that sooner or later somebody will put together enough rumors to link Ames with the Brain and the whole MASTERNET crisis, and we'll be accused of covering up."

"Probably that will be because we are," Levinson noted.

"Before that happens," Touhy said, "let's hope we're squared away vis-à-vis the Soviets. That is, of course, my major concern." He snuffed out the cigar he had been working on and took a deep breath. "All right, let's make some projections. Would you agree that we have reason to anticipate the collapse of our total data processing capacity—possibly worldwide?" He raised the question with his accustomed coolness, so casually that Heller could almost take the prospect in stride.

"That is a distinct likelihood," he agreed. The words floated from him like something said in a dream, an absurdity lacking all rational impact. "As I look down Berny's list of afflicted installations and the material you've supplied, it looks as if a wide variety of hardware has been affected. I don't see any pattern suggesting there may be equipment that's immune. That possibility is worth checking out, but I wouldn't be hopeful."

Levinson added, "There isn't a single division at the Brain that hasn't been hit by the rash, and we have quite a spectrum of hardware on the premises: old and new, big and small. As for MASTERNET and ARPANET—and DIANE in Europe —they must include every kind of computational device from every manufacturer."

Touhy continued. "I assume we all understand the gravity of such a scenario."

". . . the body politic, suffering a disease of its central nervous system," Heller said half to himself, quoting a source he could not name in this company.

"Exactly," Touhy agreed. "Possibly a fatal disease." He pulled his glasses down on his nose and stared gravely at Heller over the rims. "Have you anything to contribute that might tell us what we need to know? Facts, theories, hypotheses . . . ?" After a pause, he added, "No matter how bizarre."

Casually as the question was put, Heller knew it was the crux of their meeting. Touhy was placing the full weight of his trust and authority behind it. All cards were being ordered on the table.

"Most of what's happened to us at the Brain is public knowledge," Heller observed. "Too public, I agree. The rash, the bugs, the casualties, the shutdown. You've talked to Schifman about the bug. You have Berny's findings." He paused, then added, "That's it." Two words and he had trespassed across a hazardous boundary. Daphne Saxton's drawing went unmentioned. Touhy was eying him steadily, a mental lie detector gauging Heller's face. There was an oppressive blankness to his expression that Heller had never seen before. After a moment, he relaxed his stare. "All right, then," he said, "what are our priorities?"

"First of all," Major Kilraddin said, "we've got to make sure the Soviets are as seriously affected as we are. If the damage isn't symmetrical, we've got real trouble."

"I think we can agree on that," Touhy said. "That's the principal reason for security at this point. We can't let the Soviets know how much we're hurting until we know they're undergoing the same deterioration . . . if they are."

"A bit of a paradox there," Levinson observed. "We can't tell them until they tell us. They can't tell us until we tell them."

Touhy smiled wryly as he lit another cigar. "Fortunately, our intelligence community and theirs have developed procedures for finessing our way around that paradox. A cute little system called 'Graduated Mutual Disclosure.' It's come into play several times before as part of deterrence strategy. If I'm not mistaken, Tom helped develop the theory some years back at MITRE."

"Ralph Koenigson worked out the games theory," Heller said. "I just helped dope out the programming."

"DIA has already initiated the procedure," Touhy went on. "For now, let's assume the damage is approximately symmetrical, and that we have a way of keeping the terror balanced through the crisis."

"By 'damage,'" Heller noted, "we mean disarmament, don't we? Both sides have to recognize that they're being disarmed— suddenly, involuntarily, by the bugs. Nothing in the nuclear arsenal will work without computers."

"That's correct," Touhy said, hard-nosed to the last, trying not to betray the sensational nature of the admission. But Heller was right. Data processing was the connective tissue of the deterrence system. Everything in the nuclear war machine was wired through computers; they were the brains behind the strategy. If the bugs could not be stopped, the entire military establishment would be paralyzed.

"Well," Levinson asked, "do we cheer or weep? The bugs may be making Armageddon impossible."

"Only if the damage is symmetrical," Touhy corrected. "In any case, I think we can agree that the military aspects of this crisis should be left in our hands. We'll expect you to keep us informed of anything that might touch upon the national security—promptly."

"Of course," Heller agreed.

"We need lots of co-ordination here: where the bugs are moving, how fast, where we're being closed down, what capacities we're losing, especially of a defense-related character." Nodding in Haseltine's direction, he added, "I'm assigning Larry to liaison between the Brain and DoD. What you report to him will come directly to me."

Over the next hour, provisional arrangements were roughed out for handling the most urgent military contingencies. Touhy had already developed his plans; he was simply filling Heller in, establishing a priority. While Touhy realized the impact of the crisis on the country's economic life, its law enforcement, its social services, he was clearly relegating these problems to a secondary level, instructing Heller to pursue them with other authorities. It was the first time in his dealings with Touhy that Heller could recall such a firm line being drawn between the military and civilian uses of the nation's computer power. That had never been necessary before. Now it was. Heller accepted that. But something rankled. Was he wrong in sensing that his status, on the civilian side of that line, had just slipped a notch?

Before he could decide, Touhy had moved ahead. He would be seeing the President immediately following their meeting. If the situation were severe enough—as they now agreed that it was—he would instruct the President to appoint a committee that would oversee all non-military ramifications of the emergency. Heller would be in charge of that. It might be his most prestigious appointment, but ironically his role would be that of planning the global liquidation of information technology.

As they broke up, Touhy mused, "I wonder if anybody knows where we buried all the slide rules and adding machines."

"The hand-crank cash registers . . . the key punch . . . the comptometers . . ." Levinson contributed a few more items to the inventory of tools and technologies the computer had rendered obsolete. To Major Kilraddin he remarked, "The bombsight, Barney . . . remember that?" Moving toward the door, he pointed a finger pistol across the room. "And how about aiming your own gun and shooting it yourself? The good old days of humanistic warfare."

As he and Heller made their way through the busy E-Ring of the Pentagon and down to the River Entrance, Levinson continued his list, "The addressographs . . . the linotypes . . . the billing machines . . . filing cabinets . . . sorters . . . collators. Remember office girls, making up payrolls, keeping ledgers, writing things on index cards with stubby pencils? Remember counting on your fingers and looking things up in books? Remember *remembering* . . . and *thinking* . . . and making up your own mind? The human brain . . . there's a quaint old machine. I hope we didn't scrap all of those. Say, do you remember your multiplication tables? What the hell is eight times nine?"

9

1

When they returned to the Brain, Heller—hesitantly, almost apologetically—told Levinson of his visit to Gaia Lodge. He expected it to be a difficult report. In eight years together building the Center and through fifteen years of friendship, the two men had never discussed anything remotely like the subject he now had to raise. Words like "psychic," "ritual," "worship" had never passed between them. To his relief, Heller discovered that Levinson was making it easy for him. He was listening, not just politely but intently. Welcoming the permission, Heller relaxed into his account. He felt free to include some personal reactions—to Jane, to Leah Hagar; he even mentioned the moments of anger, bewilderment, indecision he had experienced. Confessing such weaknesses was rare for him. Levinson recognized that and helped it happen. Heller was asking for a kind of counsel he had never needed before, advice that went to the depths of his convictions.

When he had finished, Levinson blew out a long blast of pent-up breath. He rose, paced across the office, gathered his thoughts. He knew what Heller wanted: a straight, frank answer, yes or no. He did not equivocate. "Go with it," he said. "Try it. If they can undo the spell, if there's even the ghost of a chance, go with it."

It was exactly what Heller wanted to hear. Even so he felt compelled to protest. "But 'undo the spell . . .'" He laughed at the absurdity. "What are we talking about, Berny?"

"We're talking about something nutty," Levinson snapped. "Obviously, something absolutely nutty. In fact, we don't know what we're talking about. Spells, hexes, mumbo-jumbo . . . this is sheer noise without information content. But I say, go with it. Why? Because I go for fact and logic, the same as you. And here are the facts I cling to. *One:* we've seen this bug. It is not a pipe dream or a hallucination. It exists, and it is even nuttier than anything you're telling me here. *Two:* this bug has now eaten four or five people alive and is screwing up the world data system. *Three:* the little girl had the dreams and drew the drawings. These are facts, real, empirical facts—as real as this cursed rash all over my arms. Nothing you know, or I know, or Schifman, or Lyman, or this pitiful, bewildered Brain of ours can make any sense of these facts. In our world, they don't compute. So I say—logically—we go someplace else to make sense. Where? To start with, where there is at least some tenuous connection with these facts. The kid, the mother, the church . . . they're a connection. In fact, the only connection we have. Their hypothesis is wacky, but, please note, it has internal consistency. It's a coherent idea. What's crazy about it? It's predicated on . . . what do we call it? Mental projection, which is no part of our working paradigm. All right. But neither is this goddam bug. So let the psychics dematerialize it, unhex it, exorcise it . . . whatever. You fight fire with fire, maybe you fight zany with zany. If the bug goes away, we're free and clear . . . though don't ask me how we explain what happened. If it doesn't, what've we lost?"

There was no question that Levinson's argument made sense; it was a minimum risk position. But it involved concessions—emotional concessions—Heller was loathe to make. He would be granting Leah Hagar and her church the satisfaction of seeming to be dependent on them. He would be dignifying what he could only regard as utter nonsense.

"You can understand how I feel about this," Heller said. "I really can't say which I think would be worse—if their mad little ritual fails . . . or if it works."

"If it works, I won't complain," Levinson replied. "That's the difference between us, Tom. I'm a technician, you're a philosopher. I don't have my metaphysical balls on the line here. You know what I am? I'm a Chaoticist. I think reality is chaos —a big surprise package. No system, no consistency, anything goes. With this monkey brain of ours we know how to compute a couple inches of the universe—provided you just count the numbers and don't look left or right. But for all I know this bug is made of astral chicken soup. I'd try anything to get rid of it—witchcraft, voodoo, cod liver oil. Who are we to care what saves the world from another dark age?"

Heller unloaded a weighty sigh, rubbed his eyes under his glasses. He was the battle-weary executive suffering beneath the burden of decision. But in playing that familiar role now he was not being wholly honest with Levinson, perhaps not with himself. Keeping close to Earthrite, remaining open to its lore and practice, was an excuse for staying friendly with Jane Hecate. And that was far from being a burden for him; it was a positive attraction. He was a man who could only express personal gratification by translating it into the language of duty and career. Enjoyment had to come disguised as part of his job.

"Yes, of course, you're right," he said. "If by some quirk these people possess the power they claim, we'll have to know about it, won't we? But if I'm going ahead with this, I want some reliable backup. How much official research do you think there might be going on in these paranormal areas? Occultism, ESP, thought projection, that sort of thing?"

"You mean federally funded stuff?"

"Yes. Especially defense-related projects, not just academic work. Suppose I need some authoritative consultation to check out what Earthrite tells me or shows me. Where do I find it? I could easily be snowed by these people. They seem sincere, but I'm just winging it here on my own. For example, what if they demand information I'm not permitted to give?"

"I could run a fast search," Levinson said. "Shelly Byers would be the man to do it. He's got all the right contacts in the intelligence community to find the classified stuff."

"All right. Put him on it. I'd like something by late next week."

"You know," Levinson remarked as he packed up to leave, "you may be surprised by what he turns up. I recall about five years back the Air Force had a hush-hush study on levitation running somewhere in the back room. Seriously. They were flying in yogis from the Himalayas. And the CIA—Christ, they're in touch with witch doctors all over the place: keeping the tribal peoples in line. Once you get behind the façade, official Washington is a zoo."

2

Before the week was out, Heller got two important calls. One was from Lyman Touhy, confirming that the President would ask him to head up an emergency committee for data control conversion. The committee would not be officially announced until the crisis worsened in the public eye; it was a card to be played for maximum effect at the right moment. However, Heller was to select its members immediately and begin meeting with them to develop policy recommendations. "Our decision," Touhy said, "is to proceed with a 'worst-case' scenario. Assume the progressive degradation of data control facilities at the present rate to the point of zero capability. How do we cope on the way down, and what do we do when we hit rock bottom?"

The second call was from Jane. "There's going to be a gathering next Friday evening—at the church," she told him. "You're free to come. Leah would like you there."

"You've found out what you need to know?"

"Leah says she'll be ready then. It's all been in her hands. She has some people flying in from Europe—Switzerland. People she trusts." After a pause, she asked uncertainly, "Is everything . . . all right?" He understood it was an awkward way of asking if things were any worse.

He could not tell her about the incident at Ames; there would be very little from now on he could tell outsiders. He answered, "I'd say things are more urgent than ever." She waited to hear more. "I'm sorry," he explained, "I can't say anything beyond that now."

"Well, please know that Leah is also treating this with great urgency. She's more worried than I think she let you know. This is the only time I've seen her . . ."

At that point, for the first time he could recall in years, Heller allowed an undeliberated remark to escape. Too suddenly, too forcefully, he said, "Jane . . . I'd like to see you . . . before the gathering." Then, rapidly, he explained, "I mean, it would be a great help to me if I could talk with somebody, with you, about what Leah may have planned. I think I should be there . . . but, well, I feel like such an outsider."

"That's because you are an outsider," she answered, angling the fact to sound like a polite rebuff. He heard the coolness in her remark, but it did not deter him.

"Would it be possible?" he asked. "I mean, to talk with you? Lunch . . . or dinner perhaps?" No, that sounded inappropriately social. "Well, actually, just a quiet hour some time might be best."

She was more confused than annoyed by the request. "Well, Dr. Heller . . . I've told you all I can. I don't know what to expect next Friday."

"I realize that. I'm not looking for more information. I need to have some feel for the situation. I know I'm an outsider—but I'd like to come with some greater sense of familiarity and . . ." He groped for another word. She supplied it.

"Trust?"

"Well, yes . . . trust. Trust in my own judgment . . . my own responses."

He could feel her reluctance like a wall between them. He put the request to her twice more, allowing himself to plead just a bit more each time. Finally, hesitantly, she agreed to meet him on Wednesday of the following week—briefly, in the evening, at her house.

As he put down the phone, one thing bothered him. He had called her "Jane"; she still called him "Dr. Heller." Could he get her beyond that? A few days later, he phoned her in the afternoon, placing the call himself rather than through his secretary. When she answered, he said, "Hello. Jane? This is Tom." She failed to recognize the name. "Tom Heller," he explained.

"Oh yes . . ."

An awkward pause. What did he say next? He had no other reason for phoning except this inept effort to move things to a first name basis. All at once he felt disconcertingly schoolboyish. It was not his style to get stranded like this in the middle of a conversation. Lamely, he improvised a pretext, "About Wednesday . . . I may not be able to get round until after nine. I've run into . . ."

"That's when I thought you were coming."

"Well . . . just confirming." Another unstable pause. After several seconds, she said, "Yes?" with a touch of bewilderment.

"I was also wondering . . . is there anything I might read?"

"Read?"

"I thought I might read up a little . . . for Friday. Something on . . . something that might help." This time he let the pause happen. What would she do if he allowed her to sense his real motive for calling? What if he let himself seem gauche, vulnerable?

"You want me to give you a reading assignment?"

There was amusement, not annoyance in her voice—gentle mockery for the seeming pedantry of his poor excuse. It was the first time he had gotten so close to her laughter. He returned it, as if to admit his embarrassment. "Is that really why you called?" she asked.

By now he assumed she knew the answer. "I like to do my homework," he said.

After he hung up, he discovered his pulse racing, the blood hot under his cheek. He had long since trained himself to cool those impulses under pressure of anger and frustration, never expecting he might have other emotions left over to worry about.

3

The week between his phone call to Jane Hecate and the evening meeting they had scheduled was a storm of activity for Heller. Lyman Touhy's decision to draft policy from the most pessimistic premises was becoming more justified by the day. Heller and General Haseltine were in touch daily exchanging news. With each call, the number of computer installations struck by the rash grew by at least one major casualty, some dating back, unreported, for weeks. There were, moreover, three new incidents where bugs had been sighted: one in the United States, one in West Germany, one in the Soviet Union. All were at military bases or research facilities where the attacks could be concealed from the public. In the American and German cases, the injuries were minor; little was known for certain about the Soviet incident, though the DIA had unconfirmed reports that it had been a disaster comparable to that at Ames.

In the Western nations, it was now standard procedure to quarantine infested computers immediately, making no attempt to disassemble them. It was discovered that a few sharp raps on the outside casing of the affected equipment would produce several minutes of agitated chattering from within: the bugs behaving like hornets in a troubled nest. The computers at the Brain were being tested in this way daily. To begin with, after the attack at Ames, only two of its major terminals gave the telltale sound; within ten days the number had risen to five, including three of the Sygnos 7000 computers which were the core of the system.

By then, Heller and the members of his emergency committee were already in unofficial session, improvising recommendations so rapidly that none of them could have said where real policy left off and pure public relations began. Heller's office issued a steady stream of press releases filled with breezy ideas about the possible use of salves, vaccines, protective garb to block the rash or slow it down. Rubber gloves, heavy stockings, jump suits of various materials were mentioned. None of this had yet been tried. The committee brainstormed remote control methods of operating computers, devices for handling data processing as gingerly as radioactive materials. But this was a long term project involving heavy investments and an entirely new range of skills. "We have many options," Heller insisted whenever he was cornered by the media; but he no longer believed he was putting a convincing face on the claim. He could feel his confident stance becoming stiff and stilted.

The press and his growing roster of political critics were after him relentlessly for explanations and predictions—always in a tone that implied invincible distrust. How bad was the crisis—*really*? How long would it last? How far was it spreading? There was one question, constantly raised, which he was careful to evade: was the rash connected with the insects that had infested the Brain? Or were these two separate problems? Heller, obfuscating shamelessly, fended off the query, sometimes saying there was no connection between the two problems, sometimes that the matter was under investigation. The secrecy surrounding the captured insects was holding—though research on the bugs was making no headway except in piling up negatives. An elaborate series of tests had been performed on the California specimens using magnetic resonance spectroscopy. The technique pressed the level of chemical analysis down to the magnetic field inside the atomic nucleus, as close to the fine structure of matter as the human eye could approach. Still the results were negative. The "white stuff" continued to reveal no physical organization of any kind. Nor had anyone found a way to kill the bugs. The sectioned parts in Schifman's laboratory were still alive, the severed head still snapping and biting.

Before Heller's emergency committee had held its second meeting, a new dimension of the crisis unfolded. In its July edition, one of the country's leading computer magazines broke a major story about the accelerating incidence of data pox among users of small, commercial computer services—in banks, real estate agencies, universities, libraries, offices of all descriptions. Rumors to that effect had been accumulating for weeks, but no source that Heller could respect had collected hard figures. When the story appeared in *Computer World*, Heller ordered Levinson to run a quick, independent check.

On the Wednesday of his evening meeting with Jane Hecate, he learned that enough of what was recounted in the story had been confirmed. There could be no doubt that the rash was spreading through the commercial mainstream of the society. IBM's VMSHARE and the TYMNET system—networks that numbered thousands of small scale users—were riddled with the rash. IBM's main research center at Yorktown Heights, its giant Mainz processing center in Germany and AT&T's Advanced Communications System were already at the Stage 2 level of infection.

"Like some of the other commercial networks," Levinson reported, "IBM has been suppressing the information to defend its corporate image. The word I've picked up is that the company thinks the pox may be industrial sabotage on the part of its competition. It suspects the Japanese."

Levinson was also able to confirm that several airline ticketing networks and warehouse inventory services were suffering chronic disruption. Employees in a growing number of Washington and New York firms were known to be avoiding their in-house computers, complaining of the rash. Steadily, the phrase "data pox," more and more frequently used in the media, was creeping into the public vocabulary. It was coming to be recognized as a major occupational hazard. Programmers, coders, information officers were letting their equipment stand idle, objects of fear and distrust.

"It won't be long," Levinson concluded, "before the pox becomes what black lung is among miners. How's that for progress? And that will be the least of it. What happens when digital watches and pocket calculators start hatching bugs? We have rumors to that effect already."

In the course of the week, there was only one encouraging development for Heller. He had placed two crucial phone calls to the Soviet Union. They were to his Russian opposite number, Yevgeny Khadzhinov at the Leningrad Academy of Information Sciences. Heller and Khadzhinov were friends and colleagues of many years; between them there was a strong bond of professional regard. On Heller's end, the contact was carefully coached by Touhy and rehearsed to the word; he assumed the same was true on Khadzhinov's side. The calls were a pivotal part of the Graduated Mutual Disclosure policy which

Touhy and the DIA had initiated. Little specific information was exchanged, but Heller came away convinced of an urgent willingness on the part of the Soviets to pool knowledge and resources. Khadzhinov hinted obliquely at extensive damage to Russian computer power, which was far less highly developed and possessed much less depth than Western facilities.

"I'd say," Heller reported after the second call, "that they're signaling loud and clear for collaboration."

Touhy meditated over a long drag on his cigar. "All right," he said, "let's work it out with them. Start with a symmetrical exchange of damage assessment, working up from minor to major losses. Then find out what they know about the bug. From here forward we assume that the threat we face is mutual and global. If the Soviets have any likely culprits in mind, we'd be pleased to hear about it."

4

Wednesday evening, when his meeting with Jane came round, was the first time in over a week that Heller excused himself from the killing pressure of the emergency. Levinson's report that the rash had penetrated the commercial networks and the minicomputers should have struck him as a shattering revelation. And, at one level of his mind, that fact ticked away like a buried explosive. Yet he left the Brain that night with an unaccountable air of relief and anticipation. Why? He had no reason to expect solace from Jane. He still had no idea what they would talk about when they met. But he did not care. Even if the evening was a misadventure, it was a chance to be with her, and that was all that mattered.

On his way to her house, he realized that the prospect of this visit had been sustaining him through the week. It had entered his thoughts again and again, offsetting the despair of the moment. He had even considered bringing her a gift—flowers . . . jewelry. Of course he dared not do that. It could be disastrous to treat the visit as if it were a date; she had signaled no permission for that. But he could not resist toying with the fantasy. He would not allow the words to form in his mind, but he knew nonetheless what his feeling for her was. Along the way he stopped to buy a bottle of wine—an expensive French import—and arrived at her door fighting down a wave of adolescent exuberance. It was just past eight-thirty—much earlier than he had led her to believe he would be coming.

It was clear from the moment she answered the door that Jane intended to offer him little of the consolation he needed. She met him in work clothes blotched with dust, looking flushed and bedraggled, her face streaked with sweat. She registered his arrival with a faintly preoccupied air, as if she had forgotten he would be coming. Distractedly, struggling to pin back her collapsing hair, she led him to the cramped rear bedroom she used as a studio. "I thought you'd be coming late," she said.

"Things broke up earlier than I expected," he explained.

The house was dark and quiet. In one bedroom along the hall, the older daughter was occupied at a desk. She glanced up as her mother and Heller passed. Anne, the housemate, was not in sight.

In the back room, Jane returned to work immediately. She was reorganizing paintings in their racks, lifting, shoving, hauling. It was heavy work and, in the stagnant heat of the evening, the little room was clammy and oppressive. She explained, without apologies, that there were things that had to get done. She was selecting some canvases for a small exhibit; they were due to be picked up tomorrow. Heller offered to help with the task, but she waved him aside. "You're not dressed for it," she said.

"May I at least pour you some wine?" he asked, unbagging the bottle.

"Yes, I could use that," she answered. "There are some glasses on the sill."

The glasses she meant were caked with a purple residue. Was it wine or paint? He found a reasonably clean cloth and tried to wipe them out, but with little success.

"I'll need a corkscrew," he said.

"Oh . . . in the kitchen somewhere. Hanging above the sink, I think."

"Some ice, too, maybe? The bottle's pretty warm."

"There may be some in the freezer," she told him. "The kids have been making cold drinks all day. Maybe we're out."

Heller stepped across the hall into the dark kitchen. As he switched on the light, a few roaches scurried down the wall behind the sink. Words ran through his mind, Daphne's voice saying, "Kill them . . . like behind the sink." Yes, he thought, squish them all dead. If only he could.

It was a messy kitchen. Or perhaps just a well-used homey one. Heller could not say which. His own apartment was looked after by professional cleaners who kept it almost clinically sterile. He rarely cooked or ate there anyway. He searched through a jerry-built stack of unwashed dishes, came up with the corkscrew and some cleaner glasses. In the refrigerator, he noticed a collection of exotic-looking fare: plastic-wrapped sprouts, yoghurts, oddly named health foods. He scraped together a few surviving slivers of ice and dropped them in the glasses. Ice in an expensive chablis . . . He sighed, but he could not be sure he would be staying long enough to let the wine chill.

Back in the muggy little studio, he took off his jacket and tie. "Where's the exhibit?" he asked as he tugged the cork out of the bottle. She answered, and they drifted into several minutes of small talk about the show and her experience exhibiting. Heller relaxed into the exchange, only marginally noting the incongruity of the situation. He was a man at the eye of a fierce political cyclone, a crisis that had already once brought official Washington close to a thermonuclear alert. Now, here he was taking time out to sip warm wine and make idle conversation about Jane Hecate's minor art exhibit. At that moment, what most vividly filled his thoughts were the movements of her body as she bent and stretched, lifting canvases into new locations about the room. She was wearing an oversized workshirt, and each time she leaned toward him, the yawning neck fell open to reveal her breasts. Once, when she rose with a painting, she caught his eyes on her. She was not annoyed, but puzzled at his attention. He wondered: did she think of him, after all, as a kind of robot—bloodless, fleshless, incapable of sexual curiosity?

He knew she was waiting impatiently for him to get to the point of his visit. But the only point he had in mind was too absurd to mention: simply that he wished to be with her in that hot, dust-filled room, accepted as a friend. He wanted to hear her talk about herself, her work, her children . . . anything that would diminish the distance between them. He knew that was no interest of hers, and yet he was vastly enjoying her distracted, uncaring presence. Could there be such a thing as one-sided intimacy?

Finally, she stopped working long enough to take a long drink of wine and let an awkward silence settle in. "You didn't come here to watch me work up a sweat," she said.

"No . . . about the meeting on Friday. It's still on?"

"Of course."

"And I'm still invited?"

"Yes. Leah wants very much to have you there."

"Do you think I should come?" He wanted her to know he cared to have her advice.

"I think you can trust Leah's judgment. I don't know what else I can say. I'm in no position to offer any promises. Oh yes, something I should tell you. Leah would like you to bring Daphne's drawing—to show her friends."

Heller nodded. He would bring the picture. "And if I come, I can expect . . . well, what?" She had no clear idea what he wanted to know. Nor had he. "I mean," he went on, "will there be many people? Is there anything I should prepare for?"

She searched her thoughts, wondering what to say. "You've seen one of our rites . . . at the lodge. I suppose it will be something like that, with maybe a few dozen people more. They'll accept you as Leah's guest. You won't be the first. As I've told you, we aren't strong on secrecy. What else? It'll be dark . . . candlelight, probably moonlight. Chanting . . . a meditation . . . people will be undressed. All our exercises are done nude. You won't be expected to participate. Things may go on for a few hours. The woman who will probably be leading the exercise—Beata Ulrich, she's one of the people coming in from Europe—is rather special. I can't exactly tell you in what way, but you'll see. She's . . . well, gifted. I've never been through anything at the church with this urgency about it, so I'm a little in the dark myself about what will happen. You see, most of what we do together is celebration—usually seasonal things, for the solstice, or the harvest. The mood is joyous, highly aesthetic and spiritual. This is all rather different. This time we're coming together out of fear . . . and out of guilt."

"And it will work. You believe it will work?"

She shrugged helplessly. "How can I guarantee that? Even Leah won't do that. I hope it will work. I'd like this whole wretched business to be over with."

"I'm sorry I can't let you know too much more about how things stand. The situation is worse, and deteriorating. This last week has been sheer hell." He was on the brink of telling her of the pressure he was under, the relentless pace of the emergency . . . but she waved him toward silence as she poured more wine. She did not want to share his burden.

"I'm sure you're under a great strain, Dr. Heller. All that matters to me is that nobody else gets hurt. Two deaths are enough."

"There've been more," he said, trespassing upon security regulations. He had never done that before. But he wanted her to absorb the urgency of the matter, to feel his dilemma. Her face darkened into a troubled frown.

"More . . . ? Where? How many people?"

"I'm not allowed to say more. This matter has gotten tangled up with national security, so the worst of it is very hush-hush. You might not believe how high up in the government this has gone—or how scared it's got our leadership."

"More people have died . . . because of the insects?"

"Yes. Please don't ask to know more. It's as ugly as I expect you fear. I know you're concerned, but I don't think you realize, or want to realize, how serious this thing has become. It's a *great big problem*, Jane—bigger than just a headache for me

and people like me. If this thing, this bug can't be stopped
soon, the lives of millions, hundreds of millions of people will
be touched." He smiled with quizzical amusement. "Odd, how
we're sitting here, talking like this, drinking wine. What we're
discussing could be the end of the world. *My* world at least
. . . but lots of people live in my world. Even you, more so
than you may be aware. If this ship sinks, we all start swimming . . . and right now I couldn't say in what direction, except maybe backward—into the past. The world is like that
now: linked together by big, ingenious, vulnerable systems. The
Arabs close down some pipelines, and families in Kansas freeze
through the winter. Only my specialty—the computers, the
data networks—that holds more together than oil, or steel, or
airlines and telephones. The whole globe has become a sort of
electronic apparatus . . . one big computer. I used to think
that was the acme of progress."

"Now you don't?" she asked. For the first time, she seemed
interested in what he thought, intrigued by his admission of
confusion. It encouraged him to go further. Was he only trying
to hold her attention, or was she drawing out something he
wanted to say, needed to say?

"As you might guess," he went on, "I'm pretty vain about
this. I don't want to admit failure. You know my reputation
. . . one of the principal architects of the brave new electronic
world. But what can I say in the face of the facts? We were
warned about putting all our eggs in one basket when we built
the Brain. Now, the whole damned system is coming down—
and everything's tied into it. If the global data technology col-
lapses, it'll put the world back generations. Nobody could
have predicted something as bizarre as these bugs, of course.
But that's just the point. The system was supposed to be omniscient, able to anticipate anything and everything—predict,
adjust, carry on. But who can say? If it hadn't been the bugs,
then it might have been something equally unpredictable.
Maybe the world really is too big to be programmed through
my machines. Too big . . . too strange."

He thought: if anybody in official Washington heard this
outpouring of self-doubt, it would be the end of him. He lived

in a world where fallibility was forbidden and weakness lethal. Now, as he spoke to her, the burden of pretense fell away. She was not offering him comfort, but she was listening to him attentively, hearing him as a person, not a public figure. For a little while, with her, he was free to lose his nerve.

After a moment, she asked, "Why did you come here? I can't offer you any help. There's nothing I've told you I couldn't have said over the telephone."

He sipped some wine and gazed down into the glass. "You remember at the lodge, that night in the woods . . . ? Something happened there. For just a few minutes, I think I would have been willing to give up everything I've built over the last twenty years, give it up . . . never go back. Maybe it was just exhaustion, a moment of weakness. I felt something giving way . . . like walls collapsing on all sides of me. It wasn't a pleasant feeling, but it wasn't frightening either. I wasn't defending . . . just letting it happen. I was almost expectant. I wanted to see what might be on the other side of those walls. I can't remember ever feeling that way. I don't even know how to talk about things like that. I wouldn't try with someone else. But . . . you were there, you're the only link I have with that evening. It seemed to have something to do with you. I had the sense that if I trusted you and followed you, I'd break through . . . to what, I don't know. I'm not supposed to have experiences like that, you realize. Strictly forbidden. It makes me cautious about coming too close to your people."

"But you came here to see me."

"That's difficult to explain. A paradox of sorts. I'm willing to come closer to you because you're so remote. You are. You're very standoffish—with me, at least. You act as if we were two different species. Strangely, that makes me trust you. You're not out to score points or win me over. I don't think you care what I believe or don't believe."

She shook her head and breathed a low, throaty laugh. "Proselytizing has never been my strong point. In fact, I hate it. Anyway, nobody is ever going to be argued into Earthrite. It's not that kind of thing."

"You don't worry about whether it's true or not?"

"Whether what's true?"

"These rituals, exercises, beliefs . . . the things you paint . . ."

The question irritated her. She was under no obligation to explain or justify anything to him. She waved his question aside. "I'm no logician. I don't know how to prove things, except by my feelings. I'm a painter. For me, Earthrite is all images and symbols and experiences. I believe there's a way for symbols to be true that has nothing to do with words or numbers. I believe that, but I can't prove it. I don't want to be asked to."

He let a pause settle in, savoring the fact that he had moved the conversation to more personal ground. "Can you understand what happened to me there at the lodge?"

"I wouldn't call it a moment of weakness," she answered. "A ritual like that—done in the right spirit, at the right time—can be very powerful. The more you open up to it, the more it moves you. I can't give you a psychological analysis."

"Maybe it's like falling in love."

The remark caught her off-balance. She did not expect to hear words like "love" from him. For that matter, he didn't expect it himself. She kept her eyes on him steadily but gave no answer. He felt his way forward cautiously. "The jellyware. That's always been the problem."

"Jellyware?"

"In my field, we have hardware, software and jellyware. The jellyware is up here." He tapped his forehead, and then his chest above the heart. "Or I suppose the poets would say here. All the stuff that just won't compute. A little girl's fear of insects. Rituals in the woods. Falling in love. Some of my colleagues insist we'll never get a grip on the jellyware. It's too slippery. I always thought it would be a defeat to admit that. Until now."

He could feel her drawing back from him, putting miles of distance between them in the little room. But it was a movement of caution, not distaste.

After a moment, she said, more gently than she had spoken to him before, "You know what you said about us being two different species? I do feel that way with you. I know I've been remote. It's because I'm afraid of you, can't you tell? You're a powerful person, part of something I don't like and don't understand—power, official power. My ex-husband had a lot to do with official power. I hated it, came to hate living in the same house with it—the deception and secrecy and bullying. I think that kind of power is everything that makes the world ugly and unfeeling and murderous. I'm not impressed by it, just frightened. I want to get far away from it. My painting . . . the church . . . that's where I've turned to get away. It's not much space to hold in the world; maybe it's just some-place an extinct species goes to die. Maybe Leah and the rest of us are part of something old and dying, getting driven out by the computers. I don't know. But I don't think you have a right to move into that space. You have all the rest of the world—just as you said. It's tied up in your machines. You ought to leave us—people like me and my daughter and Leah —our little piece of territory.

"I suppose that's also part of what I feel toward you—resent-ment. If you needed to have what we've got, you could take it. I know you could, somehow. It might begin with your getting close, and trying to understand, and maybe even being sin-cerely fascinated. But if there's anything we've got that looks like power, you'd have to take it, wouldn't you? I resent that, and I'm afraid of it. I'm afraid of what will happen if our rit-uals *do* have power. The church, I always hoped, was so strange, maybe even so irrelevant, it could never attract the at-tention of people like you . . . or like my former husband. You see, this was as far as I could run from the things and people I loathed. I felt safer here among all these weird ideas and exer-cises than I could feel living at the South Pole. But now I'm being sucked back in by this stupid miscalculation, this acci-dent. And what *will* happen? What will you and your friends in the DoD and the CIA do if our ritual works?"

Her tone was challenging, but there was no hostility in it. She was letting her sense of vulnerability show, appealing to a sensitivity in him she now had reason to believe he could offer. Heller hastened to assure her, "I haven't told anybody about

Daphne or the drawing . . . or about Earthrite. Well, I have told one close associate, but he can be trusted. I've been keeping this to myself."

"Maybe you haven't told anybody because it's too embarrassing to talk about. And you don't know anything for sure—not yet."

She was making shrewd guesses about him. Her experience with her former husband had taught her a lot about official behavior. He felt the edge of her suspicion pressing against him. How much reassurance should he offer her?

"I'm sorry," he said, "there are things I can't promise. I wish I could."

"Yes, I know," she answered, a tone of great sadness, perhaps even pity entering her voice. "I believe you. But I know you'll do whatever you have to do to save your position, your reputation. I'm not foolish enough to believe you could offer me any special concessions. If necessary, you could be very cruel. There's a word my husband used all the time about people he worked with in government. 'Reliable.' 'Reliable—unreliable.' Paul was *very* reliable. Oh, he could have gentle feelings, warm feelings. He was capable of friendship, concern . . . love. Even moments of weakness. Just like you. You can come and talk to me about my art, talk about your doubts and fears, be friendly, human. But I've learned what it means to be 'reliable.' It means you don't let those feelings matter. If necessary, if you're ordered to, you can snuff them out. You're reliable, Tom. That's how you've gotten so far. Only reliable men receive the kind of success you have. Let me warn you—I'm *not* reliable."

She had used his first name, finally. But it came in the context of a wounding accusation, adding to the sting. Now he realized her aloofness was nothing he could overcome with patience and tact. It was not an unreasoning aversion that arose from ignorance or envy. It was grounded in simple truth. He *was* reliable, and tied by that reliability to whatever his duty or ambition demanded. She was right not to trust him. The desire he felt for her was real; perhaps it was a rudimentary love. But it could be switched off in an instant. He knew exactly how to betray his most genuine impulses, and to take pride in the treachery. He said, knowing the inadequacy of the words, his throat laboring over them as he spoke, "I'd like to think that what you're calling reliability might be called responsibility."

She shook her head chidingly. "Responsibility is between people—real people, face to face. What you're talking about is between you and . . . I don't know . . . governments, agencies, abstract things. It's just doing a job, following orders, making a reputation. I'm sorry, I don't want to sound unkind or self-righteous. I'm really just trying to protect myself. I've been through this before—from a wife's-eye point of view. I know what it's like to be mangled by that kind of 'responsibility.' It lets you hurt people and think: it's all right, it's got to be like that, this is official business. Sometimes I think that's what all these big official operations really are—excuses for hurting people and saying it's all right."

She was not being harsh with him, only severely honest. She was letting an old wound show in her eyes, hoping he would understand and ask nothing more. That much at least he could do for her. It was as simple as saying good night.

Several minutes later, as he stood on the porch with her, a wave of urgency rushed through him. He had not come expecting more than he had received—a few hours of her company, the privilege of her attention. The chance she had given him to confess his growing uncertainty was more than he could have wished for. But now, realizing how precisely she had measured the ground that divided them, a twinge of panic coursed along the edge of his mind. One thought thrust itself upon him: this might be the last time he would be alone with her, close to her. With a sad half-smile, he reached out to press her shoulder, a gesture of resignation and withdrawal. She let his hand stay long enough for the gesture to become an unspoken question. She gave no answer, but he presumed upon her silence, drew her close, kissed her lightly. She neither resisted nor responded. There was an almost deliberate inquiry in her kiss, as if she were gauging his trust, his warmth.

Warnings and reservations flooded his mind; he walled them

back stubbornly, acting without thought. He brought her tight up against him, giving his second kiss an unmistakable insistence. He could tell she was meeting his desire with little more than curiosity, and perhaps a kindness that was too spontaneous a part of her to be restrained even by wise caution.

He came away from her reluctantly, then moved quickly across the dark yard toward his car. That night she had gently but decisively drawn a line of moral preference between them which even his embrace could not bridge. Though he had held her in his arms, she was further off than before.

10

1

The memo began:

TO: T. J. Heller, Director NCDC
FROM: Sheldon Byers, Security Liaison
RE: Inventory of Federally Funded Research
           in Paranormal Phenomena

It had been delivered to Heller's office in a sealed envelope
marked "Strictly Confidential."

Heller went through the several pages of the résumé rapidly,
making quick notes in the margins. When he had finished, he
scheduled a conference with Levinson and Byers for late that
Friday afternoon.

"I was surprised to find out how much of this stuff we've got
under way," Byers explained. He was a scholarly looking young
man in his mid-thirties, hired to co-ordinate the Brain's relations with military and civilian intelligence agencies. Heller
liked his approach to the job; Byers managed to make intelligence gathering seem like a kind of academic research, having
no political overtones at all. "You'll notice that most of the
projects I've listed deal with voodoo, black magic, and so on.
That's related to counterinsurgency policy in Central America,
Africa and various tribal areas. It's generally justified on the
grounds that it provides insight into native cultures—an adjunct to psychological warfare. You get the same justification
for most of the ESP research: the only reason we're into it—

supposedly—is because the Russians are, and we have to know what the opposition is thinking. It's interesting: almost nobody is willing to admit to honest curiosity, though I'm sure it's there. I think the military is seriously interested in the possibilities of telepathy and distant viewing, for example. A few of the more academic efforts—the projects at Yale, Michigan, Chicago—seem to value the confidentiality they gain from defense-related research. Dressing things up as national security protects them against prejudicial criticism from colleagues. Incidentally, this is by no means an exhaustive survey. I'm sure there's lots more, including a few projects that are highly classified. I got some hint of that in talking to people at DoD. I suspect they have a few things going under very heavy wraps."

Heller asked, "How did you explain your interest in this?"

Byers was confused by the question. "Well . . . I understood from Berny that this was to supplement a Bibliographical Reference Base inquiry from someone at . . . where was it? Harvard?"

"Oh yes," Heller said, picking up on the cover.

"But," Byers added, "some of the people I contacted asked if we were trying voodoo to get rid of the data pox. I just sort of laughed that off." After a moment he asked, "Does this have to do with the rash? I mean, I wasn't clear why I should be giving this such a high priority, what with . . . well, you know."

"It does have to do with the rash," Heller admitted, judging that Byers could be trusted. Besides there was no other way to explain the meeting they were having. "But only marginally. That's strictly confidential."

"Of course," Byers agreed.

Heller ran over the list again. "As far as you can tell, does any of this work have to do with psychic projection?"

Byers looked puzzled at the term. Heller groped his way forward like a man speaking a foreign language out of a pocket dictionary. "Projecting the contents of the mind . . . objectifying the . . . a mental image, let's say." Out of the corner of his eye, Heller caught a glimpse of Levinson masking a broad grin with his hand. Byers was going to think they were putting him on.

"Something like telepathy?" Byers asked.

"Well, more with a view to physical effects. What is that called?" He threw the question in Levinson's direction, seeking to implicate him in the embarrassing line of inquiry.

"Uh . . . I'm not sure," Levinson replied, assuming a strenuously sober expression. "Teleportation? Tele-something, probably."

"Telekinesis," Byers suggested, flashing on the word. "I've come across that term a few times. That's like using the mind to influence the fall of dice, or to move a pith ball in a vacuum. Is that what you're after?"

"Yes . . . maybe." Heller was still groping.

"Also there's 'materialization,'" Byers went on, searching his notes for possibilities. "I gather that's making some mental entity tangible."

"Yes, that's more the thing," Heller said. "Especially as that might be related to primitive religions."

Byers was flipping back and forth through his notes. "You mean doing a hex or casting a spell?" He looked up as a bright idea struck. "Or maybe conjuring up a jinni?"

"Or an imp . . . or a goblin. Why not?" Heller sighed wearily, yielding to the humiliation of the subject. Levinson, standing off at the window, was almost audibly giggling.

"Yes, I see," Byers went on, conjecturing seriously. Another bright idea. "I saw this movie on the late night 'Creature Features' the other week. My kid watches it, you know. In the picture, this warlock would conjure up a . . . what was it? A 'familiar,' that was it. A little catlike thing. That would be a sort of imp, wouldn't it?"

Levinson burst into a loud guffaw. Byers registered confusion, then amusement. He began to doubt the seriousness of the meeting.

"All right, all right," Heller insisted, "let's try to keep this roughly within the bounds of sanity. Have you come across anything of that admittedly nebulous description?"

Byers was squinting at him over his glasses. "You think the

rash, the bugs . . . they might be some kind of psychic sabotage?"

Levinson intervened. "No, Shelly, that's not what we're after. Nothing like that. This is pretty offbeat and extremely unlikely. Tom just needs backup for some inquiries he's making. Again, that's strictly confidential."

Byers understood he was being warned away from further questioning. He returned to his notes. "Okay. There's some work on witchcraft being done by the CIA—mainly with reference to the Caribbean and sub-Sahara African areas. There's something about hexing involved in that. That would be items twenty-seven, thirty and thirty-one on the list. Also there's a joint Canadian-American project at McGill University. Item fourteen. They've been experimenting with native Americans —mostly tribal medicine men—and a number of psychics. They seem to be interested mainly in weather control and various kinds of ESP. That's an Army Intelligence project. It's been going for about four years, with pretty lavish funding. The work is densely classified. I had to dig pretty hard on that one. Even so, I couldn't find out too much on short notice, even from friends. The man in charge there is a Richard Gable. He has quite a reputation in academic circles. Several of the people I contacted mentioned his research—not always approvingly. Anyway, his project seems to be making some waves."

Heller placed a check mark next to item fourteen. "Yes, that one looked intriguing to me as well." For several minutes longer, he annotated his list with Byers' help. Then, when Byers was gone, he turned to Levinson with a vexed look. "I'm glad that amused you," he said.

"God, what I wouldn't have given to get that on tape," Levinson laughed. "I could blackmail you bankrupt."

"Poor Shelly. He's going to think we've flipped."

"And he may soon have company," Levinson added. "It won't take long for Lyman to hear about this. There's no way for anybody around here to make inquiries of this kind without attracting attention."

"So I assume," Heller agreed. "Well, after tonight, I'll know how much explaining I've got to do."

2

Heller arrived early at Earthrite. He was met at the door by Professor Samples, who told him "Leah is waiting for you upstairs." There were several people already on hand in the bookshop, among them Jane and Anne. Heller nodded to them as he was ushered upstairs.

On the way, Samples explained, "We've used the term 'church' because it avoids a good deal of public misunderstanding. Most people don't ask you too many questions about your church affiliation. Also it gives us the usual tax advantages. But you won't find Earthrite much like any church you're familiar with. Actually, we're much more at home out-of-doors—in a forested area. We think of Gaia Lodge as our real place of worship. But most of us find it difficult to get away from town too often. We're very citified pagans. A contradiction in terms, you know. 'Pagan,' in the early Christian usage, simply meant 'bucolic,' 'bumpkin.' 'Hick,' as we might say. You see the last holdouts of the Old Religion were countryfolk. Now, all the surviving bucolics in the Western world are either fundamentalist Christians or inveterate Catholics. The only pagans around are us college graduates."

At the top of the stairs they arrived at a large landing where Heller was asked to leave his shoes. He noticed a line of dark robes hanging along one wall. Samples led him through a door into a spacious, high-ceilinged loft whose only windows were two oversized skylights that were heavily shuttered against the waning daylight. An air-conditioner was quietly at work keeping the room dry and reasonably cool. Hardly a pagan touch, Heller thought, but he welcomed escaping from the humid summer heat outside. The only light in the room came from a row of dim lamps along the walls.

It was a plain, almost austere room, richly paneled in dark

wood from floor to ceiling. At the center stood a larger version of the table Heller had seen before: raw wood supported on three stones. Upon it was the horned and twisted shape that was Earthrite's emblem, the figure carved from a dark, gnarled piece of wood. Beside it stood a few ceremonial implements, the crossed knives, an unlit candle. On the far wall hung a large tapestry, the room's only décor. Its design in the faint light seemed to be a constellation of swirling celestial bodies. The colors were subdued, but stitched with a shimmering thread that here and there coruscated as one moved through the room.

Along the wall to the left, seated on a low wooden bench, were Leah and two others. As Heller approached, she awkwardly levered herself up on her cane and reached out to him eagerly.

"Dr. Heller, so very good of you to come. Let me introduce you." Her companions were a man and woman of her own age. The man rose to meet Heller, one hand firmly outstretched, the other thrust inside his jacket. He was slightly built but created the impression of being taller than he was by holding himself rigidly erect, shoulders lifted high, his massive head tilted far back so that he seemed to be gazing down at Heller from a great height. He was meticulously well groomed; despite the oppressive Washington heat, he wore a high stiff collar and a vest.

The woman who remained seated beside him was tiny and delicate, with a mousy face and nervous mouth. She was dressed in dark, matronly clothes and wore her hair piled high on her head, caged between two shiny bone combs. There was an antique, slightly dusty air about the couple; they were people from another era, a time of severe formality and seriousness. Leah introduced them as Professor and Mrs. Ulrich from Basel.

"They have come just for this evening. Together, after the war, Beata, Ernst, I, a few others—we were all that survived of *Erdrecht*. We spoke of ourselves as aboriginals of the New Earth." The three exchanged fond glances. "I have told them all we learned from you last week."

"Let me assure you, Dr. Heller," Professor Ulrich said, "we are fully aware of the gravity of this matter. Most regrettable, such a miscalculation." He spoke in a slow, ponderous baritone. His English was precise and confident with only the hint of an accent. Heller noticed that he and Leah were keeping their voices subdued. That more than anything else brought home to him that he was in somebody's church. "May I ask," Ulrich went on, "has there been any change in this unfortunate situation in the course of the last week?"

"I'm not at liberty to give you any further details," Heller explained, giving the remark a distinctly sharp edge. He wanted to put some distance between himself and these people at once, reminding them that he had stepped down several levels of official status to be with them that evening. "I expect you will understand. I can only tell you the crisis has deepened."

"Jane tells me there have been more deaths," Leah interjected with marked excitement. "This is so?"

Heller flinched, realizing he had violated security in letting that much be known. "I won't confirm that," he snapped, again trying to repel her presumption. "I've already shared more information with your church than I have any right to do. You'll have to settle for my description of things as very serious."

"We have made our plans on that assumption," Leah said. "With the help of Professor Ulrich and Beata we have composed an exercise for this evening. It has been a great deal of work. Beata will lead us; she has always been our most gifted celebrant. We are quite optimistic."

"We would have appreciated more time," Ulrich added. "This is a matter for extensive research. But tonight, we have the moon." He gestured toward the skylight. "We have subordinated everything else to that."

"A full moon," Leah explained. "Many of our exercises are keyed to the moon. It is, you might say, our source of energy." She was smiling at Heller with the fixed grin that seemed to claim more understanding and friendship than he was willing to offer. He stared back with a cool, ungiving look. "When the moon is full," she continued, "we say the goddess is fully awake to us. If we had missed this moon, we would have had to wait another lunar month."

"Yes, that is important," Beata Ulrich added, speaking for the first time. Her voice was high and tremulous, as if taut with fear. "We will need all the support we can gather, since we are unable to use the child."

The remark noticeably jarred both Leah and Samples. Heller could see a disapproving frown pass over Leah's face; she gave a slight, sharp wag of the head. Then the fixed smile returned. "Of course, there is no need to use the child. There was never any question of that."

For a long moment, an air of tension hung over the group. Heller waited for it to subside. "You will be joining our session this evening, Dr. Heller?" Leah asked, obviously moving the conversation to safer ground.

"I'd prefer simply to observe," Heller answered, shading the answer to carry a marked rebuff. She had to know the limit of his participation. She was not about to recruit him as a convert.

"Yes, of course," she agreed. "I understand. But one thing I hope you can contribute. Jane told you we would like to make use of Daphne's drawing?"

Heller took the picture from his briefcase and passed it to her. Samples and the Ulrichs examined it eagerly. "The insect looks like this?" Ulrich asked in amazement.

"It does," Heller answered, "except in three dimensions—almost like a solid, animated version of the drawing."

"Has it been examined by an entomologist?"

"Yes, but—again—I'm not at liberty to tell you the results."

Professor Ulrich gave a slight scowl of disappointment. "You cannot tell us the insect's anatomy, its physical nature?"

"I'm sorry," Heller insisted. "You must understand that . . ." He broke off, noticing that both Ulrich and Leah had turned their attention to Beata, who was murmuring something in a low, halting voice.

"*Nichts . . . nichts . . . nichts drin. Durchaus massiv.*" She repeated the phrases several times, her eyes closed, the tips of her fingers passing lightly across the drawing. "Ah!" Ulrich said, giving a small gasp of gratification.

Nichts. Heller could make out the German word for "nothing," but he was losing the rest. "What is it?" he asked. Ulrich waved him to silence as his wife went on.

"*Keine innere Struktur. Kein Herz . . . keine organe . . . alles leer.*"

"She says," Ulrich explained in a whisper, "that the insect has no insides, no inner structure. That it is completely blank."

Heller felt his stomach go hollow. The words might have been taken from his own mind. He stared at Ulrich, who was studying him with an intense gaze. "It is important to know," Ulrich said, "if Beata has got that right. Will you say so?" A new note of firmness had entered his voice, a tone of command.

"How would she know something like that—about the composition of the bug?" Heller asked with increasing unease. He began to suspect he was the victim of an elaborate hoax.

"She is quite sensitive," Ulrich explained. "Is she correct?"

"Sensitive to what?" Heller demanded.

Before Ulrich could answer, his wife spoke again in the same trance-like murmur. "*Einige tot. Zwei in der Nähe. Darauf funf in einem entfernten Platz . . . Kalifornien. Viele andere weiter weg . . . Russland, ja.*" After a moment, her eyes blinked open, and she visibly shuddered. With a gesture of disgust she thrust the drawing back into Leah's hands. "*Ein teuflischer Ding,*" she muttered. Her face was drawn and tense; her delicacy had become the tired and sallow look of illness.

Listening more carefully this time, Heller had been able to make out most of the German. She had said that several people were dead, two nearby, five in California, many more further off, in Russia. "What is she sensitive to?" Heller demanded again, allowing his impatience to show.

"Thoughts," Ulrich answered, "In this case, I presume yours. But she is not always correct."

Heller stood up with obvious agitation. He looked at each member of the group in turn. With all the authority he could muster in these unlikely surroundings, he said, "There are things about this matter I am not at liberty to disclose. I tell you that again. They involve the national security. If any attempt is made, in any way, to draw information from me, I will have no choice but to leave. I warn you, the consequences of such an attempt—to you and to your church—will be severe. I came here in good faith. I expect my request to be respected."

Leah and her companions, exchanged worried and contrite glances. "Of course, Dr. Heller," Ulrich hastened to say. "We have no right to intrude upon your responsibilities. These reactions, Beata cannot always control them. They come like natural curiosity. I will only say that we intend to proceed on the basis of my wife's intuitions. What she says of the insect—that it has no internal physiology—such cases have been recorded in esoteric literature with respect to materializations of this kind. There is, for example, one case, that of the Dutch iatrochemist Van Vechten—seventeenth century. He sought to realize the alchemical homunculus by such a means. You understand—the homunculus was a living being of small size. A test-tube creation, you might say. The alchemists spoke of this as 'the Great Work.' Van Vechten undertook to do the Great Work *internally*—without laboratory apparatus. A labor of many years. Tremendous mental concentration. The creature he finally projected, so the accounts say, was seriously flawed. Monstrous, imbecilic, only marginally human. And quite vicious. The specimen was later dissected by the great Dutch anatomist Tulp. Yes, the same as in the famous Rembrandt painting—Dr. Tulp's anatomy class. It was found to have no internal organs, no tissues, no cellular structure. There was simply a blank white surface. In the alchemical literature, this is called the *materia prima*. How to explain? It is the absolute physical, before the mind reads structure into it. Before life enters, before thought enters. There are records of this dissection. I have brought the citation."

He pulled a note card from his inside jacket pocket and passed it to Heller, who tried unsuccessfully to read it in the dim light. As he studied the card, Heller felt slightly relieved.

What Mrs. Ulrich had said about the insect, she had no doubt picked up some time earlier from her husband's research, not from his own thoughts. But how had she known about the deaths? She had mentioned California and Russia specifically. Heller struggled to recall if he had passed that information to Jane. He was sure he had not.

The professor was continuing his remarks. "Our science, to-day, of course, has no place for these traditional concepts. From the modern viewpoint, the *materia prima* is primitive meta-physics. But in the mind of a child, such ideas survive. It is all a child has to think with. I had assumed, when I first read of Dr. Tulp's dissection, that possibly the microscopes then in use were not powerful enough for this specimen. But no doubt the insect you have captured, Dr. Heller, was investigated by the best equipment."

Slipping the note card into his wallet, Heller asked, "How was this . . . creature disposed of?"

"Ah!" Ulrich answered. "This I was not able to trace in de-tail. Most unfortunate. However, it was done by a hermetical rite—so much we know. We have tried to adapt that method to our exercise this evening. You will notice the three phials there on the altar. Sulfur, salt and quicksilver—the alchemi-cal trinity. You see, Van Vechten's homunculus could not be destroyed by any physical means, even after dissection. I can-not, of course, say what your experience has been with the in-sect. But we take the approach tonight that the entity must be *unmanifested*. The science of such matters is hopelessly lost. We can only improvise. But, as Leah has said, we are optimis-tic."

Heller was closely exploring Ulrich's face and manner all the while he spoke. There was about him the same disconcerting combination of restrained scholarship and occult lore Heller had witnessed in other members of the church. Once again, he found himself off-balance, negotiating the relationship cau-tiously.

"You're a specialist in this field?" he asked. "Esoteric litera-ture?"

"No, no," Ulrich said with a quick wave of the hand. "Some

of the writings I know—but only as a hobby. I am—was—professor of medicine—pathologist. At Basel. Now *emeritus* the last six years. The seventeenth-century medical literature is a queer mixture, not given much attention except by scholars. The beginning of modern science, but with much of the older traditions still lingering. And of course much superstition. It is not easy to discriminate. Van Vechten's experiment . . . for years I did not know how seriously to take it. Then, when Leah calls us about this situation, at once I realize we may have something similar with the little girl. Let us hope we are as successful in reversing the effect."

Leah, glancing up at the skylight, spoke to Samples. "I think perhaps we begin to have some stars by now?" She turned to Heller. "We can soon begin. We must have the night sky, and then the moon. You may sit here if you wish, or at the far end. You will not disturb us."

Samples began to work a crank on the wall. The heavy shutters slid smoothly aside. The sky had become a hazy gray-purple streaked with the reflected lights of the surrounding city. The moon was not yet in sight.

Excusing themselves, Leah and her friends withdrew to the landing. Heller moved off to the darkest corner of the room near the exit. For several minutes, he could hear a rustle of activity on the landing outside. People began to enter and assemble, wearing their dark gowns. Jane was among the first to arrive. She looked for Heller, then turned to help the others place cushions around the central table. Among those who entered was an extraordinarily tall man with thick blond hair and a dapper goatee. He approached Jane and exchanged a few words. She nodded toward Heller and the man came over to introduce himself.

"Dr. Heller? We meet again. But who would have guessed on such an occasion?"

Heller did not recognize the man. "I'm sorry," he said as he accepted an overly tight handshake.

"I wouldn't expect you to remember. The name is Christopher Sperling. This is pretty flabbergasting, isn't it? We all feel painfully responsible. I hope we can bail you out. Well, not just you. We're all in the same boat, aren't we? You've met the Ulrichs?"

"Yes." Heller did not place the man's name. He studied him closely, trying to recall where they might have met.

"We're lucky to have them with us," Sperling went on. "Especially Beata. Remarkable woman. Have you read her poetry?"

"Poetry? No, I haven't."

"Very powerful stuff. I've seen her conduct an exercise once before—in Basel. It was devastating. She's an authentic sorceress, every move, every rhythm. One of the surviving few. No wonder *Der Fuhrer* tried to recruit her for the cause. Do you know the story?"

"No."

"Well, later maybe. They all wound up in the camps, you know—the psychics, the gypsies, and the Jews. Or at least the psychics who could tell black magic from white, and cared about the difference. I know you must be on your guard in company like this. But do try opening yourself to the exercise tonight. Beata is a real treat for you. Myself, I would have trusted her with Daphne."

Heller pretended to know what he meant. "But I gather you won't be using the girl?"

"Leah thought it might be too dangerous. And Jane wouldn't hear of it. So we'll have to trust their judgment. I'm certainly in no position to override them. Only I should have thought that in an emergency like this . . . well, we'll do our best."

Heller, probing, asked, "How would you have used Daphne . . . if you did?" But before Sperling could answer, Jane had come over and, picking up the drift of the conversation, plucked him away by the sleeve. There was an exchange between them as they moved across the room. Heller could not hear; but he could discern some temper on Jane's part. It was clear that Sperling, whoever he was, knew everything about the bugs. As Heller had suspected, these people could not be trusted to keep anything confidential. He had long ago learned that secrecy was either a rare talent or a difficult discipline.

More than half an hour passed as people quietly gathered in the room. They sat in concentric circles around the altar, dropping into a meditative silence. Gradually the room seemed to grow lighter. Heller realized the moon was edging into view at one corner of the skylight, bathing the loft with a chill, blue tide of light. After several minutes more, someone went quietly along the walls extinguishing the lamps. By then, there were some forty people in the room. The last to enter were Leah and the Ulrichs. They made their way through the still figures at the pace of Leah's limping gait.

When they reached the table where one candle had been lit, Beata was left on her own before the Earthrite emblem. For several moments she stood with her face turned upward into the night sky, as if she were gathering her concentration, her hands at her sides opening and fisting in a slow, tense rhythm. She had undone her hair and it fell to an astonishing length down her body; in the moonlight, it gleamed like a silver-white shawl that covered most of her small frame.

A thick, underwater stillness engulfed the sanctuary, as if the scene were slowly sinking away from the everyday world into a deep well of fantasy. Even the steady mechanical drone of the air-conditioner, instead of mocking the ritualistic pretense of the gathering, added a hypnotic ground tone. Interwoven with it, Heller could hear the husky rasp of Beata's breathing as it grew heavier, more labored. Then, with a subtle ripple of the shoulders that Heller scarcely noticed, she shrugged her gown away, letting her hair enfold her like a second costume. The others, at the signal, let their robes slip down their backs. Now she was surrounded on all sides by a small field of heads, backs, shoulders, shining dead white in the moonlight.

Leah reached out and placed something on the altar: a piece of paper, Daphne's drawing. Beata, tightening her hands at her temples, stared down at it and began a throaty moaning. A drum somewhere across the room counterpointed her chant like a dull heartbeat. Heller could not make out the words, but the intensity of her song was invasive enough to prickle his scalp. The tiny woman's voice was becoming unreal—a rough, cavernous groan. He could hear anger and anguish mixed in her chant, a storm of struggling emotions. Twice, she reached high overhead and slowly brought her fists down, first one then the other, upon the drawing, each time swelling her voice into a vibrant roar. Now Heller could just make out fragments of the words he caught as Latin.

"*Nomeno sancto . . . Luna qui . . . in imperium magnum est . . . primoque ultimo . . . vincite, vincite, vincite . . . Sapientia, Via, Vita, Virto . . . Luce, Gloria . . .*"

It was the corrupted medieval Latin Heller associated with spells and conjurations. His own Latin was still good enough for him to make out the general drift of the chant: an invocation to the moon, an appeal for power and protection.

The woman he was watching must have been in her late sixties, but, as she lost herself in her task, the assurance and uncanny energy of her performance transformed her meager appearance. She ceased to be withered with age and became a commanding and supple presence at the center of the rite, writhing, working, swaying to her words of power. In Heller's eyes, as he studied her through the blue shadows of the moonlit room, her form took on an unnerving sexual potency, a heat and impassioned authority that broke through the barriers of age. She became the priestess of a rite older than the Christian sin of blasphemy. Moving without fear or shame among the aroused powers of desire and fertility, she brought an unyielding dignity to her bizarre office. Heller could see she was no longer in full possession of herself. Her eyes were shut, her face laboring painfully with the words she uttered. Even in the cool air of the room, sweat gleamed on her brow and across her breast. In her rapt intensity, the woman had become the whole force and focus of the ceremony, drawing the attention of the group to a bright, hot point. Heller was watching a psychotic fervor that, even in his own skeptical mind, had grown to awesome proportions.

Beata's voice fell suddenly into a low murmur. She now had one hand pressed hard upon the paper and, through it, seemed to be interrogating the drawing. There was a distinct questioning lift to her voice. Heller caught the Latin for "Who?" "Where?" Then long silences between the questions. Heller sensed unease in the congregation. Another question and a long pause, after which Beata shook her head fiercely—a determined denial, her voice almost growling. Then, as her arms swung up, the group rose to its feet and joined hands. It formed two concentric circles around the altar and began to move in a slow shuffle, one circle turning to the left, the other to the right. Between the wheeling bodies, Heller could make out the naked form of Professor Ulrich. He had risen to assist his wife at the altar. He was holding a bowl out before her. Into it she poured something, materials from the three phials on the altar: the sulfur, salt and mercury. With each pouring, Beata intoned a passage, and there was a chanted response from the congregation. "*Solvite corpora.*" "Dissolve the body."

A man and woman stepped forward from the inner circle: Jane and Sperling. They knelt stiffly at the altar and took up the chant with Beata. After a moment, the others stopped and looked on. Jane took the candle and held it forward with Sperling's hands covering hers. Beata's voice swelled up with a menacing power, switching into a language Heller could no longer recognize. Perhaps it was no language at all, but a glossolalic outpouring. Words rushed from her, alternately pleading and commanding. Slowly, she raised Daphne's drawing, holding it out with stiff arms as she barked her will at it. The members of the congregation, with hands still joined, raised their arms to point inward toward the drawing. As Beata held the paper toward the candle, Professor Ulrich lightly sprinkled it with particles fingered up from the bowl he held.

Only at that point did Heller realize that the drawing was going to be burned. He did not want that; he did not wish to lose this piece of physical evidence. He stood up, but felt helpless to interrupt the ceremony. Jane and Sperling pressed the candle forward and lit the sheet of paper at the center. The salt upon it flashed yellow, the paper curled into ash. Heller heard himself say "No!"—but the words were covered by Beata's final command, a fierce blast of rage. In the trance that had taken her, she did not think to drop the burning page; it had to be knocked from her hands by her husband. She slumped down exhausted into his arms at the foot of the table.

There was a moment of drawn stillness. Then the people returned to their cushions and put on their gowns. Professor Ulrich helped his dazed wife into her costume and led her away to a bench at the far end of the room. Leah came forward to stand at the altar. She fingered the ashes of the drawing and let them float into the air. In a low voice she said, "*Malum mortum est,*" and extinguished the candle. There was a quiet meditation that lasted perhaps two minutes. To Heller it seemed like hours. He glanced at his watch; the digital numerals read ten-fourteen. He discovered a long imprisoned breath in his chest waiting to be freed. Though the room was still cool and dry, his shirt and coat lay over him like a damp hide. There was an aching need for release in all his muscles, and he dropped back into his seat limp with fatigue.

In the skylight overhead, the white disk of the moon was staring straight down into the sanctuary. "The eye of the goddess fully awake."

After his nerves slackened, Heller walked across the loft through the departing members of the congregation. No one spoke. They passed him like shadows in the dark room. Leah, the Ulrichs, Jane and Sperling were together in a group. Leah rose and hobbled toward him. "Yes, yes, Dr. Heller," she said in a loud whisper. "Very successful. There was great power here tonight. Perhaps you felt its presence. I feel very certain we have succeeded. And Beata too, she also feels it."

Beata Ulrich, leaning against her husband's shoulder, looked a haggard ruin. The exercise had drained her, leaving her a frail old woman once again. She was laboring to draw her breath. "Yes . . . I could feel a great evil passing, passing from the world," she said in a hoarse undertone. "But struggling . . . it would not die easily. The resistance . . . very great."

Professor Ulrich looked up at Heller. He too was breathing heavily, as if his energy were flowing away into his wife. "She has done a great work this evening. Never before have I seen so much power gathered in her." There was a note of tense concern in his voice. "She will need much rest."

"You destroyed the drawing," Heller remarked, showing his annoyance. "You didn't tell me that would happen."

"We took the liberty," Leah explained. "You must forgive us. There had to be such a physical link, you see."

"We did not use the child," Beata added, a note of desperate appeal in her voice. "We spared her. We have done the exercise without . . ." Her words sank into a painful gasp.

"I wanted to save the drawing as a piece of evidence," Heller said. "I wish you hadn't . . ."

"Don't you have a copy?" Jane asked.

"Well, yes. But now the original is gone."

"What use could it be anyway? Ugly thing."

Beata spoke again. "You see, we needed something of the child's. We could not . . ." Her voice fell away once more. Her husband encouraged her to keep silent, but she went on. "I think perhaps we have overcome the evil. It is worth that much."

Heller had one more question. "How many of these people tonight know what I've told you?"

"Only the few of us here right now," Leah answered. "And those who were at the lodge when you came. The others understand this was a healing exercise, nothing more. I think you can be sure of confidentiality."

Heller placed no great trust in her assurance. Still, he felt compelled to offer some token of appreciation for her efforts. Perhaps the gesture would reinforce her promise. "It must have been some expense to you to bring Professor Ulrich and Mrs. Ulrich here. I'd like to pay their travel and accommodations . . . and whatever other costs this has put you to. I hope you will permit me."

She protested, but he was resolved to send the money. "I'll have my secretary call next week and make the arrangements." As he moved away, following Jane and Sperling toward the door, Leah and the Ulrichs fell into a muffled discussion in German. Beata, grimacing and rubbing her chest inside her gown with noticeable distress, seemed to be trying to explain something the others could not follow.

"And you?" Heller asked Jane. "How do you feel? Did it work?"

She answered slowly, her face showing deep puzzlement. "I

don't know. This is new to me. I've been at other exercises
where Beata led. They were very different. I've never partici-
pated in anything so combative. She seemed to be struggling so
very hard . . ."

"Yes, against the grain, as it were," Sperling added.
"Strange, I noticed that too. It was out of keeping."

On the landing outside, there were about a half dozen people in various states of undress, changing out of their gowns.
Heller would have moved on, but Sperling held him with his
talk. His gown came off and he stood talking totally naked.
Heller tried to keep his back turned toward Jane as she
changed. "The general spirit of our exercises," Sperling went
on, "is ease and grace—flowing with the course of things. Harmony, reciprocity, give and take. There was a great deal of . . .
would you call it antagonism in Beata's work tonight? A lack
of rapport. Poor woman! She's really depleted herself."

"I'm worried for her," Jane said behind Heller's back.

"Yes," Sperling agreed. "There was something that gave unusual trouble here tonight. I gather that's what *Die Drei Altere*
in there are going over. I've seen Beata do some beautiful exercises—especially where she uses her own poetry. Do you know
Rilke?" he asked Heller.

"No."

"Very much in that vein, her work. Only with more plas-
ticity—the feminine subtlety Rilke could never quite bring
off." He spoke in a bluff, breezy manner, a forceful man with
strong opinions. He was older than Heller first took him to be.
The blond hair and beard were liberally streaked with gray.
Annoyingly, as he spoke, he left himself naked from the waist
down until the last while he fussed with his hair and tie.

"Are you a poet yourself?" Heller asked, making small talk
until he was sure Jane was dressed.

Sperling eyed him with some amusement, "Oh, I dabble."

Jane, still at Heller's back, said, "Christopher is quite a famous poet."

"Not worth mentioning actually," Sperling remarked with
mock humility that was meant to be heard as false. "I hope,"
he said to Jane, "you're not going to recite my list of awards."

"I'm sorry," Heller apologized. "I'm not much of a poetry reader."

"And I'm lousy at long division," Sperling said. "Or whatever it is computers do."

The crowd on the landing was thinning out as people drifted away down the stairs. "How about some drink?" Sperling asked. "Casting out demons is thirsty work. I've got two hours before the red eye leaves for Boston."

"Oh, you don't live in the area?" Heller asked.

Again, Sperling gave him a wry look. "No, no. I'm stuck away up in Harvard Yard. They flew me in just to provide the symbolic paternal presence. Actually, in the church, physical paternity counts for very little. But tonight, I guess Leah wanted to cover all bets."

"Paternal . . . ?" Heller made his bewilderment clear.

"I'm Daphne's father. Didn't Jane tell you? Well, you see how little it matters."

Heller stared at Sperling blankly. He was finally beginning to draw on his trousers. "Conception is carefully, almost artistically arranged in Earthrite. Though I must confess I only half believe all the lore Leah spins around the act. However, it does seem we've produced a remarkable offspring—wouldn't you say, Jane? Must prove something. I wonder if all the variables involved—the moon and stars and personal vibrations—could be programmed into one of your infernal machines, Heller."

Jane had finished dressing. As Heller turned, she said, "I'm worried about Beata. I'd like to stay with her a bit longer. You two can go on." She started back into the sanctuary, wishing the men good night.

"What do we do now?" Heller asked after her, trying to hold her presence a little longer.

She shrugged. "Wait . . . to hear from you, actually. I expect you'll keep us informed." And she was gone. Heller turned back to Sperling, who was leading him down the stairs.

"You said we met before," Heller remarked.

"Also hardly worth mentioning," Sperling said. "Ten years ago, maybe longer—at Harvard. One of those dismal science versus the humanities tournaments. AAAS I think it was. Oh, you wouldn't remember. You must attend scores of them. A batch of us marginal artistic types get invited along. The chorus of lamenting elders for all the Nobel laureates and technocratic mandarins on center stage. I recall that somebody told me you were one of the most dangerous men in American politics. A shrewd prophecy at that distance."

"I'm not in politics," Heller said sourly.

"True, you're *above* politics. That's what makes you so dangerous—operating from that godlike height beyond all petty human good and evil. 'Our Father who art a semi-conductor, hallowed be thy name.' You know, if Machiavelli were alive today, he'd be writing all his books in FORTRAN—knowing where the power lies."

They reached the front door of the bookshop. Samples, wearing an optimistic smile, ushered them into the sweltering night outside. "We're all very hopeful," he told Heller. "That was an extraordinary exercise." He and Sperling exchanged some final remarks at the door. "So, I'll be down for the equinox in September," Sperling said, "if the apocalypse doesn't strike before then." Turning to Heller on the sidewalk outside, he resumed where their conversation had left off.

"We had an encounter at that event, you and I—down a very long table at dinner."

"I don't recall. Sorry."

"Well, it was nothing to be embalmed in amber. You were saying something rather condescending about traditional cultures. Yes, that's it—that it was a pity astronomical computers like Stonehenge had to be burdened with so much excess religious baggage. And I said, on the contrary, it was a pity *our* computers weren't enhanced by such an ennobling higher purpose. Because we were doomed if they could not be. Rather a perceptive augury on my part, come to think of it."

Heller smiled. "You remember the incident in detail."

"Well, how often does one have the chance to contradict one of the most dangerous men in American politics? Actually, I later wrote a little poem about the exchange, so I remember it quite well. I'll send you a copy. Anyway, and then you said something about superstition . . . hocus-pocus, and so on. And

I said I expected that's how the true word of God has always looked to the Philistines. I think I finished calling you a vicious, nihilistic snob. I must have been drinking too much."

Now, just dimly, Heller recalled the incident—though not Sperling's part in it. He remembered it as a nasty encounter with the sort of defunct academic humanist he despised: whining, impotent, vindictive. Had that been Sperling? Stripped of its particulars, the meeting had lodged itself in some corner of his mind as a classic example of the corrosive resentment of the non-scientific intellectual. He had, in fact, drawn upon the image many times in taking his professional bearings. Yes, he remembered now, but he would not give Sperling the satisfaction of admitting the memory.

"No doubt I've blotted the whole incident out of my mind," he said. "At the time, when we were at the conference, were you a member of the church?"

"Just getting into it," Sperling answered. "Yes, about a year before that I had heard a series of lectures by Leah in Cambridge. My first significant brush with the neopagans. I thought of it as some sort of kinky cult at the time. But Leah took my defenses by storm. Remarkable woman, don't you find? God, I'd like to build a whole university around her. She's the embodiment of a liberal education. She's a brilliant biologist, did you know? Wrote a few classic monographs on morphogenesis back in the thirties. They read like poetry. I've been tempted to try a translation. Anyway, I learned from her that there really were alternative realities that could embrace modern science rather than rejecting it. Suddenly, a whole lost world of myth and metaphysics was open to me—as something more than a scholarly boneyard."

"And you've stuck with the church since?" Heller was walking slowly toward his car parked down the street.

"Oh yes. Most exciting thing to enter my life since . . . well, since sex at puberty. Earthrite has changed my poetry radically. And apparently for the better. All the recognition has come in the last five years. Leah introduced me to Goethe, Novalis, Rilke, metaphysical poetry. There's now a depth to my work where there used to be nothing more than a glittering, facile surface. You know: conventional despair, conventional resignation. One-dimensional stuff. I think you would have liked the poetry I used to write. In so many words, it was the unconditional surrender of the human cause."

Heller sighed with irritation. "It must be doing my soul a world of good to hang around here. I take so many mean knocks."

"Sorry," Sperling apologized, not very strenuously. "Own it up to envy on my part."

"Envy?"

"You forgot meeting me. I couldn't forget meeting you. How about that drink?"

Heller was eager to get away. He disliked Sperling, as he disliked most of the indignant artists he met. In his eyes, their rancor only proved they belonged to a dying breed. He admired Jane for having admitted as much about her art, and for not needing to strike out in spite. Now, least of all in his position of vulnerability, did he want to be in Sperling's company. But he did want to learn more about the man's connection with Jane. "I really can't take the time," he told Sperling. "I've actually got a heavy night's work still ahead of me. You understand." Then with his hand on the door handle of his car, he asked, "Incidentally, how long have you and Jane been . . . together?"

Sperling raised an eyebrow archly. " 'Incidentally.' Well, that's the right word. Intimately, we shared an incident just long enough to beget a child—and with no misses, mind you. All part of an arcane rite which deserves to remain the lady's secret. Though actually it was prim and proper to a disconcerting extreme. Almost clinical in its metaphysical precision. Beyond that, Jane and I meet at the various exercises several times a year and exchange notes about Daphne. That's how I came to be cut in on knowledge of your crisis. A legitimate parental concern, I think. Earthrite has odd ideas about procreation and child rearing. Sort of an etherealized eugenics. Personal emotion doesn't need to enter into it—and in this case it doesn't. The church—which is stoutly matriarchal, as you can see—is meant to be the child's family. The father is rather marginal. If you're interested in Jane—'incidentally'—I'd say you stood the proverbial snowball's chance. Any man would. She fled to Earthrite out of a marital conflagration, very badly burned."

"Just asking as part of my background research," Heller explained.

"As the professor said when he got arrested at the orgy."

Heller, shuffling through his keys, unlocked his car. Sperling asked, "May I put an 'incidentally' to you? Incidentally, what happens if tonight's exercise doesn't work? I gather civilization as we know it goes down the tubes as of a week from Wednesday. Correct?"

"Well, you can judge how dire things must be by the fact that I'm here at all. You can guess how much stock I'd put in occult rites."

"And yet here you are."

"Yes."

"Then it's that bad."

Heller had settled behind the wheel of his car. Sperling, closing the door behind him, leaned his large frame over to say a last few words through the open window. "You know, even by our eccentric standards, there's something odd about what happened tonight."

"What's that?"

"You see, this exercise was directed against some evil loose in the world. But what evil would we in the church be concerned about combating? There's a weird ambiguity here."

"I don't follow you," Heller said.

"These bugs . . . they're *your* evil, Heller. But why should they be *ours*? There's something off-center about Earthrite trying to pull your chestnuts out of the fire. If you'll excuse the comparison—could you imagine the synagogues of Nazi Germany praying to keep the trains to Buchenwald running on time?"

"I *don't* excuse the comparison," Heller retorted sharply.

"Well, all right . . . but allowing for the exaggeration, you see my point."

"I talked this over with Leah a week ago. She agreed that the bugs were a danger to everyone."

Sperling paused over a thought, still leaning in at the window. "Well, yes, fair enough. We *should* be responsible. I mean, if people are getting killed. God, it *is* horrible. But there was something unnaturally strained about Beata's performance tonight. As if she found herself working in the wrong direction. Do you see what I mean?"

Heller gave an exasperated sigh. "Sperling, I'm reluctant to talk about any of this as if it deserved serious consideration . . ."

"Yes, but you came, and you lent the drawing . . . and you're leaving, hoping to whatever it is you hold sacred that the magic worked."

Heller relented, suddenly feeling deeply fatigued by his encounter with Sperling. "Yes, that's true. I'm that desperate. In any case, Leah seemed confident afterward. Mrs. Ulrich also."

"Yes, confident that the evil would be vanquished. But *what* evil? *Whose* evil?" He stood up and backed off from the car a pace. "Do you remember your classics? The famous prophecy the oracle at Delphi gave King Croesus? If he marched against the Persians, a great army would be defeated. The king marched, and a great army *was* defeated. His own."

He gave Heller a wink and walked off.

11

1

It was just past midnight when Heller arrived at the Brain. The full moon was riding low in the southern sky; it would soon be setting. Before he headed his car into the underground garage below the Center, he paused to watch until the moon's lower edge touched some distant buildings beyond the Anacostia. Wordlessly, he was offering his own small invocation to a goddess he could not name. Having strayed so far into the lunatic fringe that evening, why not add his own prayer to the rest?

He did not have to return to the Brain that night, but he was too restless with curiosity to sleep. There was a vibrant mixture of exhaustion and exhilaration churning through his nerves, keeping him taut against the demand for rest. The security guard who met him as he left the elevator inside the lobby was not surprised to see him. Heller had been working late for over a week, sometimes at his desk until dawn or spending the night on the sofa in his office. "Evening, Mr. Heller," the guard said. "Working late again?"

"Yes, Bob. For a few hours. How has it been this evening?"

"Funny thing, Mr. Heller. About nine-thirty, a couple of the computers started makin' a hell of a racket. That sort of clickin' sound you know. But really loud."

"Which computers?"

"That sucker in GOD—and the one in Public Opinion. Sam said the one in Econ. was soundin' off too. Maybe they all were. We couldn't get around to check everywhere. There's only four of us on duty nights now." He added the remark to remind Heller that the security force was understaffed. Since Jimmy Willis' death, there had been three resignations. It had not been easy to find replacements.

"That's all you noticed—just the noise?" Heller asked.

"Hey, that was enough, Mr. Heller. I was ready to bat right outa here. Was that the bugs we heard?"

Heller did not answer. He thanked the guard and moved off toward the Government Operations Division at the far end of the lobby. A large placard on the glass door identified the room as a quarantined area not to be entered without official permission. Heller unlocked the door and stepped into the silent room. With infinite caution, he approached the cool metallic oblong of the IBM 370 core and circled it. Unlocking the door, he had tripped an alarm in Central Security and within minutes a second guard was on the scene to investigate.

"It's all right, John," Heller said. "I'm just checking a few pieces of equipment." The IBM 370 had not been used since Ziggy Champolsky's death. It had been reassembled and left idle. Several times over the past few weeks it had been examined by knocking on the exterior, and each time the clicking sound had been heard inside. Having circled the computer core twice, hearing nothing, Heller reached out and knocked lightly on its metal casing. No sound returned. He knocked again, several times, hard.

"Mr. Heller," the guard at the door protested. "I'd be careful if I was you. That computer was kicking up a big fuss this evening. You know the noise I mean."

Heller had his ear against the core. There was no hint of a sound. "How long did the noise go on, John?" he asked.

"Maybe about twenty minutes, half an hour. I called Mr. Levinson, and he heard it too. He had me send everybody who was left in the building home. Except us guards."

"And then what happened, after half an hour?"

"Well, it just stopped. They all stopped, those that was making the noise. All at once."

Heller stood back from the IBM 370 and, taking a breath,

he brought the flat of his hand down as hard as he could on the top of the casing. A loud, dull thud resounded through the room. The guard at the door leaped back, letting the heavy glass panel swing shut. Then, pulling it open, he shouted, "Hey, Mr. Heller, are you crazy?" The room was silent.

Heller turned and walked briskly back through the door, locking it behind him. The guard was still complaining. "There's only a couple of us on duty tonight, you know. I mean, if there's any trouble . . ."

"All right, John," Heller said. "But you see, there was no noise this time. You didn't hear anything, did you?"

"Well, no . . . not this time." He was following Heller across the building toward the Public Opinion Division. "Say, Mr. Heller, these machines, they aren't haunted or something, are they? I mean, it's getting creepy around here, nobody working the place. And at night, with just three or four of us on duty, it gets, well, you know, creepy."

"No, the machines aren't haunted, John. But you see, even the smartest computers in the world have some bugs in them." Heller gave the guard a wink. John returned a queer, uncomfortable look, not knowing how to take the remark. Heller wondered too what he intended by tempting fate so blatantly. He was suddenly feeling buoyantly euphoric.

Heller unlocked the glass door into Public Opinion and stepped in. The guard stayed behind. "You gonna knock on that one too? Hey, Mr. Heller, I don't like this."

"You stay back, John," Heller ordered, "and keep the door open." The Public Opinion computer was a PDP 20. Again, Heller circled the compact core of the machine, drawing his hand along the smooth casing. Then, very softly, he rapped at several points along the sides. Silence. He moved to the other side and rapped harder. Silence again. Finally, as he had done before, he unloaded a sharp slap on the top. When the echo of the blow died away, there was no answering sound from inside. He looked across to John, and asked, "Hear anything?"

"No, sir."

Heller moved across the room to the keyboard and switched the PDP 20 on. He chose a disk pack from the storage rack and

loaded it into the disk drive, then typed out some simple diag-
nostics on the keys. For several minutes, he interrogated the
computer, giving it straight queries and nonsensical ones, burning juice, waiting. There was no sign of irregularity. The machine was working normally, obediently.

"All right, John," he said to the guard. "You can leave me
with it. I'll signal if I need help."

Dubiously, the guard drew off, letting the thick glass door
swing slowly shut. He walked away, looking back several times.
Heller spent another half hour testing the PDP 20. Two or
three more times, with the power up, he circled the computer,
rapping and knocking on its sides.

The machine was silent . . . dead.

The bugs were gone.

2

By two-thirty A.M. Heller had tested the Brain's major computers, including the Sygnos 7000s in Central Processing. All
were silent. Could he take that to mean the nightmare was
over?

Of course, he must not let his hopes rise prematurely, but already his mind was busy listing the computer centers he would
call in the morning to suggest similar tests. He would start
with major installations where the bugs had attacked. It would
not be too early even now to phone through to some of the
European centers, but before he did that, he would test the
Brain's computers once more, in another few hours. And perhaps he should first have one of his machines dismantled.

The evening had taken a heavy toll of his energy; he could
feel a dead weight of fatigue pressing down upon his brow and
eyes. But there was no question of sleeping. He informed Central Security he would be spending the night and settled into
his office. He took a bottle of Dexedrine from his desk, shook
out two tablets and laid them alongside a Styrofoam cup. Then
he put on a pot of coffee to brew. Despite his weariness, he
was feeling the excitement of a man reprieved from a death

sentence, eager to make the most of his time. His mind leaped forward to ambitious prospects. When the crisis was past, there would have to be a well-designed campaign to win back the Center's lost prestige and power. He began to brainstorm a strategy that took the form of an argument with Senator Cory. The ploy would be to insist that the emergency had actually proved the reliability of MASTERNET and the Brain: the system had survived under totally unforeseeable pressures and had even grown stronger, more adaptable by the experience.

In his mental scenario, Heller could imagine Cory becoming more angry and irrationally aggressive. He could see the senator's fury building until he shouted out with impatience, crying for help from his colleagues and supporters. The cry rang in Heller's ears as he went on calmly, confidently, to explain the most valuable lesson to be learned from the crisis—which was the influence of the moon on microprocessors. What a curious thing for him to say . . . but no, Heller would brazen it out. He was fully in charge, moving from strength to strength against his protesting opposition. Again, he could imagine the senator yipping with outrage at such an absurdity. What did the moon have to do with computers? Never batting an eye, Heller, feeling almost giddy with confidence, toyed with Cory's anger. The moon, he explained, does govern the tides. And the tides travel across the shore. The shore is covered with sand, sand is silicon, microchips are made from silicon. A perfectly logical connection. And then he began to laugh at the joke while the senator did a slow burn, shouting out to the applauding audience, "No, no, no!"

But don't you see, Heller was explaining, it's all right to make jokes now. We mustn't be afraid of a little levity. It's only human. Now that the worst is over . . . finished . . . we can afford some humor. And while he was still chuckling at Cory's aggravation, his eyes blinked open and he realized he had been asleep, stretched out on the leather sofa in his office, dreaming.

He jerked himself up, rubbed his eyes and temples, stared at his watch. His own dream laughter and the senator's angry outbursts were still ringing in his ears as if they had gotten nested in the corners of the room. It was just past 4 A.M. He had dozed off despite himself. He made his way unsteadily to his desk. The Dexedrine tablets were still there, waiting to be taken; the coffee brewer, its little light beaming red, was keeping his pot of coffee warm.

No harm done, he thought. All for the best. He had gotten some much needed rest. Now he could make the rounds of the Brain, testing its equipment. He poured out some coffee and took a sip. Something left over from his dream was still buzzing in his ears. No . . . the buzzing was not in his head. It must be in the neon light above . . . a nasty electric sizzle that grated harshly on his sore nerves.

Trying to escape the sound, he took his coffee into his secretary's office, but there he discovered the buzz was even louder. It was not coming from the lights overhead but from the corridor outside. He opened the door and stepped out. The hall was filled with the unpleasant, scraping sound. He followed it around the corner and out on to the mezzanine balcony that overlooked the entrance foyer of the Center. All at once, the blood drained from his face as he stood listening. There was no mistaking the sound. What he heard echoing up from below was the chatter of the bugs, but now amplified to the volume of a pounding surf. It was washing up from somewhere out of sight on the ground level. Where?

He called out in a croaking voice still husky with sleep. "John! Bob! Sam!" None of the security guards responded; none was in sight. He leaned far over the balcony, almost losing his footing, and called again. No answer.

He rushed back to his office and tripped the alarm to Central Security, then returned to the balcony and called again. There was no reply. The chattering sound was so loud in the building it seemed nightmarishly unreal. Could he still be asleep? From somewhere downstairs he heard a huge, resounding concussion—something banging at a wall again and again. He ran to the stairs and started down. At the bottom, off to his right, he saw a crumpled form: one of the guards, lying face down against the information counter, a telephone with a torn cord still clutched in his hand. Heller rushed to him and turned him over. He could barely make out the ruined features of Bob Williams, who had greeted him when he arrived that night. The face was even more mutilated than Jimmy Willis' had been. Heller realized: Senator Cory's cry in his dream had been Bob calling out from the foot of the stairs. He began to go dizzy and numb, his throat struggling against a sickening thrust. But then a piercing pain struck at the back of his hand, at his arm. Insects from the dead guard's body were leaping at him. Another bite at the cheek, another at the ear. Heller jumped back, swatting at his arms and face, then bolted forward across the entrance foyer toward the door.

The chattering sound swelled up more loudly, off to the right. Heller yanked at the door, but of course it was locked. He fumbled in his pocket, one, then the other. Before he could draw out his key, he turned to find a living wave of bugs seething over the floor toward him. The doors of the Econ. Division were open and the swarm was pouring out of the room and across the foyer. It moved like an effervescent gray froth, bugs leaping over one another, rolling forward and down in a wild, devouring cascade.

For a moment, Heller's amazement overcame his horror; he stood gaping at the sight, holding off the realization that he would not have time to unlock the door, that he must run, find another escape. Then, as panic gripped him, he turned and darted toward the opposite end of the hall. Ahead of him, the glass double doors of the Public Opinion Division were closed, locked. He dug into his pocket again for the key, then saw that behind the glass barrier, in every part of the huge room, the bugs were gathered in roiling, chitinous heaps that swelled and fell. As he reached the doors, he saw a rolling tide of the things hurl itself over desks and tables, slamming thunderously against the quivering glass wall. With his hands against the glass, he felt the impact, a terrific blow. The wall would not hold. He could not pass that way.

A trickle of the bugs was even now seeping through the crack of the door, falling on the floor outside, scrambling in all directions like a hungry pack on the scent of prey. Heller turned. The stairs he had come down were now covered with insects making their way to the upper levels. He dashed down a central corridor that connected with the rear of the Brain. He was heading for a staircase down to the garage. But as he raced along the hall, he heard a sharp crack and the shattering of glass. Emerging from the corridor, he saw the glass wall of the Law Enforcement Division breached and splintered, broken under the massed and battering weight of the insects that were now flooding through the jagged gap like an angry sea that had breached its dike.

To his left, across the rear corridor, there was an emergency fire exit: the door that led to the garage. There was just a chance that Heller might get to it before the bugs covered the floor between. He started, made it halfway across, then pulled up short. The door ahead of him was opening. A grotesque, misshapen figure came collapsing through it. It was a man howling with pain: one of the guards, covered, heaped over with the bugs, carrying them along, trailing them at his feet. Heller could not tell which of the men it was; his head and face were a living helmet of swarming insect life. The figure was stumbling blindly toward Heller; he backed off, then saw the bugs to his right, from the shattered Law Enforcement wall, surging forward toward him. He turned and raced for a staircase that would take him to the upper levels. As the stricken guard went down, screaming, the bugs covered him like a carnivorous surf. Even muffled and distorted by pain, the voice was familiar; it was Sam Burcholzer. He must have tried to escape through the garage and had not made it. The entire lower floor now belonged to the swarm, possibly the lower levels of the building too. Heller had no choice but to go up—back toward his office. In that direction, he realized he had no escape. But there was a slender chance of safety, the one part of the Brain that could be made secure against the bugs.

As he raced up the staircase, the lights blinked, blinked again, then dimmed and went out. Something had happened to the power supply. If the bugs were at the garage level, where Sam had tried to escape, they must have penetrated to plant operations. There they could interfere with all the electrical functions of the Center.

Heller groped his way into his office, opened his desk and came up with a flashlight. He used it to locate a key in one of the bottom drawers. At the rear of his office there was a storage closet. In it was a narrow metal door and beside it a small steel cabinet the size of a fuse box. Both were equipped with electronic locks. Heller punched four buttons on the cabinet and it swung open; inside was a lockswitch. He inserted the key he had taken from his desk and turned it, activating an emergency power supply concealed in the depths of the building. Next, he punched out the lock-code on the metal door. It opened, letting Heller tug open another inner door. Behind it there was a small elevator whose light was already lit from the emergency supply.

Heller hesitated for a moment on the threshold of the elevator, then turned back into his office, following the beam of his flashlight. On the wall behind his desk was the fire alarm. As he reached it, the chattering of the insects filled his secretary's office. He shined the flashlight into the adjoining room and saw the bugs surging through the entrance from the corridor, covering the walls and floor, leaping toward his office. He had made a mistake in turning back; the bugs were coming too fast.

He smashed the tiny glass window of the fire alarm and searched for the handle inside, pulled it and turned to dash for the waiting elevator, slamming his office door as he passed. A dagger point of pain struck at one ankle, then at the other. Suddenly it was as if he were running through fire. The insects were in his office, attacking him, leaping up his body. Ahead of him, back through the closet, he could see the lighted oblong of the elevator only several feet away. Heller felt a touch of flame at his eye. Swatting at it, he knocked his glasses away. His cheeks and neck prickled with bites. He lurched toward the elevator, carrying a load of insects on his body and clothes, trying to the last to brush them from his face. There was only one button on the control panel of the elevator; he stabbed at it and the door slammed shut, cutting off the sound of the bugs.

The elevator hummed and descended rapidly. Heller knew

the door to the elevator shaft would close airtight above him. The only bugs he had to contend with now were those on his body. He threw off his coat and shirt, batting at the remaining bugs, struggling to keep them from his eyes and ears. The elevator stopped. Before opening the door, Heller ripped a fire extinguisher from its casing; squeezing his eyes closed and holding his breath, he used the force of the spray to drive bugs out of his hair and from his body. Only then did he open the door. Gagging, his throat filled with sodium fumes, he staggered out of the elevator and pressed a button to close the door behind him. There were still bugs gnawing at him; his throat was afire with pain, one eye was already swollen shut.

His vision blurred. Heller made his way into a nearby bathroom. There were showers in the room—there to wash away traces of radioactivity. Heller used them full blast to drive off the clinging insects. He kicked off his shoes and struggled to pull off his remaining clothing under the pounding spray. His ankles were so wreathed with insects, he could hardly get free of his socks and pants. As he knocked the bugs away toward the drain, his lower legs ran with blood, pierced by countless bites. The floor of the shower turned red around his feet; he was losing too much blood.

After several moments, he emerged from the shower, faint and exhausted. His body was severely lacerated from top to bottom. Shivering with shock and pain, he could still feel bugs drilling mercilessly into his flesh and muscle; one had entered his cheek just below the eye; others were somewhere in his throat. He knew he would not stay conscious long in this condition; his life was bleeding away. But if any part of the Brain could be kept secure from the insects, this was the room. He was two stories below the garage level of the Center in a concrete bunker that could be entered only by the airtight elevator shaft he had closed behind him.

He was in the underground fallout shelter of the Brain designed for its director and senior staff in the event of thermonuclear war. It was a new part of the Center, still sparsely furnished and unequipped with computers. Heller had visited it only twice before on routine drills.

At a desk in the central control room, Heller reached for a hot-line telephone. Without his glasses, with one eye swollen shut, he would not have been able to punch out a number on the phone; but the hot line was connected directly to an emergency switchboard at the Pentagon. Heller fought to stay conscious as he waited for a response. There was no immediate answer. In his ear, the phone hooted with a siren-blast urgency. Finally a tired voice came on the line. "War room," it said. His mind fogging over rapidly, Heller managed to give the message. "This is a Code Lazarus call. Heller at Station 12 . . ."

Then he fainted across the desk.

12

1

Heller remembered the hours that followed as a troubled voyage across small, half-submerged islands of consciousness. Again and again, his mind flickered awake, struggled to hold its lucidity against merciless fatigue and shock, then slipped back beneath the wave of sleep like a shell sucked from the beach by the undertow. Once or twice, he woke long enough to recognize the bunker around him, to look anxiously for any sign of the bugs. For the most part, he surfaced into a brief, delirious haze. He only faintly recalled being carried from the shelter into the open air. A face that was a blur bent above him in the sunlight to tell him he was safe. But Heller preferred the darkness that dragged at his mind; he yielded and returned, possessed by the sense that he had something still to do there in the lightless depth. "Not yet," he said, or wanted to say. Eagerly, he let himself slide away from the world.

In his hallucinatory sleep, his mind was strangely alert, expectant. He was swimming a dark oceanic current down and down, moving swiftly, purposefully, to a crushing depth. What was his task here? He was pursuing a great, taunting secret somewhere far below, knowledge he realized could be his only in this fleeting, imperiled moment. He knew exactly where it was—just ahead, at the bottom of the sea. There, he scooped up a handful of sand and let it wash away until there was one bright grain left in his palm, the one grain that mattered.

Here is where the answer is, he thought, in this single grain. It was his, but he must take possession of it now before they brought him back to the surface. Quickly, he entered the grain, piercing its exterior like a diver. He was contracting rapidly, miniaturizing himself by a process that made him feel clever and bold. He was master of the great and small, master of the great *within* the small. Now he could see: the inside of the sand grain was a microcode etched in the gleaming silicon. Expertly, he moved forward along its intricate grooves and channels, deciphering its meaning as he went. For an instant, as he plunged deeper into the labyrinth of the message, he became afraid. I am such a long way from the sun, he thought, and shivered with the watery cold. But no, he must go farther in. The secret of the code was there, at the inner compacted core, the deep inside of the world.

All at once, the darkness melted away, illuminated as if by a black flame. He could see that, within the grain, he had found an undersea cave carved in the glittering stone. He was in the crystalline heart of the code.

He struggled forward, stiff now with a sense of terrific density. He saw he was no longer alone. There were people here, rows and rows of them, tightly packed along the sides of the cave, motionless millions petrified into the brittle quartz. He paused to pass his hand over their sleeping faces; it slid as if across a glass surface. Yes, he thought, they are all finally here, like insects in a crystal hive. We have finally captured the life of the world, all the brains of all the people who ever lived, preserved in the imperishable silicon. Here, no one will ever die, nothing will be lost or forgotten. Everything will be perfect forever.

It grew harder to move. Movement was out of place here. Here stillness reigned, the ultimate solid state. But he was not ready to rest yet. There was one face he was looking for. *Hers.* He wanted to explain the secret to her, offer it to her as a gift. And, yes, there she was. He had found her among the millions, more beautiful than ever, quiescent as a crystal statue. No, not quite. Her eyes had not yet grown still. They were awake and alive, staring out at him, pleading for release. One stubborn sign of vitality in the lightless cave.

No, no, it's useless, he told her. There's no reason to struggle. There's no way back now. The sun is very far away. We must give that up. *Trust me*. We will find peace here.

He reached out to comfort her, but his hands were numb, the flesh dying into immortality. He was joining her and all the others. Did he wish to? In any case, he was powerless to resist. There was no turning back from the invincible pressure that was crushing him. Be still, he said to her. See how perfect it is.

But her eyes would not stop crying out against the perfection. He wondered why. Why could she not accept and surrender?

And then he knew—quite suddenly, as all power of motion left him and his body petrified.

This was not perfection. This was death. This was the pitiless grave of the universe, the entropic abyss. He had gotten it wrong—upside down, inside out. Here life stopped, mind stopped. And here he was stopping, with a single thought that would be frozen into his brain forever—the knowledge that the deathless crystal was the *other* eternity, the *wrong* eternity. The code was *exactly wrong*. And now it was his prison, the world's prison forever. She had known better, and he had betrayed her.

Spurred by panic, fighting against the deadening compaction, he flung himself toward her, seeking to shatter the paralytic stillness that gripped her. Under his blows, the crystal rippled into water, and the water gave way. He was back through the surface, free. His eyes fought away the sleep that covered them, and he woke clinging to the conviction that he had learned what was *exactly wrong*. Now he knew, and therefore . . . therefore . . .

The thought was lost, torn from him on the threshold of waking. But it would return to him later, the dim memory of a distant betrayal.

2

He was lying in a hospital bed. Above him, two intravenous drip bottles were methodically measuring saline and blood into his veins. He could not tell if his rescue from the Brain had happened hours ago or days ago. There was a nurse on hand to tell him that much. She said he had been taken from the bunker late Saturday morning. Now, it was mid-afternoon Sunday, a day and a half since the attack, and he was in Walter Reed Hospital. The nurse would tell him nothing about his injuries, but within five minutes there was a doctor at his side examining him.

"You're a lucky man," the doctor said. "You lost a lot of blood, and your eye suffered some damage." (Heller noticed: half his vision was gone, his left eye covered by bandages.) "But otherwise you seem in good shape. The worst injury seems to be around your throat. That's where you did most of your bleeding. You may eventually need some skin grafts there."

"There were millions of them," Heller said in a weak, croaking voice, struggling to throw off the narcotic haze that filled his head. "Where are they now?"

"The bugs, you mean? Well, there were at least four of them *in* you. That may not be all. You'll have to tell us if you feel any more of them troubling you."

"I mean . . . at the Center. Are they still there?"

The doctor shook his head. "Not my department. Your colleague Mr. Levinson will be here shortly. He's been calling in all day, waiting for you to come around."

Less than half an hour later, Berny Levinson was in the room to answer Heller's question. "They're all back in the computers, it would seem, and chattering away worse than ever. The Center is a shambles. The whole electrical system has been demolished, chewed to pieces—insulation, wiring, everything. We've closed up shop and relocated to the Administrative Services Building. It will take days to make the place

usable. The Center is under armed guard. Do you know h
the glass got smashed?"

"They bunched together, hoards of them," Heller said.
"Flung themselves at the walls like battering rams. The guards
—what happened to them?"

"Dead," Levinson said flatly. "Same condition as Jimmy
Willis. Looks as if they were taken completely by surprise.
Two of them were found in Central Security—never even got
out the door. One of them must have lasted long enough to
turn in an alarm. By the time the fire department showed up,
the bugs were out of sight."

"I turned in the alarm," Heller said.

"So they didn't even get the chance to do that. We know
what the damage was, but you know what happened inside
better than we do. Lyman's on his way over for a full report."

The doctor had finished his examination and was preparing
a hypodermic. Heller asked, "When can I get out?"

"You've lost a lot of blood," the doctor answered. "It will
take another day to get you off the IV—and longer for that
eye to heal. We really don't know how bad that is." He estimated a week or longer.

"I can't lose that much time," Heller protested.

"I understand," the doctor replied. "Fact is—we don't have
any experience with wounds like yours. At this point, we're just
treating you for shock, inflammation, possible infection—and,
of course, the loss of blood. We don't know how deep some of
those bites go, or whether they're toxic. We can't even be sure
we've gotten all the critters out of you. We'd like to keep you
under observation for a bit. What we learn may come in
handy in the future. I gather we may be in for a lot more of
this . . ." The remark was more of a question than a statement.

After the doctor left, Levinson said, "I told Lyman all I
knew. There was no way to hold back. The kid, the drawing,
the church . . . he knows it all."

"He's mad?"

"In his own quiet way, yeah. I'd say he's incensed. It can't
be because he could make any more sense of this psychic stuff

than we can. But you know how Lyman is about the chain of command. We held out on him and started our own line of inquiry."

"How did they get me out of the Center?" Heller asked.

"Lyman knew from your phone call that you were in the bunker. He guessed what the problem was and sent some Marine Special Forces to the rescue. They had to wait nearly four hours for the bugs to withdraw before they could go in. Then they just rode down the elevator shaft and pulled you out, You're lucky the bugs didn't get into the auxiliary power supply. You might have suffocated if they had."

"Also lucky we haven't installed our emergency systems in the bunker," Heller added. "If there had been computers in there, they might have been infested too. The bugs seemed to be migrating through every piece of equipment we have."

When Levinson received word of Heller's recovery, he had notified Touhy. At once, Touhy ordered a conference at Walter Reed. Waiting for his arrival, Levinson ran through a rapid review of the last thirty-six hours. The briefing did little to lift Heller's spirits. Two more major military installations that were near total closure had been placed on the Center's critical list. They were the Logistical Command Headquarters in Ohio, and the Readiness Command in Florida. At both sites, data equipment was heavily infested with bugs; scores of computer technicians were incapacitated by several weeks of intensifying data pox; errors and confusion were mounting as poorly trained personnel took over. Even routine operations were hamstrung.

"As you can imagine," Levinson said, "losing facilities of this importance has the brass in a near panic. Even where there haven't been open attacks, the military is running out of expertise to pilot the technology. DoD is talking about drafting computer talent out of the civilian economy, which would take months. We've got these two bases plugged into as much alternative hardware as we can find. There's no way we can duplicate all the data services they need. God help us if there were a serious military alert now."

Levinson shuffled more lists and reports out of his briefcase.

Outbreaks of data pox in connection with minicomputers and computer peripherals were steadily escalating, with many unconfirmed rumors of bugs. Heller, still struggling to clear his head, could not take in all the details. Recognizing that, Levinson skipped to a quick summary. "Just assume everything is 10 per cent worse than you remember. I have a rumor that the FAA is going to order suspension of all computerized air traffic control. The systems are crapping out too often; pilots won't put up with it. If that directive goes through, air transport will be cut back to 1960 levels or worse. Also, we have trouble with the unions: Office Workers and State-Federal-Municipal. They're talking up a nationwide boycott of all data processing equipment. That will probably receive official sanction early next week. It won't make much difference, actually. Fact is, everybody remotely connected with computers outside the military has been avoiding them for weeks now. Can't say I blame them."

Less than an hour after Heller came to, Touhy arrived with his crisis team—Haseltine, Kilraddin and Schaeffer. Heller at once noticed a distinct chill in Touhy's manner, a shift in their relationship that was not promising. Quickly, he reported his experience in the Center, then went back over it in minute detail. He was quizzed closely on every characteristic of the bugs' behavior. Everything he said was taken on a tape recorder by Schaeffer.

Haseltine had a question. "When the bugs went after you or the guards, could you tell what they were responding to? Motion, sound, smell . . . what?"

Heller tried to remember, then shook his head. "I can't tell. It went too fast. Certainly I was moving when they came after me. But it was as if they were searching for a human presence in all directions, blindly. When they find it, they start chattering faster, louder. Maybe that's a signal. One thing I should emphasize. My distinct impression was that the bugs weren't just coming out of the computers; they were being *generated* by them—millions more than could ever fit in the machines. They were filling whole rooms, enough of them to cover the ground everywhere. Sooner or later, they'd get to you by sheer multiplication. It's inconceivable that they could all have vanished again so quickly. There couldn't possibly be enough space in the computers to hold them."

"Yes," Touhy remarked pointedly. "It's almost supernatural, you might say."

"The broken walls," Major Kilraddin commented. "That's worth noting. They were shattered into tiny splinters under terrific impact. That's inch-thick construction glass. It would take a high caliber tank gun to do that kind of damage."

There was a pause as Touhy checked with each member of his team for more questions. Then he asked, "And before the attack, Tom—where were you?" Earthrite had finally entered the conversation.

Unblinking, Heller replied, "At a pagan ritual, Lyman. A rite of the full moon. We were trying to reverse a psychic materialization by the use of incantations and alchemical magic." He waited for the bewildered and frowning response he expected. Touhy and his team exchanged enigmatic glances, neither surprised nor puzzled. Heller asked, "If I had told you that a week ago, what would you have made of it?"

Touhy answered with measured calm. "I would have said you were on to a good thing."

Heller wondered if Touhy was ribbing him. He wasn't. He was dead serious.

"Mind you," Touhy went on, "maybe ten days earlier than that, I would have thought you were plain crazy. We began to play with the psychic angle about two weeks ago. And I do mean 'play.' It wasn't easy to touch, I admit. Not only because the idea was bizarre, but because we didn't have any connections with anything paranormal to build on. We didn't know about the little girl's drawing or the church, you see. We started consulting authorities in the field, but we were just flying blind. That's why it would have been good to know what you knew, Tom."

Heller felt the impact of Touhy's remarks, the impatience and disappointment behind them. "You never mentioned that hypothesis to me," he said in his defense. "Why?"

"Maybe it seemed too wild."

"That's how it's been on my side too. I held back becau̱ thought this might be garbage. I was too embarrassed to tell you I was flirting with the idea."

"Now you don't think it's garbage?" Touhy asked.

"I don't think it's garbage," Heller muttered soberly. "I learned the hard way."

Asking no permission to smoke in Heller's room, Touhy lit a cigar, revolved it methodically in his fingers and blew out a cloud of smoke. His manner was still remote, ungiving. He was not thawing out. "So it seems we both might have done well to let each other in on our little secrets. Now, tell us everything about Friday evening. And please don't leave anything out. Especially not the weird parts, all right?"

Heller recounted the exercise at Earthrite in as much detail as he could recollect. As he did so, Captain Schaeffer took careful notes, picking up all the names mentioned. Touhy interrupted at one point to underscore the loss of the original drawing. "That wasn't wise," he said.

"We have copies," Heller reminded him.

Touhy responded with a disapproving grunt. "Why do you think the bugs attacked like that afterward? Do you connect that with the ritual?"

"The ritual," Heller said, "was an attempt to get rid of them. If it makes any sense to suggest it, the attack could have been retaliation from a determined opposition. I don't know how else to regard it." Then, contritely, he added, "Look, Lyman, with the benefit of hindsight, I see I was wrong to hold this back. I simply couldn't imagine we'd reach this point. I'm frankly amazed, even now, that you're hearing me out."

Working at his cigar, as smooth and cool as ever, Touhy said, "You know, Tom, until the Second World War, atomic energy was regarded as so much theoretical moonshine—even in the eyes of leading physicists. That's exactly what Rutherford called it—'moonshine.' We've learned to take a lot of far-out things seriously over at DoD. We can't afford to be doctrinaire. One of the advantages of super-secrecy: it lets you take a few flyers you couldn't possibly justify to intelligent public criticism. My own policy has been: if it looks like a weapon, research it. If it works, grab it. This looks like a weapon. I want it. Or at least I want to make sure *nobody* gets it."

Heller's mind flashed back to Jane Hecate's words. "And what will you and your friends do if our ritual works?" Now he knew. Had he ever been in any real doubt?

"Incidentally," Touhy continued, "you were right in singling out the McGill project for special attention. That's the major resource we've been using. It's where we seem to be getting the best return on our mad money."

Surprise came over Levinson's face. He glanced at Heller, then at Touhy. "I hadn't gotten around to that yet. How did you know we were on to McGill?"

"I've been holding out on you a little too," Touhy answered. "The Brain processes a lot of classified material for us. We had to make sure your security was backstopped."

Heller made the connection. "Byers is your man."

Touhy nodded. "Just a sort of trip-wire safeguard. He's supposed to let us know if there are serious leaks. Since the Brain closed down, we've been checking with him regularly. Sorry, Tom. But we weren't as shocked as you may think to know you were on to psychic sabotage. Our thoughts were turning that way too."

"It isn't sabotage," Heller was quick to insist. "There's no subversive intention here. Berny must have told you: the Earthrite people blundered into this."

Touhy paused to exhale a stream of smoke. "That's something we can't know for certain until we've checked these people out."

For an instant, Heller's brain reeled. Did he really understand what was being said? In so many words, he was being told that Earthrite might have duped him, that the church might be part of a calculated effort to subvert the world's data technology. That was too wild for Heller to take in. Did Touhy believe he could be that gullible? Or was it possible that his own intellectual principles had been cunningly used against him by people who knew he would be unable to recognize their true purposes behind a veil of occult lore? Feebly,

Heller remarked, "I'm sure you won't find anything of that nature involved."

"I sincerely hope not," Touhy said. "For one thing, I haven't got the ghost of an idea how we'd interpret such a finding. We have confirmation that the Soviets are as badly crippled by the bugs as we are. Maybe worse. We're on the point of setting up some form of bilateral co-operation to go at this together. That's thanks to you, Tom. Your connection with Khadzhinov seems to have swung the Soviets behind the proposition. So if there's sabotage involved here, it's a third party operation—maybe something outside the bounds of conventional politics."

"But who . . . ?" Heller asked helplessly.

Touhy wagged his head. "Once we get beyond East, West, Third World—and I think that's where we could be with this —we're in outer darkness, at least from the viewpoint of DoD. In any case, we're bringing in our principal researcher from McGill to deal with the spooky end of this. His name is Gable. Very sharp young man. Yale and UC-Berkeley background. Strong credentials in psychology, neurophysiology, all the appropriate fields. I've been in touch with him twice now over the past few weeks. He's got a number of rather original ideas. He'll be flying in this evening. He needs to be briefed by you as soon as possible, Tom. Will you be up to that by tomorrow morning?"

Heller nodded. "Just instruct the medics here—no sedatives tonight. And tell them I have to begin taking calls, seeing people. Don't let them isolate me."

Touhy agreed. "You understand, I'll expect you to give Gable your full co-operation. We've lost a lot of valuable time. I want things to go as smoothly as possible from this point forward. You're our main contact with the Earthrite people. You've got influence with the girl's mother. That's a crucial connection for us. I want you to do all you can to strengthen it and make it available to Gable. I think you'll find he's reliable."

The word passed across Heller's nerves like a razor. He

remembered what Jane had said about reliability. He suddenly realized that, all the while he had been talking to Touhy, nothing had been so much on his mind as regaining his own reliability in official eyes. He was not sure he had succeeded. Something he could only identify as distrust lingered in Touhy. Why? What more did he expect?

Before he left, Touhy asked Levinson if he had shown Heller any newspapers. Levinson hadn't. "You were lucky to sleep through this," Touhy said, dropping copies of the Washington *Post* and the New York *Times* on Heller's bed. "We had no choice but to be co-operative with the press—once the four guards were found and the fire department was on the scene. The only thing we've been able to hold back is the damage to some of the key military installations. And, of course, the occult connection. But maybe your friends at Earthrite will leak that item for us." He gave a nasty twist to the phrase "your friends." Then, not even wishing Heller a good night, he left with his team.

Spread across Heller's bed, the newspapers screamed their headlines off the page.

FOUR DEAD IN FREAK ATTACK ON DATA CONTROL CENTER

WORLD DATA SYSTEMS THREATENED BY UNIDENTIFIED INSECTS

His own name appeared farther down the page.

THOMAS HELLER, BRAIN BOSS, CRITICALLY INJURED

The smaller print was a blur to his one working eye. Levinson came to his rescue. "I found these on the floor of your office." He held out the eyeglasses Heller had dropped escaping from the bugs. As he took them, a thought clicked into place in his memory.

"Berny," he asked, "did you recover any of my clothes from the bunker?"

Levinson shook his head. "I checked through after they brought you out. What was left of them really couldn't have been rewoven, I'm afraid."

"My wallet . . . what about that?"

Levinson opened a drawer in Heller's bedside cabinet. "Never fear. We managed to save your credit cards," he said wryly, producing the wallet. Heller searched through it and took out Professor Ulrich's note card. On it, carefully written in a heavy Germanic script, were the words:

Hieronymous Lavater, *Arcana Anatomica: Tractatus Secundus Cum Tabulam Arteriarum Corporis Humani, Ope et Beneficio Microscopiorum*, Leiden, 1637, pp. cccxxii–cccxli.

Heller handed the card to Levinson. "Do me a favor," he said. "Have somebody run this citation down. I'd like a Xerox of the pages given and a translation, if that's possible. If you can't find a copy closer to home, try the University of Basel."

Levinson read the card and cast a puzzled glance toward Heller. "A little light reading to hasten your recuperation?"

"Professor Ulrich passed it along to me. A report—supposedly —of a materialization. Let's see how accurate his scholarship is." One more thought crossed Heller's mind. "Oh yes. Will you get in touch with Leah Hagar at the Hartmann School? I owe her church some money—obviously *not* for services rendered. Ask her how much the air fare and other expenses come to for the Ulrichs' visit— and don't let her put you off." Levinson was giving him a quizzical eye. Defensively, Heller added, "You heard Lyman tell me to stay close to these people. Besides, I made her a promise about it."

3

With Touhy's help, Heller persuaded his doctors to put him back in touch with the world that afternoon. It meant he would have to do without the more powerful pain-killers that might fog his mind, but he was determined not to let his injuries isolate him. His throat and ankles, their pain dulled only by aspirin, quickly lost their numbness and became a constant throbbing distraction that left him edgy and impatient. Working against the pain, he took calls—one from his ex-wife, another from Christopher Sperling, another from Kayla Breen. They had seen reports of the attack on the Brain and phoned with messages of concern.

"I'll tell you the truth," Sperling confessed, "I'm scared shitless. Should I be?"

"You should," Heller told him. "Also you should keep quiet about your connection with this—both for the sake of the church and yourself. Don't start publishing poetry on the subject yet."

Sperling agreed. "I can't help feeling that Leah and the Ulrichs are out of their depth. They've released a jinni they might not be able to bottle up again. If I were you, I wouldn't lean too heavily on their assistance. I say that with profound regret."

Heller raised another matter. "Is there any chance you can be with Jane for the next week or so? There's going to be a lot of official investigating going on in and around Earthrite. It may worry her."

"What are you concerned about?"

"I'm not sure. It's just that I'm not on top of things now. She may need help."

"Jane's a strong lady," Sperling assured him. "And she has plenty of support in the church." There was a pause. Then he asked suspiciously, "Your people wouldn't be up to anything nasty, would they?"

"I don't know." Heller made his terse confession of uncertainty sound ominous.

"Well, I could get down early Thursday for the rest of the week," Sperling said. "Meanwhile, she can always call." Before he hung up, he added, "You know, she's not in the habit of looking to me for very much help. All she ever really needed from me she took seven years ago."

Kayla's phone call carried an even more distressed note. Heller had done little more than assure her that he was alive and conscious when he realized her anxiety was not primarily for him. She was worried about her show. The repeat broadcast of "Wonder/Wander" at the Brain would have to be canceled with less than a week's notice. "We won't even have time to change the listing in *TV Guide*." Annoyance crackled in her voice.

"Is that bad?" Heller asked.

"It's embarrassing. My department head wanted to drop the rerun last month, after those two men were killed at the Brain. I said no. I was going on your assurance. The worst thing is we've run ads for the show in lots of school publications. And we're over budget on our promotions already. I even shot the last of our Mobil oil funding for a big spread in *The American Education Review*."

Heller almost laughed. So that was "the worst thing." He wondered if he should remind her that greater matters might be at stake in the collapse of the Brain. Instead he apologized, letting a quiet sigh of weariness sound through as a small plea for sympathy.

"I wish I had trusted my instincts about this," Kayla muttered.

"Which were?"

"To cancel. I didn't think you were going to pull out of this mess so neatly."

She was working to put him on the defensive, as if he had deceived her into scheduling the rerun. "Kayla," he said, "I'm sorry about your show. But frankly it wasn't one of the things I was most concerned about."

Suddenly her tone softened. "You could make it up to me."

"Make it up? How?"

"It would help if I could do some favors around this place. You know Lloyd Briggs . . ."

Of course he did. Briggs was head of CBS News. Heller had done shows for him; their paths had crossed several times at social events in New York and Washington.

"Lloyd's putting together a blockbuster special report on the computers. He's asked to use a few segments of the 'Wonder/Wander' show for background. He wants an interview with you, something exclusive. Let me set it up for him."

"Kayla, I'm in no shape to be televised."

"A consultation, then," Kayla urged. "Something off the record." Her voice became cagey. "Don't you want to make sure

CBS comes up with the right angle? Lloyd's taking a pretty critical approach. I think he's out for blood."

Heller pondered the proposition. Kayla wasn't requesting a favor; she was intimidating him for all she was worth.

"Besides," she added, "I'd love to pay you a visit. Give me an excuse for coming down."

"All right, Kayla," Heller agreed. It was a weary surrender.

Sleep did not come easily that night. Pain kept his nerves alert despite his exhaustion. Picking his way, drowsy and one-eyed, through the newspaper accounts Touhy had left him, Heller was surprised to find a small oasis of relief forming in the middle of his troubles. The truth about the data pox—or at least most of it—was now the news of the day. It was no longer his responsibility to evade or deceive. Nor would he have to underplay the gravity of the crisis. By way of frantic journalistic hyperbole, his once private anguish was shifting toward a familiar public identity. The bugs were becoming a prime-time disaster story, *another* disaster story to take its place alongside energy shortages, oil spills, electrical grid failures, nuclear power scares. From here on, it would become almost mandatory for everybody concerned to heighten the drama. Rather than continuing to minimize the emergency, he could now push it to the limit.

Still groggy and aching from his injuries, Heller allowed himself to glean what crumbs of consolation he could around the edges of disaster. He let his mind wander back to his undergraduate reading. Gibbon's *Decline and Fall.* All the emperors who had earned their place in history by skillfully shrinking the boundaries of Roman power, leading the long disciplined retreat before the advance of barbarism and disorder. Now, in a matter of months, his empire, the vast electronic empire that had so swiftly girdled the globe with a common mentality, a common language, a universal standard of progress and well-being, was failing massively at its center and in all its provinces. Would his role at the helm of state be the same—to prepare the way for dignified defeat, to smooth the path into another age of barbarism?

13

1

When they returned to Heller's bedside Monday morning, Haseltine and Schaeffer were grim-faced and haggard, an unmistakable sign of bad news and a sleepless night. Accompanying them were Professor Gable and another, older man of immense size, wearing clerical garb and dark, blindman's glasses. Before introductions were made, Haseltine asked if Heller had received any word about WIMEX. He hadn't.

"It happened early this morning—before dawn," Haseltine said.

"An attack?" Heller asked. Haseltine nodded yes. "Bad?"

"Bad. Looks like another Ames."

Heller winced. WIMEX was the World-Wide Military Command and Control System, the Pentagon's most ambitious computerized telecommunications network. More than a score of major military command posts worked out of the system, among them NORAD, the North American Air Defense Command at Colorado Springs. Ever since the Brain had been closed down, Heller had known that cushioning WIMEX against serious disruption would have to be his highest priority. Now, apparently, the provisions he and his staff had made had been put to the test, and, to judge from the worry he saw in Haseltine's face, they had failed.

"Berny will be in to brief you later," Haseltine said. "He's been up to his ears all morning." He passed on rapidly, eager to get the interview under way. "We realize you're still recovering your strength. I'm sure Professor Gable will make this as short as possible.

Professor Richard Gable was an intense young man with doleful eyes and a badly pitted face. His mouth had hardened into a sour curl at the corner that gave him a fixed expression of acerbity and arrogance. Before more than a few words had passed between them, Heller recognized the man's type: the tough-guy academic, hard-boiled and hard-driving. It was an angular, aggressive style he had often encountered among the behavioral scientists. Insecure about the status of their discipline, and for that reason highly defensive, they frequently substituted truculence for rigor.

From the moment Gable entered the room, Heller detected an air of surly impatience about him, as if he had been summoned far too late to take charge where others had blundered and failed. The clergyman Gable brought with him was not entirely blind. His narrow eyes, squinting and flickering behind their heavy dark lenses, managed to wedge a thin sliver of vision into the world; they strained steadily in Heller's direction. He was introduced as Father Bernard Guiness, Gable's research assistant. Nothing more was said to explain his presence. Gable guided him to a chair near the head of Heller's bed; the old man awkwardly lowered his bulky frame to a sitting position and finally dropped into the seat with a loud grunt and an embarrassed laugh. His face, florid and mushy, crowned by a high pompadour of white hair, wore a perpetually impudent grin. He stuck out a hand in Heller's direction, wheezing heavily as if recovering from some extreme exertion.

"You're a priest?" Heller asked as they shook hands. The old man did not release his grip at once, but held Heller's hand firmly while he answered.

"Ah, well, once a priest, always a priest," he said, the grin becoming more exaggerated. He spoke in a hoarse, breathy voice, his accent thickly Irish. "Oh, but not of the Mother Church, it's a pity to tell. Not any longer, no, no. You might say I'm a bit of a maverick, Dr. Heller. You see, the Church will not respect any miracles she cannot own. But my vocation this last thirty years has been the world's wealth of miracles hidden in the poorest and humblest among us. The great gift of the mind, you see, that makes us all Powers and Dominions of the most high." Guiness was still gripping Heller's hand, flexing it, running his fingers over the imprisoned palm. His answer was overdone, deliberately so. He seemed to be affecting a role: the comic and garrulous old Irishman, inviting everyone to laugh at him. No one did. He was on the point of saying more, when Gable reached out to draw his arm back. The old man released Heller's hand with a soft chuckle and settled back in his chair, muttering to himself under his breath.

Gable, shuffling nervously through a stack of notes and papers, moved quickly into the business at hand, speaking to Heller without making eye contact. "This 'exercise' on Friday night—it was conducted by Beata Ulrich. Impressive. Is she still in the area?"

"I can't say," Heller answered. "Very likely. You know her?"

Gable grunted a strong affirmation. "She's a woman of some reputation—in our field of study. A highly gifted psychic. I've been trying to investigate her for years. So have a score of other researchers."

"She refuses?" Heller asked.

"Absolutely. It's understandable. During the war, in the camps, the German doctors manhandled her. Forced experimentation. The Nazis had an ambitious program in paranormal phenomena. She seems to have held out against them rather heroically—and paid the price for it. This ritual you saw her lead, it was something of her own? Something she composed for the occasion?"

"She and her husband—and I imagine Leah Hagar. That's how it was described to me. I gave Secretary Touhy a full report yesterday, everything I could remember."

"Yes," Gable remarked dismissively as he ran his eyes over a transcript of Heller's interview with Touhy. "It's not much help. We'll have to go back over some of this ground to pick up the details we need."

"Such as . . . ?" Heller asked, irked by Gable's terse manner.

"That's difficult to say," Gable answered, still without looking up from his notes. "Most of the exercise seems to be conventional gobbledegook, maybe intended to divert your attention. The central question is whether Beata Ulrich's performance could have had any influence on the subsequent behavior of the bugs. That would involve a prodigious energy displacement which isn't characteristic of clairvoyants in her category. She might have used some hallucinogenic agent . . ."

"Not that I noticed," Heller remarked impatiently.

"It might have been inhaled when the drawing was burned."

"She showed no signs of that when I talked to her afterward."

Gable gave him a quick critical glance. "Oh? Would you know what to look for?"

The question caught Heller off-guard. He stammered over his answer. "Well, I mean she seemed quite coherent when we spoke . . ."

Gable sniffed contemptuously. "A low level dose of psilocybin wouldn't interfere with her ability to articulate. It might even sharpen her faculties. Then, too, some psychics are able to cathect repressed sexual anxieties to boost their powers. It would be interesting to know if Beata masturbated during the exercise. Or if anyone else in the group did . . . her husband, the Hecate woman . . ."

Heller felt himself flush with outrage at Gable's offhandedly belittling tone. The reaction confused him. Why should he object to anything Gable said about Beata or the others? Quickly, he moved to fight down his anger and embarrassment. At his side, Father Guiness giggled under his breath, a distinctly dirty laugh. At what?

"Why should I be watching for anything like that?" Heller asked, a note of undisguised scorn entering his voice.

"Exactly," Gable retorted, "you weren't there as a trained observer. It's not your field."

Sarcastically, Heller asked, "Is there a field in lunar incantations? I didn't know."

Raising his eyes from his notes, Gable fixed Heller with a look that mixed surprise and contempt. Then, with exaggerated forbearance, he said, "Since we'll be working together, I should probably explain something about my methodological suppositions. It will help avoid misunderstanding."

"Ah, now," Guiness interrupted, "speak for yourself, Richard." Tilting sideways toward Heller, he whispered loudly, "Myself, there's not a methodological bone in my poor, weary body, not a one. That's Richard's university talk, you see."

"Father Guiness and I," Gable remarked, "do not come at the study of paranormal experience with the same orientation. I'll leave him to explain his approach for himself when time allows . . ."

But Guiness, eager to hold forth, snatched the opportunity before it passed. "Oh, and that's easily done, Doctor. I'm a happy amateur, you see. Oh yes. There's no great learning in the matter for me." Then, leaning closer, he fell into his ludicrous stage whisper again. "Only the gift. The *gift*." Turning blindly in Gable's direction, he said aloud, "But I think I can say that Richard and I, we make a nice pair. Like bangers and mash." Giggling softly, pointing to his head, he added, "I'm the mash."

The relationship between Gable and Father Guiness showed every sign of being strained and awkward. When the old man spoke, Gable's expression became one of resigned annoyance. "Father Guiness is a psychic," he explained, giving the necessary gist of his associate's turgid remarks. "Every science needs its instruments. He has agreed to be mine. He is a particularly powerful instrument and I value his assistance. But my research is entirely based in physics and neurophysiology. I work from the hypothesis that subtle forms of physical energy are operative in psi phenomena, probably of a subquantum, or even a subquark origin. I assume this energy is transmitted through the electro-chemical fine structure of the nervous system, where it manifests in a non-uniform and often random way. At best, the capacity is subject to extremely imperfect voluntary controls. As with all natural phenomena that are poorly understood, the psi capacities have come to be overlain with a variety of metaphysical and theological explanations. Specialists in the field regard these as merely folkloristic superstructures, about at the level of the Aristotelian theory of gravity."

"There you see, Doctor," Guiness interjected with a wry smirk. "Richard has no heart for the poetry of the matter. All facts and figures. Such a pity."

Brushing the interruption aside, Gable continued. "In short, Dr. Heller: no, I don't take lunar incantations seriously." (Guiness wagged his head and clucked regretfully.) "I do take empirical evidence seriously—for example, unclassifiable insects that devour people. I work in a field where such data are respected and are coming to be understood. That body of research may be essential to solving your embarrassing little problem. My impression is that those of you who have been dealing with this matter so far have been doing so in much the same way that electricity might have been dealt with in the days of Benjamin Franklin. The result has been a rather sorry waste of valuable time."

Their eyes met and held for several seconds, Heller studying Gable closely without replying. He resented being lectured to like this; he was angered by the belligerent edge the man put on his remarks. What was he up to? Why did there seem to be a contest of wills between them? Gable went on, "I had a long session yesterday evening with Secretary Touhy. I believe he understands the relevance of my work to his needs."

The remark clicked in Heller's mind. Gable had been talking to Touhy. This was an opportunistic young man, trying to place himself at the center of the crisis, to make himself indispensable to its solution. Of course, this was a great chance for him, for his entire profession—provided he had something substantive to offer. That was a long shot; in Heller's eyes, a bad risk. Still, he could not blame Gable for playing the game for all it was worth. But why the hostility, the attitude of distrust?

"All right," Heller said, yielding for the sake of getting on with it. "What do you want to know?"

Again, Gable submerged himself in his notes, speaking without looking up, almost offhandedly. "One thing to begin with —just to clear the ground. How strong is your emotional attachment to the girl's mother?"

Heller was jarred. The breath caught in his throat. He stared at Gable. Oddly, Gable was not looking back; his eyes were on Father Guiness.

"You understand the importance of the question," Gable added, glancing back and forth between Heller and Guiness. "We have to know what part your personal involvement with this group plays in your perceptions."

Heller's answer burst from him. "There is no personal involvement. What are you talking about?" He could feel the blood flaring hot at the edge of his ears and in his eyelids. "What the hell are you getting at?"

"I'm only going by the file," Gable answered.

"What file?" Heller asked indignantly.

With a weary sigh Gable ticked off the facts from his notes. "You've visited Mrs. Saxton—excuse me, Ms. Hecate three times." He gave a sardonic buzz to the "Ms." "Once overnight at a mountain retreat, twice at her house. Most recently last Wednesday night. You stopped to buy wine or whiskey for the occasion. When you left, you embraced on the porch. 'Embraced' . . . yes, that's the word they use. Quaint."

Heller turned to glare fiercely at Haseltine. Touhy had held out on him in more ways than he had admitted. How long had he been under surveillance? Haseltine stared back unabashed, the trained intelligence officer to whom privacy meant nothing. "After that couple from Pittsburgh were attacked by the bugs," Haseltine explained, "Lyman ordered all senior staff at the Brain to be monitored."

"This is ridiculous," Heller protested. "I won't be . . ."

"You're not going to say your privacy has been violated, are you?" Gable challenged, meanly.

Heller was trapped. Washington's Peeping Tom was hardly the person to protest against government surveillance. Weakly he said, "I deserve more trust than this."

"All we're trying to do," Gable went on, "is to clarify the degree of emotional investment you have in Earthrite. That could have a lot to do with the value of your reports. It could influence your willingness to believe what you were told."

"That's absurd," Heller snapped. "I have no commitment to these people."

"So it wouldn't trouble you if we proceeded from the premise that Earthrite's world view, its rituals and so forth, is so much cosmic bullshit." He shot the remark out sharply like a probe meant to strike a raw nerve. Heller was coming to despise Gable's arrogance. But he realized he must not appear defensive of Earthrite. He put his answer as strongly as possible. "You might have taken the words right out of my mouth." But as he spoke the words, he felt a slight twinge of remorse.

"Ah, it hurt to say that, didn't it?" Guiness remarked close at his side. "You wouldn't have wanted the lady to hear that."

Heller realized his reactions were being gauged by Guiness, as they had been by Beata Ulrich. Either that, or Gable and the priest were collaborating at a ruse, trying to convince him that his mind was being read.

"I don't know what you mean by that," he protested. "I don't normally bother insulting people's belief systems that way. Why should I? It's a cheap shot to take in company like this."

"Then how *would* you characterize your involvement with Jane Hecate?" Gable asked, clearly pressing to irritate Heller. The session was becoming more like a grilling by the minute.

"How about pure lust?" Heller shot back. "Will that do?"

"Under the circumstances, it's one of the safer answers you could give," Gable answered. "And reasonably credible. She's a foxy woman." Gable was studying a photograph he had taken from the file.

"Is it true, Dr. Heller," Father Guiness asked, "that the church of the Earthrite performs its worship as naked as our Mother Eve?" There was a mocking, prurient whine to the question.

"I believe I included that piece of information in my report to Secretary Touhy yesterday," Heller answered dryly.

Gable, flipping through the transcript he held, wagged his head. "Actually, you didn't."

"I'm sure I did," Heller insisted.

Gable held out a stack of papers to him across the bed. "Not in the transcript."

Heller did not reach for the document. "I'm certain I mentioned it . . . in passing. It must have been omitted." He glanced at Haseltine and Schaeffer.

"I don't recall your mentioning it," Haseltine said.

Heller's temper flared. "I did. I wouldn't suppress it. Why should I?"

Gable shrugged, his eyes once again on the file. "It's not a matter of suppression. It may have slipped your mind. But it's the sort of item that helps us understand something of the psychology of the people we're dealing with. Often such an uninhibited sexual display . . ."

"There's nothing sexual about it," Heller burst out. "Besides, if I didn't mention it, how would you know to ask about it?"

Gable gave no answer; Guiness chuckled smugly to himself, as if over a private joke.

Gable passed on to another question. "The mother wouldn't let the child—Daphne—be used in the exercise. That was her decision, was it?"

"Hers and Leah Hagar's. I have no idea how they would have used the child. They thought it might be dangerous."

Gable gave him a shrewd look. "That's what they told you— that it was dangerous? And Beata Ulrich went along with that?"

"Yes, she seemed to. That's why they used the drawing in the ritual. I'm afraid I don't follow that part of it."

Gable sighed wearily, "No, I can see you wouldn't." Then, after a moment, his eyes drilling into Heller's face, he said with cold aggressiveness, "You were duped by them, Heller. Do you realize that?"

Shaken, but struggling to stay calm, Heller asked, "Oh? How so?"

Gable fished a pack of cigarettes out of his pocket, then realized he was in a hospital room. "Do you think I can get away with this?" he asked. Heller shrugged permission; Gable lit up. The cigarette seemed to soften the tension in him. "As I've said, the lore, that metaphysics, that accompany psi phenomena are so much negligible superstructure. The energy isn't in them; it's in the nervous system. In this case, the child's nervous system. Apparently the girl was raised from conception under hothouse conditions in order to prime the psi capacities. The kid's brain—that's where the bugs have to be checked. Working from the drawing would have to be a gimmick, a trick. It has no relationship to the materialization we're dealing with."

Heller was bewildered by the point. "But the people at Earthrite don't share your paradigm. Why do you assume they were deceiving me?"

"Because even in terms of their own assumptions, it makes no sense to avoid working with the child. That's the direct and immediate target. The exercise was an elaborate pretense of cooperation deliberately designed to mislead you."

"That's ridiculous!" Heller objected. "I know they want to get rid of the insects."

Gable gave him a dubious squint. "Yes? I wonder how you know that—other than being told by them. You see, that's where Ms. Hecate's feminine influence may come into play."

Ignoring the insinuation, Heller asked, "Would it pose any danger to the child to be used in such a ritual, or in any effort to get at the bugs?"

There was a strained pause. Drawing deeply on his cigarette, Gable said, "Is it your understanding that that is a central policy priority?"

Heller gave no immediate answer. He noticed Gable checking with Guiness out of the corner of his eye. "What am I supposed to believe he's telling you?" he asked Gable sharply.

Father Guiness answered for himself. "Ah, Doctor, I have the impression you're a man with a good heart, a heart of gold. You don't want to see this child hurt. Not that any of us do, mind. That's admirable, admirable. It's a pleasure to be working with a good, kind man like yourself."

At once, Heller forced himself to blot every reservation out of his mind, to hold only the words he spoke in his awareness. "What matters to me is resolving this crisis. Nothing else matters worth a damn. Nothing." He lined the statement out as forcefully as possible, realizing he must demonstrate absolute conviction. He fought the image of Jane and Daphne out of his thoughts ruthlessly.

Gable said, "I'm sure we're all agreed on that, as we are on not taking any unnecessary risks with the child. But we will have to see the girl. There's no way around that. Can you be of any help to us in that respect?"

Again, struggling to block out any sign of reservation, Heller answered. "I've been in touch with Miss Hecate—last night by phone. She'll be visiting tomorrow with Leah Hagar. I'll advise her to give you all the help she can."

"Good," Gable said. "We want this to go off smoothly, with as much voluntary compliance as possible."

"Otherwise . . . ?" Heller pressed him. "What happens if I can't persuade Miss Hecate to co-operate with you?"

Gable exchanged glances with Haseltine. The general answered, "Let's assume she shares our concern for bringing this crisis to a speedy resolution."

Through the glass wall of his room, Heller could see Levinson coming along the corridor. He entered with an armload of papers and was quickly introduced around the room. The shadows of a hard, sleepless night darkened his face. Haseltine looked to him eagerly for news of WIMEX. Levinson handed him and Schaeffer a few photocopied sheets of paper. "That's the latest we have—as of ten-forty-five this morning when I left the office—100 per cent shutdown."

"How many casualties?" Schaeffer asked.

"Eight dead at NORAD and REDCOM. Maybe twenty more injured. SAC also lost an Avenger bomber in bad weather over Kodiak Island when the computerized ground control was taken out by the bugs. That's another five deaths there."

Haseltine asked, "Was the plane carrying any nukes?"

"Yeah. They're going to have to be recovered from the sea."

As Haseltine ran through the report, Gable asked, "You don't mind if we continue with the interview? I'm nearly finished."

"Please go ahead," Haseltine answered, busying himself in Levinson's papers.

Gable, rapidly resuming, asked Heller, "I can assume, then, that you'll provide the liaison we need with Miss Hecate?"

"Yes," Heller said with clear reluctance, feeling he was being pushed too fast. There was still a question in his mind: what did Gable intend to do with Daphne? Seeking to slow the discussion, he remarked, "It's hard to believe an effect of such magnitude could stem from any one mind, especially a child's mind. Can you help me understand that?"

Gable drew a number of journal reprints out of his briefcase and laid them on Heller's bed. "These may give you some background on our research. In this field, as in most of modern science, one has to leave behind intuitive perceptions of size and quantity. An atom is infinitesimal, but we know its energy potential is vast. A strand of DNA is microscopic, but its information content is immense. And I needn't tell you about the storage capacity of a microchip.

"The same is true of psi phenomena. The neural structure underlying them is superminiaturized far beyond anything so far studied in nature. We work from a holographic model of the brain. Which means the whole structure is reproduced in every part down to the last molecule. We hope to prove that such an ultraredundant storage capacity can be transformed into a form of energy—by way of resonance gain, as in the familiar case of electronic feedback. The contents of the brain —an image, word, idea—get resonated through the system instantaneously, until all gross empirical limits of time and space, all dimensionality are annihilated—crushed like matter in a black hole. That's what a psi event is: a mental black hole, but at the deep subatomic level. We don't know what the rules are in such conditions of matter or energy. Far and near, past and present—they all get compacted into a point, a singularity. Then anything goes. Usually a psi event lasts for a split second. In most cases, this just produces the random noise we interpret as a dream, a hallucination, a schizophrenic break. But if the event could be contained, extended, controlled . . . well, we could write our own rules for the universe, just as we do in dreams."

As Gable explained his research, a childlike exuberance came over him that offset his arrogance. Heller recognized it as the intellectual passion of a man championing a big, new idea. In other times and places, that had been his stance in the world as one of the bright, young talents in computer science. He listened closely, struggling to glean what he could from Gable's explanations, resenting his ignorance of the field. Where his own knowledge of physics and brain anatomy connected with Gable's theories, they sounded preposterous. He was certain the man must be exaggerating his findings. Yet, if Gable now enjoyed Touhy's support, Heller had to tread carefully or he would not stay close to the key decisions.

And where did Father Guiness come into things? He was clearly not a scientist; nothing about him seemed compatible with Gable's style. Several times while Gable talked, the old priest wagged his head in amused bewilderment, chuckling and muttering under his breath. At times, Guiness seemed almost imbecilic.

"You don't accept Professor Gable's theories, Father?" Heller asked, probing.

The question startled the old man, breaking in upon some interior monologue of his own. Heller had to repeat what he had asked. "Ah, well," Guiness said, "there's a problem for us. To tell you the truth, Doctor, I haven't got much of a head for Richard's science. No, I'm just the old workhorse on the farm; it's the old rites for me. You can't have the magic without the poetry, so I say. Nor without faith. Faith, Doctor. And I can tell you, the old rites was making the world go round before there was the *para - this - ology* or the *para - that - ology*. And there's nothing the devil wouldn't do to have the power of them if he could. It's the old magic that put the curse upon us, and it's only the true faith that will take it off."

Gable registered annoyance that Heller should bring Guiness into the conversation. He visibly winced at the words "magic" and "faith." Heller had the impression that Guiness enjoyed baiting Gable with such remarks, jibing his scientific convictions. "And how will you be using the child to do that?" he asked casually. He expected that if he put the question to Guiness, he would get some sort of response from Gable. He was right.

"Oh, just routine psychological counseling," Gable answered quickly before Guiness could respond. "The girl has a phobia for insects. That seems to be the operative factor. If we can condition her out of that, we should be able to use the same mental dynamics to reverse the materialization she's produced. That should have been done as soon as the connection between her and the bugs became clear. It's a pity all this time has been lost."

"But why are Leah and the others so fearful about using the child?" he asked.

Gable was unconcerned by the problem. He shrugged. "I've suggested that they may, for their own reasons, wish to allow the insects to extend their damage. There are lots of atavistic elements like Earthrite in the modern world capable of such willful subversion. On the other hand, since they work out of an irrational frame of reference, there's no telling what sort of chop logic they may be burdened by. There's a point where inherited metaphysical systems like theirs simply won't bear empirical analysis. I suppose, in the days of Stonehenge, the old Druids might have thought it would screw up the universe if they moved one of their rocks to correct an astronomical reading. They might have thought you needed to resort to human sacrifice to shift a stone an inch. Superstition always overdetermines its effects."

Heller was struck by the reference to Stonehenge. It brought to mind what Sperling had said of their encounter ten years ago. Gable might have been Heller himself, holding forth about the ancient monuments. He wondered: had he ever been so obnoxiously cocksure and pushy? Yes, he had. In his time, he had been a ruthless competitor, using information science as his peculiar weapon to clear the way toward high professional success and political power. Now, here was another brash young man using his expertise in the same way to become king of the mountain. It was ironic enough to bring a small, bitter smile to his lips.

"I can tell you this much," Heller said. "Daphne is a very delicate child. She'll have to be handled with great professional care. I'm sure you'll want her mother to be with her during the counseling."

"Oh yes, yes," Gable answered, but his tone was hollow and unconvincing.

"And Miss Hecate may also want the girl's psychiatrist there," Heller added.

Gable flipped through his notes. "You mean this man Fritsch. Hm, yes. Jungian background. More superstructure. Look, Heller, promise her everything she wants. Make her feel secure. As long as she brings the girl in."

"Is that the deal?" Heller asked. "I can assure her of that? She accompanies the girl and brings along whatever support she wants. And you agree to obtain her consent for whatever you do?"

"Yes, yes," Gable tossed off the words. "Anything she asks for. We can't be very choosy now, can we?"

"You might mention to her," General Haseltine suggested, "that we can guarantee her absolute security and seclusion. She may value that once the media get on to the church. It can't be kept a secret forever."

It was a good point. The only chance Jane might soon have to shelter her daughter would be to co-operate with the government. "May I assure her and her friends," Heller asked, "that they will have access to me whenever necessary? And that I'll be in touch with all aspects of your investigation at my own discretion?"

"Anything!" Gable snapped, showing his exasperation.

Heller pressed further. "I can assure her that I'll be involved in the investigation, that she can appeal to me for advice or support at all points?"

Gable threw him a fierce look. "You're not seriously suggesting that you act as a consultant to my research. You don't know the field."

"You're asking me to gain the woman's confidence for you.

I've got to know what guarantees I can give her. For example, does she have the right to leave—with her daughter—whenever she sees fit? You understand," he said to Haseltine, "if I can't guarantee her that, you may not gain access to the child at all."

Haseltine weighed Heller's request. "I don't think there's any question but that Miss Hecate's rights will be fully respected. We want this project to work voluntarily. Of course, we'll have to let Dick decide on his own needs and procedures. With regard to that, you can communicate to Lyman through me and raise any questions you find necessary."

Heller raised the key question. "But I'll have no direct connection with Gable's work? No power to intervene and veto?"

"Oh, be reasonable, Heller!" Gable burst out. "I'm not asking to screw around with your conversion plans."

Haseltine quickly placed himself behind Gable's objection. "We do have to keep some orderly division of labor here," he said.

Heller saw the emerging pattern. The crisis was being divided into two self-contained projects under Touhy's direction: his work with the computers, Gable's work with Daphne and Earthrite. Gable would not be operating under him, but independently of him and on an equal footing. If anything, Gable's area was now being favored with a higher priority. Perhaps that made administrative sense, but it was psychologically all wrong. It was bound to make it difficult for Heller to gain Jane's trust. But how far could he press his point with Haseltine without seeming—in Gable's phrase—"emotionally involved"?

"Tom"—Haseltine put the remark with intimidating weight —"we don't want to have to work around you in this. We need your help with the woman. It's the only way things can proceed smoothly, without . . . embarrassment."

Heller was being pressured; that hurt his pride. But this was not the moment to take a stand. Grudgingly, he nodded assent. "All right. I'll do my best with her tomorrow. But you may be exaggerating her trust in me."

At once, Gable and Haseltine began packing up to leave. Father Guiness suddenly came alert in his chair where he had been dozing, occasionally murmuring or chuckling to himself. "Ready to go," Gable said to him, taking his arm and helping him lever his bulk to a standing position. As they moved toward the door, the old man turned back toward Heller. "Yes, I have in my time also been a hammer of witches," he declaimed. "'A desolation, an astonishment, a hissing, and a curse.' But we are not without resources, Doctor. Of that I assure you."

As Gable ushered the priest into the corridor, Heller offered him a final dubious glance. Gable stared back without a hint of apology for his colleague's conduct.

2

After the others were gone, Levinson, tense and angered, said, "You know what's happening here?"

Heller knew. He had moved in the upper levels of political life long enough to recognize the signs of official disfavor. He nodded sullenly. "We're being frozen out."

Levinson punched a fist into the palm of his hand. "Christ! Just like that. Shit-listed all the way to the top. They can't handle this mess without us."

Heller wondered how much of Levinson's rancor fell upon him. "My own fault," he said, not apologetically but objectively. "I just couldn't see myself bringing up the subject of Earthrite with Lyman. It's not the sort of thing someone like me takes seriously."

"Someone like you!" Levinson repeated, his voice crackling bitterly. "There's nobody *like* you, Tom. There's just *you*. Even that image on the TV screen—Horatio Heller defending the bridge of Reason—that's still just *you*. You make up your own mind, nobody else. Maybe if you hadn't been so damned worried about your reputation . . ." Then, relenting, he said, "Excuse the lecture."

"Okay," Heller agreed. "No alibis. I thought the ball was out of bounds and let it drop." He shuffled through the reprints Gable had left on the bed. "What do you make of Gable and company?"

Levinson gave a sneering chuckle. "He's a son of a bitch and a first class bullshit artist. Which means he's got a great future in Washington. The old priest gives me the creeps. What the hell is he all about?"

"Gable says he's a clairvoyant, uses him in his research."

Levinson blew out an exasperated breath. "A senile psychic yet. That's what they replace us with!"

"Something I'm curious about," Heller said. "Do you remember me mentioning yesterday that Earthrite performed its rituals in the nude?"

Levinson thought back. "You told me that before. No, I don't remember you telling Lyman about that. As a matter of fact, I recall thinking you wanted to hold that back for some reason. Why do you ask?"

"Never mind," Heller said, worrying over the answer. Where else could Guiness have picked up that point of information? "Let's hear about WIMEX."

Rapidly, Levinson sketched in the broad outlines of the disaster. "It's a total crap-out. By all accounts, as bad as what happened at the Brain—but with more people on hand. There were some personnel at NORAD who were ordered to stay on duty until their equipment was literally overwhelmed by the bugs. They had some luck with using hard suits—the gear they use for fire-fighting at oil well blowouts. Apparently, there were technicians that held out for an extra half hour or so against the bugs wearing those. But they had the same experience you had at the Brain: the computers finally generated enough insects to knock people down by sheer weight of numbers. Also the bugs finally bit their way into the air supply for the suits. We had a total shutdown of WIMEX by 6:45 A.M. That's less than four hours after the first bugs were sighted at the National Military Command Center here. From there, they permeated the entire system. NORAD was knocked out within two hours. We've rerouted to a half dozen other facilities. The plan is essentially the latest revision of RE-DIRECT that you doped out, with a few last minute adjustments by yours truly. Seat of the pants, it may be, but pretty brilliant for what we've got left to work with. Jesus, we're running the national air defense, or what's left of it, out of university computer centers and commercial air traffic controls, which were in critical shape already. Fact is: if the Russians weren't just as badly off, we'd be dead ducks."

Heller ran through the reports, then sat back in his bed, his eyes heavy with fatigue and despair. "You realize what this adds up to? It means nobody East or West can launch a thermonuclear attack. The system's that crippled."

"You could call it the *Pax Entomologica*," Levinson said. "Maybe all the more reason to hope this snotty bastard Gable falls flat on his face."

"Which is likely. Lyman's not going to get any help out of this stuff." He tossed Gable's reprints on his bedside table.

"You're so sure?" Levinson asked. "Have you read any of that?"

"Have you?" Heller asked back.

"A bit of it, just since yesterday. Haseltine passed along the professor's bibliography. There may not be a lick of hard science in it, but you've got to admire the guy's chutzpah. He's got all the state of the art technology stuck away in the brain somewhere. Holograms, lasers, superconductors, x-ray diffusion . . . Wait until you read the stuff on the quantum computer—to be modeled, mind you, on the telekinetic capacities of the brain. It uses tachyons instead of electrons. Faster than the speed of light, understand? So the computer model redefines the historical past. Wild."

Heller sighed disconsolately. "Lyman's not the sort to go for airy-fairy material like this. What is Gable promising that he can possibly hope to deliver?"

"Could be something buried in the classified research at McGill," Levinson speculated. "The important thing is—he's a man with an idea, and nobody else has one. Let's face it. We're up against something spooky. And spooky is Gable's schtick. Meanwhile, all we're doing is barely holding the fort. So, of course, this guy comes on looking like a solid gold savior."

"That's not all that's working against us," Heller observed somberly. "Lyman has stopped trusting me. And maybe I've stopped trusting myself."

"It shows," Levinson commented with poignant frankness. "So whatever became of your own messianic aura?"

Bitterly, Heller answered, "It got eaten for breakfast by a billion little bugs."

14

1

Bending above Heller's bed, Kayla Breen offered a kiss that was expertly balanced between friendship and familiarity. There was a noncommittal "darling" attached to the few brief questions she asked about his injuries. Then, abruptly and rather too grandly, like the hostess at an exclusive dinner party, she turned to introduce Lloyd Briggs as if he and Heller might be strangers meeting for the first time. They weren't. A simple phone call would have been enough to put them in touch. Heller assumed it was as clear to Briggs as it was to him that Kayla was intruding herself between them. But just as clearly, neither of them was going to say so.

There were few people Heller had met on the political scene who blended power and candor as gracefully as Briggs. He had the principled newsman's gift for currying favor in high places without surrendering the leverage of critical distance. Since he had taken over CBS News six years ago, the network had featured Heller in two major documentaries on data technology, one of them a grand tour of the Brain just before it began operations. They were solid, probing reports; all the hard questions about civil liberties and computer reliability were raised. In both cases, Heller came away looking extremely good under investigative pressure. He knew that was thanks to Briggs' editorial control over the shows, and for that he remained grateful. Briggs' support in the media was an important vote of confidence; he did not want to forfeit it now.

Still, he harbored a nagging resentment for the status that news barons like Briggs enjoyed. They were the self-appointed referees of American politics, mixing thickly in the action, bargaining on all sides, but always reserving the right to assess stinging penalties against their closest allies. They could, whenever it suited their interests, invoke an authority that was shallowly rooted in Heller's sentiments—the people's right to know.

Tall, distinguished, almost unnervingly smooth, Briggs might have passed muster as a senior diplomat. His ambassadorial calm clashed sharply with Kayla's highly strung assertiveness. In style, they were polar opposites. But by now Heller could read Kayla's manner with some precision; he knew there was more than a purely professional relationship between his visitors. She settled herself beside Briggs with just enough of a proprietary air to let it be known that he had joined Heller among her trophies.

"I don't know how much Kayla has told you about the special report we're planning," Briggs began.

"Just enough to convince me it would be wise to co-operate. I gather you intend to rake me over the coals."

"Well, I wouldn't put it that way," Briggs assured him tactfully. "But I think you will agree that the role of computer technology in our society is going to have to be rigorously re-examined."

"Agreed." Heller surrendered the point, though he was hardly convinced that it was the place of CBS to undertake that re-examination on the television screens of America.

"The program we're working on," Briggs continued, "will air a week from Friday, with an excerpt run on 'Sixty Minutes' this Sunday. The full show may go two hours, prime time. Our top staff is involved, plus the best computer expertise we can round up, including yourself if we can persuade you. This is one of the biggest efforts the department has undertaken since I took charge. Tentatively, we're calling it 'Data Quake'— probably with the subtitle 'End of the Electronic Age—question mark.' Hope that doesn't sound too journalese for your tastes. As things are shaping up now, we'll probably start with the Detroit welfare center tragedy. That's the best visual coverage we have of the bugs . . .''

He paused, noticing Heller's questioning frown. "You haven't heard?"

"Not about anything 'tragic.' I'm a bit behindhand picking up news here." Glancing at the still folded newspaper by his bedside, Heller explained apologetically, "I slept a little late. It's the sedative. I need it to get through the night. And then I was on the phone most of the last hour with the Pentagon. Problems with the B-MEWS system."

Kayla leaned forward to spread a copy of the New York *Times* across his bed. The lead story carried the headline: COMPUTER INSECTS OVERRUN DETROIT WELFARE CENTER. THREE KILLED, SCORES INJURED.

Quickly, Heller skimmed the report while Briggs spoke.

"We realize the military side of this crisis poses the most serious risk. We intend to emphasize that in our report. But most of the defense-related material you're concerned with is classified. And, in view of the delicate situation we're in, we want to respect security limits. That leaves the welfare centers as the most dramatic and visible aspect of the story to reach the public. As of this morning, seven major cities have had to close down welfare operations, four of them since the weekend when the Brain was taken out of commission. That hits people where they live. Food, rent, Medicare. Sooner or later something like Detroit had to happen. As I understand it, there just isn't enough spare computer capacity left to keep the systems going."

Heller knew that much of the story. For more than a month, computerized welfare services, many of them routed through the Brain, had been malfunctioning across the country. Wrong payments to the wrong people at the wrong time—or usually no payments at all. Then, some ten days ago, in New York, where the confusion had reached its extreme, overburdened welfare officials pulled the plug. Detroit and St. Louis quickly followed. The machines were shut down, the checks stopped coming.

At once, frustrated recipients—the poor, the aged, the unemployed and handicapped whose fate had been entrusted to the computers—converged on the welfare centers, demanding payments, receiving none. In Washington, Heller's staff, monitoring the breakdown, fed him daily reports on the mounting public pressure. But there was no backup equipment available to handle the overload. The technology was approaching depletion. More and more of what was left had to be diverted to military uses. It was Heller himself who had finally given the order to cut welfare services out of the nation's data transmission network. Official explanations were sent out in carefully drafted administrative memos, but they did no good. Instinctively, the crowds that milled through the idle welfare centers knew that their lives were locked up in an electronic vault whose keys had been lost.

Inevitably, a flashpoint was reached. In the week when Heller was scheduled to attend the ritual at Earthrite, there were demonstrations at welfare offices in New York and Los Angeles. In Philadelphia, a sit-in turned violent. Windows were broken, desks overturned, welfare officers attacked. The report in the *Times* supplied Heller with the latest chapter of the story. Late last night after he had fallen into a well-sedated sleep, angry crowds that had been besieging the downtown Detroit welfare center for two sweltering days, forced their way into the building. A fire broke out, computers were set upon and smashed. From several of the battered machines, bugs emerged, attacking firemen, policemen, people on the streets. The insects soon scattered and vanished as they had at the Brain, but a policeman and two National Guardsmen were left dead and mutilated.

When Heller finished reading, Briggs said, "It's the first time the public at large has seen the bugs. It's also the first public attack upon the computers. That makes Detroit a sort of benchmark in the crisis. We have a lot of videotape from the scene of the riot. We intend to feature it. But we want to do more than a scare show. We want a full analysis of the problem, its history, its causes, the future . . ."

"That's a lot to cover in a couple of hours," Heller commented dryly. "Much of what you want to know is highly technical—too technical to be packaged for the general public."

A challenging light came into Briggs' eyes. "That's exactly the problem we want to highlight, Tom. How did we get caught in this technological trap? What we're talking about here are jobs, welfare, economic survival, the military security of the nation. These aren't technical fine points for experts at MIT and Cal Tech to kick around the seminar table. These are matters of political life and death for millions of citizens. How could we permit so much that's so vital to get beyond our control, even beyond our understanding?"

Feeling the weight of the questions, Heller sighed heavily. "All our politics is technical fine points, Lloyd. Where do you draw the line? Energy is technical. Inflation is technical. Nuclear war is technical. People don't even understand where their food and water come from any more. They don't know what their money's worth, what's in the pills they swallow. Our whole way of life has become a big black box. People don't know what's in the box. They don't care to know. It's too much for them to handle. The computers are . . . or *were* the most efficient way to keep the box working. People wanted that. We gave them what they wanted."

"Are you willing to say that on television?" Briggs asked. "Are you willing to be quoted?"

Heller threw a sharp look toward Kayla. "I understood this was to be off the record."

Briggs agreed. "Of course. But we need somebody authoritative to strike that note—to tell us how we got where we are."

Heller returned a firm, level gaze. "Lloyd, I think you're out to draw up an indictment. You want a scapegoat to blame the problem on. The computer scientists. Maybe me."

Briggs looked wounded by the accusation. "The network has always treated you fairly, Tom. In any case, I don't believe in using the news as a public pillory. We're not looking for simple answers."

"In two hours, all you can get are simple answers."

"I grant we can't be exhaustive," Briggs conceded. "But a

concise report can have its own value. It can cut through to the core of the issue. There's a difference, I think, between simplifying and clarifying. We want to go back over the development of computer technology—the promises that were made, the expectations that were raised. Maybe it was an honest mistake, but we *were* led to believe the computers could solve all our problems."

"That's what Lloyd wants to use from our 'Wonder/ Wander' material," Kayla added with undisguised pride. "The section where you tell the kids all the good things the computers can do. All the conveniences, the glowing possibilities. Remember the House of Tomorrow sequence?"

Her enthusiasm bewildered Heller. Did she expect him to relish the prospect of having those words thrown back at him now? "You know how foolish that will make me look."

"Well, you did say it, Tom. You practically scripted the show yourself." There was a serves-you-right spitefulness to her words that embarrassed Briggs. Noticing that, Kayla rushed on to add, "The important thing is that 'Wonder/Wander' is the last major media document on the Brain—before the deluge. We can't let it go to waste. It's a collector's item."

She might have been a broker describing a smart investment. It occurred to Heller that Kayla's "Wonder/Wander" material might be paying her some handsome dividends. He recalled her telling him that she wanted to move out of children's programming into the news department. Had she perhaps found a convenient bridge into Briggs' good graces?

He asked her, "Will you be assisting on the show?"

"Well, I was the last network person to handle a production on data technology . . ."

"Kayla's joining the news department," Briggs said, as if that might reassure Heller. "We do plan to make extensive use of the material she filmed with you."

" 'Wonder/Wander' was done for an audience of children," Heller protested hotly. "It's a kindergarten level presentation. In light of what's happened since then, it will sound ridiculous. Do I have any control over the material you filmed?"

Kayla, jarred by the question, hastened to remind him, "You signed a release to the network."

Heller looked to Briggs. "That's law. I'm talking ethics."

Kayla's tone took on a fierce edge. "You were willing to use the media to boast about the Brain when we gave you the chance. Is it fair to ask us to forget that now and just let you off the hook?"

Bitch! The word almost forced itself from his mouth. Aloud he answered, "I'm not on the hook. Our whole society is. This isn't a Watergate scandal, it's a public emergency, and we're all in it together." He appealed to Briggs. "Ask yourself what's fair and responsible here. There's no way to get out of this mess without drawing on the best brains we have. If you use your show to vilify computer science, where does the public turn for help?"

Briggs lifted an eyebrow wryly. "Is that the way you see it, Tom? The more the technology fails us, the more we need the technicians? That's rather neat."

Heller made no apologies for his position. "Those may be the facts of modern life."

"So the technicians never lose," Kayla observed sardonically.

"The way I'd put it is: if the technicians lose, we all lose." Turning to Briggs, Heller asked pointedly, "Incidentally, how is your own television technology holding up? Are you even going to be able to splice this show together on your VTR? If so, it will only be because somebody with the know-how has kept the hardware functioning."

Briggs gave a troubled smile. "Now that you mention it, we are having our problems. Lots of them. Almost everything that uses satellites and long distance computerized transmission facilities is flaking out. We're as deeply embedded in the technology as everybody else—the banks, the hospitals, the schools. Maybe that means we were as gullible as everybody else. We bought the same bill of goods."

"If it *is* a bill of goods," Heller insisted, "it's a very old and honorable bill of goods. As old as human reason. You believed what the best scientific minds in the society told you. Maybe that's the wrong way to go. Maybe the world is really a big bag of circus tricks. But we've been on the path of reason since the days of the lever and the wheel. What other path does a sane man choose? Look, I'm not asking special favors for myself. I'll take my share of the blame. It was a mistake to make our society so dependent on a single technology. It was a mistake to centralize that technology in the Brain. The world is just too damned unpredictable to be tied up in any one human package. Colleagues of mine warned me about that when we began planning the Brain. With hindsight, I can see they were right. They were right because they were more rational than I was, more logical about the probabilities. You've got to be careful about letting my bad judgment discredit the entire profession. There are plenty of atavistic types hiding in the woodwork who would love to use a crisis like this as an excuse for going back to mumbo-jumbo and black magic . . ."

He was jolted to a stop by his own words. After all, where had Thomas Heller been the evening before the Brain was overrun? He must be careful to steer clear of even the remotest reference to Earthrite. But Briggs had already fielded the remark. "Interesting you should mention that. We've picked up rumors that some people in the Defense Department think there may, in fact, be something psychic about these insects. Is there any truth to that, Tom?"

Heller could tell that Briggs felt embarrassed to be raising the question. He used the advantage that gave him. "I hope that's not the level at which you intend to pitch this program. If you scratch around enough, you'll find people who blame the bugs on UFOs."

Briggs backed off deftly, but not Kayla. "That's something I've been curious about, Tom. Remember when you asked me to trace the little girl . . . Daphne what's her name? Her mother is connected with this rather exotic church that does ritual numbers. Were you working out some kind of psychic angle along those lines?"

Briggs was paying uncomfortably close attention. Heller shunted Kayla's question aside. "You've been doing too much children's programming, Kayla. I doubt we can get the wicked witch of the west in on this show."

Defensively, Kayla pressed further. "Well, what came of that? Did you find the mother?"

"It was a dead end," Heller said flatly. Kayla and Briggs were waiting for more. "I simply wanted to find out if any of the kids had seen some insects around the Brain while we were filming. They hadn't."

"Perhaps we should talk to the little girl too . . . and her mother." Briggs was fishing to see Heller's reaction.

As casually as he could, Heller passed the suggestion off. "You won't find anything there." Quickly he shifted his ground. "Does what I'm saying here about the use of the 'Wonder/Wander' material make any sense to you, Lloyd?"

Briggs studied him like a judge deciding a point of law. "I want to be fair, Tom. If we agree not to use whatever 'Wonder/Wander' footage you feel is inappropriate, will you give us some help with the show?"

"You mean on camera? I may not be up to it. Even when I'm out of here, my time will be very restricted. I've got lots of catching up to do."

"I understand. We wouldn't need much from you to lend weight to the show. Do you mean what you said about the world being too unpredictable for the computers?"

Heller gave a bitter little laugh. "The Brain almost killed me last Saturday morning. It did kill four men. None of my computers predicted that. None of them could have. Life has too many ambushes."

"It would mean a great deal to have someone of your authority tell us that. The world is suffering a high technological hemorrhage, Tom. People have a right to learn something from a disaster like this. Perhaps the best lesson computer science can teach us—its own limitations."

Under Briggs' unwavering gaze, Heller felt like a penitent who was being given a chance for public contrition. He did not know Briggs well. This might be the sort of ethical intimidation he used on every tough customer he confronted when he was out for a story. Or perhaps what Heller heard in Briggs' voice was his own conscience. "All right," he answered softly. "If I'm up and around when you need me . . ."

"We'll wait until the last possible moment," Briggs said. "We can even try something live on the night of the broadcast —if our equipment is still working. After all, there may be more to ask you about then."

Before she and Briggs left the room, Kayla stopped at the door to ask a last question. "What *was* her name?" Her notebook was in her hand.

"Whose name?"

"The little girl. Daphne *what?*"

Heller shrugged her off coolly. "I can't recall. Are you sure her name was Daphne?"

2

In the late afternoon, Jane and Leah arrived. Both looked burdened by fear and confusion. They came with their defenses raised, knowing what Heller would ask of them, yet without any awareness that they might be in a position to bargain or make demands. Instead, they readily admitted their sense of responsibility for Heller's injuries and the disaster at the Center. Heller was almost embarrassed by the moral leverage this gave him in dealing with them.

All the while he talked, seeking to win their consent for Gable to examine Daphne, he realized he was carrying out a distasteful assignment. If he did not gain access to the child, he would lose his value to Touhy, surrender his influence over policy. But if he did persuade Jane to turn her daughter over to Gable, what was his position then? He was clinging to the margins of power, serving Gable's needs, not his own, making promises he did not believe and could not guarantee.

"Sooner or later," he told Jane, "the press will get on to Earthrite and to Daphne. Just this morning I talked to some people from CBS News who may already be trying to track you and Daphne down. They're bound to succeed. What will you do when they finally ferret out the whole story? I don't want to alarm you, but you must realize that you, Daphne, the church, could be identified in the public eye as some kind of Satanic conspiracy. The media wouldn't have to try very hard to make this a supersensational story. That could place all of you in the greatest danger."

Leah's face tightened with concern. "You think there could be a public outcry against us? Some form of persecution?"

"I think you would be wise to find a dependable seclusion for Daphne. Away from reporters, away from the public. Somewhere we can deal with her quietly and humanely. If the people I'm working with now can succeed where your exercises failed, the crisis may pass without Earthrite being drawn in at all."

"But what will they do with her?" Jane asked.

Heller offered Gable's description of the procedures, presenting it almost as if it were conventional medical care. Leah listened respectfully, but was stubbornly reluctant. "There could be dangers in this," she warned. "The child has never been subjected to these psychiatric techniques."

"But surely," Heller argued, "you'll agree that there could be dangers in allowing Daphne to continue as she is, possessing these strange powers. What do you have in mind for her future? You can't control the effects she produces. And these are deadly effects. How long can that go on? Do you realize what damage she might eventually do?"

Jane shuddered. "I don't want anybody treating her like some kind of monster."

"Of course not," Heller said. "Professor Gable and his people aren't like that. They're scientists, doctors." He fought against his own doubts as he spoke. Before his mind's eye there was the image of Gable's arrogant, unfeeling face . . . and Father Guiness advertising himself as the hammer of witches. He blotted out the thought and went on. "She'll be treated with every professional consideration. You can be there with her. And you too," he assured Leah.

"I must tell you, Dr. Heller," Leah replied. "I have talked to my friends Ernst and Beata. We no longer believe these events are due to some quirk of the little girl's mind. Beata, in her exercise, became convinced: the problem is not in the child, not in the insects. No. It is in your machines."

"How do you mean?" Heller asked, startled at the remark.

"You recall the first time we spoke—at Gaia Lodge. I suggested there could be more behind this than one child's unfortunate misunderstanding. That possibly Daphne has only served to focus the fears of many children, many people. So, we go a little further now with this line of thought, yes? How are we to understand such a remarkable development? Could this be a *warning* to us, a warning born from the fears of children? Something special, unique, even therapeutic. Something that goes to the heart of the evil."

"Evil . . . ?" Heller smarted at the word and let it show.

Leah continued, but not nearly apologetically enough. "You must forgive me for being so tactless. I do not wish to offend. But I wonder if perhaps even you have not sometimes feared that we have gone too far with these computers which you call 'brains,' 'intelligences.' It is not the same with these as with other machines. We do not ask these machines to work for us, but to *think* for us. We give away to them something so distinctly, so preciously human. And yet, it is not the whole human mind we can give them, but only a part—the purely logical part divorced from tenderness and compassion, divorced from all the past and from the deep knowledge of the earth. We entrust too much to these counterfeit brains. Bombs. Missiles. The choice of apocalypse. It is too much power for any one man, any one government to possess. A great power is a great evil."

"Or a great good," Heller insisted. "These data processing systems are no better or worse than the people who use them, Miss Hagar. They are tools. Sophisticated tools, but still tools. They can be used to harm, to kill—but also for beneficial purposes. There's a lot of superstitious fear surrounding computers. I don't subscribe to it."

Leah nodded, granting him his point. "Yes, surely on such matters we can disagree, I hope respectfully. But perhaps, after all, it is not up to us to decide on things so grandiose. In nature, always there are reciprocities. Always there is balance, the circle returning to its beginning. Our church, Earthrite, is a worship of balance. The two knives you have seen us use, they are a symbol of that balance for us. The black knife and the white, always together, crossed. This reminds us that good and evil are not *this* or *that*, but *too much* of this, *too much* of that. I only mean to suggest that evil may be anything that becomes too much.

"Your machines, the computers, are, at this moment, too much. So there is need of balance. The moment comes for that. And how does it come? Maybe like this—from where we do not expect it, from the fears of children, the foolish things that confound the wise. They bring us this warning that we have gone too far and now must return. You and I —learned people—we might argue forever and not agree. And all the while the power of the machines goes on growing, growing, until it is beyond our control. But now, you see, there are these bugs in your computers. You use this curious, childish phrase—'bugs.' And suddenly they are there, just as a child would imagine them. So now everything must change. It is taken out of our hands. I think something like this lies behind this strange happening."

Heller allowed a long silence to follow her words. He wanted to give a patient, considerate reply, despite the anger he felt boiling up inside.

"You call the computers evil," he said. "But it's the bugs that are doing the killing, the bugs your church helped release. And it isn't simply people like myself who are being injured— people you might feel are responsible for this 'evil.' Many of the people killed so far have been innocent security guards, military men, ordinary people who don't know anything more about computers than you do. I would say these bugs of yours are behaving quite indiscriminately—more blindly and brutally than the computers have ever acted."

Leah was frowning over her thoughts, struggling with the conviction she wished to voice. "Yes, yes, I understand. It is horrible. I know you will believe me if I say that never would I deliberately release such a power if I had known the consequence. But nature must often strike out in such severe ways.

Human beings are hard to teach. Our pride is hard to break. We are creatures of fear and violence, and of great arrogance. You will excuse me if I observe that this is especially true of the men, men in positions of power. Often harshness, violence is all they will respect.

In the folktales and religious teachings of the world, many times a necessary instruction is placed in the mouth of a dreadful being—an ogre or dragon. Sometimes furies must be sent to chastise the wrongdoer. Also, there are forbidden places, sacred ground where a terrifying guardian must be posted. You have seen the gargoyles of medieval cathedrals, yes? Such ugly things. Yet, they are there in the service of God —to ward off evil. The bugs, I think, are the same. Gargoyles, guardians. They make us afraid, but they are not the evil. The evil is what they defend against. This is what came to Beata in her exercise. She felt so strongly she was working in the wrong direction—*contra naturam*."

Her remarks worried Heller. "Does this mean," he asked, "that you no longer wish to help with the problem? Are you telling me you're willing to let the bugs take over?"

"I cannot speak for Jane. She must do as she sees fit. I only say we confront something far greater than we realized. It is not simply a matter of curing this one child, altering her fears or dreams . . . 'deconditioning' her, I think would be the word your brain technicians use. No, it is not a matter of simple mental engineering, but of recognizing this child's mission and, I think, acquiescing. Yes, acquiescing."

Heller glared at her with rising contempt. What she was saying was weak and treacherous. She was surrendering to the insects. She was, after all, a superstitious old woman. "You misjudged before," he said. "You were mistaken about Daphne's dream to begin with. How can you be so sure now? I'm afraid I can't agree that we should simply lie down and give up. The insects are ruthless, destructive, alien. We *must* try to destroy them. We have the right to do that." He turned to Jane. "Do you agree with her?"

Jane looked back at him in blank and pitiful confusion. "I

don't know, I just don't know. I'm willing to try what you want . . . but I'm afraid for Daphne."

"Why?" he asked impatiently. "What harm can come to her?"

Jane looked from Heller to Leah and back. Anxiety strained her features. "I didn't tell you everything about Daphne's dreams," she said. "Neither of you. There was something more. You see, they weren't just dreams."

"Jane, what are you saying?" Leah asked.

"Night after night her dreams became more vivid, more real," Jane went on. "Daphne dreamed of being attacked by the bugs. She said she could feel them in the bed with her. One night when she called out in her sleep, I found the bugs there—in her hair, on her body. I thought I was hallucinating at first. But no, they were actually there. I could . . . touch them. So you see, I was the first person to see them. I didn't know what they were, where they came from. Except I knew they were *her* insects, her dream breaking through into our world. It was ghastly. Not simply that they were there, but what it meant about my daughter, the terrible power that was in her, that I had helped create in her."

Leah stared at her in hurt astonishment. Apologetically, Jane said to her, "I didn't want anyone to know, not even you. I felt terrified . . . and ashamed."

Heller asked, "The bugs didn't harm her?"

"No, they were simply on her, hardly moving."

"What happened to them?"

"I picked her up, and when she woke, they . . . just vanished. They were gone."

"They didn't bite you?"

"No. They seemed . . . slow, drowsy. They hardly moved. I just brushed them off her, and they fell. But I'm afraid it might be dangerous to bring her back to that memory. She'd be so frightened."

"Yes, I agree," Leah said. "If the insects could once be so real to her, what might happen now if this process were reversed?"

Heller was stymied. He could not say how Gable's methods would come to grips with the problem. What promises could he make? "Look," he said, moving forward cautiously on shaky ground, "isn't it possible that Professor Gable might have an approach that avoids that danger? Isn't it worth a try? None of us wants to hurt Daphne. But sooner or later, as long as the bugs are there, she's going to be at risk. You'll be dealing with responsible, rational men who want to eliminate that risk."

"We will also be dealing with powerful men," Leah said shrewdly. "Men in official authority, trying to save their way of life. Excuse me, Dr. Heller, but I have had some experience with such men in my life. Would they let the life of a child stand in their way?" At her words, Jane winced visibly. Heller could feel her drawing off, retreating toward cover.

"But you'll be there," Heller insisted. "Both of you. Dr. Fritsch can be there, Sperling can be there."

"Yes," Leah agreed, "a handful of little people without power."

"*I'll* be there," Heller blurted out the promise, playing it like a trump card. "I'll be there if you need me. You have my word: I won't let them hurt the child."

"You have the power to stop them?" Leah asked pointedly.

"Of course I do," Heller insisted almost boastfully. "For God's sake, how much of a risk do you think these people would run with their reputations? One word from any of you, one word from me to the President or to the press . . . You must be reasonable about this. You're implicated in a grave public emergency. You can't simply opt out."

Leah nodded knowingly. "Ah, yes, Dr. Heller. Of that I am certain. Do we really have any choice in this matter? If we say no, you cannot have the child—what then? Would we be left in peace, left to ourselves? Would your friends simply make the best of it?" She fixed him with a penetrating gaze. Heller did not answer. He knew what she feared. "No, I think not," she went on. "Also I think there is no chance for us to hide. Perhaps already we are being watched. I am right, would you say, that what is really being said here is: we must accept the best arrangement we are offered?" She turned to Jane. "You understand, my dear? It is better they take the child on Dr. Heller's terms, and us with her. Otherwise . . ." She shook her head resignedly.

Jane's eyes were on him, placing all that Leah had said to him as a question. Chagrined, Heller admitted, "She's right. I don't think there's much chance you can walk away from this. Please trust me. Choose what will allow you to protect Daphne the most. I give you my word . . ."

His voice faltered and fell. He was pleading for her trust in the midst of a lie, and he felt deeply ashamed. He could not guarantee anything that happened outside this room, not even his own powers of intervention. More humiliating still, he knew no way to counsel resistance, even in the face of what Leah had now exposed as naked intimidation. Opposition to authority was nowhere to be found in his moral repertory. More than anything else, he was toiling to make himself useful to Touhy, to the President, to men of power whose favor he craved.

In another moment, Jane, wearied and beaten down, agreed to his proposal. She would be ready to leave with Daphne tomorrow. Leah and Robert Fritsch would come with her; she would also arrange for Sperling to visit. As she rose to leave, she reached across to press his hand. "Get well," she said. And her eyes added, silently, Let me trust you. Don't hurt me, don't betray me.

After she had gone, a vague memory stirred at the back of his mind, an image that still belonged to a dream. When had he pleaded for her trust like this before? Somewhere sealed away from light and warmth. He had reached out to her, touching a smooth and icy surface between them, a lethal barrier.

The image faded, except for her eyes, begging to trust him. He would have preferred to drive those eyes from his thoughts, to free himself of their claim. But he knew that could not happen now. Some distant, half-real memory of her had become part of his conscience.

15

1

The long, chauffeured limousine that stood outside Jane Hecate's little house was more than an automobile. It was an emblem of official power. Nearly blocking the narrow street, it waited at the curb like a dark predatory beast, its engine rumbling impatiently. Children on their way to school paused to stare and point.

Captain Schaeffer, professionally cheerful and courteous as ever, walked briskly to the door and knocked. Jane was expecting him; a few pieces of luggage waited on the porch. They had talked on the phone the previous day, making arrangements for a "short stay" as guests of the Defense Department. Jane and Daphne would be going to Mount Rose; Schaeffer described it as an army medical facility closer to Richmond than Washington; safe, secluded, quiet. "You'll find it very comfortable," he assured her. "Almost like a resort."

Inside the car, Richard Gable sat waiting, filling the back seat with cigarette smoke. Introduced to Jane, his mouth curled into a small, stiff smile. His eyes were on Daphne at once, intent and penetrating. It was clear he did not know how to talk to children. The effort he made sounded hollow. "And how's our special little girl this morning?" he asked.

Daphne did not answer; childishly, she contorted her body into a reluctant posture and cringed at her mother's side. Jane maneuvered in her seat to place herself between Gable and the girl. As she did so, she caught sight of Father Guiness in the front seat. A priest in dark glasses. Who was he? She looked to Schaeffer for an introduction; none was offered. Guiness did not turn to greet her. He sat facing forward, his massive head of white hair nodding and wagging as he mused to himself.

"You'll be picking up my friends?" Jane asked. She meant Leah and Dr. Fritsch, who were to accompany her to Mount Rose.

"Oh yes," Schaeffer said. "Another car is calling for them." He perched himself in front of her on a fold-down seat. "They're already on their way."

He reached to pull the car door closed; Jane held back, leaning against it. "Did you forget something?" he asked, smiling, as if he were ready to whip back into the house for some final item.

"No," she said uncertainly, "but I thought . . ." Schaeffer tugged the door against her weight, forcing her into the car. "Sorry," he said, still smiling. He knocked on the glass partition behind him, a signal to the driver, a man in an Air Force uniform. The car pulled into the street immediately.

"I thought," Jane continued, "my friends would be riding with me."

"I don't believe that was the arrangement," Schaeffer said. "Much faster this way, using two cars."

Jane rubbed her arm where the car door had knocked against her. It did not hurt, but she knew the lingering sensation she felt there belied Schaeffer's smile. The closing of the car door had been a small, ambiguous act of coercion, and she had yielded to it.

"What about Dr. Heller?" she asked.

"He'll be along in a few days. He's still laid up, you know. I doubt they'll check him out until the weekend."

Daphne, drawing away from Gable's insistent gaze, buried her head in Jane's lap. "Want to go home," she whispered, pouting. Jane hugged her close; together they sank deep into the soft leather seat. Peeping out from under her mother's arm, Daphne stole a glance at Gable. Nobody saw her hands, hidden from view, form into tiny finger pincers. Under her breath she mouthed the words, "Pinch, pinch . . ."

"I've been in touch with Daphne's father," Jane said, uncomfortably aware of the nervous tremor in her voice. She tried to swallow it away. "He will be flying in tomorrow morning from Boston. He expects to join us for a few days."

"Yes, I had a call from Dr. Heller last night about Professor Sperling," Schaeffer replied. "He'll be met at the airport and driven to Mount Rose."

Several streets beyond the house, the car entered the expressway—Route 95 toward Arlington. At once, it surged forward with a smooth, eager thrust that settled Jane more deeply into her seat. With the windows closed and the air-conditioning on, the car moved almost soundlessly, bulleting past the morning traffic at well above the speed limit. The narrow, tinted windows gave the rear seat a cozy, unreal seclusion. Jane was in a moving fortress, a high-speed citadel designed to shelter busy men of affairs from the grime and noise of the world outside. Here, great questions of state could be discussed in subdued tones. There was a telephone embedded in the leather armrest at her side, a link with distant centers of government. Floating buoyantly over the road, the car surrounded her with a sense of quiet, efficient power that was more impressive, more intimidating than she might have experienced in an airplane. Here, one did not leave the world behind and out of sight; one cleft one's way neatly through it, through its struggling traffic, its slums and shopping centers, its industrial parks like a speeding phantom—in the world, but not of it, not bound by its law or courtesies.

Jane had often seen these powerful official cars racing through the city on their privileged missions, obeying no law but their own, carrying ambassadors, senators, presidents, who expected all barriers to yield magically at their approach. It had once struck her that they were like the Black Riders in the Tolkien stories she read to Daphne and the children at school —ominous and mysteriously empowered travelers, dispatched on inscrutable assignments for a remote dark lord. For them, the police cleared away all obstacles, invoking special rules. At one point along the way, where the cars thickened into a jam, the limousine swerved into the narrow shoulder lane and, at undiminished speed, arrowed past a few miles of stalled commuters. A dangerous maneuver not even noticed by Gable or Schaeffer, taken in stride. Rocked gently, disarmingly in the cushioned comfort of the back seat, Jane knew she had entered another world, *their* world, a domain of practiced official arrogance. She did not belong here. She hated being here. It was a subtle trap, and it had already closed upon her.

Little was said in the car. Jane stroked Daphne's hair in her lap and gazed vaguely out the window. A few times, she caught Captain Schaeffer's eye; he smiled back with well-trained amiability. He possessed a classic masculinity: cool, handsome, politely domineering. He reminded her of the airplane pilots who visited passengers in mid-flight to show off their status and self-confidence. When they were several minutes under way, he offered her coffee from a silver thermos carried in a serving tray at his side. A little later, as they were skirting Arlington, the red light on the telephone blinked and he reached out to take a brief call. She heard him say, "Yes . . . yes . . . on schedule." He replaced the phone and smiled again.

Several times, when her eyes wandered in Gable's direction, she caught him studying Daphne furtively. Once, noticing her look, he dug into his briefcase and drew out some journal reprints. "Would you care to read through some of my research?" he asked. She nodded and took the literature. Flipping through, she found it filled with a language she could not fathom. Passages that read like physiology alternated with passages about atomic particles and electronic apparatus. The titles suggested studies of the brain and the nervous system. There were obscure calculations and many charts. What could this cadaverous research have to do with her and her daughter?

Her mind went back six years to the day the little girl she held at her side had been born. She remembered the rites that had accompanied the event—a women's ceremony borrowed from many sources like a crazy quilt made by many hands. There had been poetry and song, invocations to the earth and moon. The birth had taken place in the grove at Gaia Lodge, in a cabin the women of the church had built themselves. A priestess-midwife, one of many Jane called sister, had performed an American Indian smudging of the mother and newborn using incense of sage. Candles ringed her about; sanctified water was poured over her belly and breasts. Yes, there was pain, there was unbearable expectancy, but never fear. The baby had been born to the sound of her mother's crying out; blood had streamed over her thighs. Yet the moment brought a fierce, clean joy. It had been the right beginning for her strange, gifted daughter. She had been born into the company of women, passed from hand to hand around the circle, surrounded by love and wonder.

Now, suddenly, with too little thought, she had delivered her child into another world, the quintessential world of men where soldiers, politicians, scientists ruled. And she was quietly terrified. Not by any show of force or by any weapon—but by the towering walls of cold male logic and unfeeling precision she sensed closing in upon her, blocking out the earth and sky and the powers of sisterhood. Heller's work, Gable's work, her former husband's work—it was all fleshless abstraction, bound up with matters of state. There was nothing here that touched the senses, nothing that made the imagination dance.

Across from her sat a soldier under orders to take her, confine her. His face had been trained to smile just as his hands had been trained to kill. The courtesies he offered were no more than instructions handed down, the sort of lie men understood to be necessary, important. If it came to it, he would as soon take her in those hands and force her to do his will, break her, crumble her. Like Heller's computers, he was a machine. Gable's learned papers also carried plans for machines, arcane instruments designed to probe the mind, measure the soul. What nonsense! No wonder these men placed such faith in machines, told the world that machines were superior to people. They *were* machines. They had already mechanized themselves. None of them knew the true depth of their lives, the wisdom of their bodies. None of them knew the earth, its patient and insistent power. How she despised them for the false, ugly things they had made of themselves! For Heller, in his confusion and helplessness, she had begun to feel the warmth of pity. Something in her had reached out toward him, a tentative gesture. Now she saw how he had betrayed her, turning her over to these robots.

The first hour of the trip passed quickly. Daphne, half-dozing in Jane's lap, looked up now and again to glance from Gable to Schaeffer and back. Finally, her eyes were drawn to Father Guiness, still a massive, unnamed presence in the front seat. Squinting hard, she studied the back of his head for several minutes. Then, reaching up, she drew her mother down to her. Pointing at Guiness, she whispered in Jane's ear, "He prays to the bugs." Gable caught the remark. His eyes went at once to Jane's. She turned away to discover that Father Guiness had turned in the front seat, straining behind his dark glasses to see her, a wide, hard grin across his face. Quickly, she looked away out the window, a chill flashing over her body.

Soon afterward, rocked in the spongy rhythm of the car, Daphne fell asleep. Jane nodded a little herself at the window, watching the swiftly moving landscape. Then, registering the signs they were passing, she asked, "Shouldn't we be going south, toward Richmond?"

Schaeffer looked up as if the remark had distracted him from his train of thought. "Um?"

"The signs say Wheeling. We're heading west," she said.

"Yes," he answered, agreeing to the fact as obvious. And then, as if seeing her point, "We won't be going directly to Mount Rose."

A twinge of anxiety plucked at her mind. "Where *are* we going?" she demanded.

"We're stopping off at another facility along the way—just for a few preliminary things."

"This isn't 'along the way,'" she observed. "We're miles to the west. What 'preliminary things'?"

Schaeffer passed the question over to Gable. "A brief physical exam," he answered. "A few lab tests. It's a better setup for that than Mount Rose."

"You didn't tell me that." She let her irritation show.

"Hardly seemed worth mentioning," Schaeffer said, unperturbed by her annoyance. "It's just a brief stop."

"How long will we be there?"

"Very briefly," Gable said. "Probably not more than over-night."

"Overnight?" She stiffened with anger. "But the others will be at Mount Rose."

"Yes," Schaeffer said. "You'll be seeing them soon. You don't mind, do you?" Amiably, never losing his smile, he was telling her she mustn't mind, that she had no choice about minding. She sank back in her seat. She did not feel frightened, but frail and resigned, realizing she had expected this all along. So this is how they do it, she thought. This is how they get their way. She had entered their province, and she was not supposed to mind anything they cared to do. Wrapped in the cushioned plush of the sleek limousine, she and her daughter were morsels in Leviathan's belly.

2

"How does it feel?" the doctor asked.

"Fine. No problem," Heller answered, lying for all he was worth. He was taking his first steps in nearly a week, limping around his private room. His ankles were swollen thickly under heavy bandages; his throat was an inferno of pain. Stripes of fire shot through his body with each movement. His face censored the anguish. "Good as new."

The doctor looked uncertain. "We haven't gotten the swelling down very much. I don't see how you'll get your shoes on."

Heller did a little hop and skip. His ankles shivered almost enough to make him fall, but he held his balance. "There," he announced, grinning broadly against the pain. "Really, it's nearly painless. I'll just stay off the tennis court for a few weeks."

"And your eye?" the doctor asked.

"A little light shy," Heller answered. "But I can wear sun-glasses." In fact, he could hardly keep his left eye open. He forced the fluttering lids wide apart. Tears clouded his vision. "It's my weak eye anyway."

"I don't know," the doctor said dubiously. "It doesn't look good. Any more flare-ups like on Wednesday?"

He was asking about a sudden, severe onset of pain Heller had experienced Wednesday evening. For over an hour, he had felt hot, jagged thrusts at his throat and around his left eye where the doctors suspected the bugs might still be lodged. He had tried to hold out against the distress, but finally called for help. He was given heavy doses of codeine and was sedated for the night. What he had felt was a sensation like needles being driven deep into his muscle tissue: the insects still at work, tunneling farther in. But why then? And why did they stop all at once? The next morning, though he did not say so, the vision in his wounded eye had beome noticeably dimmer.

"No flare-ups," Heller answered. "I'm sure that was something freakish."

"It's all freakish, the whole thing," the doctor commented. "What we're most concerned about is any internal damage the insects might still do if we didn't get them all out—as, apparently, we didn't. They might lie quiescent . . . well, we can't say for how long. Nothing shows up on x-rays or in the probes we've done. And, as you know, there's no way to knock them out. We've got you on a heavy course of antibiotics to check possible infection. If we released you, that would have to continue. And you'd have to come in pretty frequently to have your dressings checked. It would really be advisable to have you stay . . ."

"The team needs me, coach," Heller insisted.

"Yes, I know. Well, we can't hold you here against your will. Will you agree to report to out-patient every other day for the next week or so—at least until we're sure there's no chance of infection?"

"Regular as clockwork," Heller promised.

It was Friday afternoon. Heller had been at Walter Reed for seven days. He was still in fragile condition, but with each passing day, he felt the crisis slipping from his influence. He was desperate to leave the hospital and resume his responsibilities. His stoic performance convinced the medical staff; they agreed to discharge him the next day. On Saturday morning after breakfast, Levinson came by to pick him up. It was not until they had pulled away from Walter Reed that Heller dropped his pretense and for a moment let the pain show in his face.

"You're sure this is smart?" Levinson asked. "You really look hobbled."

Heller ignored the remark. "What's happening with Gable?" he asked.

"I surmise nothing dramatic. I get daily calls from Barney Kilraddin at Mount Rose. Very cordial, very upbeat. He's been programmed optimistic, but he's making no predictions. He tells me precisely nothing; Barney's good at that. Incidentally, this week my liaison at DoD has downshifted from Haseltine to Kilraddin: general to major. Our status would seem to be slipping. Or maybe it's just my low grade presence on the job."

"They're still at Mount Rose—Jane and the rest?" Heller asked.

"Uh-huh, as of this morning."

"You haven't talked to Jane or Leah directly?"

"No, but I never asked to. I thought I'd leave that for you. You speak their language. And, besides, we're overwhelmed at the Center as it is, without trying to keep track of our psychic friends. Whatever progress Gable may be making isn't showing up on our end. On the contrary. The catch phrase around the new, economy-sized Center for Data Control is 'a transitional period of accelerated compulsory restructuring.' Meaning we're racing like hell to keep ahead of the avalanche. You might deduce that much from the newspaper accounts. I'll give you the big gloomy picture when we get to our new home away from home—which, as you'll see, is quite a comedown from the Brain. Remember that old movie where Bette Davis walks on and says, 'What a dump!' I expect a similar response from you when we get there."

3

The emergency headquarters for the NCDC was a rapidly converted upper story of the old Administrative Services Building, a slightly decaying WPA remnant in the no-man's land south of the Anacostia River. Planes from Bolling Air Force Base roared over the building loud enough to interrupt conversations. Heller and his senior staff had been allocated desks, files, typewriters, telephones—little more. Most of the office space was squared off with frosted glass partitions that ended at head level. The quarters were cramped and dismal: bare walls painted a glossy institutional beige and high-ceilinged light fixtures. The neon tube above Heller's own small office was troubled with what seemed like terminal flicker. "Tried to get that fixed," Levinson said. "The maintenance up in these reaches of the building isn't too prompt. They seem to get to us after the ladies' room in the typing pool."

Surveying his provisional office, Heller felt a numbness at his heart that momentarily eclipsed the physical pain in his body. It was a moment of crowning depression. "I'd agree with Bette Davis," he said. "It looks about that vintage." He lowered himself gingerly into an old wooden swivel chair behind his desk and rocked back and forward. The chair creaked abrasively. Heller pulled a sad face. "Didn't get around to that," Levinson apologized. "There were a few more pressing matters."

Heller was not one to conceal the gravity of the crisis he was in. He had faced up to the implications of Touhy's "worst case scenario." He was the captain of a sinking ship. Like a glamorous ocean liner foundering on the high seas, the once lordly technology he administered was going under, driving himself and his surviving crew into any miserable little lifeboat they could find. But nothing he had confronted so far captured his plight as poignantly as this dingy, antiquated office. Everything the Center for Data Control represented had been crudely swept into a dusty corner of Washington. The Administrative Services Building was a notorious bureaucratic graveyard where defunct agencies and moribund bureaus came to die. Now the NCDC shared their sad space. Only the impressive battery of telephones that lined Heller's desk served as an indication of work to be done, vital business at hand. The office had been well and quickly equipped with first class telecommunications. But he noted that the only computers in sight—a few desk-top minis—stood disconnected, shoved off into out-of-the-way corners. He asked why. "Can't we use them even to crunch some numbers?"

Levinson explained. "That's the latest addition to the catalogue of horribles. I took the liberty of holding off until you were back on the job—a small concession to your delicate condition. We can't trust any computational hardware any more —not even the modest minis. You can't touch them without picking up the rash. It's like working with poison ivy. In addition, they're glitching all over the place, even on simple arithmetic. It's sometimes hard to tell if it's actual hardware failure or human error due to the distraction of the rash. But I've had several pieces of small- and middle-range equipment checked out, actually torn down and inspected. Where there weren't bugs—we found a few small infestations—there was actual physical damage to the microprocessors and circuitry."

"What kind of damage?"

"They were chewed up—the way the electrical wiring in the Center was chewed up. Just random destruction—microchips with pieces broken or bitten out of them. We're better off counting on our fingers."

"How widespread is this?" Heller asked.

Levinson took a deep breath. "Okay, if you're up to it, let's review."

Within half an hour, Levinson had assembled the senior staff in a makeshift conference room. Two large wall charts were brought in. One was a map of the world with major computer centers, private and governmental, picked out by colored flags. As the facilities went from unaffected to afflicted but usable and finally to inoperable, their colors changed from blue to red to black. A scattering of white flags indicated uncertain or unreported centers, these mainly in Eastern Europe, Russia, China. Heller's eyes swept over the map. He could not find a blue flag anywhere; the majority were red, about a third were now black. As he surveyed the scene, he felt like a field marshal tracing the steady onset of defeat as his outposts fell to the enemy.

The second chart was a graph measuring in both absolute numbers and percentages the steady downward path of computer power in defense, heavy industry and other major sectors of the economy. For each category, there was a committee of consultants co-ordinated out of the makeshift Center, struggling to devise alternative processing routes and methods. Heller requested brief reports from several members of his staff. In giving the statistics of decline, their responses were crisp, professional, objective. But behind the tidy façade of exact numbers, Heller had no difficulty imagining the spreading daily chaos that was disrupting the lives of hundreds of millions: the power supplies and public services that would not be provided, the sewage and water that could not be properly monitored, the transport that had slowed to a crawl and was nowhere on schedule, the money, goods, resources that were simply being lost in countless dead ends and forgotten corners of the society where it was the computer's job to remember.

Next to several items on a list of priorities he had drawn up for the conference, Levinson had penciled in the word "hopeless." By the end of the morning when all the briefings were finished, Heller agreed with his pessimistic judgment. There were sectors of public life that were doomed to much worse than confusion and inconvenience; because they had been so thoroughly entrusted to the safekeeping of the computers, they would now be subtracted from history. The welfare accounts of the society, the credit references, very nearly all the nation's banking and insurance, countless records and archives . . . all these were pure data. They had seemed perfectly suited to the new information technology. Accordingly, they had been coded wholesale on microchips and memory tapes where they existed as nothing more than magnetic signals. No human eye or hand could any longer intervene to retrieve what was locked away in these tiny electronic repositories. What had been placed there would vanish forever amid the deteriorating silicon and polyvinyl from which the computer's memory tissues were fashioned.

4

It was late afternoon before Heller found time to place a call to Mount Rose. He asked for Jane. After a lengthy wait, he was put through to a man . . . Major Kilraddin.

"Hello, Barney," Heller said. "I'm calling to talk to Jane Hecate."

"Good to hear from you, Tom. Are you calling from Walter Reed?"

"No, I was discharged today. I'm at our temporary office in Administrative Services."

Kilraddin began to ask about his injuries. Heller promptly reminded him of the reason he had called. "I promised Miss Hecate I'd stay in touch with her."

"Yes, of course. I'm sorry I can't put you through to her just now. She's having a session with Dick Gable."

"When will she be finished?"

"It would be best to call tomorrow."

"May I talk to Leah Hagar? Or Dr. Fritsch?"

"They're all in on this. Sorry. Try tomorrow."

"I see. Has Christopher Sperling shown up there?"

"The father? Oh yes. On Thursday. He's nicely settled in."

"May I talk with him?"

"He's with Gable too. Sorry."

"All evening long?"

"I'm afraid so. We don't like to interrupt these sessions."

"Sounds pretty intensive."

"We're trying to make the most of the time. Seem to be making some progress."

"Oh? May I know what?"

"Well, I'd rather have Dick explain it."

"It isn't showing up with us. In fact, things are running down fast."

"Well, I wouldn't know about that."

After a pause, Heller asked, "Barney, I'd like to drop by there tomorrow."

"Tomorrow? You're sure you can spare the time? Sounds as if you've got your hands full."

"Tomorrow's the sabbath," Heller joked. "You don't mind me visiting, do you?"

"Of course not. Simply clear it with Lyman's office."

"Clear it? Why do I have to do that?"

"Orders, I'm afraid. Just routine."

Heller put in a call to the Pentagon—first to Touhy's office, then to Haseltine's. He could tell at once that he was being stalled. Nobody he wanted could be contacted short of a national emergency. When would they be available? Nobody could say. Would he try calling back Monday morning? Heller asked about Mount Rose. Was there anyone on hand who could give him clearance to the hospital? Nobody recognized the name. Would he please phone back on Monday?

Heller hung up in anger. What did he do now? Call Kilraddin back and demand admission to Mount Rose? Or should he simply go there directly? He might put through an emergency call to Touhy; he had the code and authority for that. Did he dare attempt it with nothing more to request than permission to make a visit? That was bound to seem pesty and distrustful. Above all, he must tread carefully, avoiding confrontation. Clearly, he was being screened out of Gable's work. But he must try to change that before he challenged it.

He decided to let the matter slide—at least until the next day. The truth was: he was feeling weak and tired, ravenously in need of rest. The pain-killers he was using were building up in his system, making him lightheaded, insecure in his responses. He knew he was taking longer than normal to answer questions. "Sorry," he had apologized to his staff more than once that day, "I'm feeling a little cloudy up here."

At the end of the afternoon, Levinson offered him an invitation to dinner, but Heller turned him down. He wanted a quiet evening, the chance to turn in early. He took a taxi to his townhouse, carrying away with him two briefcases filled with urgent business. He knew he would be too weary to look at it, but there was one item he was determined to read. Levinson had secured a photostat of the pages cited by Professor Ulrich from Lavater's *Arcana Anatomica*. There had not been time to solicit a translation; Heller would have to apply his own rusty Latin.

The text proved to be straightforward and posed few problems beyond antiquated technical terms. Despite his fatigue, Heller picked his way through the ornate seventeeth-century typeface with keen attention.

The excerpt recounted a dissection performed by the Dutch physician Claes Pieterszoon Tulp. The specimen under study was referred to by several names; most often it was called *monstrum parvum* or *incubus parvus*—little monster or demon. But it was also called *homunculus miser*—wretched little man. There was a description of its discovery or creation—the Latin word *inventio* had that ambiguity about it, meaning both something found and something made. The account was couched in more alchemical lore than Heller could follow. The "*inventor*," Henrik Van Vechten, was identified as a "spagyric philosopher" and treated as a somewhat ominous character. There were hints in the text that he had come to a bad end, falling under the Church's anathema. As for the creature itself, its nature and appearance were left shadowy. The adjectives *ferox* (fierce) and *horrendus* (hideous) were used many times; it was also characterized as *carnivorus* (meat-eating) and *larvalis* (goblin-like). At one point, it was said to be *quasi reptilis*—reptilian; but it was also credited with the ability to speak.

With a chilling uneasiness, Heller realized he was peering back into another world where rudimentary science and ancient superstition mingled. It was an age that ought to be buried forever in the past. Yet, here he was now, living through a similar interval, a time of intersecting realities.

Many of the anatomical terms in the passage eluded him, but Heller could recognize the general drift of the account. There was a Latin negation connected to every physical feature mentioned: "no this, no that." Nothing was found inside the body. Scrutinized under a primitive seventeeth-century microscope, the uncanny little being was only *vacuum album*—a white void. The author commented:

All concerned would have considered the prodigy a
hoax or a humanly crafted automaton, if they had not
witnessed its wildly vital behavior, and if some had
not been attacked and bitten.

It was unclear from the report if the creature had been alive
or dead during the dissection. The description of its dema-
terialization was even more obscure. There was only a brief reference to an alchemical ceremony and, at the conclusion, a
prayer offered up, imploring God never to let such an unnatu-
ral horror appear again on earth.

"Amen," Heller said to himself, drifting off toward sleep on
his couch, still dressed in his street clothes. He was brooding
about Jane and Leah, worried that he had not lived up to his
promise to stay close to them. Well, tomorrow for sure, he
thought . . .

5

He woke with a start to a persistent buzzing in his ears, suddenly fearful that it was the sound of the bugs once again. It
was the telephone. Groggy with sleep, he groped his way
through the now dark living room and picked up the receiver.
The voice at the other end of the line was not familiar to him.

"Dr. Heller? This is Rod Goren. You may remember me.
We did an interview about a year ago on channel four."

Heller strained to sharpen his dull attention. Yes, he vaguely
remembered Goren. A newsman on local television. They had
met a few times at press conferences. But why was he calling
now? Heller switched on a light and peered at his watch—two-
thirty in the morning. He had been sleeping for some three
hours. Outside, the weather had turned windy and wet. There
was hard rain against the windows. The voice on the phone
continued.

"Sorry to disturb you at this hour. I wouldn't do it if it
wasn't urgent. I wanted to confirm that Christopher Sperling is

with me, that I do have a tape cassette from him, and that I'll follow his instructions."

Heller, deeply puzzled, started to ask a question, but Goren had left the phone. Another voice, overloud and angry, suddenly drilled its way into his ear. "Heller, this is Sperling."

Heller's mind reeled. Why was Sperling calling him now? From where? "Listen to me, Heller," the tight, abrasive voice went on. "We're going to do this my way, understand? Or the shit hits the fan tonight. You heard Goren. He means what he says. I mean what I say. I'm coming over. I want to see you alone. The cassette Rod's got contains everything I know, including everything about Mount Rose. He has instructions to play back and broadcast if anything happens to me, or if your people don't co-operate."

Heller could not take in what what he was being told. "What are you talking about? Where are you calling from?"

"No questions!" Sperling shouted into the phone. "Just let me in when I get there. And don't call anyone. Don't do anything. Remember, I'm a rank amateur at intrigue. I could easily do something we'll all regret in the morning. What's your address?"

Heller gave it. He was instructed not to hang up; Goren would keep the line open until Sperling arrived. Heller was to make no calls out.

When Sperling left the phone, Heller slumped back into his chair trying to order his rambling thoughts. He became aware of a heavy throb in his head and the blaze of pain at his throat. He went into his kitchen to take some tetracycline capsules, then shook out a few codeine tablets from the supply he carried. He decided instead to use plain aspirin to keep his head clear. He made coffee and waited. A half hour later there was a buzz from the night doorman. A Mr. Sperling was in the lobby. Heller said, "Let him come up."

When he entered the apartment, his clothes wet and rumpled, Sperling stood with his back against the door looking like a trapped animal.

"Son of a bitch," he growled, staring at Heller. "Treacherous son of a bitch. You better believe what I say. I'll blow this story wide open if you don't let Jane and Daphne go free. Goren will spread the word to every newsman in town—everything I know." His voice rang with a high, strained note of hysteria, the sound of a frightened man unused to making threats, uncertain he was in a position to threaten. "Are we alone here?" he asked before he would enter the apartment.

"There's no one here but us," Heller said softly, trying to bring down the level of tension. He realized he was in the company of a desperate man. He was also beginning to suspect what Sperling had to tell him. It was turning his stomach soft and sick.

Entering the living room, he offered Sperling the telephone receiver. Sperling moved through the apartment, glancing in other rooms, opening a closet or two. Then he took the phone, assured Goren at the other end all was well and hung up.

"They held you at Mount Rose, didn't they?" Heller asked, afraid to hear the answer. "You and the others . . . they kept you confined."

"You think that's the worst?" Sperling asked in a dry, raspy voice. "I was *shot* at. Shot at! They might have killed me. Just who in hell do you people think you are? Christ! I'm so mad . . . and so scared! Oh, Jesus, I could wring your neck." He was on the edge of panic, trembling and tense, glaring at Heller. He held his hands clenched in his lap, the fingers laced together tightly. Heller noticed that his hands were bandaged; some of the fingers showed raw cuts.

"Do you want a drink?" Heller asked. "Whiskey? Coffee?"

"Yes," Sperling snapped. "Lots of both." He took out a handkerchief and began to mop his dripping hair. Holding out his damaged hands, he muttered, "I went over the barbed wire. Imagine that . . . like a goddamned prisoner of war." He made the remark as if he were telling himself something he could not believe. Heller brought him some scotch, a bottle of soda, a cup of hot coffee. Sperling drank off a mouthful of whiskey without using a glass and finally seemed to relax into his exhaustion. "Christ," he sighed. "I'm no good at this kind of thing. This is barbaric." He scowled at Heller. "Barbaric, you hear? With all your push buttons, computers, laser beams, speed of light . . ." He was rambling in his anger and confusion. Staring at his hands again, he said, "I could get tetanus. I should get a shot."

"I tried to get a call through to Mount Rose yesterday afternoon," Heller explained. "The man in charge there—Barney Kilraddin—gave me the runaround. That made me think something was very wrong. I'm being blocked out of this whole affair. They regard me as unreliable."

"Ha! *You're* unreliable," Sperling gave a bitter little laugh. "Then what's reliable? Absolute zombies?"

"Tell me about Mount Rose," Heller went on, ignoring the crack. "What are they up to? I was considering driving out today to see Jane, just presenting myself at the door."

Sperling eyed him distrustfully. "I'm supposed to believe you don't know Jane isn't there?"

"Not at Mount Rose." Heller was jarred by the news. "Where is she?"

"That's what I want to know from you," Sperling answered aggressively. "I want you to get her released and brought home —Jane and my daughter, and Leah, and Fritsch. Either that or I spill the beans."

"Look," Heller said, showing a little temper, "stop threatening me long enough to tell me what you know. I tell you, I'm in the dark about this. I don't know anything about Mount Rose. I'm not running this operation anymore; maybe I never was. Just for five minutes, believe me and tell me what happened to you."

Sperling gave a grudging "okay," drew a breath and calmed himself. "You know I was picked up at the airport Thursday morning. One of those hearse-sized limos with square-jawed military chauffeur. Lots of 'yessir,' 'nosir.' You did arrange for the transport, I gather."

"Yes," Heller said. "You were to be taken to Mount Rose to meet Jane and the others. That's the agreement I made with General Haseltine. He's high level military intelligence, pretty much in charge of the show now."

"When I got to Mount Rose," Sperling continued, "Leah and Roger were already suspicious. Who wouldn't be? The place is a fucking dungeon. Chain mesh fence ten feet high, barbed wire, armed guards at the gate. They had been told Jane and Daphne were spending a few days at some other facility. I asked to call you about that, and they gave me some story about your not being available at the hospital. That's when I realized we were prisoners. We couldn't make phone calls, we couldn't leave the grounds. It took me the rest of the day to realize that sheer indignation would get me exactly no place. This brute Kilraddin just kept bullying the hell out of us with consummate politeness. Sorry, we couldn't do this . . . sorry, he couldn't permit that. I think he would have cheerfully disemboweled us if those were his orders. How do you people produce a specimen like that?

"Finally, Friday morning I tried to force my way out the front gate. I gave one of the guards a big argument. He wasn't even taking me seriously enough to be careful. When I saw a chance, I grabbed his keys and started running for the gate. Heroic stupidity. The bastard pulled a gun and actually shot at me. The bullet went right past my ear. I gather he only meant to scare me. He did. I went back to my assigned quarters and began scheming. As it turns out, the place isn't that tightly patrolled. It's a vast estate, miles of fence and only a few guards. Probably they didn't think any of us looked up to climbing the fence. Well, goddam if I didn't—last night, I just walked out of the hospital after dinner and kept going until I got to the fence. Nobody stopped me. I thought for sure I'd be shot in the back. But I got over with surprisingly few puncture wounds and headed for the highway; flagged a lift into Washington and got in touch with Goren."

"Why him?" Heller asked.

"Who should I have gone to? The FBI? I assume your people own the police around here. I wanted to check in with somebody in the press I knew and trusted. Rod's an old student of mine, from years back. He's an honest, gutsy newsman. He won't hesitate to let the story out. I don't know if that concerns you, but it's all I've got right now to bargain with. All I want is to see Jane, my daughter, Leah and Fritsch released unharmed. You're crazy to think you can hold us anyway. People know I've come to Washington. I'm expected back in Cambridge on Monday. How the hell did you think you could get away with something this heavy-handed? This isn't even clever."

Sperling was right. This was a risky move. It smacked of desperation. That worried Heller. "When you were at Mount Rose," he asked, "did you see someone named Gable?"

"I met Smilin' Jack Kilraddin and a few of his myrmidons. That's all. The place looks deserted. Obviously nothing's happening there at all. We were just being held off the scene. Who's Gable?"

"Somebody who's taken my place in favor. He's calling the shots. He means to use Daphne to deal with the bugs."

A suggestion of alarm passed across Sperling's face. "But how? You don't mean he's a psychic?"

"I have no idea what he intends to do. I'm not getting told such things these days. Gable himself is an academic psychologist—very hard-nosed type. But he works with a clairvoyant of some description—a batty, old Irish priest named Guiness. What I know for sure is that Gable has been given carte blanche, right up to the point of kidnapping Jane and Daphne. He must assume he can get fast results—in a few days, before you and the others would be missed."

Sperling's eyes blazed at Heller. "How much of this are you to blame for?"

Sheepishly, Heller admitted, "More than enough. I told Jane to co-operate with them. I thought I'd struck a reasonable deal. I was supposed to be in touch with her at all times. They've lived up to none of that. I'm as much on the outside as you are."

Pondering the way he had been used and deceived, Heller discovered a tide of outrage rising in him. Over the years, he had grown accustomed to the possession of power. He had been entrusted with secrets, consulted on policy, envied, even hated for the privileges he enjoyed. Now, for the first time since he came to Washington, he knew what it was to be powerless, marginal. It was especially galling to appear this way to Sperling, who expected him to take action. But all Heller could think of was to appeal to Touhy to be heard and trusted, to have his status restored. He had no conviction that would happen. And if not, what did he do next? How much trouble was he prepared to make?

"Tomorrow . . ." he began, then glanced at his watch. It was nearly 4:30 A.M. "I mean later this morning I'll contact Touhy and ask that he let me see Jane. I'm sure if I can get through to him . . ."

"Touhy . . . ?" Sperling asked. He clearly did not recognize the name. Was that possible, Heller wondered. He had mentioned the second most powerful man in American politics, and Sperling seemed to have no idea what he was talking about. Were there people so far removed from the political realities of life? "Lyman Touhy," Heller explained. "The Secretary of Defense."

Sperling was unimpressed. Instead, his eyes flashed with exasperation. "Secretary of Defense! Why are we fooling around with flunkies here? We go to the President, man. We go straight to God. And we don't 'ask' for anything. We *demand*. Heller, I didn't come here to have you hold my hand and soothe my fevered brow. I came here to save lives, starting with my own. You know what I am? I'm a bomb ready to go off. I'm telling you: let my people go, or I make all the fucking noise I can all over this town."

He was on his feet now, pacing back and forth in front of Heller, haranguing him in a high, tight voice. "Jesus! The United States Army tried to kill me yesterday because I wouldn't sit quiet in a concentration camp. Look at me! This is pure rage you're looking at. If you knew how crazy with rage I am, you'd be scared stiff. At the best of times, I'm a borderline psychotic. That's no kidding. There's only so much I can take. Now, I expect you to get on that telephone and tell the President he's dealing with a raving maniac who's threatening to blow up his Administration. Remind him of Watergate. Tell him that's what's coming down by the break of day. And he's got just two ways of saving his ass. Either he releases my friends, or he bloody well liquidates me."

Heller felt himself going slightly faint with Sperling's intensity. He was oppressively weary, his mind working sluggishly. Sperling did look psychotic, his eyes wild, his mouth flooding over with threats and abuse. "Sperling," he pleaded, "that's not the way it works. Touhy's the man I've got to talk to. You've got to let me do this the way I know how."

"No, no, no!" Sperling insisted, bending over Heller, his face hot and twisted. "I'm not going to go pussy-footing around the corridors of power, filling out forms in triplicate. For all I know, my daughter is being carved into little pieces by these witch doctors of yours. I swear to you. I'm ready to run screaming through the streets. Out in the open, I feel safe. Your way, waiting for an appointment a week from next Wednesday, maybe I disappear down an elevator shaft. Am I making myself sufficiently irrational? Is my paranoia just possibly scaring the shit out of you? Good!"

Trembling with anger, he took hold of Heller's shoulder and began pulling him up out of his chair. "Now move, man! Pick up that telephone!"

"Sperling!" Heller cried, trying to calm him. It was useless. He could see the hysteria welling up in the man's face, turning ugly. Sperling, shouting incoherently, gave him a hard push toward the telephone, forcing Heller to stumble against a low coffee table. With the collision, pain flared sharply in his injured ankles. Maddened, Heller spun and struck out. His fist, coming around with all his force, caught Sperling on the cheek. There was a dull, fleshy thud, and Sperling reeled back, sprawling across the sofa. For the moment, he was unconscious; Heller was surprised at the effectiveness of the blow. It was the first time he had ever thrown a punch.

He sank down in the nearest chair and struggled to gather his thoughts. Was Sperling's urgency justified? What if Daphne's life *was* at stake—and Jane's? He no longer felt sure of his terrain. The methods he knew—administrative jockeying, bureaucratic pressure and leverage—no longer applied. Things were becoming plain brutal. Perhaps Sperling was right; he had confronted gunfire and forcible detention. He had been up against what Heller was still trying fastidiously to ignore: raw power, the ultimate sanction that stood behind all authority. Heller had never before been forced to look beyond the public façade of political life. Now, the rationality he had championed looked like a fading cosmetic that could no longer disguise the predatory face beneath. The essence of government was not, after all, statistics and information neatly assembled. It was the muzzle of a gun forcing people to do as they were ordered. He felt painfully naïve; even more so, he felt paralyzed, unable to act against men who had for so long held his allegiance, rewarded his service.

Like a screaming shell, the phone broke in upon his thoughts. He flinched with surprise. Taking up the receiver, he heard a familiar voice speak his name. "Tom?"

"Lyman . . . ?" Heller asked. "Yes, it's me."

The voice snapped, "Is Sperling there? Just say yes or no, if you can't talk."

How could Touhy know about Sperling? Heller, struggling to understand, answered, "Yes, he's here. It's all right, I can talk."

"He won't scare off?"

"No . . . no, he won't be running off just now. He can't hear us. Lyman, what the hell's going on? Sperling says you're keeping the Earthrite people against their wishes. And where's the girl and her mother? He says they're not at Mount Rose."

Touhy did not register the questions. Abruptly, he said, "Just keep Sperling there. I'm sending over to get him." Irritation and fatigue crackled in his voice.

"No, Lyman," Heller blurted out the words, speaking before he thought. "What legal right have we got to do this?" With difficulty, he said "we," hoping feebly to keep himself associated with decisions he had played no part in shaping.

"We'll go into that later, Tom. Right now we've got to secure Sperling."

Heller's mind raced to find some way to intervene and delay what Touhy was ordering. "Lyman, Sperling's been in touch with the newspapers. He's left information with them. If you take him against his will, it will all come out. He's charging us with kidnapping."

"Who has he told besides Goren?" Touhy demanded. "We've got Goren covered."

"You followed him to Goren?" Heller was laboring to piece the situation together. How could Sperling have been tailed from Mount Rose? Why would he not simply have been stopped?

"Anybody besides Goren?" Touhy asked again.

Then it became clear—the only way Touhy could know about Goren. Dismally, Heller answered, "That's the only person he mentioned to me. Lyman, we have to talk. You can't keep me locked out like this and expect my co-operation. You're totally wrong about my relationship to Earthrite. I've never . . ."

Touhy cut him off; he was on the brink of hanging up. "We'll talk about this when there's time, Tom."

"No, Lyman, wait. This is kidnapping we're talking about, isn't that so? I have to have some justification for that."

"There's no time," Touhy insisted.

"*Now*, Lyman!" Heller shot back. At the word, he realized he was placing himself across Touhy's path, thwarting an urgent line of policy. He could almost feel the impact of his resistance physically, a hard pressure upon his chest and throat. "You're asking me to make myself an accomplice to a felony. Is this a presidential decision? I have to know that much."

"You're going to have to trust me just now," Touhy answered.

"Trust?" Heller spat out the word bitterly. "Lyman, I've been under surveillance for weeks. I found that out from Gable. I was followed to the Hecate house . . ." He fought down a rising wave of anger. "Trust works both ways; what have I got to go on here? You're simply using me as a lackey in something I had no part in deciding."

There was a strained pause. Touhy's voice came back sounding grudgingly deliberate, a tone of carefully phrased concession. "We're getting some important results from Gable. We need more time, maybe only a few more days. That's why Sperling and the others must be neutralized for that period. Gable's work has been given top secret classification; detaining

Sperling and the others for a period is a reasonable extension of security precaution. That's a presidential decision, Tom. It's that big."

"What sort of results do you mean?" Heller went on. "There's nothing showing up in our work at the Center. All the data systems are still deteriorating."

"I can't go into this on the phone," Touhy answered.

"Why not?" Heller retorted impudently. "Would anybody else besides your office be tapping this line? It *is* tapped, isn't it? That's how you knew about Sperling and Goren."

Touhy made no reply. On the couch, Sperling shifted his position, groaned and swallowed. He was coming around.

"Listen, Lyman," Heller raced on. "I want to see Jane Hecate and the girl—today . . . Sunday. I want to know what sort of results Gable is getting."

"Sorry, Gable won't go for that," Touhy answered. "He wants to keep this under his own . . ." Heller picked up the hint of a voice off the phone, someone intervening. Touhy wasn't alone. His end of the line went dead silent—a hand over the mouthpiece. Touhy was consulting with somebody. Sperling's eyes blinked open, looking glassy and dazed. His hand went to the red welt on his cheek.

"Lyman?" Heller called into the phone. "Where is she? I want your guarantee I'll be able to visit her today. You can't expect my co-operation if you . . ."

Touhy's voice came back on the line. "All right, Tom. I'll arrange the visit. Is that agreeable?"

He sounded smooth and ingratiating. Heller knew the tone: a dead giveaway. He had heard it more than once before. Touhy was lying, trying to put him off until Sperling was taken. Suddenly, a deep chill ran over Heller's body. He would have preferred outright opposition from Touhy. To be lied to like this was the definitive sign of rejection. His stomach feeling hollow, Heller sought to disengage himself from the phone. "All right, Lyman. Later today. Good."

"Just keep Sperling there—any way you have to. That's authorized . . ."

Heller put down the phone, realizing that with the gesture,

his career had come to an end. The break between himself and the Administration was now complete. He was being deceived, manipulated, used far beyond anything he could permit himself to tolerate. The anger that gathered in him was cool and deliberate. Mixed with a keen sense of fear, it sharpened his thoughts.

He moved quickly across the room and began helping Sperling revive. He had not been deeply unconscious. In several seconds, he seemed reasonably alert, massaging his sore jaw, groaning to himself. Heller, pouring out a large whiskey for him, spoke quickly and intensely. "Listen to me carefully, Christopher. We don't have much time. Minutes, that's all. My phone has been tapped. I didn't know until just now. Your call was intercepted—by Touhy and his people. They're on to Goren; they won't let him do anything. They're sending around to pick you up. I'm not going to co-operate with that. I'm breaking with them. But we've got to do things my way, understand?"

As he recovered full consciousness, Sperling grew steadier, more sober. The hysteria had been shocked out of him. He was glaring sullenly at Heller, but taking in every word.

Heller asked, "How did you get here? By cab?"

"I took Goren's car." Sperling flinched to use his battered jaw.

"Where is it parked?"

"Around the corner . . . down a few blocks on Q Street."

"Good. We'll use it. I don't want to try moving my car; for all I know it's being watched, or it's been bugged. We're getting out of here right away." He was helping Sperling to his feet. "Are you all right? Can you make it? We'll use the stairs, down to the garage and out through the back alley. I don't want to risk being seen."

Quickly, Heller gathered a raincoat and hat from his closet. He paused to think what else he might need.

"Why should I trust you?" Sperling demanded, his tone surly and bitter.

"Because, damn it, all I had to do was leave you unconscious another ten minutes and you'd be back in their hands. I'm letting you go—against instructions. That finishes me in Washington—just like that. I'm putting my head on the block for you, for Jane and the others. Is that enough?"

Sperling was studying him shrewdly. "I still think we should start screaming in the streets right now."

"Argue with me a couple more minutes about it and we won't have any choices left. I warn you—we do this my way, or maybe somebody gets killed. I think things are that close to the edge. Are you ready?"

Sperling began to move slowly after Heller, acquiescing sulkily. Before he was out of the living room, Heller's buzzer sounded, the doorman ringing from downstairs. "That's it," Heller said. "They're here. We've got to move." Suddenly, for the first time, there was a "they" in his life, a faceless, official "they" capable of wielding an unapproachable and punishing authority. And he was one of the little people who had to flee before their displeasure. Ignoring the buzzer, he opened the door and stepped into the hall with Sperling.

"Wait here one second," he said, and darted back into the apartment. The buzzer rang again. In his bedroom, Heller threw open a bottom drawer in his dresser. He searched inside and came out with a small automatic pistol and some cartridges. He jammed them into his pocket and raced back to the hallway. At the door, wincing at the pain in his throat, he realized he should take some medication along . . . some antibiotics. But there was no time. The buzzer began to ring insistently, the doorman showing urgency. Glancing toward the elevator as he closed the door to his apartment, Heller noticed the dial moving. Touhy's agents were coming up without permission. Down the corridor, Sperling, his face now strained with fear, was already at the fire exit, holding the door open. The two men rushed through and down the stairs.

16

1

Beata Ulrich's hand passed slowly over the photograph again and again, tracing a slow circle. Surrounding her at the table, her husband, Heller and Sperling waited expectantly, silently, as her trance deepened. For ten and twenty minutes at a time, with eyes closed, she had explored the picture with her hovering hand—a snapshot of Jane and Daphne from Sperling's wallet. Now, her hand rose and, for the third time, a map was placed beneath it. It was a highway atlas of Washington and its surrounding area. Beata's hand circled, searched, then descended. One finger touched lightly, tentatively, on a highway running west from the city. Route 211. She had chosen this road twice before, following it out of Arlington, toward Warrenton, stopping there. This time her finger traveled further, westward to the Blue Ridge and Shenandoah country, then returned, moving like a slow pendulum in ever smaller arcs, and finally stopping at the town of Sperryville. After several seconds, her finger moved slightly north along a small, unnumbered road. There she pressed down until her knuckles whitened. After that, her hand did not move. Her body grew tense, alert. Under her breath she murmured Jane's name, then Daphne's inquisitively, uncertainly. Then she was silent, her body relaxed.

Before her hand could slip away from the map, Professor Ulrich reached forward to mark the place she had chosen. He showed it to Heller. A small town called Flint Falls. "I do not think she can do more," Ulrich said, taking his wife's hands in his own. "When her hands grow so cold, it is a sign."

It was late Sunday morning. In the dining room of Leah Hagar's home where they had been staying, the Ulrichs had been with Heller and Sperling for over two hours, using Beata's powers to locate Jane and Daphne. "It is not an exercise at which she is proficient," Ulrich had explained at the outset. "We are asking after something unknown to any of us. We can give her no help in her task. She will have to make contact directly with Jane or Daphne, perhaps at a great distance. But if the emotion on their part is great, if perhaps they are also reaching out . . ."

It had been Heller's idea to consult Beata. After fleeing his apartment, he and Sperling had checked in at a motel across the river from Georgetown and spent the last scraps of the night planning their next move. To Sperling's surprise, Heller had already formed a clear design. It began with Beata.

"You're willing to follow her guidance?" Sperling had asked.

"What else have we got?" Heller answered. "I'm working from the outside now."

Searching the road atlas where Beata's finger had touched down, Heller found a hopeful possibility. "There's a military hospital indicated on this road—just outside Flint Falls. Braddock Veterans Hospital."

Sperling was talking to Ulrich. "Can she tell us anything more? Any other impressions?"

Ulrich, massaging his wife's hands, spoke to her softly in German. Beata, still groggy, answered.

"She says it is a clear impression . . . very strong, very unpleasant. Jane—not Daphne. She receives nothing from Daphne. But Jane, she feels, is alone, in a strange room, all white, like a doctor's office."

Beata spoke again. Ulrich reported, "She says the insects are there. Very dangerous."

"Beata," Sperling said to her, "you're sure about this? It's a long way for us to go."

She was fully alert now, her eyes deep and anxious. "Yes, yes, very vivid. Also there was another power—like my own. It was blocking . . . like a wall."

"You mean another mind?" Sperling asked. "You could sense another mind?"

"Yes. Something dark, twisted, a danger to the child. It was there with her, very close. You will have to be careful."

The Ulrichs agreed to remain at Leah's house until they heard from Heller. He might have to ask for their help once more. Then he and Sperling left, taking care not to be seen by anyone who might be watching the house. At a nearby liquor store, Heller used a pay phone to place a call to Braddock Veterans Hospital in Virginia. He did not use Leah's phone, fearing it might be tapped. The operator's voice came back saying she had no listing. He made a second call to the Medical Hot Line at the Veterans' Administration, inquiring for the number. After being transferred to three people, he learned that the hospital had been closed five years ago.

"What do you make of that?" Sperling asked.

"Makes it more likely for us. They seem to be using abandoned facilities—like Mount Rose. I'd say it's a good bet. Let's trust Beata's intuition."

Despite his fatigue, Heller's mind was working sharply, snapping off decisions. Anger and fear were sparking his system like adrenalin; he could feel himself flowing forward through the plans he had laid with a strange, reckless confidence. Together, he and Sperling sought out the nearest rental car agency, where Heller acquired a car for himself. Then he sent Sperling back to their motel in Goren's car to wait for a phone call which he would place later in the day.

As he headed west out of Washington, a sense of unreal exhilaration took hold of him. He was moving outside the tight professional pattern of conduct he had long ago assigned himself. He was no longer burdened by considerations of career and duty, no longer struggling to hold his place in the rigid hierarchy of official life. He had become something of an outlaw, living from moment to moment by his wits, rebelling cunningly against the masters he had once served. Despite the risks he was running, he was buoyant, expectant. He wondered: was there a name for this remarkable feeling? Yes, he decided at last. It was called freedom.

2

The only thing about Braddock Veterans Hospital that looked as if it were still being maintained was the chain metal fence that surrounded the scruffy grounds. The main reason for the fence was apparently to display the signs that read "US GOVERNMENT PROPERTY—NO TRESPASSING." The decaying buildings behind the signs seemed hardly worth vandalizing.

In a small wooden cabin at the gate, Heller found a soldier on duty doing an efficient job of staying out of sight. Heller brought his car to a stop and hailed the guard through the fence. "I'm here to see Professor Gable," he said.

The soldier looked bewildered. "Who?" he asked. Heller repeated the name. "Sorry, sir. The hospital is closed."

"I know that," Heller answered, assuming a commanding tone. "I came to see Professor Gable. Will you let him know I'm here please?"

Hesitantly, the guard picked up a telephone and dialed a number. "Who are you?" he asked.

"Tell him Dr. Heller is here."

The soldier, his eyes steadily on Heller, delivered the message to someone at the other end of the line. There was a long pause. Then he put down the phone. "Wait here," he said. After a few minutes, the front door of the hospital opened. A figure in uniform stepped out and walked toward the gate. It was General Haseltine. At the gate he greeted Heller courteously but coolly.

"Hello, Larry," Heller answered. "I'm here to see Jane Hecate."

"Sorry, Tom," Haseltine answered. "I have no authorization for that."

Inwardly, Heller gave way to a glad sense of relief. Haseltine's answer confirmed that Jane was there; Beata Ulrich had been right. "You may have no authorization, Larry. You also have no choice," Heller announced. "If you don't let me in, I'll have this hospital surrounded by every television station and newspaper in the area before nightfall. Do you want to have that on your head?"

For a long moment, Haseltine studied him. "Sounds like a threat, Tom."

"I think if you were to ask Gable or Lyman, you'd be instructed to handle me rather carefully. I'm willing to respect your need for security. I'd like to see Gable's effort succeed, for all our sakes. But I must insist on seeing Miss Hecate. That's all I'm here for. The last time I talked to you, I was given to understand that would be permitted."

Haseltine deliberated, then ordered the guard to unlock the gate. "Don't you want to bring your car in?" he asked as Heller stepped onto the hospital grounds.

"No. I'll be using it again soon," Heller said.

Together he and Haseltine walked back toward the rambling boarded-up hospital. Haseltine asked, "How did you manage to locate us here?"

Heller gave no answer. Instead he said, "I haven't come to cause trouble, Larry. You know what my views are. The government has every right to protect itself in this crisis. But I did give my word to Miss Hecate that she would have access to me and to her friends. I was led to believe that guarantee would be respected."

"Unfortunately," Haseltine replied, "there were other considerations at stake that were regarded as more important than your promise to Miss Hecate. Sorry to put it so bluntly, Tom, but I'd expect you to understand that. What you're doing is extremely unwise."

Haseltine unlocked the front door and ushered Heller in. He closed and double-locked the door behind them. The entrance hall of the hospital was dimly lit, a musty cavern of a room obviously unused for years. The air was stale. For a moment the two men stood in silence. Then Haseltine said, "I'll have to let Lyman know you're here."

"It might be best if I talked to Miss Hecate first," Heller answered. "Then we may all know where we stand."

Haseltine had been studying him curiously, waiting for some clarifying piece of information to be offered. Finally he asked, "And why am I supposed to do that, Tom? Why am I supposed to let you leave here before we're ready to release you?"

"For one thing, because it would be illegal for you to do anything else," Heller said.

Haseltine answered as if he were reciting the ABCs to a child. "What we're doing has a national security cover. It's being done under presidential orders."

"All right, Larry," Heller said, "the arrangement is this. It's nearly one-thirty now. By three this afternoon—no later—I'm scheduled to receive a phone call. If I do, and if I say everything is satisfactory, then you'll have no difficulty. You can go ahead with your plans. If I don't answer that call, the media will be notified of where I am—and of what's happening to Miss Hecate and her daughter."

"You don't know what's happening to them," Haseltine objected.

"I have a rather good idea," Heller answered, pressing his bluff. "You're using the girl to investigate the bugs. In fact, you've got some bugs on the premises." Haseltine's poker face told him he had guessed right. Beata Ulrich's information was holding up. "Now, whatever sort of legal cover you think you have—and I'd say it was damn flimsy—I'm sure you don't want any of that known until Gable has given you the results he's promised. And I'm not eager to interfere with that effort."

Haseltine was clearly impressed with the accuracy of Heller's assessment. "You're expecting a call here?" he asked.

Heller shook his head. "There's a little grocery store at the head of the street. I stopped there on my way in and left that number with my contact—who is using pay phones, incidentally, just as I am. A different one each time."

"Your contact is Sperling?" Haseltine asked.

Heller ignored the question. Glancing at his watch, he said, "I'd say we have about an hour to play with here before I have to get back to the store. Let's not cut this too thin."

Haseltine's face was stiffening with exasperation. "You're pushing me too hard, Tom. The woman's in no shape to see you now. She's angry and upset that we brought her here. If you talk with her, she'll insist on taking her daughter and leaving. I can't allow that."

"You *are* holding her against her will," Heller said. "You know what will happen if that gets out. Christ! Who talked you into this idiotic scheme? Gable? Lyman should have had more sense than . . ."

Haseltine interrupted, finally showing signs of worry. "Tom, we're on to something big here. We need a little time—maybe just another day. You must give us that."

"I didn't come this far and take these chances to back down now," Heller warned. "I mean what I say."

Haseltine fixed him with an anxious stare. "If you disrupt things now, it may cost the little girl's life."

"What do you mean?"

Haseltine reached a reluctant decision. "Come with me," he said, and led Heller quickly up the stairs into a long neon-lit corridor where the windows were shuttered. This part of the hospital had been kept in working order. It was swept and scrubbed, freshly painted, air-conditioned: a secret, but well-maintained facility. Midway along the hall, guards were stationed in front of two large swinging doors. Taking their salute, Haseltine directed Heller through; inside, they took a narrow flight of stairs to the left into a dark, glassed-in observation area. Before they went forward to the large windows at the front of the balcony, Haseltine said, "Get a grip on yourself. The girl's in no immediate danger. She's under sedation."

He led Heller up to the windows. Spread below was a brightly lit operating amphitheater that looked to be fully equipped and ready for use. There were about a half-dozen people coming and going in the crowded room; they were wearing some form of radiation-protection garb as they moved among the several pieces of electronic gear that surrounded the operating table. On the table itself something lay covered by a white plastic material.

"What's under the cover?" Heller asked at once. "The girl?"

"Look again," Haseltine said, handing him a pair of miniature binoculars. Heller used them to bring the covered form into sharp focus. He recognized the texture immediately.

"Where did they come from?" he asked. "How are you keeping them immobilized?"

What he saw through the binoculars was not a plastic cover; it was a solid sheet of bugs packed tightly together. They were absolutely motionless, forming a small mound on the table. Heller quickly surveyed the equipment in the room. "You haven't got any computers in there. Where did they come from? Why aren't they attacking?"

"Gable will have to explain that. He's found some way to produce them and keep them under control. Since they emerged, they've been dormant like that. They make a little noise now and then—if there's a sound in the room, or if anybody tries to disturb them. But they haven't moved. They just sit there and cling."

"Cling?" Heller asked.

Without looking at him, Haseltine said, "The girl's underneath them."

Heller's mind blurred out of focus. He stared at Haseltine blankly. "Gable and his staff started working with the girl on Wednesday," the general explained. "They've been using hypnosis, drugs, some special techniques of their own. I don't understand it, but I can assure you it has all been humane, considerate. They haven't forced anything. Then, Wednesday night, they managed to . . . materialize the insects you see there. 'Materialize'—I guess that's the word we're using. The bugs just emerged and covered the girl—over a period of about an hour. They've been clinging there since. Frankly, I'm not sure Gable really knows what he did to produce them."

Heller slumped down into the nearest seat. He felt hollow and sick inside. "You mean Daphne is underneath that heap? How do you know she's alive?"

"Before the bugs appeared," Haseltine explained, "Gable had her vital signs monitored on his equipment, including all her brain wave readings. The indications are still that she's alive and well. Everything is functioning normally, except she's in some kind of deep trance or coma. She's doing completely without food or water, using absolutely minimal oxygen. The bugs seem to be letting the air get through. Otherwise, they make a tight seal. I know the girl was lightly sedated early on, but I don't think Gable was responsible for the trance. That came after the bugs appeared. My impression is that Gable is still feeling his way here, though he seems confident enough. In any case, there's no indication the insects are harming the child."

Heller's mind flooded with questions. Before he could speak, Haseltine moved into the seat beside him, glancing urgently at his watch. "You see what the situation is, Tom. The girl's been like that since Wednesday evening. Gable must be on to something to produce that result. Lyman flew in Thursday morning to check out the operation and he's convinced we're making important progress. You can see, we can't just break off now. If you tried to move the girl, she might be injured seriously. And we can't let her mother see her like that. We have to have more time to work our way out of this."

Heller glared at him, enraged and fearful at the same time. "You mean you've blundered into something you don't understand and can't control. Now the girl's life is in danger."

"*Everything's* in danger, Tom," Haseltine corrected. "All of us here, the computers, the defense of the nation, maybe the human race. That pile of insects has been increasing in size since Wednesday. Very slowly, but steadily. We don't know how to stop it or make it go away. We don't know if or when the bugs will attack. We need more time. What happens if you bring the media in here? Are you willing to take responsibility for that?"

3

Sperling's call came just several seconds past three o'clock. Heller was in the little grocery store waiting. At the first ring, he snatched up the receiver. "Christopher," he whispered hoarsely into the phone. "Jane and Daphne are here. Beata was right."

"Then get them out of there fast," Sperling ordered.

Heller had not decided how much he could tell Sperling. "I'm going to need more time. I haven't had a chance to talk to Gable."

"What the hell has that got to do with it? You're not there to hold a conference. Just get Jane and Daphne out." Sperling's tone was tightening with anger.

"Christopher . . . we can't move that fast."

"Why not?" A note of suspicion entered his voice.

"You're going to have to trust me. It's a difficult situation here. The worst thing we can do now is to disrupt their experiment."

"What experiment? What's going on?"

"I can't go into this on the phone. I don't understand all of it yet. Give me until tomorrow morning. This place opens at nine. Put through a call at nine-fifteen."

"Fuck you, Heller! I'm not going to sit quiet while my daughter is vivisected by these goons of yours. For all I know, you're just trying to wangle a consulting fee out of this."

"Christopher." Heller struggled to restrain his voice. "The bugs are here—just as Beata said. I haven't found out yet how they got here. They're in some kind of dormant state. If they're disturbed, they may attack. Daphne's life would be in danger—and Jane's. I can't tell you more until I've talked with Gable. The man has produced some kind of effect . . . maybe even he doesn't know how. I suspect he's painted himself into a corner. If we don't let him work his way out, it could be tragic for everybody here. I'll bring Jane and Daphne out as soon as it's safe. Believe me, the best thing you can do now is give me time. Please, wait until you hear from me tomorrow."

There was a strained pause. Finally, Sperling replied, "Heller, you're really overreaching my trust. Also my sanity. How do I know which side you're on here?"

"Why would I call to tell you this much?" Heller answered, laboring to sound as forceful and sincere as he could. "Why would I tell you Jane and Daphne are here? I didn't have to.

For that matter, I could have turned you over to them at any time. I'm playing square with you. Look, when we talk tomorrow, I'll have Jane with me. You can discuss this with her. Please give me that much more time."

Reluctantly, Sperling agreed to the arrangement. But he warned, "Don't push it too far. Don't ask more patience or courage from me than I can give."

Heller left the phone knowing that in Sperling he had, at best, a weak and unpredictable ally.

4

Back at the hospital, Heller was eager to see Jane. But he held off, knowing she would expect him to tell her about Daphne. He had to find out more about the girl's condition and Gable's plans.

Haseltine led him into a small surgical prep room alongside the operating amphitheater. Between the two rooms, there was a large window. Haseltine mentioned as he opened the door that he had been in touch with Touhy. "I don't need to tell you what he thinks of your action."

"Did he ask what I think of his?" Heller retorted.

"You can tell him yourself. If Gable gets set up by tomorrow, Lyman will be coming in to observe."

In the prep room, Gable was surrounded by a steady traffic of assistants and medical technicians: his own people from McGill supplemented by military personnel. Haseltine had already explained Heller's presence, apparently with advice to handle with care. While Gable remained as arrogant and hostile as ever, he proved surprisingly willing to talk about his work. It was not wholly because of Heller's capacity to threaten; Gable seemed eager to justify himself in Heller's eyes. He needed to be right. That was a clear display of insecurity. The man was worried, groping his way forward in the dark.

"We administered some standard tests to the girl on the first day—physical and psychological. The child has problems—very definitely so. There's a strong indication of incipient schizophrenia. Overactive fantasy life—with delusionary tendencies. Of course, a marked phobia regarding insects. Interestingly, there was an even stronger aversion to machinery of any kind, even commonplace electrical appliances. She proved highly susceptible to hypnosis, which is unusual at this age. Indicates advanced intelligence, a remarkable capacity for strong and prolonged concentration. We initiated a time-regression process, moving her back very gradually toward the origin of the problem. That would be her visit to the Brain last March, the day you mentioned the bugs. The idea was: we might isolate the trauma and erase it. We've developed a deep deconditioning technique for doing that. As yet, we haven't been able to reach the traumatic experience. We got as far back as the ritual exorcism that was performed by the church, and then things bogged down. It proved extremely difficult to get past that without destroying the hypnotic trance. She has a stubborn defense mechanism working at that point, no doubt something left over from the ritual. We had to use drugs to get through that—mainly Thorazine to lower her resistance. Father Guiness was of great help at that juncture. There's an uncanny similarity between the two of them, psychologically speaking. Extremely similar psycho-encephalographic mappings and neural responses. That's something I was banking on; it will be important when we . . ." He broke off, obviously holding something back from Heller. "Anyway, it was pretty much like forcing a locked door open to get into the pre-exorcistic period. We had no idea what we would find there. Once we were through . . . that's when the insects materialized."

"How?" Heller asked. "From where?"

"It's a classic materialization. A spontaneous projection of neural energy. The bugs simply appeared on the skin surface. They formed, hardened . . . and multiplied. That's where we broke off. The bugs drove us away. But we were videotaping the session all the way through. Here, I can show you."

He spun his chair around and began rewinding a videotape cassette attached to a television monitor against the rear wall.

"You've regressed her to the point where the bugs first appeared," Heller said.

Gable's eyes brightened with interest. "What do you mean?"

"Her mother told me. The first materialization happened in their home, while Daphne was asleep—dreaming. That was the night before the healing was performed."

"Christ! If I had known that . . . Why didn't you . . . ?"

"You haven't been inviting me to help. Besides I only found out about the incident the last time Jane and I talked."

On the small television screen, there was a grainy image of Daphne on the operating table. The tape was running without sound. It showed the girl under sedation, with Gable and Father Guiness at her side. Electronic sensors were attached to several parts of her head and body; a white-gowned nurse was standing nearby holding a syringe in a metal basin. Gable was speaking to Daphne close up; Father Guiness, his eyes closed, his face screwed tight with concentration, was stroking the girl's forehead. Suddenly, he jerked his hand back with what must have been a cry of pain. Simultaneously, Gable leaped back from the table, upsetting his chair, brushing at his hair and face.

"There," Gable said. "That's where they appeared. One of them nipped Father Guiness. I felt one land on my cheek—but I brushed it off. We were driven back from the table."

The camera jiggled, drew off, then came back into focus, drawing in tight upon Daphne's upper body. Across her brow, over her cheek, along her throat, small white nodules were forming like beads of perspiration on warm flesh. In less than a few minutes, they took the shape of the bugs gathering in scattered clusters; in less than ten, they had covered most of her body like a second skin.

"Here's where she began to slide into deep trance," Gable commented. "Remarkable. Her spectral density plot downshifted to nearly one-half Hertz—right through the Theta level like a stone falling. But she's maintaining a high amplitude reading on the scalp. That's a unique state of consciousness—somehow both comatose and yet subjectively alert."

There was the thrill of discovery in Gable's voice. Heller,

watching what happened to Daphne on the television monitor, found his conduct ghoulish. The recording camera bore in close to show Daphne's arms and shoulders taking on the same living film of insects. Then, their number began to grow here and there, becoming knots and lumps. By the time the tape ran out, very little of her body showed beneath the amorphous white pile. Heller, gazing with horrified fascination, shuddered. Deep in his throat and below his eye, he could feel a cold tingling, the movement of the buried insects he carried in his body.

"When did this happen?" he asked. "What time of evening?"

"From about nine-thirty on," Gable answered.

Nine-thirty Wednesday. The hour Heller had experienced the sudden upsurge of pain at Walter Reed.

"They attacked you and Guiness, but not the girl," Heller remarked, pondering the significance of the fact. "They drove you off and covered her over. No sign of any harm to the girl at all."

"No," Gable said. "Her metabolism has slowed almost to a state of suspended animation, but there's no indication she's suffering any sort of physical deterioration. You see the delta waves here." He showed Heller an oscilloscope where a bright sine wave held steady. "That's actually a spectacular reading. Up to Wednesday evening, even under hypnosis she was registering considerable tension. But this . . . this is deeper relaxation than I've seen in mature yogis."

After a pause, Heller asked, "And now what?"

"I'm having more gear brought in," Gable said, rewinding the videotape. "Including some equipment from McGill. It's coming in by military transport. If what you say is true about the first materialization, we may be at exactly the right point."

"The right point for what?"

"Where we get beyond the girl's purely subjective experience. The apparatus I'm having delivered from McGill might just do the trick."

"You mean to erase . . . eliminate the trauma?" Heller asked. "Wouldn't it make sense to go back to the first dream for that, or back to the point where I mentioned the bugs to the children on the 'Wonder/Wander' show?"

Gable did not answer. He was studying the tape again, the point where the bugs first emerged on Daphne's skin surface. Behind them, in the far corner of the room, Father Guiness could be heard breathing strenuously, muttering and chuckling. As he watched with Gable, Heller mused, "It's almost as if they're protecting her, driving you away . . . shielding her."

The remark suddenly snagged Gable's attention. "What?" he snapped, turning sharply from the monitor. "What did you say?"

This time it was Heller's turn not to answer.

17

1

Haseltine unlocked an upstairs door not far from the operating theater. Inside, Jane rose from her chair and backed off against the far wall. For a moment, as Heller entered, her face brightened; then, suddenly, her eyes went cold with suspicion. It was the expression he remembered from the first time they met.

Haseltine said, "There's a bell. Ring when you want me." He closed and locked the door.

"Where's Daphne?" Jane asked at once. "What are you doing with her?"

Heller tried to calm and reassure her before he told her more. He wanted to explain his own position and his arrangement with Sperling, their single hope of release. But he could see there was only one question on her mind. He did not want to alarm her, nor did he want to deceive her again.

"We're in a lot of trouble, Jane," he said, reaching out to take her hands. She drew away, giving a quick, angry shake of the head. "There's no immediate danger to Daphne," Heller assured her, "but it will take me a while to get you out of here. That's why I've come—to take you and Daphne away."

"You lied to me," she said, a flat objective accusation. "You said I'd be with Leah and Roger. They brought me here, locked me up. They took Daphne . . . just took her."

In the small, quiet room, Heller began to feel the full burden of his fatigue. Over the past two days, he had not slept more than a few hours. The codeine he was using to hold off the pain of his injuries was a steady distracting pressure upon his attention. For seconds at a time, he was blanking out, losing touch. Even the urgency of the situation at hand was not fully contacting him any longer. Vaguely he wondered if the room might contain any listening devices. That was not likely; it was only designed to hold one person, and his arrival could not have been foreseen. In any case, he did not have the energy to do more than check the most obvious hiding places—a precaution he had never taken before. Surprising how swiftly distrust had already reshaped his conduct.

Finding nothing, he sank down on the bed heavily. "They deceived me too," he muttered. "They went back on the deal we made. Never told me they were bringing you here. I thought you were at Mount Rose . . . found out from Christopher yesterday . . . no, today . . . this morning, early. What time is it? God, I'm so tired."

He squinted hard at his watch. His injured eye was more blurred and thobbing than ever. It was going on toward eight o'clock. Outside, the sky was heavy with rain clouds and a hard wind had come up.

"What are you doing with Daphne?" she asked again, as if she had heard nothing he said.

He looked up, training a frank look upon her. "What are *they* doing, you mean. I'm not in on this. I'm finished with them, the whole thing. I've come here to get you out, you must understand that."

"I want to know about Daphne," she demanded.

"Yes, I'll tell you—give me a moment," he said, a commanding edge to his voice. "Please, sit down and listen. You've got to get one thing absolutely clear. There's been a change since I saw you last. I'm working against them now. That's very dangerous for all of us."

Straining against immense fatigue, he told her about Sperling, Mount Rose, finally about Daphne's situation in the operating room. He told her slowly, cautiously, but truthfully. He could see a sick terror falling across her face. Her hands went to her throat. "They're *on* her . . . those things? Oh, God."

"Jane"—he reached out and took her hands, holding them tightly—"would it make any sense if I said I think the bugs are protecting her?"

She gazed at him as if the question startled her. He asked again, "I mean—can you recall the first time this happened? Did the bugs look . . . angry, threatening? Were they going to harm her?"

"I only remember being terrified, trying to sweep them away. No, they didn't bite her. They were slow, sluggish . . ."

He was fighting to keep awake, to piece together an idea. "That's the way it is now. The bugs have had plenty of opportunity to harm Daphne. They haven't. Not that they can't. They've driven Gable off, attacked Guiness. Then, afterward, they covered her again, but without hurting her. They're letting her stay calm and relaxed, holding down her metabolism. Maybe . . ."

"We've got to *do* something," Jane insisted. "What are we going to do?"

His mind turned more and more slowly, weakening before his need for rest. "All right," he said, "let's see if we can fit this together. There must be some reason why . . ." He relaxed across the bed, his head propped against the wall. For a moment, his attention went to his shoes. He worked to remove their grip from his swollen ankles. It occurred to him that he needed antibiotics . . . he should ask Haseltine for some. Before he could kick his second shoe loose, his thoughts flickered out like dying embers.

2

He woke with a fierce pain in his throat. The room was dark. The evening light had gone from the windows, replaced by a drab, steady rain. The room felt overheated, close. Or was he perhaps feverish? He sat up and called, "Jane . . ."

A voice came back from close beside him. "I'm here."

"What time is it?" he asked.

"Late. After midnight."

Heller felt his way across the small bedside table, found the lamp, turned it on. His watch read two-thirty. "You shouldn't have let me sleep," he said.

She was curled up uncomfortably in an upholstered chair near the window. "I tried to wake you. You were so tired. Then I fell asleep myself."

"I'm on some heavy medication," he explained. "For the pain. It makes me groggy."

"Captain Schaeffer looked in—before I dozed off. He saw you were asleep, said he'd wake you in the morning for a phone call."

"Oh yes. I have to take a call from Christopher. So do you. Remember? That's what I'm holding over them." Heller collected his thoughts. Was there any point in ringing for Haseltine now? He judged not. Gable had said they would go no further with their work until tomorrow morning. He could see Jane was tense. He sat next to her on the arm of her chair.

"You know more about intuition than I do," he said softly. "I have an intuition about Daphne. You tell me if it makes any sense at all. She's the only person who has been in direct physical contact with the bugs—on two occasions—without being harmed. As afraid as she is of them, they haven't hurt her. Right now, they're actually keeping Gable from approaching her. Not only that, but since they emerged in the operating room, she's gone into a deep trance-like sleep—which is a great mercy for her. Now put that together with what Leah and Beata believe—that the bugs are a sort of warning. They arise from Daphne's fear, but they're addressed to us, to the world. They're here as guardians, Leah says. Wouldn't it make sense that they should, first of all, be Daphne's guardians? She may be in less danger than anybody else."

Jane searched his face, wanting to believe what he said. "You think that's true?"

"I don't know. I *feel* it. When Gable was talking to me, the thought flashed across my mind: Perhaps he hadn't produced this manifestation at all. Perhaps it was a protective reaction against his meddling, a shield he couldn't penetrate." He sighed and sat back, giving a small weary laugh. " 'I feel it.' Maybe I've been associating with too many mystics lately. I never put much stock in intuition before."

"You don't think we should be doing anything now?" she asked.

"We have time. I want to talk to Gable again—and to Lyman Touhy. We can't leave here with Daphne in the state she's in. Here's what I'm thinking: if nothing has changed for the better with her by morning, I'm going to demand that Leah and the Ulrichs be brought down here to work on the problem. It was never my intention to see the child taken out of their care. Now, it's clear Gable can't handle the matter on his own; maybe he can't handle it at all. If I can convince Haseltine of that . . ." An amusing thought crossed his mind. "When Schaeffer looked in earlier, did he ask you if it was all right for me to spend the night locked in your room?"

"No."

"Didn't that make you wonder?"

"I didn't know what to make of it. Just taking more liberties, I assumed. I don't expect much consideration from them."

Heller smiled wryly. "Military intelligence—you see what it's like. Dumb and stubborn. You may be amused to know, even in these depressing circumstances, that, in the top secret files of the Defense Department, you and I are characterized as being on such intimate terms." She frowned with confusion. "The night I kissed you on the porch—remember? I had been followed; we were observed. That's when my downfall began."

She still did not follow him. The connections were too bizarre. He explained. "It's simply a matter of putting 2 and 2 together so that they add up to 119. Kiss means intimacy. Which means I'm on your side—obviously seduced, because why else? Which means I am not to be trusted. So, rapidly, I am frozen out of all policy consultations. Other, far more idiotic counsels prevail. Bring in the parapsychologists, kidnap the child, consign Heller to outer darkness. That's how we arrived where we are. I suppose that every hour longer I stay here confirms their interpretation."

He made his way back to the bed and stretched out. "A great lesson to me," he went on. "It doesn't matter how smart you make the computers. They're still working in the same old human world, running in the same old grooves. Behind the most brilliant programs we can design, there are all the same vices—greed, unkindness, paranoia. It all comes down to human will, human weakness. All the computers do is make it look logically sound. Mad rationality. Remember . . . how the code came out wrong, *exactly* wrong?"

She stared back bewilderedly, not placing the reference. What was she supposed to remember?

Suddenly he realized. Of course she could not remember. It was a dream he was talking about, and it was only returning to him now. Gingerly, for fear of losing it again, he coaxed it back into his mind.

"After the attack on the Brain, I became delirious. I had this strange dream. Something about a cave at the bottom of the sea. I was trying to cram the whole world into a microchip. You were there. You were telling me to stop, it was wrong. You wanted to escape. And then I saw that it *was* wrong, all wrong. But it was too late."

Now he recalled it all. The two of them lost in the world of the petrified dead, the sunless kingdom his science had built. His fault she had been there, trapped in that dark prison. His fault she was here now. He shuddered with deep shame.

"Odd," he said, "that's the first dream I've remembered in years."

The pain sharpened in his throat. "I really must get hold of some antibiotics," he murmured. "You're not supposed to break off in the middle of the course. I left my pills back at my apartment. Except for these." He fished a small bottle of codeine out of his pocket and took the last two tablets in it. "I hate to use them. They make me woozy. But . . ."

She stepped over to the bed and examined the wound at his throat where the bandage had loosened.

"You left the hospital too soon," she said.

"Where would we be now if I were still lounging around Walter Reed?"

She settled herself beside him. After a pause, she asked, fearing the answer, "These men—Gable, the general, the others . . . how far would they go? I mean, are our lives really in danger?"

"You recall what Leah said about desperate men of power," Heller reminded her. "She was right. I'll be honest with you— I'm way out of my depth here. This is what they call 'hard ball' in Washington. The intelligence agencies, the military— that's where things get rough and ugly. We're way beyond the rule of law here, way past rational discussion. Nothing in my line of work relates to this. I'm just a sort of superbureaucrat, when it comes right down to it. Sitting around long tables, exchanging facts and figures, lining up influence, maybe a little political arm-twisting—that's what I know. I'm good at that. I usually win. But this . . . this is plain street fighting. I feel as if I'm holding off a lynch mob with a popgun. If either Christopher or I make one wrong move in this amateur cloak-and-dagger arrangement we've cooked up . . . I should have warned you of the risks. You had a right to know. I wanted to believe we could work around the nastiness without anybody taking any losses. That wasn't smart. And it wasn't fair to you."

She reached out to place her hand on his forehead. "You feel warm," she said. "You might be running a fever. There must be doctors and medicine here. Shall I ring for . . . ?"

She was close enough for him to take hold of. He drew her near; she did not resist, though her body was tense with anxiety. He pressed her against him, then gave her a soft, tired kiss of gratitude for not judging him as severely as she had the right to. Only as his mouth closed on hers did he realize how important her approval was, more important at last than any authority he had served with all his talents. Ironic, how the government's ignorant suspicion had finally validated itself by driving them together, locking them away in this room. His reliability had evaporated in his need for her. She was right: he should call a doctor. But he did not want to leave her side. There was a comfort in her nearness that meant more than medicine.

"No doctors," he said, holding her to him. "Some sleep would do me more good. And . . ." But there was nothing more he had the right or courage to add. He did not have to. Gently, needfully, she folded him in her arms and stretched out beside him. The movement was almost impersonally generous, a desire to shelter and be sheltered from the evil that threatened them.

For a while—he could not tell how long—he dozed in her embrace. Then, distantly, he became aware of a soft tremor in her body. She was weeping soundlessly—for her daughter perhaps, or simply out of fear and despair. He gathered her deeper into his arms. The brief and timid gesture of love they exchanged passed vaguely through their awareness, a moment of quiet intensity that brought transient release from peril and then dissolved, almost unremembered, into sleep.

He accepted her tenderness as a silent appeal for loyalty, nothing more, nothing he could presume upon if they ever escaped this room. She was a strong woman, holding up bravely against the danger and indignity that surrounded her. But she found herself in a political jungle where her resources were scarcely adequate. She clung to him for the only security she could find, even though—paradoxically—she was more strongly drawn to him by the vulnerability they shared than by any power he might still possess. More vividly than he would have wished, she sensed how fearful he was of the confrontation that would come with the morning.

18

1

The next morning, Jane and Heller waited together in the little grocery store for Sperling's call. It was the first time in five days she had been out of the hospital, away from the watching eyes of General Haseltine's guards. As she and Heller had walked through the gates, she had to fight down a giddy impulse to run without stopping, never turning back. But there was Daphne to hold her to her grim confinement, still in danger, not even capable of rescue.

Sperling's call came late. Phone connections were becoming hit and miss, deteriorating with the rest of the country's computerized services. When he finally got through to Heller, Sperling sounded a nervous wreck, cursing the phones, overflowing with questions and incriminations.

"It took me four tries and two operators to make this connection," Sperling raged into the phone. "This isn't going to work, Heller. The world's falling apart on us."

Heller did his best to calm Sperling before he passed the phone to Jane. Her voice soothed him immediately. Heller had carefully coached her for the call. She had to make the situation at Braddock sound critical without frightening Sperling into any impulsive action. She succeeded. Reluctantly, Sperling accepted her appeal to hold off on contacting the media, but not before he quizzed her closely. "Please," he insisted, "no more long delays between calls. I go crazy waiting to hear. Can't you guess what runs through my mind?"

Before the phone was hung up, Heller arranged for the next call. It would be at three in the afternoon. He reminded Sperling to use a different phone. "For all I know," he warned, "they have ways of tracing these calls instantaneously. So keep moving around."

"Are you kidding, Heller? The way these phones are working, they'd probably trace this call to Siberia. What happens if next time I don't get through at all?"

"We may have to resort to carrier pigeons."

Sperling found no humor in the remark. Nor did Heller. If his phone link with Sperling failed, he lost the only weapon he held.

Back at the hospital, Heller was allowed to take Jane up to the observation balcony above the operating room. Captain Schaeffer and an army nurse accompanied them. Heller escorted Jane slowly up to the window, staying close at her side. "Be strong now," he said. Hesitantly, she followed his gaze down into the room below. The scene she witnessed there had a surrealistic eeriness to it. Several figures dressed in boxy, white fire-fighting suits were moving cumbersomely about the crowded space, engaged in examining various pieces of equipment. At the center, on the operating table rested the shapeless, jelly-like mound, wholly covering the tiny body beneath it.

"But where is she?" Jane asked. Before Heller could answer she realized from his description the night before where Daphne was. With a small, sick moan, she sank into the nearest seat.

"Are you sure you want to stay?" Heller asked. "I have to go down to talk with Gable. I don't know what you may be seeing from up here today. It could be unsettling. You can always go back to the room, if things become . . ." But he knew she wouldn't leave, especially if there was danger. He left her with Schaeffer and the nurse and went to join Gable in his booth.

On the way, he stopped to swallow another codeine table—his third of the day. Haseltine had arranged with the medics on hand to supply him with antibiotics and pain-killers. A doctor, examining Heller that morning, wanted to have him put to bed, a suggestion Heller waved aside. He settled for having his dressings changed. The pain in his throat and legs was becoming more persistent, and there was a slight fever holding out in his body at all times. But he was determined to get through the day undeterred.

Before he got down the stairs, Schaeffer caught up with him. "Dr. Heller," he called. "Excuse me, I'm curious about one thing. Last Saturday morning and this Wednesday in the evening, I had some difficulty with one of these bites I picked up. Really very painful—as if I might still have some of the bugs in me. It occurred to me that each time there was some extraordinary activity with the insects. On Saturday, the attack on the Center, and on Wednesday, the incident here where the bugs went for Professor Gable and his assistants."

"How do you interpret that?" Heller asked.

"Maybe the bugs have some way of staying in touch during times of stress. They all work together."

The thought had occurred to Heller too. If it were so, it gave him a built-in gauge to measure the anxiety of the insects. More worrisomely, it meant the bugs were part of a sensitive network; even inside the body they stayed active indefinitely. "Have you mentioned this to Gable?" Heller asked.

"Yes, just the other day. He thought we might check with some of the other surviving victims of attacks. We're doing that with the people back at Ames. And I guess I'm checking with you now."

"I've experienced the same thing, Captain," Heller said. "On Wednesday about nine-thirty in the evening."

Inside the observation booth, Heller found Gable busy with his equipment. He looked drawn and nervous, more so than usual.

"I understand your apparatus has arrived from McGill," Heller said. Gable grunted yes without looking up. He gestured across the operating theater to the observation booth on the opposite side. "It's set up there. Been working on it most of the night."

"The girl's mother will be watching," Heller informed him,

pointing toward the balcony window. "May I tell her what Daphne's condition is?"

Gable glanced up at the window and made an irritated face. "You think that's wise—to let her see this?"

"She was imagining even worse," Heller answered. "She has a right to know."

Gable shrugged and continued his work. "The girl's in the same condition as yesterday. Deep trance, no sign of distress. There are more bugs on her, that's all."

"And you're planning to do what?"

With a petulant sigh, Gable stepped back from his work. "We need to take a few more readings from the girl. We can't get any more electrodes on her. The bugs have her sealed off. They're on her as tight as a metal shield. So we're wiring through the encephalograph and these other monitors, making the necessary corrections. We need to get what we call a DNC —a Dynamic Neural Contour. That's a three-dimensional holographic scan of the brain worked up from a selective stimulus schedule."

"What will you use that for?"

Gable mumbled his answer. "It's basic to our approach—like getting the blood type for a transfusion. We can't make a transfer without it."

"Transfer . . . ?" Heller asked, fishing for more information. Gable volunteered none. The door opened and two of the hard-suited figures bumped their way awkwardly into the booth, moving like strange, unearthly animals. They struggled out of their helmets. One of them was Father Guiness, the other a young medical orderly who had been guiding him. Heller had noticed one of the figures in the operating theater standing very still for a long while at the head of the table where Daphne lay. He gathered it had been Guiness. Once his protective hood was removed, the priest's near-blind gaze was drawn intently in Heller's direction. For one brief moment, there was a stern concentration to Guiness' face that Heller had not seen there before. Then Guiness chuckled and wagged his head, playing his comic part again.

"Perseverance," he remarked. "It will take perseverance, Dr. Heller. Oh yes, the bastions of evil are never left undefended. Snares and pitfalls."

"Bernard," Gable called, "come over here and rest." He was obviously trying to hush the old man up.

Guiness tapped his way across the room and dropped heavily into his seat. "She's resting so peacefully, Richard," he reported. "All the fear is gone from her, the innocent soul. It's a blessing to rest so deep."

"There are no dreams?" Gable asked.

"Only the tiniest flicker now and again. It's a dark sleep she's in."

"Why is she being defended?" Heller asked Guiness.

Before Gable could intercept the question, the priest answered, "Because she is their source, Doctor. She is their portal and passage. Oh no, they did not come to harm the child. Her danger is not from the little imps."

Gable, piqued by Heller's interference, said, "I'll fill you in on things later. We're at a highly speculative stage right now."

"The child has a tragic vocation," Guiness went on, nodding tendentiously. "It will not be easy to take this power from her. But we must *persevere*." He repeated the word with a schoolteacherish wag of the finger.

"What is he saying?" Heller asked.

"You'd be wise to take your information from me, Heller," Gable said. "You must have noticed, Father Guiness' perspective on these matters is . . . eccentric."

"I suppose especially because he thinks what you're doing here has something to do with good and evil," Heller observed.

Gable returned a blank, bemused stare. "Superstructure," he muttered.

"Well, suppose you explain it to me, then," Heller suggested. "Without the superstructure."

Overhead, as he spoke, he could hear the roar of aircraft coming in. A helicopter landing nearby on the grounds. Gable stopped his work and looked up. "Unless I'm mistaken, that's Secretary Touhy. I'd prefer to have him in on this."

2

Several minutes later, Lyman Touhy was in the building, moving through the scene with his usual brusque efficiency. He quickly checked Daphne's condition in the operating theater. It was his second observation of the girl; he had been there Thursday morning after the bugs first emerged. That was what convinced him that Gable was producing "results." He took a rapid briefing from Gable in the terse, telegraphic style he preferred. Gable mentioned Jane Hecate in the balcony overhead. Touhy shot a quick, displeased glance at her, then led Gable, Haseltine, and Heller into an adjoining room. Father Guiness, still murmuring to himself under his breath, was left seated in the observation booth like an obedient pet.

So far Touhy had not acknowledged Heller's presence. Heller was familiar with the treatment; he had seen it used on others regarded as disloyal or unreliable. When he had settled in his chair and lit up a cigar, Touhy looked across at Heller with undisguised animosity. It was clear that the break between them was beyond repair. Heller suspected the rancor directed at him was more than a little grounded in insecurity. The government was taking a reckless gamble on a high risk policy that demanded absolute solidarity. That made Heller's opposition a mortal sin.

"We want to know where Sperling is," Touhy said, his opening remark simple and blunt, without preparation. "The man's unstable. If he goes to the media . . ."

Heller cut in, wagging his head firmly. "Nothing doing, Lyman. He's all I've got to bargain with."

"You know what you're doing, bucking us this way, sheltering a potentially subversive element?"

Heller flushed with insult. He was outraged to have such a patently paranoid cover story unloaded on him. "Potentially subversive!" he echoed. "Next you'll tell me that your action at Mount Rose represents preventive detention. I'm certainly not going to turn anyone over to you to be illegally detained. I'll take my chances on this side of the law."

Touhy shrugged him off contemptuously and turned to Gable. "Are you ready to proceed?" he asked.

"Just about," Gable answered. "I'd prefer to get one more wire on the girl. There's a reading that isn't coming through clearly on the encephalograph . . . here in the occipital region. But I think I can correct for that through the synthesizer."

"Good," Touhy said. "We have full presidential authorization to go ahead. Can we get right down to it?"

Heller spoke up sharply, "I think not until I have some questions answered. I'd like an explanation of what you plan to do —the risks, the benefits, all the rest. I've promised to convey that to the girl's mother."

"We don't owe you any explanations," Touhy snapped, rising from his chair with marked impatience. "You opted out of this. Now you're *out*."

"I was squeezed out," Heller protested hotly. "Forced out by an asinine intelligence assessment—of Earthrite, of my relationship to the group and to Jane Hecate. That was stupid. It was even more stupid to lie to me as you did. That's no way to hold loyalty. In any case, I think you realize I'm in a position to make more trouble for you than you want. All I have to do is *not* answer a phone call this afternoon."

His eyes fixed coldly on Heller, Touhy gave Gable an abrupt nod of permission. "Tell him."

Gable proved only too ready to tell, as if he wanted to rehearse the design carefully, explain it, justify it. His manner was both eager and anxious. "The idea is simple, though there's fifteen years of hard research behind it. We're going to carry out a deep neural pattern transfer. The psi capacities— where they are as highly developed as they are in Daphne— have a distinctive contour. They show up vividly on a thermal density plot. We use that to isolate the target structure and compare it with a finely discriminating typology. That's what the equipment I've brought down from McGill does. We call it a Multi-dimensional Synaptic Synthesizer. With it, we can map the holographic brain contours, erase them, alter them or, as in this case, transfer them to another, compatible subject. That ought to relieve the girl of her phobias. You might think of the process as a kind of electronic surgery. In effect, we're transplanting neurological patterns."

"Have you tried this before?" Heller asked doubtfully.

"Oh yes, many times." But Gable sounded as if he were bluffing.

Heller pressed him. "On humans?"

"Mainly animals—including higher primates. A few humans. The procedure is perfectly safe, if that's what you're concerned about."

"Yes, that's what I'm concerned about," Heller snapped. "I'm concerned that you've got no consultation going here with other specialists."

Gable's temper flared. "You're observing a full team of specialists—the most highly qualified people in the field."

"Your staff. Your people," Heller said. "I'd hardly call that outside consultation. Has the procedure ever failed? How often? How seriously? For example, have you ever erased too much . . . maybe an entire brain?"

Uneasily Gable replied, "Of course there have been complications. I've discussed them with Lyman."

"He has," Touhy agreed. "I'm prepared to run the risks."

"You're prepared to run the risks." Heller gave a sardonic laugh. "You're not the one lying out there on the table covered by the insects." He rushed on to raise another point. "You say the pattern will be transferred. To where?"

Gable looked to Touhy for permission. Again Touhy nodded. "From the girl to Father Guiness."

The answer jarred Heller. Gable explained. "The two of them share a remarkably compatible neurological profile. It's really a beautiful overlap. They're the same species of psychic —the same 'blood type' you might say. That's extremely rare. In fact, I was astonished. So was Guiness. He said it was almost as if he had been waiting a lifetime for this opportunity to come along. The transfer ought to be absolutely smooth."

"I don't understand." In his bewilderment, Heller stammered over his words. "You're going to transfer the girl's psychic powers to Guiness—her ability to call up . . . to materialize the insects? Why? Why not simply erase it, obliterate it?"

Gable did not answer. He deferred to Touhy to explain the assignment he was following out.

"We want to salvage the capacity," Touhy said gruffly. "We're going to store it in Father Guiness."

Heller only marginally grasped the nature of the operation, but a sense of sickening unease began to descend upon him. He could see what Touhy was after; nevertheless, he wanted to hear it said. "But why?" he asked. "Why store it?"

Touhy was angered to be forced to admit the obvious. "Because it's a weapon. We want it."

It was no worse than Heller had expected. But it was not until now, in one concentrated moment of insight, that he had faced the truth: the horror of the bugs was going to be appropriated by the military. The prospect of eliminating them was available, but that choice would not be made. "Lyman," he protested, "we might be able to get rid of them. We might be able to save the world's computer technology, undo all the damage."

"That's exactly what we intend to do," Touhy answered, pressing his point aggressively. "But the only way we can do that is to take control of this power. That's the only way we can secure it and use it. If something like this can happen once —either freakishly or by design—it can happen again. Another little girl with psychic powers might come along, or someone especially trained and developed in those capacities. The Soviets, the Chinese—we assume they know about the girl by now, or will soon enough. The Soviet military program in paranormal psychology is considerably in advance of ours. If we don't move on this fast, we know they will. You might mention that to Ms. Hecate when you talk to her. If her daughter weren't in that next room, she might be under study in a laboratory in Moscow, with a lot less concern for her well-being and survival. What we've got here is like atomic energy, Tom. You can't wish it away; you can't subtract it from human history. You have no choice but to master it."

Heller's eyes went to Haseltine, a futile appeal.

"The bugs are a practically unstoppable force," the general added. "Our laboratories have been running an intensive research program on the specimens we've captured—as we assume the Soviets are doing. Nothing kills them, nothing deters them. As far as we can tell, they can go through anything except solid concrete or inch-thick steel. And even then, where they're physically blocked, they can use an electrical vector to relocate across or through any barrier, across any distance. That means they can be directed at any target at the speed of light. They could be the deadliest invasive agent ever deployed in battle. If we harness them, we'll be in a position to selectively disable any computerized economy or weapons system in the world."

Quietly, but with absolute determination, Touhy announced, "We're not going to lose this opportunity." His tone was stubborn and final. With a dispiriting sense of impotence, Heller realized how puny his threat to Touhy was. He was witnessing an eager rush toward an ultimate weapon; the fascination and greed of that effort were like a running tide thrusting him back. Ultimately, these men would not let him or Sperling stand in their way—nor the media if they should be summoned to the scene. Cautiously, Heller edged back from direct confrontation, taking another tack. "Lyman, what reason have you to believe you can pull this off? Why do you think you have any chance at all of controlling the insects?"

"I'm satisfied with the progress Dick is making," Touhy answered, a bit too pompously.

"You mean the bugs that have emerged on the girl?"

"Yes. He's found a way to produce them and to immobilize them. What you see here is already half the capacity we need."

"And once we transfer the girl's capacity to Father Guiness," Gable added, "we'll be dealing with an entirely co-operative instrument. There will be unrestricted possibilities for experimentation."

Heller's face twisted into an expression of disgust. "That pathetic old man—you're willing to entrust this power to him?

He's an obvious psychopath. He talks about witches and curses. He's a nut case, Lyman."

Gable choked back his anger. "I told you, whatever Father Guiness thinks about his powers is mere superstructure. It doesn't make any difference what he believes about the girl or my work. It's his nervous structure that matters, his brain, which is a meat machine, nothing else. We're at the point where we can take that machine apart and put it together, use it any way we want. Guiness is an instrument, a receptacle— like any computer you use in your work . . . or *used* to use in your work. He can be programmed with absolute precision. I've worked with him for years. I can fine-tune him to my specifications."

Again, Heller backed off, trying to find a persuasive route forward, a point of common interest between himself and Touhy. "Lyman, you're assuming Gable produced those bugs out there. You think his approach yields results. What if that's not so?"

Gable flashed out at him. "What do you mean?"

Heller went on. "What if the bugs are here *in spite of* Gable? Not because he produced them, but because they're defending the child? What if they're here to obstruct what he's doing—like an army ready for battle? That's why he hasn't been able to get more electrodes on her. He can't get near her; the insects are fending him off."

"That's nonsense," Gable half-shouted. "I've found a way to materialize them; I just need more time to learn their control mechanisms. That's why we need to transfer them to Guiness. That gives us the time we need."

"And I'm saying you're dead wrong," Heller rushed on. "The bugs aren't there because of anything you did—except to threaten the girl. They appeared of their own accord as some kind of defensive reaction. Be honest. You heard what Guiness told you. The child's being protected and very effectively."

For the first time since he had arrived that morning, a shadow of uncertainty passed over Touhy's face. "Is that possible?" he asked Gable.

"Even if it were," Gable answered nervously, "that's still a point of contact with the phenomenon. We can work with that, go forward from there."

"How can you be sure?" Heller challenged. "What if their whole purpose is to thwart you?"

"We don't know that," Gable insisted.

Touhy made a grudging concession; he asked for Heller's opinion. "What would you propose, then? Starting from where we are?"

Heller's mind raced, fighting against malaise and fever to find a convincing formulation. "Gable's gotten some important readings from the girl already. That's something he can work with in future research. Settle for that. Make it your first priority now to get rid of the bugs—at least to clear them off the girl. Bring in the people from Earthrite, especially Beata Ulrich, to go over Gable's findings and work with him. They enjoy the girl's trust, and they can bring you powers neither Gable nor Guiness can supply."

"Absolutely not!" Gable hurled the remark at Heller fiercely. He was drawing his line. "You bring them in, and I pull out—me, Guiness, my staff, my equipment, the works. I can't accommodate my methods to gross superstition. There has to be one consistent line of approach here. We don't even know what the intentions of these religious fanatics might be. For Christ's sake, Lyman, we could bog down for weeks trying to negotiate a *modus vivendi* with them."

Heller asked the obvious question. "If you can work with Guiness, why not with Beata Ulrich?"

"Because I control Guiness. With him, I set the priorities. There's no resistance."

Touhy deliberated: two long drags on his cigar. "Dick's right," he decided. "We can't afford the time; we can't risk confusing our methods of operation. We've got some strong indications of success for his approach. We'll go ahead from there. We're set up for that. I see no reason for delay. I don't see what objection you can raise, Tom. Our purpose is to free the girl, to take her out of the picture. That seems to be your major concern at this point as the Hecate family's self-appointed ombudsman. If Dick's experiment works, you and the mother will have what you want—and we'll have what we want. Fair exchange."

Touhy rose decisively, meaning to close off discussion. Heller gave no sign of assent. "I want the Ulrichs in on this," he insisted. Gable released a hiss of exasperation. "That's my demand," Heller said, determined to hold his position.

"Look," Gable snapped. "Will you at least agree to let me get through this morning's work? We're all set up. There's no danger to the girl. We could be close to something big here."

"You mean the transfer?" Heller asked. "You want to try that?"

"We're not up to that yet," Gable answered. "We need a preliminary test, a trial run—just to see if I can align the neurological contours of the girl and Father Guiness. That's a few hours' work right there. If I can't, then everything we're arguing about here is moot. We'll have to back off for a while—a few days, maybe longer. I'll have to put Guiness through a battery of preparatory exercises. At that point, there'll be time to reconsider contacting the Ulrichs."

Touhy studied Heller. "I think you can agree to that much. Let's find out if we really have something to argue over here."

Heller reserved his answer. "Let me look at your setup," he said. "I want to know what you'll be doing, and how much of it I can expect to follow."

Gable led them across the hall toward the operating theater. This time, he went to the other observation booth where the synthesizer was installed. Father Guiness was already there. Two assistants were working over him, attaching electrodes to his body: his head, along his neck and spine, at the eyes. Heller entered the booth after Touhy and at first his eyes went to Guiness, watching his preparation. It was only when Gable moved out of his line of sight that Heller saw the synthesizer. He gazed at it across the small room, experiencing a slow-motion double-take. The synthesizer was a PDP 14 computer. It sat in the far corner of the booth, a neat and shining oblong box wired into several detectors and visual display units.

"It's a computer . . ." Heller said, observing the obvious. "You've brought a computer here. You're going to use that with the girl?" His astonishment choked his voice to a near whisper.

"Of course it's a computer," Gable answered. "What did you think it was?"

Stupidly, Heller wagged his head. It had never occurred to him that Gable would be reckless enough to bring a computer near the girl. He had assumed the synthesizer was some form of encephalograph, an electronic monitor.

Gable was going on, "We use it to correlate the readings. The parameters that have to be calculated to build up the holographic model are enormous. We couldn't possibly . . ."

Heller stared at him in painful disbelief. "You're mad. You're absolutely mad. You don't dare bring a computer near that child. How do you know it isn't infested?"

"Because it isn't," Gable answered. "There's no indication . . ."

"When's the last time you used it?" Heller asked.

"I've been working with it all night."

"Before now."

"It's been in constant use at McGill, until I got heavily involved in this situation about a week ago. Saturday before last —that's the last time I used it personally. It's never malfunctioned."

"What about the other equipment at McGill?" Heller pressed him. "I know for a fact the university computer center there has been affected by the rash."

Gable admitted this was true. "But our facilities are independent. It hasn't hit us. Look, it's a small change computer."

Heller turned to Touhy. "I can guarantee that computer will generate the bugs if you put it in operation. You've brought a live bomb in here."

Gable appealed to Touhy. "This is a stall. The computer has never given trouble."

But Touhy was willing to take Heller's warning seriously. "What makes you so sure, Tom?"

"Of course the bugs haven't infested every mini and medium computer yet," Heller explained. "But they're moving in on them fast. So far Gable may just have been lucky with his equipment. But the bugs are here, in the next room. They're protecting the girl."

"We don't know that for sure," Gable protested.

"Ask your partner." Heller threw off the remark heatedly, nodding toward Father Guiness. "He says they're defending her—and doing a damn good job of it. What do you think will happen if you plug that computer directly into the child's brain? Every piece of electronic equipment you've got here will be infested. Don't you understand? The bugs are after the machines, the whole technology. The girl's mind is their source, the computers are their target. You're hard-wiring them into each other." Heller was tense and trembling with urgency. He could feel sweat tickling his brows and throat. Touhy was studying him closely.

"He's bluffing, trying to stall us," Gable sneered. "You know he's not to be trusted. We're a couple of minutes away from proving something he wants to prevent."

"What is the man saying there?" The voice—hard and commanding—came from behind them. Father Guiness, his head and face trailing wires, was staring blindly across the room at Heller. "Ah, Doctor, it's a shame to see your great talents put to such a wicked use." He reached out to his side to touch the synthesizer, stroking it like the head of an animal. "The machine is not the evil, Doctor. The machine will serve its master. It has been consecrated to the Lord's service. It is a poor dumb beast. It has no soul, you see. The soul that brings it to life is the gift of man. And if that man's will is corrupted, the beast is not to be blamed."

Something was wrong, out of focus, off-key. Heller fought to clear his head and regain control of his perceptions. Guiness had ceased to be the doddering old Irish clown. His face was severe, his voice sober and level. Behind his dark glasses, Heller was convinced the man was watching him, piercing him with a relentless hypnotic gaze.

"Your protest is not honest, Doctor," the new voice of the new Guiness went on. "There is nothing in your mind but

Self. Envy and spite, the gall of a wounded pride. We do the Lord's work here. Depart." He flailed his tapping stick in Heller's direction.

Before he could finish his admonition, there was a shrill scream from the operating theater. Everyone turned to look. Two of Gable's assistants in hard-suits were on the floor not far from Daphne's table, writhing, scrambling about for safety. The bugs were on them. Not many, but they had penetrated the protective garb. Others in the room rushed to their aid, dragging them back from the table, beating off the insects. On the table the mound that covered Daphne had become a voracious, living jelly. When Gable opened the door of the booth to shout orders, the chattering could be heard, harsh and angry. But the swarm held to its position; only a small number, perhaps some few hundred, could be seen leaping about the bodies of the fallen assistants. As they were beaten away, they jittered and skipped back to the table to rejoin the undulating heap. Just for a moment during the excitement, Heller felt a swingeing jab of pain—at his throat, behind his wounded eye: the buried insects in his own body responding sympathetically to the threat.

The downed assistants were dragged into the corridor outside the operating theater and their suits were roughly stripped off. One of them, a man, was severely chewed up along one arm. The other, a woman, carried a nasty red welt under one eye. The suits, as they were cast away, revealed a number of punctures where the bugs had drilled their way through.

The woman explained what had happened as Gable bent over her. "We were trying to adjust the electrode attached to the occipital region. That's the one that's giving faulty readings. We thought we might work our way under the insects . . . just a few inches." She broke off, gasping with incipient hysteria. "I thought they were all going to attack. They started . . ."

"You shouldn't have tried it," Gable said angrily. He turned her over to one of the medics for treatment. "That wasn't necessary," he said to Touhy, who was standing nearby. "We didn't really need the adjustment. We can work around it. No need to disturb the bugs at all. The synthesizer can give us a corrected reading of the data we initially collected from the girl. It's just another calculation to feed in." To Heller he said, "That's what I spent most of the night doing. We'll get an enhanced facsimile of the occipital contour."

"You surely don't intend to go ahead after what just happened," Heller protested.

"There's no need to delay," Gable insisted abruptly. He turned back into the observation booth, Touhy and Haseltine following briskly. Schaeffer, who had raced down the stairs from the balcony, started in also just behind Heller. He was rubbing a swollen welt near his eye where his own wounds had flared up during the incident.

Heller rushed toward the booth, appealing to Touhy. "You saw the pattern. The insects drove off Gable's people—no mass attack, just enough to obstruct them. Then they returned to the girl. Don't you see? It's a defensive maneuver. They respond to any intrusion upon the child. What do you think will happen if you release the whole force of this apparatus? Lyman, I've seen these bugs overrun an entire building—in minutes. The computer will generate them."

Touhy was wavering, making up his mind. Heller recognized all the gestures: the hand playing at the jaw, the abstracted stare. Turning to Gable, who stood at his controls tense and waiting, Touhy began, "I wonder if it might not be best . . ."

But his voice trailed off; Heller hastened to press his advantage, but he found his mind slack, wandering. He began to speak and went dry. Why? Was it the infection he carried, worsening? He centered himself, straining to focus his thoughts. He was fitting his words together like pieces in a jigsaw puzzle. "All I'm asking . . . all I'm asking is that we bring in some outside consultants before . . . It needn't be the . . . Ulrichs. An objective . . ."

An objective *what*? He reached for the word, but it perversely escaped him. He saw that Touhy was slipping away from him, turning his attention elsewhere.

"Richard," Father Guiness' voice spoke from the corner, soft

but commanding. "Richard, isn't it time we started? I'm sure
Mr. Touhy is growing impatient. He knows how close we are
to the results he wants. They could be in our grasp today, this
morning. There's no need for further delay, is there?"

Heller peered across the room as if through a thickening
haze. He could just barely make out the figure of Father
Guiness seated there, looking larger, more formidable than
ever, his blind eyes making their dark vision felt. Heller wanted
to say no, wait, I haven't finished . . . But the words were
locked in his throat. Touhy had turned away, toward Gable,
who was nodding, agreeing with Guiness, starting his experiment. He and the others seemed to Heller to be moving in a
dreamlike slow motion, drifting out of touch.

"That's right, Richard," he heard the low, insinuating voice
saying. "Begin, begin. There's nothing to stand in our way."
Guiness went on speaking, crooning encouragement, but his
words were growing muffled in Heller's ears. Only one clear
perception still came through to him. He knew it was Guiness
who was dimming his mind, bullying him toward confusion
and silence. That was the source of the terrific, unsettling
pressure he felt. The old priest was moving into the center of
things, taking charge. From here forward, it would not be
Gable who was in control. Gable would be the instrument,
making his knowledge available to Guiness for some stranger
and darker purpose.

Could that really be so? Heller was fighting to clarify his
thoughts—or rather to unify them. It was as if he were seeing
both the surface of things and an x-ray picture of forces that
moved beneath. He must align the two, make sense of their
juxtaposition. Something both fearful and fascinating about
Guiness gripped his attention. The things that thronged in the
priest's mind—ancient emblems of supernatural good and evil,
demonic forms, images of twisted desire—flooded into his own
thoughts becoming vividly, persuasively real.

Suddenly, Heller recognized that here, before him, was an
insatiable hunger for power, an appetite that was timeless,
deep and vastly malevolent. It belonged to the mythic past,
and yet it was in this room filled with the instruments of

precise science. Now, it was reaching out to gather in that science, along with Touhy's politics, Haseltine's soldierly violence. The four men he was watching rose up in Heller's eyes like four dark fires that were being drawn together, burning into each other. Soon, if nothing intervened, they would merge into a single invincible conflagration. The evil of that prospect was a matter of absolute clarity in Heller's mind, as certain as any result reached by cold logic. He could not say *how* he knew what he knew; but there was no question of its truth. It was the one spark of conviction he could cling to in the dizzy vortex Guiness had set swirling in his head.

For months, since the bugs had first appeared, Heller had been fighting his way through a jungle of events, searching for the right and wrong of the matter, knowing that somewhere near him there was an evil to be faced and fought. He had thought it was the insects, the menace they posed to everything reason and civilized life meant. But no, the matter went deeper; it belonged to a far older and stranger dimension of life. And now he had found it, there in the person of this bizarre old priest who played the part of a bumbling imbecile; at last, he had penetrated the charade. Whatever it was Heller had to resist, it was before him, wearing this unlikely human shape.

Quite coolly, Heller thought to himself: no doubt this is some kind of hallucination. I'm breaking under the pressure. But that did not matter, because even at the core of that hallucination, there was a commanding certainty. He was seeing things oddly—as he had in his dream of the crystal doom, but he was seeing them truly. There was simply no question but that these men had to be stopped.

Stepping back against the wall, Heller rammed his left ankle into the metal bracing of the counter beside him. The pain was immediate and explosive, cutting its way through his clouded perceptions like a razor's edge. Again, he drove his ankle against the sharp corner. The pain worked as he wanted it to, purging his mind, forcing away the other pressure that was there distracting his attention. The words he wanted finally rushed from him. They were simply "No! Stop!" The two kicks he had delivered to the counter had jarred Gable's delicate equipment. All eyes were on him; the experiment stopped.

"Tom!" Touhy roared at him. "Get hold of yourself! We're going ahead."

"No, Lyman," Heller answered with absolute determination. "This is wrong. You're not making up your own mind here. You're not in charge."

They would think he was crazy. He could see that. They were right, he was crazy. But that did not matter, as long as he stopped them. And he would do that, because there was a gun in his hand. They would obey a gun in the hands of an irrational man, a man they thought was irrational.

At the far end of the room—it seemed a very long way off down a hazy tunnel—Father Guiness stood up. Heller's gun was pointed at him.

"Don't you think you're feeling a bit tired, Dr. Heller," the old man said in a kindly, whispering tone. "Don't you think you should put down that heavy weapon? You're not a man of violence now, are you?"

If he comes at me, Heller decided slowly and logically, I'll have to shoot him. Then they won't be able to continue. Good.

Guiness was coming toward him, his stick forward, his massive head wreathed in electrodes, streaming wires. Heller wanted to shoot, but his finger would not tighten. He could not kill a man like this, coldly, up close. It was not in him. But as he stared across the room, just for an instant, he saw the computer by Guiness' side become the dumb beast the priest had called it: a small hideous incubus crouching at its master's heel, leashed to him by its buzzing wires. The image came and went in a flash; Heller almost wanted to laugh at the tricks his hallucinating mind was playing on him. Of course, he said to himself, I can kill the beast, the ugly little monster.

He swung the gun around toward the synthesizer and fired once. Before he could shoot again, he was aware of a fast blur of movement charging at him from the right. He turned to catch a glimpse of Captain Schaeffer coming through the open door. Heller had forgotten he was there, still outside, waiting. Schaeffer jammed him against the wall, then moving with expert dexterity, drove his hand against Heller's temple. The darkness reached Heller before the pain of the impact did. The vortex thickened and closed in. He went down beneath the wave.

19

1

Sperling had made up his mind. As he placed his phone call that afternoon, he was determined to deliver an ultimatum. He would accept no more stalling from Heller. He wanted a guarantee that Jane and Daphne would be back in Washington that evening. The truth was: his nerves were rubbed raw with anxiety. He had spent two days holed up in his motel or roving the streets, killing time between phone calls. He could not take more tension.

He phoned from a gas station near his motel. It took three tries to complete the call through the collapsing circuitry of the telephone system. Then, to his surprise, Jane answered. "Really, Christopher, everything is fine now," she assured him. "We're all safe. It turned out all right. Daphne will have to stay a few days, just to rest up. She's been through a lot, but she's in fine condition."

Sperling began to unload questions, but Jane interrupted. "Tom thinks you should come and visit—this evening. Please do. It will set your mind at rest."

He was baffled, but relieved. His only thought was to depart at once for Braddock. He announced he would start out immediately.

As she hung up the phone, Jane felt a shiver of guilt ripple through her body. Standing beside her, smiling as always, Captain Schaeffer complimented her on her performance. "Good," he said. "He'll come?"

"Yes," she answered sullenly.

"Good," he said again, as if she valued his opinion. He took her arm and guided her out of the store, back to the hospital.

2

When she returned to her room, Jane found Heller there, still recovering from the blow Schaeffer had given him. It had been a solid, professional hand chop from a trained fighter. Heller had been unconscious for nearly twenty minutes, groggy and nauseated for another two hours afterward. He was held in a separate room under guard until Jane took Sperling's three o'clock call. Even now, hours after taking the punch, his head was jangling with confusion.

"Feeling better?" Schaeffer asked Heller as he escorted Jane into the room. He offered no apologies; Heller gave him no answer. "Ring if you need some attention," Schaeffer said with all the courtesy of a hotel manager as he moved to leave the room. "There's a medic on duty."

Before the door closed, Heller asked, "Did I get the synthesizer?"

"Fortunately, no," Schaeffer answered with a smug grin. "You did nick one corner. Not bad for a fast shot. If you had done it any damage, I think you'd regret it now." Chidingly, he asked, "Why didn't you waste the priest? That was your best move."

Heller turned away without answering. Schaeffer shrugged and drew the door closed behind him. There was a sharp click as he locked it from the outside.

Jane had seen nothing of the scuffle in the observation booth. She heard the one shot Heller had gotten off, and then saw Heller being carried out into the operating theater and away. She assumed he was dead, shot. Soon after, a guard returned her to her room and locked her in. Nobody answered her questions about Heller or Daphne. Toward one-thirty in the afternoon, Haseltine and Schaeffer had visited her, insisting that she take Sperling's call when it came.

"They said if I promised to do that, they'd let me see Daphne," she explained to Heller. "They said she was all right, that the experiment had been a success. I promised to take the call, and they took me to her. She's in a room along this hall. The bugs . . . they're gone. She's safe and well."

"You're sure?" Heller asked. "It wasn't some kind of trick?"

"I don't see how it could be. She was still asleep—under sedation, they said. But they let me hold her, be with her a few minutes."

"She was . . . alive?" Heller choked on the question.

"Yes, I touched her. I felt her breathing, her pulse. She seemed to be resting peacefully. They said I could see her as soon as she woke up. The general—Haseltine, is that his name? —said if I wanted to ensure all of us got away safely and soon, I had to bring Christopher here. They wanted him to see that Daphne was well. They didn't want him bringing the newspapers into this—for Daphne's sake as well as theirs. I did what they wanted. Christopher is on his way now. I don't know if that was the right thing to do. I only know I wanted to see Daphne."

Heller's head ached too much to let him hold to a line of thought for more than a few seconds. Everything about the last twenty-four hours was fragmented, blurred out of focus. No thanks to him, Gable's experiment had gone forward. The synthesizer had done its job. The bugs were gone, Daphne was safe. Is that what Jane was telling him? Then he had been totally, humiliatingly wrong. Touhy and Haseltine had been justified in cutting him out of the picture. Suppose he had succeeded in destroying the synthesizer, or in bringing the media into a delicate situation. At the thought, he felt weak with embarrassment.

At the same time, his mind kept returning to the incident in the observation booth. He could not free himself of Father Guiness' voice, the old man's crooning, hypnotic words, his uncanny menace. For just those few moments, Heller had pierced the world about him with another power of vision. He had seen the meanings that move events. And he had seen evil embodied in a human form. Or so he thought at the time. He had obeyed his intuition, and he had been almost disastrously wrong. Now, at this distance, the experience looked like a failure of nerve, as well as a sorry delusion. Apparently his mind had crumbled under the stress of pain, fever, fear. He had panicked; the others hadn't. He deserved to lose, to pay the full price for losing.

"I tried to stop them," he confessed to Jane. "I had a gun . . . I tried to destroy the computer they were using. That's why Schaeffer laid me out. I guess I got things all wrong."

She sat close beside him, taking his hands in hers. "I don't care anymore who was right or wrong," she said wearily, but charitably. "They've saved Daphne. We're going to be sent away from here. That's all I care about." Then, seeing his despair, she said, "I'm grateful for what you tried to do. You've given up a lot. It was a great risk, I know. It isn't easy to make such choices."

He warmed to her sympathy. "But if things had gone my way . . . if I had crippled the computer . . . God! You don't know what was going through my mind at the end there . . . what I saw, *thought* I saw. I've taken too much of a beating."

For a long while they said nothing. A silent bond was growing between them, flowing from her hands into his. In his helpless confusion and failure, he had taken on a humanity in her eyes that all his previous power and status could never have lent him. Whatever else he had lost, he had gained that, the one thing that might survive the wreckage of his life's work. His grip tightened on her hands.

There was a knock at the door, then a key in the lock. Haseltine stepped into the room. "We can let you see your daughter now," he said to Jane. She leaped up. Heller followed her out of the room. Two doors down the hall, a door stood open. Inside, on a bright, clean hospital bed, Daphne was propped up on pillows. A nurse and doctor were beside her. Jane rushed forward to hug the girl. She was groggy, unable to keep her eyelids apart. There was the flicker of a smile as she dimly recognized Jane, then she fell away toward sleep again. Heller watched from the doorway with Haseltine.

"She's all right . . . ?" he asked.

"The doctors say completely. They've checked her over thoroughly. She's still heavily sedated to prevent any sort of shock, in case she remembers anything of what happened. But it looks as if Gable pulled it off."

"How much can you tell me about it?" Heller asked.

Haseltine replied sharply, "Everything that's happened here is classified, you understand. You have no clearance any longer."

"I know, I know." Heller acknowledged the fact with a deep quiver of shame.

"But I guess we can let you know enough to satisfy you that we made the right decision. You're going to have to agree to keep this secret, and persuade the others to do the same. I mean Sperling and the people at Mount Rose. I hope we can have that much co-operation from you."

Heller nodded sullenly, following Haseltine toward the operating theater.

"One more thing we'll have to ask of you," Haseltine added. "Lyman thinks it's imperative that the child be kept under wraps for at least the next several months. You understand what he's concerned about; the girl could look like quite a prize to some of our competitors. Gable's convinced that she no longer possesses any special powers—which ought to make her life a lot more settled. But the opposition may want to do some research of its own to find out if that's so. For the girl's own good, we'd like you to persuade Miss Hecate to take her on an extended vacation. Incognito, of course. There are several suitable places she could choose from . . . Latin America would seem the best area. The government would pay all the bills, provide education, medical care, and so on. You might want to accompany them. We'd lay on full security. Don't get the wrong idea, incidentally. This would be completely voluntary, but I hope you can see the necessity."

Heller did. He nodded again, a broken man taking orders. In the operating theater, nobody was wearing the hard-suits any longer. There were no insects in sight. On the table at the center of the room lay Father Guiness, still attached to the synthesizer by several electrodes. Gable was working beside him, taking readings from his apparatus, occasionally speaking to the priest. The central area of the room was now cluttered with electronic gear.

"We've moved everything in here," Haseltine explained. "A bit more room. Gable says he'll be working here for several more days, wrapping up the results. Then we'll want to move him to a more comfortable research facility."

"You're sure the bugs are gone?" Heller asked.

"Um-hm. We videotaped the whole procedure. Gable will show it to you. It looks like the first tape run backwards. The bugs just sort of melt away. Eerie . . . but a beautiful sight. When we first saw the kid again on the table, free of the bugs, I think everybody felt a million years younger. They sent up a cheer."

Heller approached the operating table cautiously. When Gable caught sight of him, his contempt was absolute. He gave no sign of recognition. Haseltine mediated. "I think it's important that we send Tom away convinced that we've brought our project to a successful conclusion."

"He isn't going to pull a knife on me, is he?" Gable snarled without looking up.

Contritely but still firmly, Heller demanded one piece of information. "Where are the bugs?"

"No thanks to you, they're under control," Gable muttered. "*Our* control." He continued with his work. He was administering stimuli to Guiness, taking readings, asking questions. "Now?" he asked as he delicately adjusted a switch.

"Oh, just the barest tingle," the priest whispered. "Just above my tired old eyes."

Heller pressed to know more. "When you say 'gone,' what do you mean? Gone where?"

Gable cast a quick glance at Haseltine, seeking permission to answer. "I don't know how much of this you're cleared to know." The general replied with an indulgent nod. Gable shrugged and reached out with the tip of his ballpoint pen to tap the bright screen of an oscilloscope. "Well, my best guess right now is that your bugs are here." He was tracing out an oddly skewed sine wave that contained a tiny, persistent jitter.

"Right there, in that little electrical kink. An absolutely novel configuration. You might think of that as a cerebral cage."

Guiness giggled softly to himself on the table. "Oh, we've got him by the tail, Doctor," he murmured. His manner had returned to that of the eccentric old Irish character. Had it ever really changed, Heller wondered.

"Do you mean the insects, the power the girl had . . . it's stored in him, in his brain?" Heller asked.

Smugly, Gable replied, "I think all you have to be concerned about is that your computers have been debugged for you. As far as your work is concerned, or *was* concerned, they're gone."

"How can you be sure of that?"

"We're in touch with Berny back in Washington," Haseltine answered. "He's running a preliminary check for us. He says there was a minor upsurge of noise from the bugs around noon. That's when we carried out the transfer. Then the machines went silent. He's made a fast check of the computers at the Brain—including disassembling one of them. He called from there an hour ago to say it looked clear."

From the table, Father Guiness spoke in a low voice, "They're in the Lord's hand, Doctor. They have become His rod. Never fear, never fear."

"What does he mean?" Heller asked.

Gable gave no answer. His hand went to Guiness' lips to silence him. Heller surmised that the transfer had been accomplished. The insects were stored somewhere between Father Guiness' psyche and the synthesizer, safely locked away in some subtle vault of the mind.

"Satisfied?" Haseltine asked. "I'd say everything worked out rather neatly." They were not going to tell him more. Heller surveyed the equipment which Gable and his assistants were tending. There was little he could learn from it. It belonged to another technology, one that would now take its place at the human frontiers, shouldering aside Heller's once-proud information science. Perhaps, in comparison with the marvels that would be worked in the future by psychic technicians like Gable, even the most sophisticated computers would soon look as comically cumbersome as the steam engines and dynamos of the past. Heller could feel his dawning obsolescence in his bones, a sagging weariness. He was an interloper here. It was time to go. Yet, even as he turned away, he shuddered inwardly to remember Father Guiness as he had once seen him —a dark force working for its own ends, exploiting the resources of Gable's science, twisting them into the service of an ancient and alien purpose.

He had moved off only a few paces when he felt the small, prickling tingle at his throat. He reached to scratch at it before he realized its significance. One of the wounds made by the bugs was acting up—an early warning signal. He stopped, waited. A few seconds more and the tickling became a sharp needle of pain. His hand shot to his throat.

"What is it?" Haseltine asked.

Heller spun around. Gable, to one side of the table, was working with an assistant. "More," he was saying. "Give it another few points." Over his shoulder he asked, "How's that, Bernard? Can you locate that?"

Heller rushed back to the table, the pain in his throat growing and now beginning to throb behind his left eye. "Gable," he cried. "Stop! Stop now!"

Gable turned to glare at him. "Heller," he snapped angrily, "we've been all through this. Give it up, man. You're finished and you're out. If you want to take this up with . . ." He could see Heller was in pain. "What is it?" he asked. But before Heller could answer, Guiness' body stiffened on the table into a high, rigid arch. He gave an anguished grunt, opened his mouth wide, gulping, fighting for breath.

Gable was beside him at once. "Bernard, what is it?" Reaching behind, he gave a quick gesture to his assistant who turned several dials immediately.

"Whatever it is you're doing," Heller half-shouted through his knotted throat, "stop! I'm feeling them . . . they're . . ."

"I've stopped," Gable said. "There's nothing, no stimulation."

On the table, Guiness' vast, flabby frame was going in and

out of wracking spasms. His breathing grew jerky and labored. He was sputtering something, broken words. Heller, bending near, thought he heard "Rod . . . Lord . . ." several times. Then, as suddenly as the reaction had begun, it ceased. His body slumped heavily. His eyes flickered, his lips continued to toil, struggling to speak. "What is it?" Gable asked, coming close. Then, with a yip of surprise, he pulled back. Heller looked down into Guiness' twisted face. What seemed to be a tiny drop of saliva drooled over the edge of the priest's lips. Then another. And another.

They were bugs, making their way sluggishly out of the open and choking mouth. A few, then several, a thickening stream. Others began to issue from his ears, his nostrils, moving to cover his face and slide down his body. Heller jumped away, bumping into Haseltine behind him, then clattering into a piece of apparatus. It tipped over and fell to the floor with a brittle crash.

Like a puppet suddenly jerked upright, Guiness shot into a sitting position on the table. His hands were at his head, clawing at his temples. He was trying to speak, but his mouth was so clogged with bugs, he might have been speaking a foreign language. He was trying to lower himself from the table. His arm slipped under him and he fell ponderously to the floor. For a moment, he seemed unconscious.

Heller shouted, "Disconnect him from the computer!" But there was nobody to obey the instruction. Everyone in the room had drawn away from the table or was fleeing through the doors. Gable had backed off against the far wall of the operating room, rubbing furiously at his eyes. Streams of insects were pouring from all the electronic gear that had been wired into the synthesizer.

Heller tore from the room, the pain in his throat mounting by the moment. At the door and in the corridor outside, he collided with a crowd of people trying to enter the operating theater to see what had happened. He fought clear and dashed toward the room where Daphne and Jane waited. "Leave!" he shouted, or tried to shout. His throat was too tight to let the word out clearly. Two medics rushed to help him but he shook them off. He took Jane by the arm and forced the words out, "Take Daphne. Leave. Now."

A doctor intervened. "You can't take the child yet . . ." He would not let Jane lift the girl's sleeping form.

"The hospital . . . under attack," Heller cried. "Jane, the insects . . . they're here, worse than ever. Leave now."

There was shouting in the hallway: orders, warnings, a cry of pain all overlapping in confusion. The high, fierce chatter of the bugs was filling the building. A nurse darted into the room, screaming. The bugs were already on her, at her throat and cheek. Heller roughly thrust the doctor back from the bed and took Daphne in his arms. She was limp and unresponsive. Jane followed him into the corridor. Outside the doors of the operating theater, there were already bugs leaping across the floor—just as Heller had seen at the Brain. A guard and a medic were writhing along the corridor toward the stairs; then there were others, rushing from the operating room, blocking the way. Heller turned to the right, away from the tumult, having no idea if he would find an exit. His vision was blurring badly as the bugs he carried within him bit deeper into his tissues. Along the way, he and Jane threw open doors looking for stairs, an elevator, some means of escape. They found nothing but small rooms, closets, locked doors. In that direction, the hall was a dead end, its windows shuttered.

Turning, they saw a small crowd of soldiers and medical personnel at the opposite end, stumbling away, falling to the floor. Some were already thickly covered with bugs, tearing and beating at them. Among them, Heller saw Touhy crashing against one wall, rebounding toward the stairs. Passing Daphne to Jane, he attacked the shutters, tearing them open. The windows behind them were guarded by metal screening. There was no way out except back along the hall, past the operating theater. They would have to dash through the swarm to find their way out.

Frantically, Heller looked for some way to protect Jane and Daphne. In one of the rooms along the corridor, he found

plastic bedsheets. Quickly, he wrapped two sheets around
Daphne, while Jane tried to cover herself. Then they started
back up the hall.

"We'll have to move as fast as possible—down the stairs,"
he said, leading Jane behind him.

"There's no way," she protested. "No place to step. It's
all . . ."

As they rushed forward, bracing for the attack, the swinging
doors of the operating room burst open, and a vast, only
vaguely human shape shambled through into the hall before
them. It was Father Guiness, heaped over with bugs. He was
not being attacked by them; there was no sign of blood. Now
Heller saw: the source of the bugs was not the computer. It
was Guiness who had taken Daphne's powers into himself. He
was generating them, pouring them in torrents down from his
mouth and nostrils. Gable had concentrated the entire infestation in Guiness' brain; but the cerebral cage could not hold. It
had burst, and now the priest was bloated with the insects,
swollen full and exploding. For a moment, he stood in the center of the hall, his teeming head turning this way and that.
Then he swung around heavily in Heller's direction and groped
forward, hands outstretched, more blind than ever beneath the
living pelt that covered him. In his wake, the bugs slid and
cascaded to the floor, leaping ravenously.

Heller and Jane shrank back helplessly from his approach,
flattening themselves against the shuttered windows. In Jane's
arms, Daphne stirred and moaned as if the wild chattering of
the insects had penetrated her sleep. The bugs, falling from
Guiness' body, scrambled toward them, filling the hall in all
directions. Heller threw his arms around Jane and Daphne;
they flinched back, waiting. Jane hid her face in Daphne's neck
and gave a small, panicky cry.

On the wall across from him, Heller caught sight of a
fire extinguisher, and beside it a glass case containing a fire
hose. At once he remembered his escape in the Brain—how he
had managed to drive the bugs from him in the elevator. The
insects could not be killed, but, until their numbers became in-
surmountable, they could be forced away.

He raced to the fire equipment, smashed the glass with his elbow. With one hard tug, he uncoiled the hose inside; quickly, he spun the wheel that would turn on the water. It spurted at once from the nozzle, a sharp, hissing spray. Steadying the hose firmly under one arm, Heller used his free hand to detach the fire extinguisher and carry it away. He shouted to Jane to follow behind him. The current of water he shot out ahead of him swept a slippery path through the bugs. As the powerful spray struck them, they leaped and bounded wildly away. But Heller could see the swarm collecting and regrouping in bulky clusters along the far wall; he and Jane would have to move quickly, before they attacked in more massive formations. Struggling to keep their footing on the slick floor, they worked their way cautiously around Father Guiness. Like some great blind beast, he seemed to be listening in all directions, searching for prey. Was he still himself under the mountain of bugs? Or had he become some new, monstrous form of life, a murderously prolific insect-bearer?

As Heller led Jane and Daphne past him, Guiness lurched round toward them, a low animal growl sounding in his stifled throat. The priest's face was a crawling caricature shaped from its deadly mask of insects. Heller shot the stream of water at his ankles, toppling Guiness from his feet. He went down, sprawling. At the end of the corridor, Heller's length of hose ran out. With the final jet of water, he cleared the way as far as he could toward the stairs and then readied the fire extinguisher for use. The insects were not as numerous here, but, even so, the spray from the extinguisher could not drive back many of them at once. They were soon on Jane's legs; she gave a whine of pain and hugged Daphne closer. "Quickly!" Heller commanded, trying to escape the building before the extinguisher gave out.

Ahead on the stairs and in the lobby below, there were cries of panic that pierced the resounding chatter of the bugs. Bodies lay along the way—soldiers mainly—covered with bugs, some still writhing, calling out for help. The front door of the hospital stood open; most of the people in the building had fled that way. The bugs were thinning out, but some were already springing out of the door and onto the porch and lawn.

From behind, Heller heard Guiness' hoarse growl. On all fours now, swollen to inhuman size by his cargo of insects, the priest was starting down the stairs, feeling his way. He negotiated the first few steps, then miscalculated, slipped and fell the full length of the staircase. His plummeting body went past Heller and Jane, and plunged to the floor of the entrance lobby below. It lay there, unmoving except for its quivering overlay. The priest was still streaming insects, an endless living torrent now using Guiness as its passage into the world.

Bolting forward, Heller pulled Jane and Daphne down the remaining steps and out the door. Their clothes swarmed with insects, but they were free of the building, racing across the lawn. Everywhere about them as they ran, people were fighting to clean themselves of the bugs, raking and clawing at their bodies, tearing away pieces of clothing. Several yards beyond the hospital porch, the bugs stopped their advance, as if at a fixed perimeter. There, on the path to the gate, Heller rested. At once, Jane lay Daphne on the grass and unwrapped her from the plastic bedcover. There were bugs on her, but they were easily brushed away; her body was unmarked. Jane, still struggling to sweep the insects from her face and hair, looked up at Heller. He stood over her, brushing at her clothes. "She's all right," Jane announced, her eyes filled with tears, her cheeks pinpricked with tiny bites.

"Yes," Heller said. "They wouldn't harm her." He was remembering what Father Guiness had said about Daphne— that she was the bugs' portal and passage, that they did not come to harm the child. It was not easy for him to speak; the bugs were still working at him. His throat was an inferno of pain, and his left eye was swollen shut.

At the end of the path, near the gate, Heller could make out a small knot of uniformed men. Among them he saw Touhy and Haseltine, both badly bloodied about the face. There were three soldiers with them holding rifles—guards from the hospital grounds. Under orders, they started forward toward the hospital, moving cautiously. They were frightened men. What could they expect to do against the insects? Heller wondered. They moved past Heller and Jane, then stopped just short of the perimeter the bugs were holding.

Through the front door of the hospital, the thing that had once been Father Guiness groped its way forward across the threshold. The shape was still a grotesque fountain of insect life. It stood flooding the porch and lawn with its fierce progeny. Was anything human left within that deadly chaos—a mind that lived and thought and willed to be saved?

Heller slumped to the ground, too weak to stand even in Jane's arms. He lay there, squinting to see, taking in the full horror of the moment. His one-eyed vision was now little more than a blur; but in that surviving smear of light, Guiness' awful presence had already been transformed. What Heller now saw in the bright corona of consciousness that surrounded his darkening mind was an apocalyptic emblem. In spite of himself, Guiness had become what the bugs would have him be: a man-shaped gargoyle guarding the boundaries, turning the world away from a forbidden path.

From the gate, a voice barked an order; the soldiers raised their rifles and fired. Several shots. The bullets did not easily penetrate the chitinous armor that encased the thing on the porch. A final barrage of shots; a great roar rose from the thing. The roar went on and on, long after the echo of the gunfire died away. And then it stopped dead. Heller watched the terrible form buckle, waver, fall. Before his mind went dark, he realized the pain that had tormented his body from within had ceased. The bugs slept, and he could rest.

THE END

1

It was the first week of April, the mild beginning of an early spring. On a bench beside the Tidal Basin where the cherry trees were returning to life, Heller sat watching the concrete mixers as they labored across the river toward the site of the Brain. He came here many times to spend the occasional quiet hour, witnessing the strange, sad work that was now approaching completion. Sometime later that week, the trucks were scheduled to deliver their last load of cement, and the National Center for Data Control would vanish from sight for generations to come. The most ingenious and fragile machinery ever invented by man—the cunning replica of his own intelligence—would lie brutally crushed beneath the most primitive technology of all, the heaping up of earth and stone.

The previous month, as the Brain's vast, featureless tomb had begun to assume its dismal shape, a congressman from New York had introduced a bill commissioning murals to decorate the structure. He had proposed images of hope and confidence in the future, the rebirth of progress. No one expected the bill to pass. There was even less hope and confidence in the country than there was federal money for superfluous ornamentation. The collapse of the computers had drained both the nation's treasury and its spirit. The Brain would be left to rest beneath the monument the public believed it deserved: a blank, forbidding monolith whose only decoration would be a succession of small, metal plates that succinctly informed future generations of the dangers that lay buried within. "Warning," the plaques said, referring to the bugs as "dangerous insect life." Nobody assumed a more detailed description was necessary: the bugs were not likely to be forgotten. They would be remembered—a permanent scar across the face of human history.

The task of sealing the Brain had taken nearly two months of round-the-clock work. The building held nearly all the computer equipment in the Washington area, compacted like so much debris into its offices and corridors, its garage and storerooms. Armored vans, requisitioned by the army engineers, had spent weeks traveling the streets of the capital, Arlington, Alexandria, Baltimore, Richmond, Philadelphia, scouring every corner of the region for computers great and small—much the same way the dung carts had once gone through the streets of plague-stricken cities to collect the dead. On designated street corners and in open lots, police guards had stood protecting the computer dumps until the vans came. Cordoned off from the public for a block in all directions, the elegant machines were roughly heaped up in the raw winter weather, stacked high, cracking and mangling under their own weight, waiting to be transported to the Brain. Whatever space remained inside once the computers had been packed into their final resting place, was rammed solid with rubble. Finally, the exterior of the dome was encased in a cement hide four feet thick.

Elsewhere, in America and abroad, smaller computer facilities proved easier to seal. By the end of the year, every major city in the industrial world contained at least one computer graveyard where all the data hardware in the region had been dumped and interred. The tombs would stand as grim, universal landmarks of modern life—like the burial pits of ancient and medieval towns, where the human remains of famine and pestilence were covered over.

The Americans had taken longest to begin the program and to complete it. There were so many more computer facilities in the country, it was important to make the right choice for their elimination. There had been feverish debates and hurried research that echoed the still unresolved discussion of nuclear waste disposal: where to put the deadly materials? In the depths of the sea . . . in salt domes . . . under the polar ice cap? A contingent of computer scientists and the data industry mounted a determined lobbying effort to have the equipment warehoused while research continued seeking ways to combat the bugs. In reaction to their effort, an impassioned national campaign was launched demanding the immediate, permanent entombment of all computers; it was led by Senator Cory, rising to the heights of his practiced liberal fervor. Galling as it was to make the alliance, Heller supported Cory in pressing for "the final solution" which ultimately prevailed.

There was a model for the program; it was provided by one of the modern world's other, great failed technologies. A number of malfunctioning radioactive power plants had been similarly terminated, capped over by solid concrete ziggurats. Heller knew it was the only decision an irate and frightened public would accept. People demanded the destruction of the diabolical machines; they wanted to *see* them destroyed, wanted to have the evidence of their obliteration visibly before them. He also knew it was the only way the bugs could ever be pacified and contained.

At first, there was a great deal of trepidation about moving the infested computers to their burial sites. Elaborate precautions were taken for their transport. Special vehicles were designed for the project, and a small army of trained personnel was recruited. But Heller's guess was that the bugs would remain dormant while the technology was interred. It was their mission to break the power of the computers; they were the blind, instinctive agents of that purpose, and where it was pursued, he felt convinced they would remain docile.

He was right. Everywhere, the program went off without incident or injury; the bugs remained silent, withdrawn. Toward the end, the big cleanup became so casual that conventional city refuse services were used to collect the last, stray computers as part of their routine rounds.

One day in late March, while he was driving through downtown Washington, Heller found himself behind a garbage truck transporting an IBM 3033 mainframe. The sleek machine was bouncing along covered with banana peels and coffee grounds. He quickly turned off the street to escape the sight.

2

In their last attack, the bugs had been more merciful than Heller would have predicted. At a few minutes past four in the afternoon on September 27, when the final infestation had exploded out of Father Guiness' brain, the bugs had emerged from every computer seen by a human observer—a worldwide retaliatory strike against Gable's nearly successful effort to appropriate their power. Even long defunct and abandoned computers spawned swarms of the insects; small terminals in private homes, many of them unused for months and stored away in closets and basements, disgorged minor invasions that forced families into the streets. The Brain was once again overrun, a massive onslaught that drove out the small crew Berny Levinson had quickly assembled there that afternoon to examine the computers.

The bugs poured out to fill whole buildings and penetrated to the streets beyond. Wherever they appeared, panic ensued. Offices, factories, administrative centers, government operations slammed to an abrupt halt. Air traffic was thrown into nearly catastrophic chaos. Serious accidents were avoided only because flight controllers had long since developed contingency plans for working around failed equipment.

The worst disruption came in neighborhoods near major computer facilities. There, in scores of cases, the bugs overran homes, and wholesale evacuations were ordered. Yet, there were few injuries, little more than superficial bites—except where there were determined efforts to hold out against the attack, as there were at critical defense installations. Among the military, there were deaths in many parts of the world; at least a handful of security guards at computer centers were also seriously maimed or killed. Otherwise, where there was no resistance, the insects simply took possession, driving off their human antagonists by the sheer force of terror. For three days they held fixed perimeters around their computers or in the streets surrounding important facilities like the Brain—armies of minuscule occupiers, bringing urban life everywhere to a standstill. In effect, the cities were under siege *from within*, the hostages of an insidious invader.

Then, on the third day, the bugs slowly withdrew again into the computers—out of sight, but still ominously audible for several days more. By then, it was clear the computers would have to be scrapped, the big installations permanently closed. The entire technology had become socially intolerable; it would have to be expunged from the culture.

3

At Braddock Veterans Hospital where the last scene in the crisis was played out, the attack ended when Father Guiness was gunned down. The building remained occupied by the insects for another three days; finally, they drew back into the synthesizer and were gone. In the search that followed, Gable's remains were found along with three members of his staff; they had never made it to the staircase. Captain Schaeffer's body was found in the downstairs lobby. General Haseltine and Lyman Touhy were severely lacerated by the bugs. Jane was among those who suffered light injuries: Daphne was the only person in the hospital to go completely unharmed. Heller, plagued to the last by the insects he still carried from the first attack upon the Center, lost the sight of his damaged eye; the optical nerve had been chewed through.

As he looked back across the last troubled year, it occurred to Heller that, besides himself, Gable, Guiness and their assistants at Braddock—all of whom had acted in direct opposition to the bugs—the only people who had been killed or seriously injured were men at arms—security guards, military personnel. It was as if the bugs had been rigidly programmed to strike at human targets who bore the emblems and instruments of violence. The pattern made him wonder if armed violence might not have been the bugs' real quarry all along.

That was, after all, the single most important use the world had chosen to make of the computers and of the remarkable science that had built them. That was where most of the money and the genius had gone. The computers were the nerve center of the thermonuclear war machine. Whatever else they promised the world in the way of wealth and convenience, first of all they belonged to the technology of death. To the general public, they may have looked like science fiction come true—a push-button luxury, endless fun and games. But that was not why the computers had blossomed like a miracle growth in the middle of the twentieth century. Every innovation of the science, every astonishing refinement, flowed into the powers of genocidal violence, giving the forces of war a scope, a speed, an annihilating efficiency that was rapidly passing beyond human control. The computers were an alien mind, an unfeeling intelligence to which a weaponry of universal doom had been rashly, irresponsibly entrusted.

Day by day, as he watched his life's work sink beneath a slowly rising tide of concrete, Heller pondered the strange ambition that had brought the Brain into existence in the first place, the obsession that had captured him and his fellow computer scientists. To outsmart and outdo the human brain in every area of life, to replace people with progressively more cunning forms of artificial intelligence—as if people were irrelevant, embarrassingly incompetent, an obstacle to the quickening pace of modern industrial life. Well, was not thermonuclear holocaust the ultimate means of achieving human obsolescence? In its connection with the war machine, the essential inhumanity of computer science showed through unmistakably. Heller had spent his best gifts helping to create an intelligence that could not be trusted to serve its creator.

Now, as the computers were being buried amid unparalleled social confusion, one paramount fact was slowly breaking through to people everywhere. The arsenals of the nations had lost their deadliest weapons. The war machine was broken. The factories that might reconstruct that machine were themselves crippled without their microprocessors and computers. It would take years to convert, rebuild, replace.

Yes, it was still possible for nations to make war, and no doubt they would. But at least for a time it would be war on a lower scale of violence, fought with the weapons of an earlier generation. Meanwhile, until the world *re*armed, it was *dis*-armed—or very nearly so. All the systems of command and control were inoperable, all the logistical networks and supply lines in disarray, all military research and development at a standstill. Predictably, the worried generals were scrambling to retool and retrain, but that would not happen soon. For a precious interval, the bugs had brought an unexpected and awkward gift. The prospect of peace. There were at least a few responsible leaders who were determined to make the most of the opportunity.

4

Heller's role in the Washington of the postcomputer era was an odd and peripheral one. He was one of the world's leading authorities on a defunct technology. It was like knowing all there was to know about medieval water clocks or Inca medicine. He was no longer a scientist or technician, but an antiquarian of sorts—an expert on things irretrievably past. Someday, perhaps, he would write on the subject, a fat Gibbonesque volume on the decline and fall of the world computer empire. Perhaps. But he must wait to see how the story came out. How would the world adjust to the sudden, total collapse of a global technology? Just now and for the foreseeable future, the answer seemed to be: not very well. The dislocation was universal, the demoralization and resentment immense. Heller, frozen out of government service, now worked for a small, private think-tank in the city whose main task was to make the dislocation survivable. There were no experts in the matter, but it was assumed that someone who knew so much about what computers could do, might also know what human beings could do to live without them.

He was not sure he had much to contribute, but he enjoyed being free of politics for the first time in twenty years. He had little choice about that in any case; Touhy would never forgive him for his disloyalty, even though it was Heller who finally prevailed upon Jane, Sperling and Leah to hush-up what had happened at Mount Rose and Braddock. He argued that they must do that for Daphne's sake—to keep her out of the public eye. The government made the proposition attractive, arranging for Jane to take her daughter into comfortable seclusion for an interval. How long would it be? A year . . . two years . . . until there was no danger of the child being hounded by the media or abducted by foreign intelligence agencies. Touhy had urged a hideaway someplace in Latin America, safely within the American sphere of influence. But Jane chose Switzerland, where she could live with the Ulrichs and continue Daphne's education in the church.

The girl was being closely watched by Beata, who was convinced that her abnormal powers had been stilled. Before she was old enough to understand the importance of those powers, Daphne had changed the course of history. Now, with that purpose fulfilled, its burden had been mercifully lifted from her. The little girl who played in the streets of Basel was like any other child, no longer cursed or gifted. As far as Jane could tell, the very memory of the insects had left her. Since the deep sleep had worn off on her way home from Braddock Veterans Hospital, she remembered nothing of Gable or Father Guiness, nothing of the hideous experiment for which she had been the focus. Even when Heller visited, she seemed not to associate him with anything in her past. Perhaps to that extent, Gable's effort had worked after all; the trauma of the bugs had been erased from her mind forever.

Heller planned to see a great deal of Jane in the months to come; his visits to Basel were running one to a month. He and Jane were still not entirely easy with one another, but the memory of shared dangers was there, a tenuous bond. He knew he must not expect too much of her too soon. It was enough that he could visit and have her trust, even in silent moments when they found little to say. They moved in different worlds, and there was not much in his life that touched her, little he could tell her of the assignments he pursued that would engage her interest. Still, she understood that his work was now of a different character. He was outside the government, a marginal figure, one of the many once-important men of power who moved in a twilight zone of diminished influence, advising, consulting, preparing studies and papers. He might never again wield the official power she had learned to hate and fear; she admired the grace with which he had surrendered that status in life. In her eyes, the act had made him more gentle, more humane, a man she could now at least imagine loving.

5

There was one memory to which Heller's mind often returned: the encounter with Father Guiness that had driven him to use his gun. Had it been a hallucination brought on by fatigue and fever? Or had he seen something invisible to the others, concealed from them? The insinuating words, the demonic aspect of the old priest haunted him. The experience had been either a moment of madness, or of privileged vision.

Heller could never ask Touhy what he had seen or not seen, but he had once tried to draw Haseltine out. Thinking back to that moment of the crisis, Haseltine recalled nothing extraordinary on Guiness' part.

"The old man just sat there waiting for Gable to begin. Then you pulled your gun . . ."

That was all the general remembered. When Heller hinted at something closer to his own recollection, Haseltine frowned dubiously. "You were under a lot of pressure just then, Tom," he said indulgently. "We all were."

Leah Hagar and the Ulrichs thought differently. When Heller related the experience to them, Beata nodded knowingly. Yes, she said, she was certain there had been another powerful psychic intelligence at work, seeking to counter her own when she tried to locate Jane and Daphne. And she had been all too familiar with its quality. She had struggled against such a force through most of her life, had often been tempted to yield to its demands—in the Germany where she grew up, in the death camps, and later in the world all about her. "*Das Gegen-Leben*" was the name she had come to use for it. *Anti-Life*. Its agencies were many, but its goal was always and everywhere the same—simple, clear, insistent. Annihilation.

"It was perhaps more than this old man knew," she speculated. "Something that used him as its tool to steal the child's power, to save the weapons, the dark forces. The poor soul—he thought he did the Lord's work. But did he know *which* Lord? Perhaps not."

The autopsy that was performed upon Father Guiness found his body to be an empty husk—skin and bones burned hollow, like some monstrous doll waiting to be stuffed. "No," Professor Ulrich assured Heller, "the bugs did not leave him so." It was, he claimed, the common condition in which bodies of the possessed were found—empty shells, rotted out, used up and abandoned by a will beyond their own.

Heller remained neutral about interpretations of this kind. He had learned not to be automatically skeptical when such possibilities were raised, but he was far from willing to accept and endorse what he was told by Leah or the Ulrichs. While he had found a new respect for them and had delved into a number of their studies, theirs could not be his style.

Gable would have called such views "superstructures," never realizing that his own science was every bit as much of a superstructure—and a rather cowardly one at that, since it refused to face the moral dimension of life. Heller confessed he was no better equipped than Gable to speak of such matters. He envied the Ulrichs their connection with a tradition that could give good and evil a name, a face, an embodiment. But he could not borrow their language, their imagery.

So he simply rested with the facts, overshadowing them with no superstructure. *This* he had seen, *this* he had done. He committed himself no further. But for those who listened carefully—as Jane did—there was a certain arresting resonance to his words whenever he spoke of his experiences over the last year. He was a man who had, for one terrifying moment of his life, stood face to face with absolute evil, and had chosen to resist it.

He had no idea why he chose as he did. Even now, he could not explain his decision to the people he had once served—or to himself. The truth was, at the moment, he seemed not to have done anything, but to let the act flow from him. He had opened himself and turned the impulse free to do its work.

6

Now, as he watched the vast cement tomb close inch by inch upon the few, still visible surfaces of the Brain, he thought back to that moment once more. Where had he found the vision to see, the strength to act? It was as if he had been another person in that instant, someone he could never expect to be again. The power he had known had died with the danger that called it forth. More than dead machinery was being buried in that crude mausoleum of stone and sand. A remarkable piece of himself would rest there, sealed in the darkness among the insects, watched over by those fierce, unsleeping guardians.